THE STOLEN BRIDE

FORGE BOOKS BY TONY HAYS

The Killing Way
The Divine Sacrifice
The Beloved Dead
The Stolen Bride

THE
STOLEN BRIDE

TONY HAYS

A TOM DOHERTY ASSOCIATES BOOK
NEW YORK

This is a work of fiction. All of the characters, organizations, and events
portrayed in this novel are either products of the author's imagination
or are used fictitiously.

THE STOLEN BRIDE

A Forge Book
Published by Tom Doherty Associates, LLC
175 Fifth Avenue
New York, NY 10010

www.tor-forge.com

Forge® is a registered trademark of Tom Doherty Associates, LLC.

Library of Congress Cataloging-in-Publication Data

Hays, Tony.
 The stolen bride / Tony Hays.—1st ed.
  p. cm.
 "A Tom Doherty Associates book."
 ISBN 978-0-7653-2629-4
 1. Arthur, King—Fiction. 2. Great Britain—Kings and rulers—
Fiction. 3. Knights and knighthood—Great Britain—Fiction.
4. Britons—Fiction. I. Title.
PS3558.A877S76 2012
813'.54—dc22

2011025189

First Edition: April 2012

Printed in the United States of America

0 9 8 7 6 5 4 3 2 1

Acknowledgments

On April 12, 2011, I had a health crisis that, left unresolved, would have killed me. And with me would have died not just Malgwyn, but all the characters that I have created and breathed life into over the years. I want to thank those folks who have had an integral role in keeping me alive and healthy. Dr. Michael Smith, Lisa Smith, Cassie Robinson, Selena Dickey, Natisha Guthrie, Dawn Atherton, and Wanda Franks. Also, Ann Moseley, Christy Doyle, and Grace Brown. The emergency room folks at the Hardin Medical Center and the team at Air Evac. All the folks in the Surgical ICU unit of Jackson-Madison County Hospital, and as always, Red and Carrie Nell Shelby, who found me and saw that I got the assistance I needed.

Right there with me, sending me their prayers and best wishes, were my editor, Claire Eddy, assistant editor, Kristin Sevick, and publicist, Aisha Cloud. And, of course, my agent, Frank Weimann, and his assistant, Elyse Tanzillo. I thank you all for the good vibes you sent me as I fought.

Tony Hays
Savannah, Tennessee

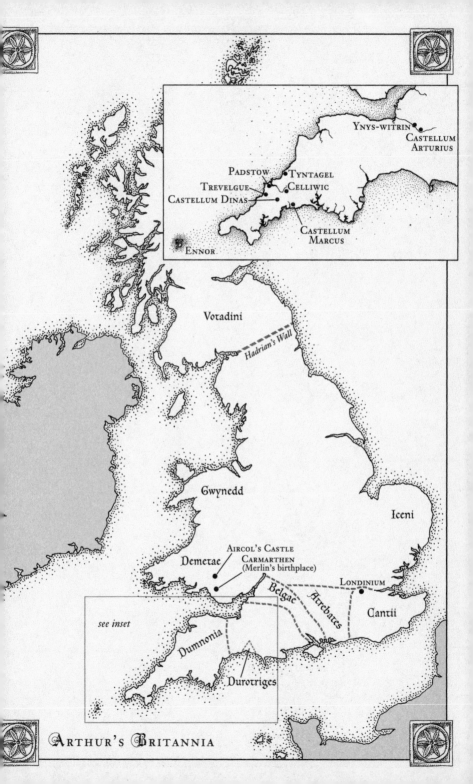

ARTHUR'S BRITANNIA

THE STOLEN BRIDE

ℭELLIWIC

In the Eighty-second Year from the Adventus Saxonum

*A*mbition, lust, power. They are the deadliest things. In my ninety and more winters of life, I have seen them bring low both the great and the lesser. But so long as there are men and power, ambition will be a part of life. And as long as there are men and women, there will be lust, which is as strong a call as ambition. And when you compare the two, lust seems to be the strongest combatant. When you combine the two, the result is nearly unconquerable. And when the lust is fed by ambition for power, God help us all.

I do not travel much anymore. The aches and burning in my joints make it too much a chore. Indeed, the furthest journey I make these days is from my hut at Glastonbury, near the abbey, to the abbot's feasting hall. The young abbot pretends to need my advice, but I think he just pities me. Occasionally he will ask my thoughts on the Saxons, but he is a well-mannered man, for an abbot. Otherwise, I spend my days in contemplation, helping the monachi copy manuscripts when my one hand allows. The damp weather, and we have much, pains both it and the stump of my right arm.

I am all that is left from the old consilium, *that alliance of nobles that tried to govern Britannia after Vortigern betrayed us all.*

But when the messenger came from Celliwic, advising me that my first great-great-grandchild was to be born there, I knew that I must go, one last time.

Celliwic. My favorite place in the far west. So much of my time was spent there in the years just after I entered the service of Arthur ap Uther, the Rigotamos, the high king of the Britons. He traveled there often, using the old fort as his base. From there, he could ride north to Tyntagel, as they now call it, to visit his mother, Igraine. Or he could ride southeast to Castellum Marcus to check on Lord Mark's lands.

I asked Arthur once why he did not use his lands at Tyntagel as his seat. "In my mother's house, there is room for only one crown, her own."

"But she does not hold a title," I had answered, still confused.

Arthur smiled at me. "Exactly."

But Arthur is dead now, and my cousin Guinevere, and Kay and Bedevere and Merlin. Many lies are now being told of those long-ago days. Gildas, for one, twists the facts to fit his own agenda and understood little. So I have set myself the task of chronicling something of those times, when Arthur was king and we tried so hard to bring order to the chaos.

But it was at Celliwic that I first met a lad who was to become very important to all of us—Culhwch, as it was spelled in the old way, Culhwch ap Cilydd. He was just a child then, and it was Cilydd that caused us much grief on that journey. And it was that journey that taught me what I know of Arthur's birth. And that knowledge came to cause us all grief.

Spring had arrived. I remember that. Arthur and I were at odds as we were so often. On that occasion, it was because beloved

Ygerne was near her time to deliver my son, or so the fortune-teller told her. I wanted to be there, at Castellum Arturius, but there was unrest in the lands of the Dumnonii and Arthur's mother was ailing at Tyntagel.

The first flowers were blooming, and we had brought Morgan ap Tud, Arthur's physician, to minister to Igraine. I remember because it was the first time he joined us on such a long journey. Yes, the flowers were blooming, and I thought it a good omen. . . .

CHAPTER ONE

My belly roiled and threatened to revolt. Bodies lay prostrate on the ground, in the lanes. Flies buzzed about them, feeding on the blood that reddened their wounds. The sickly sweet scent of death lay heavy in the air. For a moment, just the briefest of moments, I was not here, in this city of death, but staring instead at my own village, at my own cottage, at my beloved Gwyneth, freshly killed, freshly ravaged. I almost rushed into one of the silent huts to find my daughter, Mariam, but I knew that these raiders had been more thorough than the Saxons.

I climbed down from my mount and walked a dozen steps up the lane into the village. A day, no more, had passed since this abomination. The cool night had staved off decay a bit, but the bodies would soon bloat in the sun.

A pair of carcasses in front of one of the huts drew me. 'Twas a woman who had been nursing her baby. I knew because her breast was bare and the child lay a foot away, its skull crushed, the crimson of blood and yellow of old milk crusted on its cheek. The woman had been beheaded, and in a macabre twist of chance, her head, some three feet away, was turned toward her baby. But the eyes saw nothing.

Behind me, a voice, as familiar as my own, broke the near rhythm of buzzing flies and snorting horses.

"This is why I demanded that you come. This is why it is so important for you to be here."

I could hear the pain in his voice. The Rigotamos of all Britannia, Arthur ap Uther, was a compassionate man, though I had accused him of the opposite only the previous day when he ordered me to accompany him on this journey. My woman, Ygerne, was near to time to deliver our son, or so the fortune-teller said, and I wished more than anything to be there, not here.

Arthur was still talking, but though I heard him, I did not hear him. My eyes were fixed on the images before me. Rubbing the aching stump of my half arm, I spoke. "This was a provisioning raid."

"How do you know?"

"Do you see chickens or pigs or cattle, my lord?"

"Surely the people would have surrendered those to an armed force," my friend Bedevere said, "rather than be murdered trying to protect them."

"The killing was a message to all other villages these demons visit."

"Do you understand now, Malgwyn?" Pause. "Do you understand?"

I nodded, my eyes unable to leave the dead. Nearly three years before, the thought of me, Malgwyn ap Cuneglas, following Lord Arthur's banner would have seemed impossible. For I had hated him with every drop of blood coursing through my veins. And part of me still did. But to hate with that sort of passion means that once there was adoration. That part came before Tribuit, before I left one arm lying in a bloody field.

And though Arthur had not left me to die on that field, as I longed for, but had condemned me to life as half a man, it was also Arthur who took a whoring drunk and made him his councilor.

At that moment, my long grudge with Arthur was forgotten. All that I could see were the bodies of my fellow Britons, slaughtered. I squatted in the lane, took my one hand, and grasped a handful of dirt, letting it slowly drain from my fist. Arthur knew me well; he knew that my heart would not let this savagery continue, no matter how much I wished to be elsewhere.

Behind me, I heard Arthur's voice again, pulling me back to the present, back to this village.

"Morgan, take two soldiers and see if any yet live."

I nodded; Morgan ap Tud was Arthur's *medicus*, trained in Lord David's lands by the famous doctor Melus, though I suspected that the short, neat little man was more spy than physician. I pushed those thoughts from my head.

"Tell me again," I said finally, "of what is happening in these lands."

In another lifetime, I had been Malgwyn ap Cuneglas, the farmer son of another farmer. A wife, a baby daughter. A sturdy hut. Pig and chickens. Land to farm. It had been a good life.

Arthur ap Uther was just a name to me then, a boy soldier praised by my father for his *Romanitas* and his talent as a commander. Our farmstead was far to the west of the fighting, near unto the old Roman town of Lindinis. Our lives had not been touched by the war with the Saxons.

And then, one day, my neighbors and I were returning from market to find a scene much like that before me now. I found my wife, Gwyneth, spraddle-legged, ravaged until her womanly parts were red with blood, in our hut. She had succeeded in hiding our baby, Mariam, in a storage pit. I took the child to Castellum Arturius and gave her over to my brother, Cuneglas.

The other men, there were ten, and I then rode off to find Lord Arthur, *Dux Bellorum*, general of battles, for the *consilium* of nobles that tried to govern our fractious land after Vortigern's disgrace.

And now I faced that young lord again, only this time there was gray creeping into his hair and beard. And now he was the Rigotamos, the High King of All Britannia, a title more fantasy than reality, as we were more a collection of feuding tribes than a united nation. But Arthur was trying, and much good could be said for that fact alone. We were tied by more than that, though. My cousin, Guinevere, was Arthur's consort.

"These are Lord Doged's lands."

Doged was an old man, a contemporary of Lord Cadwy, who had been dead for many winters, and Ambrosius Aurelianus, the former Rigotamos, who had retired to his fortress in the north, Dinas Emrys. Doged held dominion over a sizable but poor territory in the far west, and he had no heir. But he did control our busiest ports at Trevelgue and Tyntagel. And now, in his last years, he was facing the very real threat of rebellion.

"The two primary factions are led by brothers, Cilydd and Druce," Arthur continued. "Though no one can be certain, this travesty is the work of one or both, I suspect. Doged has sent me word of provisioning raids made on his outlying villages and in the border villages with his neighbors. But until now there has been no killing, just theft."

"Until now," I repeated, glancing back into the lane at the poor dead villagers. "And Doged has no heir, you said."

"No, and that is what has spawned these factions. Doged is old, nearly as old as Merlin. But Doged is not ready to give up his title, and he has recently taken a young wife to give him an heir."

Although the position of Rigotamos was one elected by the lords of the *consilium*, the nobles from the individual tribes held their rank and titles and land by birth.

"Good fortune to him," I said grimly. "And may it happen soon."

"Don't wish him good luck yet," Arthur countered. "He has married Ysbail, sister of Ysbadden Penkawr."

That spelled trouble. Ysbadden was a minor lord far to the south. Not of noble birth, he held his title by virtue of his sheer size and cruelty. Said to be the tallest man in our lands, taller even than Kay, Ysbadden had recruited his men from among the worst, including Scotti pirates. One day he walked boldly into the former lord's chambers and cut his head off. Emerging, with his retinue of thugs at his back, he thrust the still-dripping head in the air. From that day forth, no one questioned his assumption of power.

I felt a hand on my good arm. It was Arthur, guiding me to my feet. He jerked his head to the side of the lane and Bedevere joined us in the eaves of a roundhouse. Once out of earshot of Morgan and our soldiers, Arthur reached into the leather pouch he wore around his neck.

"Malgwyn, we are in a difficult position here. Aye, a difficult position throughout our lands. That idiot, Lauhiir, set our tin-mining efforts back two years because of his greed. Aircol is a good ally to the north, but he is suffering border incursions from what he thinks are David's men. The Saxons under Aelle have begun to claim the lands around Londinium. The cost of refortifying Castellum Arturius has been much higher than I expected, but it had to be done. Ambrosius has already abandoned his seat to the east of us. He has been urging me to construct a defensive ditch to better guard against the Saxons. And that will cost yet more."

"And what does Doged have to do with this?"

Arthur reached into a pouch dangling at his side. He looked around quickly, motioned Bedevere in closer, and held his hand out.

In his palm lay four rocks, three of which I knew immediately. One was, plain and simple, agaphite, highly prized for its use in jewelry but rare in our lands. A second was a brown ore of some sort, looking something like a tree turned to rock. I had not seen its like before. The other two needed no explanation; they were the sort of rocks one found near gold.

"Doged sent me these by his fastest rider last night. They were found in his mines near Castellum Dinas."

"I heard no rider enter camp." We had left on this journey the day before and camped on the road that evening.

"You were asleep, and Merlin has told me how dangerous it is to awake you." But Arthur's joke did not ring true. Something beyond this business of Doged and his rocks was bothering the Rigotamos. I shrugged the jest aside.

"Why did you not tell me of this in the morn?" It was not like Arthur to hold information away from his closest advisors.

"I have scarcely had time, Malgwyn," he snapped at me. "And I feared spreading the word that there might be gold in

Doged's land. I love my soldiers and trust them, but gold does things to a man's thinking."

I could not argue with that. Men were unpredictable about two things—gold and women. But gold held no allure for me. Not two years before, I had refused a title, lands, and a seat on the *consilium*, a reward for my service during the recent rebellion. But something in Arthur's manner told me that the temptation of gold was not the only reason for his reticence.

We were interrupted by the diminutive Morgan ap Tud, running with his patrol to rejoin us. His tunic bore the colors of Arthur's service, and his clipped, brown beard was of the old Greek style.

"We found no one alive, Rigotamos," Morgan reported.

"How many dead?"

Morgan paused for a second, pursing his lips. "Thirteen that we found, but there were a handful of blood trails leading off in different directions."

Arthur, Bedevere, and I exchanged swift glances. At least eight roundhouses marked this village. Thirteen souls were too few a number. But had the remainder fled in fear, or had they been taken captive? And, if so, for what purpose? To be sold? To be ransomed? None of these questions had to be voiced; all three of us were thinking them.

"It smells of the Saxons or Scotti raiders," I said finally, "but that does not feel right to me. We are far to the east for such Scotti raids and far to the west for a Saxon party. If either the Saxons or Scotti are striking this deep into *consilium* lands, we will soon have more than a single, ravaged village to mourn. No, there is something else at work here."

From the corner of my eye, I glimpsed a shock of blond hair, painted with crimson, and I was swept away.

I was no longer standing; I was walking, toward the door to the hut, toward the blood-soaked blond hair. Behind me, beyond me, I heard the screams of pain, of devastated lives, as my friends found their wives and children dead. Stepping in, I saw my Gwyneth, eyes open but unseeing, naked from her waist down, blood streaking her body. In a corner, at the back of the hut, I saw a simple wooden cover move. In a single movement, I swept the cover away with one hand and scooped up little Mariam with the other.

"I have her, Gwyneth," I said softly. "I have her."

"Malgwyn?"

Arthur.

I blinked and once again I saw the village, not of yesterday but of today.

Storm clouds were already blackening the western sky, and I detested traveling at night in bad weather. But I knew that there was yet more for me to do here, to see here. "Leave four soldiers with me as an escort, Rigotamos. I will join you at Celliwic late tonight. I would send for Merlin. He knows about such things as these rocks."

"I agree. Very well. Sort this out, Malgwyn. There is something dark in the air. It troubles me. And I'll have him bring Kay as well. We may need some field commanders." Arthur's face took on a bit of that darkness then, and we exchanged a look that needed no explanation. But Kay, Arthur's chief steward, had been difficult to deal with of late. He felt that his value as a warrior was not appreciated. Perhaps this would help. "I am not a prophet or seer. But ever since I received Doged's dispatch, this business has weighed heavily on me, and I did not know why. Now, I see that my concerns were justified. That Doged has troubles with insurrection and rebellion I knew. And

I wished to take the role of mediator. But that the struggle had turned to this sort of bloodshed I did not know."

"Perhaps Doged does not yet know either," I pointed out. I paused and looked down the lane again, at the bloating, fly-buzzing corpses.

"Then he will learn quickly," Arthur concluded behind me.

One body, one that I had not noticed before, caught my attention then. A man lay facedown in the middle of the lane, his arms outstretched as if reaching for something. I moved closer and saw that the killing blow had split the back of his head open.

I pondered what Arthur had said, even as I went to lean against an old roundhouse. I smelled something truly evil in all of this too, but probably with less reason than Arthur. Coming along on this trip had not been my pleasure at all. Glancing at the sky, I saw that we had been on our journey nearly two days. And already we were deep in death and tragedy. I knew that Arthur could not have known that this village had been sacked, but it would have been just like him to direct us through such a place to marry me to his plans. Perhaps I was being unkind to him, perhaps not. But, as usual, I needed to plant my feet on solid ground. "Rigotamos."

And he stopped and turned back toward me.

"I will do this not for Doged or you or the *consilium*, but for them."

Arthur studied me closely; he wanted to scold me, to reprimand me for my insolence. But that melancholy he felt was rooted too deep. "I will take you on whatever terms I must, but remember that this is not your village. And your Gwyneth is not among these unfortunates. That is behind you."

"That will never be completely behind me, Arthur."

A few moments later and I was alone in the village with my escort, four of the older soldiers. Arthur chose well. Two of the four had been among those in my command during the rebellion two years past. Our respect for each other had been born on the battlefield; I did not need to prove my value with them in a world that held little regard for a one-armed man.

"Scatter out," I instructed. "Follow the blood trails. If you find anyone alive, be gentle with them. They have weathered enough fear. I will be here."

As the men separated, I returned to the body in the lane, the man with his head split open. Something about this one called to me. It was as if I had been there, watching him rush across the lane, until an arrow took him in the back and down he went. But that had not stopped him. I looked at his outstretched hands and saw the marks in the muddy lane where he had tried to pull himself further, his fingernails torn and dirty.

Until a battle-axe, wielded by an enemy standing over him, halved his skull, ending his flight forever.

Directly in front of this unfortunate man was a small hovel, hardly big enough for one person, let alone a family. I wondered what he would be rushing toward in such an unprepossessing house.

Crossing the lane, I ducked into the entrance, covered over only with a fur. Once inside, I saw what the poor fellow had been racing for.

A woman lay face-first on the hard-packed, earthen floor, an arrow protruding from her back. I crouched to see her better. She had been a handsome woman, if a bit young for the man in the lane. Perhaps she was his daughter. Perhaps not. I would never know the answer, and that saddened me.

And as I squatted there, another daughter appeared to me.

"Must you go, Father?"

My darling Mariam was growing up. Once her hugs had hit me at knee level; now her head snuggled comfortably into the hollow below my breastbone.

"The Rigotamos needs me to help him. You know he is quite lost without me." A simple jest.

Mariam looked up at me with her bluest eyes. "But so am I, Father."

And I hugged her ever tighter with my one arm. "Do not worry, little one. I will not let Lord Kay or Master Merlin use you for a sacrifice." Another simple jest, one used too often, I feared.

But it earned me the gift I desired; Mariam released me and slapped me in the stomach. "Oh, Father!" And then she stomped off into a back room.

Then, I felt warm breath on my neck.

Ygerne.

"Why is Arthur so insistent that you attend him on this journey?" Ygerne asked me. She had been my brother Cuneglas's wife, but he was long dead and we had come to love each other deeply. We stood in her house in Castellum Arturius. Her full belly stretched the limits of her wrap. She would deliver within a week at the most.

"He wishes me to counsel him as he negotiates a peace between Doged and his rebellious nobles."

"Bah!" Ygerne's red hair glowed in the flickering lamplight. "He wants you there so that he has someone to blame if the negotiations do not go well."

"You should have more faith in the Rigotamos," I answered, with none of the certainty my words implied.

And she swept me about and pulled me against her breasts, and against our child. Her lips tugged at mine, pulled them into her mouth. "Go then, and see to your duty," *she said.* "I do not welcome your departure, but I understand that Arthur does need you."

She paused, brushing her hair from her eyes. "But do not forget that we need you as well. You must hurry back," *she whispered, her hands exploring my* braccae *and reddening my face.* "You will have much to make up for."

The memory of the bittersweet leave-taking faded as something about the arrow in the poor girl's back pulled me away from Ygerne's warm house. The way the arrow was fletched was familiar. Holding her down with my stump of an arm, I wrestled the arrow free from her body so that I might study it in better light.

But when I worked the point free, I fell back on my haunches in surprise. It was a Saxon point, of a kind that I had seen before, designed to penetrate chain mail. Aye, I had pulled an arrow just like this one from a victim of a Saxon bow, right before Arthur's election as Rigotamos. The fletching, though, was not Saxon work.

This was an unexpected twist, and I tried to fathom its meaning. But before I could begin to reason it, the hide door flew open and a soldier's voice broke my thoughts.

"Master, we have found someone."

Chapter Two

She was a woman of twenty or twenty-five winters. Her face was bloody from a dozen scratches, product of hiding in the underbrush, I supposed. The simple dress she wore was as torn and dirty as her face. The thing that haunted me the most was her eyes, cold, blank, vacant.

"We found her huddling behind a tree down near the stream," a soldier named Sulien explained. He was one of those who had fought beside me in the rebellion.

Another of the soldiers had started a fire at the side of the lane. "Take her near to the fire," I directed. "Bring her *cervesas*, some bread and cheese."

As I spoke, she looked at me, blinking her eyes and mumbling. She offered no resistance as a soldier led her away, just continued to mumble something impossible to understand.

I did not know if I could persuade her to talk to me. Many times during my warring days, I had seen such as she. Their world as they had known it had ceased to exist, and the shock was so great that it rendered them silent. Sometimes, they never recovered.

Following the woman and the soldier to the warmth of the

fire, I squatted next to her as a soldier offered her some *cervesas*. She did not move, just kept mumbling.

"What are you called?" I ventured.

She stopped mumbling.

"What is your name?"

She turned her head and looked at me, still no expression in her eyes. "Daron."

"Can you tell me what happened here?" I spoke as gently as I could. Somewhere in the village, a dog barked, and that, more than my question, seemed to put a spark in her eye.

"They killed us. They killed us all."

"Not all, Daron. You yet live."

She shook her head. "No."

"Who did this?"

"They came in the night. Some spoke our tongue, but some did not."

"What language did they speak?"

Daron shook her head again. "I had not heard it before." Her eyes began blinking and her head twitched. It was almost as if she had been brained with a club and was just then regaining consciousness. And, indeed, that may have been exactly what left her in this state.

I reached out my one hand to see if there was an injury, but she drew back, the bright light of fear sparking in her eyes. "I do not wish to harm you. I only want to see if you have been injured."

Slowly, she returned to her original position, though she flinched ever so slightly as my hand again approached her hair. Her skin was pale, marked only by the blue veins that carried her lifeblood.

I found no injury on her head, nor did I really expect to.

Her hair was so fair that blood would have been obvious, but it could have been a glancing blow that did not break the skin. Yet my brief examination revealed no knots or swollen areas.

"Do you have a man or children?"

Tears welled up in her eyes at that question, and I was glad to see it. Tears signified that she was beginning to feel once again.

She wiped her eyes. "I had a man, but he was one of the first to die."

"How came you to live?"

"When my man, Deiniol, was killed, I ran and hid in the forest."

"Did others run with you?"

At that, her eyes glazed over once more, and she stared off into the forest. "No. The children and some of the women were taken."

I did not know what she was seeing in the darkening forest; perhaps her mind was taking her back to that horrific event of which she spoke.

"Master?"

Sulien was at my side. "If we are to reach Celliwic tonight, we must leave soon."

I nodded. There was little more I could learn here. "Very well." Standing, I felt a tug at the bottom of my tunic.

"You will leave me?" Poor Daron. To leave her in this village of death was punishment.

"No, you will come with us."

Sulien looked at me as if I were mad. "What need have we of her, master?"

"She is the only person who can identify those who destroyed this village. And I tell you now that I will find the devils behind this. Besides, she needs us as much as we need her. There is nothing left for her here now." I paused and noted how much she resembled my Gwyneth. "She can ride with me."

Somebody was speaking. Somewhere. My eyelids were so heavy that I could but barely open them. Nor did I want to. "Another word and I will drown the room with your blood."

"Malgwyn."

I reached for my sword.

"Malgwyn."

But my sword was not there.

"Malgwyn!"

Groaning, I struggled beneath my furs. It seemed that I was forever being awakened by someone, anyone. The air was chilling. My nose twitched.

This was not home.

No hint of that horrible scent of woad making painted the breeze.

Nor the smell of bread freshly baking at Arthur's kitchen, across the lane from my house.

And the voice was different. 'Twas not Merlin, Ygerne, nor even young Mariam or Owain.

I blinked an eye open, slipping the fur away just enough to see who I intended to kill.

Ah. Morgan. Morgan ap Tud. Arthur's new physician. I remembered then, the journey, the ravaged village, our late, late arrival the previous night.

"Arthur has sent for you."

I looked out the door. "The sun has not yet arisen, Morgan, and I did not arrive until after the midnight. I fail to see why I should answer his summons."

"Malgwyn!" He was shocked, too fresh to Arthur's service to understand my relationship with the Rigotamos. In truth, despite my fears that Morgan was a spy for David, I liked the little fellow. He was smart and eager to please. Merlin, with his enormous store of knowledge about herbs and healing, had done much of our healing work before, but David had persuaded Arthur that he needed someone trained. Hence, Morgan was summoned.

Throwing back the furs, I stretched and yawned. "Why are you about so early?"

"Arthur wishes to leave for Tyntagel within the hour. A rider came in last night. Lady Igraine is declining."

At that news, I truly shook the sleep from my eyes and rose. In the morning chill, goose bumps had arisen on my skin and I shivered. Morgan offered me a cup of watered, warm, spiced wine.

I took it, telling myself that it was only to warm me. Once, I had nearly lived on wine and mead and *cervesas*. But at least it was not that horrid soldier's drink, *posca*.

A rustle sounded just outside the door. Then, a head poked around. A head topped with blond hair. For just a minute, I was confused.

Then I remembered.

Daron.

"Here, child," I said. "Take some warm wine."

She looked fearfully at Morgan and skirted the wall to stay away from him as she drew closer to me. A cloth-wrapped bundle was clutched in her hands and she proffered it to me. Bread. Cheese.

"No," I said softly. "You take your fill first."

For the first time, a half smile lit her face, and she sat back against the wall and took small bites from the food.

Morgan watched us with the raised eyebrows of amazement. "She slept in the corner with but a single fur for cover, within arm's reach of you."

"She has suffered a great shock. Have you any valerian extract? It might ease her."

The little doctor nodded and began rummaging in one of his leather pouches.

"Any word from Doged?"

Morgan shook his head. "No."

That was more than unfortunate. Mediating between these disgruntled factions in Lord Doged's lands was more necessary now than when we had set out on this journey. And as we had recently learned, what had begun as a few provisioning raids had now turned to bloodshed.

And upon our success depended much, for Doged, a staunch ally of the *consilium*, and for the *consilium* itself.

After the Romans had abandoned us, a group of nobles gathered together and formed a *consilium* to establish some sort of order. The first Rigotamos was a strong northern lord named Vortigern. Faced with a shaky alliance between the tribes and the constant raids by the Picts and Scotti, Vortigern hired Saxon mercenaries to aid us, granting them lands among the Canti for their service.

And they did help with the Picts and Scotti. And they

loved our lands, loved them so much that they betrayed Vortigern and the *consilium* and began expanding into other tribal regions. They were a savage people, worshiping the pagan gods and ignoring the Christ. I hated them with all my heart for what they did to my family.

Ignoring the Christ; I shook my head at the irony. I was not ignorant of the Christ, but neither was I a believer. I found much good in His message and much good in His followers. But I was not yet ready to add myself to their numbers.

At any rate, I joined the banner of Arthur, Arturius in Latin, who had once been a tax collector for Lord Cadwy. He had risen to command of all *consilium* forces, and was successfully pushing the Saxons back. I came to be known as "Smiling Malgwyn," for the pleasure I took in killing Saxons. A chance encounter on the eve of a battle brought me to Arthur's attention and soon I commanded my own troop of horse.

Then came that horrible day at the River Tribuit. Surrounded on a grassy knoll, my men and I fought savagely, but the Saxons outnumbered us, and one by one we were cut down. I did not see the blade that struck my right arm at the elbow, but I felt the shock as I slid to the ground, the scent of new grass filling my nostrils. And I was content. I had sent more than a score to whatever life their gods provided for them after this one. I would die with my men, an honorable death. But that was not to be my last breath, no matter how much I wished it so.

"Malgwyn?"

Morgan's voice brought me back from that hateful day.

"Yes."

"Is the Rigotamos always so angry?"

"Why do you ask?"

Morgan tugged with both hands to straighten his tunic. "He sent a boy to summon me, and when I arrived he fair cut my throat for being slow."

"You are still fairly new to Arthur's service. It will take time for you to understand his moods and for him to accept you. But you should know that Arthur is always irritable when we come to Celliwic."

"Why? Are these people not of his own tribe?"

"Yes, they are. He is said to have been born at Tyntagel. But I have never seen him in a more ill mood than when we come here."

Morgan started to ask another question, but I held my hand up. "And I do not know why."

In truth, Arthur was probably frustrated still with me as I was with him. Our history was a stormy one. I had not died on that grassy knoll at Tribuit. Just as I was about to join my men in whatever lies beyond this life, I was snatched from the ground, my stump of an arm bandaged to stanch the blood, and whisked away to the brothers at Ynys-witrin. By Arthur.

One-armed men were seen as cursed in our world. Many believed that such a wound was a sign of disfavor by the gods. Since I could no longer farm, or thought I could not, the brothers taught me to write to strengthen my left arm and hand. They were good, charitable men. I did not view Arthur as such.

In my mind, he had condemned me to half a life, and a life dishonorable. I should have died with my men at Tribuit. That Arthur saved me stole what honor I possessed. And left me as a pitiable creature. So, I hated Arthur with all the passion I had once reserved for the Saxons. And I dedicated myself to drinking and whoring my way into oblivion.

Until, that is, my dead wife's sister, Eleonore, was found murdered in the lanes on the eve of Arthur's election as Rigotamos. I had had a hand in resolving a similar matter at Ynys-witrin, and Arthur came to me for help in this one. Like two hungry dogs we had circled each other, but in the end, though there were other deaths, I rediscovered respect for myself and reclaimed my daughter, Mariam. And I agreed once more to serve Arthur.

Ygerne had been my brother's wife, until he was killed in the affair surrounding the death of Eleonore. I had always been taken by Ygerne, and she with me apparently, but even after my brother was gone I delayed joining with her. Coroticus, the abbot at Ynys-witrin, often told me that I was sinning, that the Word of his God spoke against taking your brother's wife as your own. I told Coroticus that his god was obviously not a Briton, as that was more common than not in our lands.

In truth, by our oldest laws, a woman was free to join with more than one man, as long as he was of proper stature. But first the Romans changed it, and then the believers in the Christ changed it, and now no one knew quite what the true law said.

Had it been just his mother's illness, Arthur told me, I would not be needed. But this affair with Doged was exactly why Arthur had pledged me to his service, or so he said. Doged's lands lay south of Tyntagel, encompassing two of our ports from whence much of the trade goods for our northern lands flowed. A disruption of those supply lines would severely reduce the *consilium*'s trade in tin and lead. One of the few factors that kept the *consilium* bound together was the lead and tin mining; both required much labor, more than any one lord could muster. So, a dispute that threatened something of such importance meant Arthur would need all of his men. As was customary, Arthur won out. Though it was Ygerne who made the decision. "I have delivered babies before, Malgwyn. The one thing I do not need is you pestering me. Go."

And I did.

In truth, Arthur was no more anxious to travel than was I.

It had not been many months since he had reconciled with Guinevere. They had fallen in love many years before when Guinevere had been a sister of the Christ in the women's community at Ynys-witrin. When their romance was discovered, Guinevere had been cast out in disgrace for breaking her vows. Arthur's patrons, Lord Cadwy and Ambrosius Aurelianus, saved him from any punishment, but Guinevere had suffered much.

Arthur truly loved her, though, and he gradually brought her to court. But about a year before this journey, Arthur had been forced into a politically convenient marriage with the daughter of a northern lord. Needless to say, the marriage ripped Arthur and Guinevere asunder. But when the marriage ended tragically, Arthur reached out to Guinevere. It took time, but they had finally come together.

Now, I shivered in the morning chill and watched my new charge, Daron, nibble at her food. Morgan, being his over-solicitous self, scurried about hunting more food for all three of us. I sat heavily on an old chair and glanced about. Arthur should really do something about his hall, I thought. We were lodged in one of the private chambers, but the hall at Celliwic was in sore need of repair. And that was not all.

The ramparts badly needed refortifying; they would not stand an assault by children with wooden spears. The gate was of single width and the wood was rotting at its mounts. There had been no chapel for Arthur's worship, but he had set soldiers to building a simple timber hut on our arrival. I would have put them to work on the ramparts, but I was more concerned with my neck than my soul.

"Perhaps I should tear it down and build a new one," I heard Arthur say as he entered the room.

"Perhaps," I agreed. "Morgan tells me we leave soon."

The Rigotamos lowered himself into a chair, his tunic bunching at his hips. He leaned forward, his chestnut hair falling in front of his face, his wool-wrapped hands propped on his knees. I took note, as I always did, of his short, stubby fingers, the middle one on the left hand half the size of the others, victim of a well-aimed Saxon spear. Arthur never shrank from battle.

"Yes, we have no choice. Lady Igraine sent a messenger with word that she is failing fast. And Doged sent one as well. A second village has been raided; this one by Cilydd, but it was only a provisioning raid. Just simple thievery."

"We offered them all that we had," came the soft voice of Daron from the corner.

The Rigotamos turned and studied her carefully. "Is this our lone survivor?" he asked. I had briefed him quickly upon our arrival.

I nodded. "I did not want to leave her there. That would have been as cruel as the raiders that killed her people."

"You are in good hands here, child," Arthur said. He moved to touch her head gently, but she jerked her head back as if stung.

"Daron," I started to scold her, but Arthur held up a woolen-wrapped hand.

"Anyone that has been through what she has is allowed certain liberties. No one here wishes you harm, child. I will assign a soldier to watch over you."

Her pale face grew dark and she shook her head fiercely. "No. I will stay with him." And to my alarm she pointed at me.

"Daron," I began again, but again Arthur stopped me with a hand.

Arthur gently and kindly shook his head at her. "Child, your safety is important to me. That is why I wish to protect you with one of my bravest soldiers."

"Rigotamos . . . ," I began, but before I could say aught else, he grabbed me by my tunic and eased me across the chamber.

"Malgwyn, you must be free to fulfill your duties for me. As important as she is, she would be a hindrance to your un-fettered movement."

"Think, for a second, Arthur. Soldiers talk. Soldiers gossip. I can control the four soldiers who were with me. But if we set her apart as special, with her own guard, word will more quickly spread, drawing unwanted attention. And when I do find the scum responsible for her misery, I will need her alive and handy to prove their guilt."

"Do not forget that your primary mission is to help me mediate for Doged."

"And do not pretend that those dead villagers mean nothing. Whether you wish it or not, I will have justice for them."

We stood there, glaring at each other for a handful of seconds. Then Arthur did something unexpected. He chuckled. "We are a sight of wonderment, Malgwyn," he said, drawing one end of his mustache into his mouth, chewing on the end as he did when in thought. "What do you suggest?"

My mind raced quickly. "Let us do this: She is already dressed as a peasant. Let her play the role of a *servus* for me. No one thinks twice about *servi*. And give me Sulien. He can help me in my quest and keep an eye on her as well."

"Very well." Turning back toward Daron and Morgan, he said, "You may stay with Malgwyn. He will explain all to you soon." He hesitated. "Malgwyn, I would talk with you privately."

"Morgan, would you and Daron go and fill my pouch with food for the day's travel?"

Though Morgan cocked his eye in suspicion, he led Daron from the room. To my surprise, she went willingly, Arthur's decision apparently allaying her fears.

Arthur nodded. "Doged sent other word as well. A Saxon ship has sought permission to send a party ashore for trade negotiations."

"Under whose banner?"

"Aelle, king of the southern Saxons."

"We do have troubles then." Aelle had risen to *bretwalda*, high king in their accursed tongue, of the Saxons in the south after the deaths of Hengist and Horsa. He was said to be a mighty warrior and crafty. Indeed, he had already adopted a strategy of approaching individual lords with his proposals, but not Arthur. Aelle hoped to work cracks in our unity. While Arthur could punish those who parlayed with the Saxons, he chose not to. "Chastise them," he told me once, "and they will resent you." It had proved a sound tactic, so far. "Will Doged look with pleasure at their entreaty?" I asked.

The Rigotamos shook his head abruptly. "Doged, no. Ci-lydd and some of the others, perhaps. Especially a young lord named Druce, some kin to Cilydd. They need weapons and supplies to wage their war against Doged. Expediency may send them to the Saxons without regard for the future."

"It has come to open warfare then."

Arthur shook his head. "We cannot know that until we find out who massacred that village. Doged marrying this girl was unexpected. My agents tell me that Cilydd and the others could not control their curiosity, so they returned to Doged's seat to attend his wedding."

"When was that held?"

"Two new moons past."

"Is there any sign that the bride is with child?"

"Not yet. But it is still early." He stopped and chuckled. "I am told that his new woman likes being a queen, a little too much."

"Then I pity old Doged."

"But I am also told that she is exceedingly beautiful."

It was my turn to laugh. "Well, I trust her beauty is sufficient to offset the trouble she will cause."

"My lords."

We looked up to see an old friend in the door—Ider. Once a monk at Ynys-witrin, Ider had fallen afoul of *episcopus* Dubricius some months before, after Arthur's marriage to the Demetae princess Gwyneira ended in tragedy. Ider had proved himself a brave and loyal friend, and when Dubricius had him cast from the Christ's service Arthur took him into his service. For my part, I believed it a good trade.

Now, I hardly recognized the once thin, almost ascetic monk. Freed of the *monachi's* harsh diet, he had gained weight. And where once his carefully shaven tonsure marked his head, now a tangle of dirty yellow hair held sway. But his eagerness to please was still there, and for that I was glad. I would not want him to change so much that he ceased to be Ider.

"The horses and wagons are ready, Rigotamos," he reported breathlessly.

Arthur rose and slapped my shoulder. "Come, Malgwyn. We are keeping both Mother and Doged waiting."

Standing and awkwardly straightening my tunic with my one hand, I had to wonder if they were the only ones that were awaiting us.

Our plan was to stop first at Lord Doged's seat to the south, Castellum Dinas, pay our respects, and then Arthur would move on to Tyntagel in the north. 'Twas only a few hours' ride from Castellum Dinas, and when we had reached the proper moment in our mediation efforts Arthur would be sent for.

But Arthur surprised me just as we were to begin. "I wish you, Bedevere, and Ider to go to Lord Doged. I will go with Morgan straight to Tyntagel."

"Are you certain? You may need Ider."

"Is Ider a *medicus*?" he snapped, but he quickly softened his tone when he saw how my head reeled in surprise. "I am sorry, Malgwyn. My mother is a difficult person at the best of times. I doubt that lying on her deathbed will have cured that." He stopped and dropped his head. "You may need Ider more than I. It is in the *consilium*'s best interest that Doged continue in possession of his lands."

Arthur's statement made me stop and think. What I knew of Doged was that he was a generally congenial old fellow. His seat was but three Roman *schoenii* from Trevelgue, where he maintained another residence. Much of our goods came in through the port there, but we had other ports.

The Rigotamos saw the look in my eye. He reached into his pouch and removed something from his pouch. I needed no explanation for this rock. Though but a small bit, it was unmistakable. Gold.

CHAPTER THREE

So, it isn't just a possibility." The little nugget in my hand told the tale too well. First, there had only been a chance of gold. This proved it beyond doubt.

"Doged's man found only this one bit, but it makes the situation all the more serious."

"Who else knows of this?"

"You, Bedevere, Doged, of course. The rider he sent with these samples."

"When did you receive them?"

"Late, late last night. I have sent for Merlin as you suggested. He knows of such things and may have more answers for us."

I wandered over and watched two troop of horse prepare to leave. "So Lord Doged's seat truly sits atop a gold mine." The only other gold mines anyone knew about in all of Britannia were the Roman mines in the far north.

The Romans had discovered that gold, but, to my knowledge, none had been found in the lands of the Cornovii, though we had found plenty of tin and lead. But gold. Suddenly Doged went from being a mildly interesting lord of little consequence to a man of great import.

"Perhaps. There has been but this one bit of gold yet. But there has been agaphite, and its value is unquestioned."

Turning back to him, I frowned. "You should not have released Illtud." Our old friend Illtud, a cousin of Arthur's and one of the finest officers to serve him, had entered the Christ's service. At last word, Illtud was studying in a monastery in the Breton lands, across the great channel. "We could use him right now."

Arthur grunted. "I know it all too well. But I have also called for Kay."

"Who will command at Castellum Arturius?"

"Gawain."

"Not Paderic?" Paderic was Arthur's cousin and a good man, but slow of mind.

Arthur chuckled at that, and that was what I hoped to see. This journey had already become like a heavy burden to him. "No, I think Gawain will serve well."

I nodded. He was a good choice. Though a brother of Mordred, Gawain had none of Mordred's conniving nature and more than a touch of his cousin Arthur's nobility.

Mordred. We would need all of the gods' help if he caught wind of gold in Doged's land. Arthur had given up assigning Mordred special commands. At last word, he had left his own lands in the hands of a young noble and was far to the north in Lord David's lands, probably plotting Arthur's downfall, but at least far enough away not to cause immediate mischief.

Mordred had played a role in the death of Eleonore, nearly three years before. He coveted the Rigotamos's crown with all his heart, if he had one. But unlike some of the lords, Mordred was clever, clever enough not to be found out.

"What are your orders?"

Arthur paused for a second. "Kay will come to me at Tyntagel. Merlin will join you at Castellum Dinas. Take the measure of Doged and this Cilydd. Aye, and take the measure of the girl, Ysbail."

"Arthur, this . . ." I put thoughts of Ysbail out of my mind and returned to staring at the rocks.

He smiled grimly. "This is more headache than I need, but it could also be an opportunity. I have long wanted to build a merchant ship capable of trade, and we desperately need warships to stave off the raids by the Scotti."

"So, I am to lend assistance to Doged, for he is more pliable than the younger ones?"

"No, you are to lend assistance to Doged because he has been a good and faithful servant to the *consilium*. Doged is a good man, wise. There is far more to him than you would think. No lord has served the *consilium* as well or as courageously as Doged. I would rather support a proven friend than a young rebel who might become thirsty for my crown. And with gold, he might be able to purchase my downfall."

Pulling his cloak about his neck and securing it with a great fibula, Arthur headed for his horse. "Call for me if you need me. Otherwise, I will join you when my mother's health is better, or . . ." He did not finish or I did not hear his last words.

I worried for Arthur. My own mother had lain gravely ill for weeks before she passed into the shadows, as had my brother, Cuneglas, horribly wounded in the affair surrounding Arthur's election as Rigotamos. Their suffering had haunted me for many a night.

Poor Cuneglas, caught up in affairs for which he cared nothing. He had aroused just moments before he died, causing my enemies to say that he was healing and that I killed him to have Ygerne, and later that Ygerne and I had both killed him. A man's enemies will say anything to harm him.

As we rode along, the sun began to warm the land. You could see fewer pieces of the old Romans here. An occasional villa still marked the earth, some narrower roads. They had never fully populated this part of Britannia, not like the eastern lands. But they had improved many of the harbors, critical to trading in lead and tin and importing their amphorae of wine and olive oil, the interminable olive oil. But the absence of such kept these lands from looking like skin marred with scabs and blotches of ruin. It was a welcome change.

I felt a presence and twisted in my saddle to see Bedevere riding up to join me. His long tunic was bunched about his waist, held tight there by a wide leather belt decorated with iron studs. Where Kay was tall and given to fits of temper, Bedevere was stocky and taciturn. In a land that seemed often to have lost all honor, if Bedevere gave his word he never broke it. All three of us had warred under Arthur's banner, and since I had returned to the Rigotamos's service we had grown close once more, in a way only war comrades can.

"What think you of Morgan?" Bedevere asked, drawing even with me.

I shrugged. "He is typical of the northerners I have known, oversolicitous."

"That is why they make good physicians," Bedevere grunted. "Always seeking favor, not honor."

"Oh, Bedevere, every lord on the *consilium* save a handful spends more time currying favor than seeking honor."

"And other things," he said.

"How so?"

"Once, when Arthur, Kay, and I were hardly men, more boys really, we were returning to Cadwy's seat from taking messages to Ambrosius. We stopped near the crest of a high hill to eat, one that gave a good view of the land below. A maiden was feeding chickens near a poor hut in the distance.

"We noticed her, as boys will, spoke of how much sport she would be. Arthur leaped to his feet; he was always impetuous then. He announced that he would have her, by fair or foul.

"Kay lunged for Arthur and caught him about his shoulders, pulling him to the earth. 'NO!' he shouted. 'We have honor. We protect such as she, not molest them.'

"Arthur was not convinced. 'What good is it to have power if you do not use it to please yourself?' he said.

"Then a voice spoke, a new one. 'Can I help you, young masters?' It was an older man, walking with a staff. He wore a threadbare cloak of thin wool, fastened about his neck with a bit of wood. His tunic had holes in it, and he was barefoot. But that wasn't what struck me the most. He was thin, more skeleton than man. I feared the breeze might carry him away.

"I remember that Kay and Arthur scrambled to their feet, embarrassed at being caught fighting. The old man smiled at them. 'We have little to eat, my lords, but you are welcome to share it,' he said.

" 'Is that your home?' I asked him, pointing at the farm below.

"He nodded. 'Aye, that is my daughter. Please, join us.'

"Arthur had lost that hunger on his face. And he asked the question we were all thinking: 'Are you ill? You are so thin.'

"The old man's face reddened like a ripe apple, and he hung his head. 'I need but little to survive. I wish my daughter to grow strong,' he said.

"We thanked him for his offer and left quickly. Never again did Arthur speak of power, or lust, only honor."

I had never heard that tale of Arthur. In truth, stories of the young Arthur were scarce. Sometimes it seemed to me that he had been born on the edge of manhood. Asking about his youth and origins brought either a clever joke or a scowl. Merlin knew much, but he was ever faithful to Arthur and kept his secrets well.

The journey was uneventful, save a rain and blustering wind that swept across us for a few moments and then was gone. Our western lands held long, wide wastelands where the remnants of those who went before could still be seen. From the circular mounds where they buried their dead to the circular rock footprints of their houses, they dotted the bleak green landscape. I did not know why the old ones would have chosen such desolate places to live, or die. Perhaps in those olden times they were not as dismal and wind battered as today.

We approached Doged's lands a little warily. Bedevere posted a defensive screen of horse on either side of our main party to flush out any ambush. We were not too distant from the sea, and despite our best efforts, the gods' tears soaked us. "The gods' tears." That was something my mother used to say when I was small. Even then, I could not help but try to understand.

"But tears are salty. If they were tears then nothing would grow."

My mother had pursed her lips as she lowered a bucket into the well. "That's the difference between man's tears and the gods'. Ours kill things; the tears of the gods make things grow."

Though that answer did not satisfy me, I accepted it. And the driving rain on this day did nothing to dispel my dissatisfaction. Daron, riding behind me, never spoke a word. All seemed dreary and unpromising. Until a rider appeared from the west, from the crest of a low hill to our right, carrying a banner.

Bedevere raised a hand and brought our party to a halt. Ider rode forward and joined us.

"Trouble?" I asked of no one in particular.

Ider stretched forward in his saddle and squinted. "No. It is Doged's banner."

The three of us exchanged glances as the rider sped forward until, nearing us, he jerked on the reins, bringing his mount to a halt with a snort.

A big man, he wore an old Saxon helmet. I wondered if he won it in battle. Something about him was familiar, though I could not quite discern what. As his horse continued snorting, catching its breath, he removed the helmet to reveal a huge scar running across the left side of his face, from cheekbone to chin.

"My lords, please . . . forgive my appearance," he gasped, nearly as out of breath as his horse.

"You have a message for us?" Bedevere asked.

"Yes, my lord. Lord Doged wishes you to join him at Trevelgue. He has gone there to meet with the Saxon envoy from Aelle."

Part of me was grateful; going all the way to Doged's seat and then having to turn around and go to Trevelgue would have added another half day or more to our journey. Another part of me was bothered. Merlin would be delayed in joining us. The rocks were at Castellum Dinas or near there.

The rider was saying something else; I tried to shut it out and plan the most expedient way to assess the ore without drawing too much attention. But then Bedevere barked angrily, nearly like a dog.

"Mordred? What is he doing here?"

That brought me back as if a thunderbolt had struck me. "Mordred?"

The poor rider must have feared for his life, as he backed up his horse and seemed about to bolt.

"Hold, rider!" Bedevere's shout brought the poor messenger's panic to a stop. He reined in his horse and calmed it. "Repeat what you said about Lord Mordred."

The rider gulped. "My lord, the envoy says that they have Lord Mordred as a hostage and are prepared to release him to Lord Arthur as a sign of good faith."

I looked at Bedevere, feeling the grin then spreading across my face. "Can we refuse this gift?"

Bedevere was not smiling, at all. His eyes flickered at me, nearly a glancing blow, but enough to give me pause. When and where had Mordred been taken prisoner and why did we not know of this already?

"Consider your message delivered," Bedevere said to the rider.

He jerked the reins to turn his horse, and something in the gesture was familiar.

"Wait."

The rider looked over his shoulder and pulled up.

"Your name is Gurdur."

"It is, my lord."

I had seen this man before, but I could not remember where. Usually a name will spark some memory.

"You look familiar to me as well," said Bedevere.

The rider hid a smile behind his hand.

Why did I know this man? It was frustrating. Then, behind us, one of our soldiers said something in the Scotti tongue, and the rider answered him.

The soldier, Aidan, then joined the laughter. "Master Malgwyn, this is Gurdur, the boy who spoke all languages, who joined Arthur's banner before he could yet grow a beard."

And then it was plain to see. He was older by several years and had finally grown into a man. The lad had a gift for tongues, and within a few days could pick up almost any tribal dialect or foreign speech. After the war, I had lost track of the youngster and he had faded in my memory.

"How come you to serve Doged now?"

"I was from these lands, and after the war it seemed only meet that I should return. Lord Doged needed someone to serve as a translator; I was recommended to him."

"Go, and tell your master that we are coming," Bedevere ordered, as much to give us time to confer as in any haste.

Gurdur rode off; we did not.

"Mordred was with Lord David at last word," I said, studying Bedevere's face. It was expressionless. He hated Mordred nearly as much as I did.

But he remained silent.

"I can see only two ways that Mordred became a hostage of the Saxons. Either he was taken by force (an event we should certainly have heard about) or he went willingly, which seems odd even for Mordred," I said into the quiet.

"Unless it happened since we left Castellum Arturius."

He was right. But if it happened so recently, how did

Mordred appear in the company of a Saxon envoy so quickly, so far from David's lands?

"It does no good to worry about these things now," I said. "Let us go to Trevelgue and find out."

Another day passed before we entered the fringes of the coastal village of Trevelgue. I was glad that Gurdur was at Trevelgue; the speech of the far western peoples was almost incomprehensible to me, though it was said to be the same as ours. The westerners, the Cornovii, though, did not speak any Latin, which most of us still did. Oh, there were a few in each port who had some Latin; they had to since so much of our trade came from those countries. But our children were not learning much Latin, and I suspected that it would fade away over time.

I turned on my horse and motioned Sulien forward. Daron favored me with a smile. "Remember that when we enter the village you are my *servus*. Here, Sulien, take her onto your horse."

We made the exchange with little problem. "Our task is simple, Sulien. We are to keep Daron safe."

He nodded quickly, and I felt happy with my choice of a bodyguard. Sulien was mature and experienced. He did not chafe for war, but he would not shrink from it either. I urged my horse forward.

The lanes were lined with people as if some great festival had been declared. Booths lined the road, selling wine and mead and *cervesas*, rabbit and chicken. An odd variety of odors drifted across the lanes, spices that I did not recognize, warm and musky scents. Beneath the shouts of the merchants, hawking their wares, was the clink of coins changing hands. People here had more coins than we had further east. The trading ships brought them and used them in the village.

Trevelgue, though but a small place, was a seaport. And as such it boasted facilities that we did not have at Castellum Arturius—*ganea*, where men bought sex; and public houses where food and *cervesas* could be bought, where men played at dice and ships' captains recruited men for their next voyage. And coins clinked.

We were not better people to the east, but we had fewer foreigners. Those who chose to journey east from our western ports took grave risks. While many of the *civitas*, the cities of the Romans, functioned still, the land was yet lawless. Strangers were easy quarry for the bands of *latrunculii* that roamed the forests and for the petty tyrannies of lesser lords.

But Castellum Arturius had a public house, in the lower precinct near the northeast gate, more to serve the soldiers of the lords who visited the Rigotamos. Arthur would not suffer the *meretrices*, the whores, however, to establish their own house within our walls. Rather they used an old building in the Roman village to the northeast.

Most lords of the *consilium* had such laws. Though I had heard it said that David allowed *ganea* in his domain, and Mordred too. I doubted that Mark did, since our *episcopus*, Dubricius, was in residence at Castellum Marcus.

We had been noticed. A gaggle of Doged's soldiers were loitering outside a public house. Their tunics were dyed a deep brown, with a single chevron stitched in yellow at their center. But their clothes held tears and ragged edges. They were poor specimens. As Arthur's officers and councilors, we deserved their salute, but they did not give it. Rather, they turned their heads and sneered.

"It seems we are not very welcome," I said to Bedevere.

"Or these men are but wolves in sheep's clothing."

"Speak plainly."

"Everyone knows that Arthur will support Doged's authority. We know that he has rebellious men. Perhaps these are among them and they view us as enemies."

He was right.

And then yet a new party sent my hand reaching for my sword. Saxons. Beside me, Bedevere swore. We knew they were here under a flag of truce and hence we were forbidden to harm them. This was fortunate. For were I to have my way, I would personally have cut each and every Saxon throat I could find, and bathed in their blood. I tried to push those thoughts away, and much of the time I was successful. But the sight of even one greasy topknot sent the bile boiling into my throat.

"Steady, Malgwyn," Bedevere cautioned me.

"I'll start no wars today," I grunted.

The village was laid out on either side of this lane, which ran out to the headland where Castellum Dinas stood. A second lane split off just before the gate and ran down to the harbor. Shops lined that route as well: a lumberyard for the shipbuilders, a wine merchant who preferred not to have to carry his amphorae very far, a public house, a dealer in olive oil. The scents of this area were both richer and fouler. Raw sewage ran through the gutters. A tanner's stench drifted across the lane with the breeze. And beneath those lay a more appealing odor of cooked pig.

We stopped before the gate and dismounted. Two of the

Pictish *servi* that we had brought along hurried forward to take our horses. This was my first journey to Doged's coastal seat, and an impressive one it was. Its being situated on a headland, connected to the mainland by a narrow bridge, with six massive ditches and ramparts, made it a nearly impregnable fortress. Within, I had been told, were several of the old, circular burial mounds favored by our ancients.

But as we crossed the bridge and entered the fort, I noticed the signs of age and neglect. Even the bridge creaked and groaned under our weight. Weeds grew from the dirt embankment and up into the wooden ramparts. Some of the timbers had been recently replaced, but several showed signs of sagging and rot.

None of the guards challenged us, though whether out of laziness or lack of concern I couldn't tell. But the grunt from Bedevere told me that he was not happy. My companion was an excellent soldier and outstanding officer. He demanded much of his own men, and to see others so ill behaved rankled him.

Ahead of us, striding down the lane from a large timber hall, came a tall, elderly man, dressed as a warrior, spear and shield in hand. His tunic bore the yellow chevron of Doged, and his cloak, fastened about his shoulders with a circular brooch, was of the same brown fabric. The old fellow had once been a powerful man, but he was now stooped and walked with a limp.

On reaching us, he nodded and said in a voice that crackled like knotty wood in a fire, "I welcome you to my home, Lord Bedevere."

So this was Doged. I had never met him before. His warring days had ended before mine began, and he had warred, riding with Ambrosius in the days after Vortigern's disgrace and proving himself an able warrior.

Behind me, I heard a chuckle. Yes, Doged had been a great warrior in his day, but his being attired as one now made Doged look weak and addled. He should have been attired as a senior lord of the *consilium*, with a fine tunic and a strong leather belt, dotted with iron studs.

I turned to see who was making sport of Doged and saw a pack of young nobles swilling mead and jostling each other. One in particular caught my attention, a short, stocky man of about twenty-five years. His nose was the most remarkable feature, as it was crooked with a good-sized hump. I had seen such noses before; it had been broken. A closer look revealed a long scar down one side of his face. Though young, this man had seen some trouble.

"Malgwyn."

I turned back to Bedevere, who was trying to introduce me to Doged. He was easily older than Ambrosius by ten winters, his skin stretched so tight over his bones that he looked more like a skeleton than a man. Thrusting out his hand to take mine, he noticed my missing arm. He narrowed his eyes in apparent confusion.

"I was told that Lord Bedevere was missing a hand, yet I see both of his but only one of yours."

Bedevere and I both chuckled. Since Arthur's elevation to Rigotamos, word had spread about his one-armed councilor. And because Kay's role as his steward kept him from being oft afield, Bedevere was my more constant companion, and the people often confused us.

"Surely, a lord of your experience knows that you cannot believe all that you hear," I answered in greeting.

Doged threw back his head and laughed deeply. "I have

never been called old so diplomatically. Come, and enjoy my hospitality."

And he threw his arms about our shoulders and ushered us up the path and into his hall. I chanced to glance over my shoulder and saw that the band of young nobles was fast on our heels.

And Sulien nodded quickly, slightly, dismounting and taking Daron in tow.

CHAPTER FOUR

Doged was a congenial sort, more so than I would have been. All of his nobles, including the group of young toughs, trooped into his hall behind us, intent, I suspected, on assessing Arthur's lieutenants.

I noticed immediately that you did not see the trappings of the Christ here as in Arthur's hall. In truth, from the ancient burial barrows to the bear on his shields, Doged seemed a lord who clung to the old ways. Of the chevron on his tunic I did not know. Perhaps, I thought, it was some ancient symbol of his people.

Doged arranged his hall much differently than Arthur. No round tables here. One long one at the front of the hall for Doged and his family, and then a series of long ones down each side. I had been told that this was common in the western lands. Seats were assigned. The closer you sat to the lord, the more influential you were. This seemed rather silly to me. A lord's time was better spent governing his lands, not deciding who would sit where, but as I saw that Cilydd and his followers were relegated to the furthest seats, it struck me that upon such decisions rebellions were founded.

If I thought Arthur's kitchen well stocked, Doged's was astounding. Oysters, fresh fish from the sea, pig, beef, loaves of freshly baked bread. Doged had so many amphorae of wine that they were stacked around the walls. I immediately suspected that those were the price of docking at his port, not that that would be unusual. By the *consilium*'s orders, each member should receive a portion of any import tax, but it was an order seldom obeyed, and an abuse that Arthur did not speak out against.

"Ider!" I called for my young friend.

"Yes, Malgwyn." His voice sounded at my shoulder and I fair jumped. Turning, I thought once again of how he had changed since he had left Ynys-witrin. But of all the changes, I reflected on how bright and alive his eyes were now. Before, they had been the frightened, humbled eyes of a small animal, when it hides from its enemy. I wondered at a faith that stole the life from a man.

"Circulate among the people. I see no sign of a chapel here, no religious house. The Rigotamos will want to know about such. And see what gossip you hear about Doged's new bride."

"What of Sulien and the girl?"

"They will stay with me."

He nodded and slipped away.

"He has come far," Bedevere said.

"Aye, and I am grateful for his presence. He reminds me of you."

Bedevere cocked his square-shaped head at me. "How so?"

"He is a true and faithful friend. When mine and Guinevere's lives were threatened by Melwas at Pomparles, he willingly put his own in danger to save us."

"That makes him a better man than I," Bedevere countered.

I just laughed. But then Doged began to speak.

"We wish to welcome our cousins from the east," Doged said, his voice crackling like a fire of dry twigs. "They tell me that we will soon be joined by the Rigotamos."

A cheer went up and flasks were thumped on the tables, though the cheers were louder from those tables nearest Doged.

Then, a hush fell over the room. A door at the back of the hall, leading, I presumed, to Doged's chambers, opened and a woman glided out. She was of average height but well figured. Her hair was what caught everyone's eye. It was the whitest yellow I had ever seen, so white as to almost be silver. Her eyes sat above a queen's nose, slender and pointed and noble, and they were of a blue unlike any I had seen, and life danced in them. Her skin was as fair and pale as a spirit, and she used no crushed berries to redden her cheeks or lips.

"My lady Ysbail," Doged began, taking the woman's hand in his. "Please greet our visitors from Castellum Arturius—Lord Bedevere and Master Malgwyn."

She stepped toward us, averting her eyes, but not from modesty, rather from apparent disdain. "So you are what the Rigotamos has sent us rather than visit himself." Her voice was icy, destroying, for me, her beauty. Arthur was right. She did enjoy her new station.

"Yes, my lady," Bedevere said with a forced smile. "I am Lord Arthur's Master of Horse. But be assured that the Rigotamos will be here shortly. Until then, we must do."

"And this," she replied, indicating me without looking at me, "is your servant?"

"No, my lady," my friend answered patiently. "He is Malgwyn ap Cuneglas, senior councilor to the Rigotamos."

She turned that frigid gaze to Doged then. "Arthur must

be in serious trouble if this is the best he can muster for a councilor."

"Now, my dear," Doged began, but I shook my head.

"Do not worry, my lord," I said. "A 'woman' should not be expected to recognize the Rigotamos's advisors."

I did not need to see the look she gave me then; I could feel it piercing my chest with all the fury of an arrow shot in anger. But that was only in my mind. Beside me, I heard a slight gasp escape from Bedevere. I regretted my words almost as soon as I had spoken them. First, I did not believe them myself. But more important, she was the wife of Lord Doged and she deserved my respect. And I had insulted her.

Once more my temper had spoken over the voice of common sense. "My apologies, my lady," I tried a more conciliatory tone.

"The next time you appear, Lord Bedevere, leave your pets at home."

Doged rolled his eyes.

Ysbail nodded to Bedevere and ignored me. I deserved it. "Let us feast now and talk later," proclaimed Doged, in a hurry to move to other topics.

We all sat then and the *servi* began filling our cups anew. I jammed my dagger into the plank of pig on my platter and ate hungrily. Until I felt a tug at my sleeve.

Looking down, I saw a wisp of a lad, perhaps five winters old, with straw-colored hair and high cheekbones. "May I help you, young master?"

"You have but one arm," he said, his voice filled with curiosity.

"I do," I confirmed.

"But why, master? Why have you only one arm?" I could not be offended; his tone was not insolent.

"He lost it in battle, Culhwch," a new voice said. "This is the great Malgwyn of Tribuit, who slew Saxons by the dozens."

The newcomer placed his hand tenderly on the boy's shoulder. It was the broken-nosed man with the scar on his face. I saw immediately that the boy was but a fairer miniature of the father.

He extended his left hand to me, and I took it in mine. I found his smile infectious.

"You do me great honor, sir."

"Only because it is deserved. I am Cilydd, my lord. This is my son, Culhwch."

So this was the rascal Cilydd, who threatened rebellion against Doged. Bedevere and I exchanged quick glances. Cilydd was not what we expected. Traitors, in our minds, were more like Mordred, greasy, ambitious, and likable in a common way. This man seemed a genuinely good sort, and his son was charming and without guile.

"Would you sit with us?" I asked, without thinking.

Cilydd shook his head and smiled again. "I think Lord Doged would not approve. I am relegated to the far shores of the hall."

"Then attend us in our camp tonight," I offered. Our troop of horse was establishing our camp even then, beyond the walls of the fort.

Cilydd bowed. "It would be my great pleasure."

"And bring your son," Bedevere answered. "He seems a good lad."

Again, we were greeted with that infectious smile. I hoped that it was not the plague Cilydd carried.

The rest of the evening passed without the usual speeches, boasting our host's battle prowess, of which our people were so fond. I assumed they were saving those for Arthur's arrival, and I was glad. I had seen too many battlefields to find glory in any of them. War was a terrible, though sometimes necessary, thing. I am not a learned man; I have not studied with any great *philologus*, but that much I knew.

As was my charge at Arthur's table, I spent my time watching the people, and I saw much. Cilydd's men showed little interest in anything but their food. Except for Cilydd himself, that is. He seemed very interested in the fair Ysbail, and to my great surprise, I caught her meeting his looks with a faint smile and a coy expression. That did not bode well for Doged at all. Another group of nobles in the last aisle regarded Doged with equally ill-disguised disdain. I asked Bedevere if he knew them.

"They are from Ennor and Ynys Scilly."

"The lands which were flooded?"

"Aye. They have wandered for a generation, seeking a new home. In truth, they are cousins to Lord Mark, but he refuses to settle any lands on them."

In my grandparents' time, the great islands of Ennor and Ynys Scilly were connected to the mainland by a giant swamp. Older tales said that all had once been dry, and there were the remnants of great trees, stone walls, and even a chapel. But then, about the time of my father's birth, a giant wave rose, submerging the swamp and those last bits of a great and noble people, and splitting Ennor and Ynys Scilly into a myriad of smaller isles.

It had been a horrible event; thousands were drowned, swept away. Whole villages disappeared beneath the wave. Some people remained, but most fled to the mainland. Thus dispossessed, they journeyed throughout our southwestern lands, seeking a place to call their own.

"Perhaps they are hoping that Doged will grant them lands?"

Bedevere shook his head. "I do not think so. He is fighting now to keep his lands together; I doubt that he would willingly part with any."

I nodded and resumed eating the excellent grilled pig, noting as I did the intense exchange of looks between Ysbail and Cilydd.

Later in the evening, as the nobles began to leave, or pass out from the mead and wine, Doged motioned for us to join him. As we maneuvered through the wreckage of the feast, one of the nobles from Ennor stopped us.

"My lords, you serve the Rigotamos?" He was a pleasant-enough-looking fellow, neatly attired in tunic and *braccae*. His hair was neither red nor brown but something in between, and it hung below his shoulders. But his face was clean shaven and his smile showed a full set of good teeth.

"We do," Bedevere answered.

"I am Trevelyan, of Ennor."

Something in the name was familiar.

"How can we help you?"

Without Bedevere's leave, Trevelyan slumped into a chair and hung his head. "My lord, since my grandfather's time we have been attempting to find lands to settle on. Some people have found sanctuary with their kinfolk."

I nodded. It was common knowledge that Lord Mark's grandfather had taken in a large group of cousins, among them Mark's first wife, mother of Tristan. "Why do you not settle on the islands that remain?"

Trevelyan grimaced. "They are small, and who knows when the sea might swallow them as well. No, it is better that we seek safer lands."

"Have you considered the regions near the great wall in the north?"

Again, Trevelyan grimaced. "And subject ourselves to daily raids by the Picts? No, that is not the answer. I am hoping that you will press the Rigotamos to grant me an audience when he arrives."

Bedevere looked to me and I shrugged. There was no harm in it. "Very well, Trevelyan. We will arrange a chance for you to press your suit."

The young man leaped up and embraced Bedevere, much to my friend's dismay. Bedevere stepped back quickly, embarrassed, and I stifled a chuckle.

Trevelyan saw Bedevere's reaction and was immediately humbled. "I am sorry, my lord, but it is not often that we find anyone willing to listen to our plight."

Bedevere's stone face cracked a bit. "I will commend you to Lord Arthur. Perhaps your cause will find a friendly ear with him."

At that, Bedevere broke away and followed after Doged with me at his heels, leaving Trevelyan standing alone in the empty hall.

"Well, Bedevere," Doged began in his crackly voice. "You have seen the rocks I sent to Arthur?"

"Aye, my lord."

The old warrior crossed the room and sat in a chair. Behind him was the door to his private bedchamber. I guessed that Ysbail was closeted there.

"I will not lie to you. It complicates an already complex situation. Should word escape that there is gold and agaphite in my lands, then my old white head will be laid upon the chopping block for every ambitious noble in these lands and perhaps beyond."

"Is it not already, my lord?" I asked.

Doged jerked back in surprise, and then smiled. "That is true. But I have held Cilydd and his fellows off by marrying Ysbail."

"Any signs?" Bedevere did not have to explain any further.

The old lord shook his head. "Not yet, but it has only been two new moons."

"Still, the sooner she conceives the sooner you can smother these sounds of rebellion."

"Oh, well, unless she is barren, she will conceive." His certainty seemed . . . wrong, somehow. But then was not the time to question him.

"What is the current state of affairs here?" A much better question.

Doged shrugged. "You have seen my court. Of my own nobles, Cilydd is the most powerful, though his brother, Druce, is also very strong, and it is Druce I fear more than Cilydd." The old lord reached up and fiddled with the brooch holding his tunic in place, a circular one, common and unpretentious.

"Why, my lord?"

Doged cocked his head to the side. "Both are ambitious men, but Cilydd has some honor. Druce has none. He will do whatever is necessary to bring strength to his banner."

That moment seemed to be the right time to bring up the village massacre.

"Lord Doged, as we journeyed here, we passed through a village near your border with the summer country. The people were killed and all their goods and animals taken. I cannot describe the devastation inflicted on those poor people."

Doged dropped his head, and I noticed that his fist was clenched so tight that his knuckles were white. Finally, he raised his head. "Could you determine when this happened?"

"The bodies were still fresh. Dead less than a day before we arrived."

"And there were no survivors?"

Bedevere and I exchanged glances. I was most hesitant to tell anyone of Daron, but Doged's reputation was beyond reproach. And that feeling in the pit of my stomach said that I could trust him. "One, only. She says that those who weren't killed were taken captive."

Doged turned and slammed a fist into a wall, rattling the entire building, it seemed. "Druce. It had to be Druce or his brother one. They are the only two of my rivals with a will to act. The others are feckless whiners who would run in fright if they saw a dagger aimed their way." He paused, turning back toward us slowly.

"Malgwyn, Ambrosius speaks highly of some skill of yours."

"Ambrosius is kind."

"I have no one with such abilities about me. My *vigiles* are more drunks than watchmen. Would you take my commission to see that the savages who did this are punished?"

It was only then that he turned full face. A blood vessel pumped angrily at his pale temple. The wrinkles that cratered his face seemed to deepen as we watched. The redness in his eyes had grown tenfold and tears glistened. This was a good man, a proper noble.

And though I had already set myself on that course, I readily and happily nodded.

Doged turned away again, embarrassed, I am certain, at his tears. We stayed silent until he faced us once more, his eyes still red, but no hint of moisture in them.

"What of this Saxon embassy from Aelle?" Bedevere ventured into the quiet. "And their claim of holding Mordred hostage?"

Our host chuckled. "They may hold him forever for my part. I know that Mordred, when posted here by Ambrosius, incited Cilydd to revolt. But no, I have no proof of their present claim, though I have heard rumors that he is being held along the coast between here and Tyntagel.

"I have chosen not to admit their party into the fort itself," he continued. "I cannot keep them out of the town, but my problems are quite serious enough without allowing the wolves into my sheep pen. Besides, I am no fool. They are here because Arthur will be here. If there will be negotiations over Mordred, it will be Arthur negotiating. When he arrives, I will give them leave to enter the fortress.

"But until then they enjoy my hospitality in the *vicus*. I keep four of my men watching them, rotating the hours. As yet, there has been no sign of Mordred."

Bedevere nodded. Obviously Doged was not the fool that rumor held him to be. "We are not certain as to when Arthur will be here. He is visiting his mother, who is very ill."

Doged smiled sadly. "I knew Igraine when she was still married to Gorlois."

"Truly? Arthur rarely speaks of his mother and father," I said.

The old man laughed again. "Then I shall not, but did you know that Celliwic is where Gorlois was killed, freeing Igraine to become Uther's woman?"

At that, even Bedevere, Arthur's oldest companion, shook his head. "I knew only that Igraine had been married before," he said.

"Then we shall leave it at that. As to the issue of the gold and agaphite, I have decided to convey all rights to the *consilium*, provided that they take responsibility for the mining."

Bedevere and I exchanged swift glances. Doged was indeed clever. By giving the rights to the *consilium*, he essentially made them all business partners in the mining, and he eliminated the need for the other lords to contrive against him.

"Master Malgwyn," Doged continued. "I know that you are a scribe, and I hoped that you would prepare a document to that effect. I wish to present this gift to the Rigotamos immediately upon his arrival."

I nodded. "It will be my pleasure, my lord. I assume that you intend for any profits to be shared equally among the other lords?"

This time he nodded.

"Harrumph." Bedevere cleared his throat and we turned to him. "You realize, Lord Doged, that signing away what might be the greatest treasure in your lands will further enrage Cilydd and your own nobles?"

"I realize that my actions will not be popular, but imagine for just a moment what would happen if I gathered these to my breast and did not share with the *consilium*. I would make enemies of every lord of the *consilium*, to which I have pledged my allegiance. Better the enemies at home, who I know well, than enemies stretched across the land.

"And more importantly, I have always agreed with Ambrosius and Arthur. We are far stronger unified than we could ever be as individual tribes. Vortigern was wrong to enlist the aid of the Saxons. Had we truly worked as one in those days, the raids of the Picts and the Scotti would have been as the mulings of pestilential children, annoying, but not a true threat. I told him this myself." He stopped and hung his head. "I always believed that Vortigern himself profited by bringing the Saxons, that perhaps he had parlayed for the Saxon crown itself."

I reeled at the words. "You knew Vortigern? You sat in his councils?"

The ancient lord grinned at me. "Vortigern was my friend. We met as young lords at a gathering in the early days of the *consilium*. I was proud to call him my brother," and Doged spoke then through clenched teeth. "Until he recruited the Saxons. We broke on that issue, and I was denied my seat on the *consilium* for a time. It was later that Cadwy and Ambrosius petitioned for my return."

I was impressed. Doged was rarely spoken of. From what little I had heard, he was just an older lord who rarely ventured outside his lands. He was staunchly loyal and faithful to the *consilium*, seemingly unambitious, and could be expected to answer any summons quickly. In brief, he was predictable, and predictable lords caused little discussion and were trusted with the most necessary of positions.

But now I saw that there was much more to the man, and I liked what I saw. I valued fidelity and loyalty, almost as much as I valued the truth. This was a good man, clinging to all that he held dear with both wit and wisdom. And unlike many that

I encountered, he had not treated me as less than a man because of my missing arm. That counted for much with me.

It was Bedevere, though, who answered for us both. "How
can we serve you until the Rigotamos arrives?"

Doged smiled. "If Malgwyn will prepare the conveyance
and then lend me his counsel, I would ask you, Lord Bedevere, to review my troops and tell me where they need training and preparation. From what you report of those poor
villagers, I fear that I will have to use them sooner than I
would hope."

Before either of us could answer, shouts arose from the
feasting hall, voices raised in fierce anger.

The three of us rushed out to find a truly remarkable sight,
at least for Bedevere and myself.

A straw-haired soldier had twisted the arm of one of Doged's
soldiers behind his back and held a dagger to the throat of the
hapless man. With a deadly grimace, he was walking the man
awkwardly into the hall as the few stragglers about melted against
the walls.

"Lord Doged," I said. "Meet the newest recruit to Arthur's
banner—Ider."

And it was Ider.

"Why are you trying to kill one of Lord Doged's men?"
Bedevere asked.

Ider relaxed, a grin spreading across his face, and he released the soldier. "He tried to prevent my entry."

Since being cast out from the community of brothers at
Ynys-witrin, Ider, once a quiet, simple *monachus* and callow
youth, had immersed himself in the soldier's life. Obviously, he
was learning his lessons well.

"Something I am certain he will not do again," Doged

replied. The old man turned to us. "The night is upon us, and I need my rest. I will speak with you again tomorrow." At that, he disappeared into his private quarters.

The onlookers peeled themselves off the wall and resumed their drinking and carousing. I noted Cilydd considering our little trio with a smile, but quickly he returned to his drinking. I saw too that he was sharing a pot with the hapless Trevelyan.

We moved to one of the tables and sat with Ider while a *servus* filled our pots with mead.

"What did you find?" I asked. Though he had been with us for almost nine moons, I still found the sight of Ider without a tonsure unsettling. It was like I was looking at a different man. And perhaps I was.

Ider combed his hand through his unruly mop and shook his head. "You will not be happy."

"How so?"

"Doged has no chapel, aye, no church at all."

Bedevere screwed his face up in confusion. "But is Doged not of the Christ?"

"I found one *sacerdote*, an old fellow, who said he ministers to Doged. He says that Doged does not display his faith in the usual way for fear that the people will turn against him. The old gods are strong here. In truth, Ysbail, Doged's new wife, is not of the Christ. The Rigotamos will not be happy."

I agreed. Arthur's faith in the Christ was one of the best-known things about him. The Cross graced his tunic and his shield. And it remained a point of contention between him and me, as if we needed yet another. I had not embraced the Christ, and at that point did not plan to. Despite my misgivings, though,

I often thought that if it attracted believers such as Arthur, Bedevere, and Kay, it must be worthy. Merlin had never pledged his faith to the Christ either, but Arthur and Merlin's bond was strong, easily surpassing that of religious faith.

"This land is not empty of believers in the Christ," Ider said. "Doged simply does not use the Cross or the *chi roh* which came before it."

"What does he use?"

"A yellow chevron."

The symbol on Doged's shields and tunics. But I had never seen or heard of it before, at least not in that way.

Bedevere must have seen the confusion in my face. "They say it was the first symbol of those who followed the Christ, that Joseph the Arimathean brought it with him."

One small mystery solved, but it answered none of the major questions we still had. Could Cilydd and his brother be persuaded to halt their infant rebellion? Could the gold in Doged's lands be mined profitably? And did the Saxons truly have Mordred as a hostage? And why should they choose now to send an embassy to Doged? Finally, but most important to me, who had killed those villagers, and what had happened to the ones they took away? Too many questions and, I suspected, too little time to sort them out. Perhaps when Merlin arrived we could resolve at least some of them.

Merlin. He had changed in the years since we renewed our acquaintance. For many winters, Merlin had been considered a kind old man whose mind wandered. While Arthur loved him dearly, more and more, over time, Merlin had been left out of the councils. But since we had been sharing a hut, I had noticed that his "wandering" grew less frequent. All who knew him had seen this. And, over time, just as he had once been excluded, Merlin's sage advice brought him back to the fire.

Anyone who removes himself from other humans loses a part of himself. I had. I doubt that living with me brought Merlin's senses back to him, but he had earned his return to Arthur's councils and my respect along with it. He had always held my friendship.

"How does Doged stand with the people?" Bedevere queried.

"Well. He is a kind lord, and the common people will not desert him while he lives. He treats them with a fairness that they do not expect to receive from any of those who would replace him. They are very fond of him."

"What of the Saxons and Mordred?" I asked.

Ider shook his head. "I found out nothing. The Saxons are not looked upon kindly here. They are encamped some-where north of Trevelgue. I did hear that one of Doged's nobles, Druce, had visited them, but no other." I resolved to meet this Druce. He seemed to be a man that needed much study.

We had little else to discuss. Ider was assigned to find out what he could about the Saxon envoy. Bedevere and I would continue to represent Arthur at Doged's court, at least until Merlin could join us and free me to do some searching on my own.

Just as we were leaving the now-emptied hall, I remembered my charge from Doged. "Ider. Would you find some parchment? I promised to prepare a conveyance for Doged, and I would do it tonight when few are about."

"You will not do it in the camp?" Bedevere queried.

I looked around. "The light is too dim there, and I need a table such as one of these to work on."

And so, within the space of an hour, I had scraped a parchment and begun carefully lettering the conveyance.

Beyond the scratching of my quill, the only sounds in the hall were the crackling of the fire and the gentle snoring of the *servus* left behind to see to my needs.

I looked up at about the midnight, if my reckoning was correct, my hand cramping and the nub of my arm rubbed raw from holding the parchment in place. I still had three lines left to inscribe, and I would be glad to see them done.

The main door to the hall scratched open and Doged came stomping through, his cloak flapping about him and his head bowed.

Jumping to my feet, I gave him the salute, but he waved me off.

"I did not realize that you had left, my lord."

But Doged ignored me, walking like a man enraged and entering the door to his suite of chambers and slamming it behind him with such fury it shook the timber walls of the hall.

No matter the cramps in my hand, I finished my chore quickly. I suspected that Doged's queen was the cause of his anger, and I had no desire to involve myself in his marital problems.

Carefully folding the parchment, I tucked it in my pouch, dismissed the weary *servus*, and headed toward our camp, beyond the walls.

I could not stop yawning as I navigated the path to the gates. Two of Doged's soldiers were posted there, looking just as weary as I.

But then something very strange happened.

Lord Doged, dressed in the same tunic and cloak, came flying past me, running faster than anyone his age should be able to, leaving the guards reeling in his wake.

And then, even as I was watching Doged flee across the rickety bridge, a cry arose from near the timber hall.

"Lord Doged is dead!"

CHAPTER FIVE

T hat cannot be!" I shouted, to no one in particular. The guards looked at me questioningly, as if they knew something I did not.

I spun on my *caligae* and ran back up the rise to the hall, where the *servus* who had waited upon me was screaming the alarum.

Grabbing him by his tunic, I jerked him around. "Lord Doged just left the fort. He cannot be dead."

The poor fellow cringed, his eyes looking away. "He is dead, master. Come, see for yourself."

A host had gathered, and I grabbed one of Doged's soldiers. "Go to the gate. Let no one in or out."

"What right have you to give orders here?" the soldier, suddenly remembering his duty, questioned my authority.

With no hesitation, I released the *servus* and took the soldier by the throat, lifting him off the ground. People were often amazed at my strength, but when you have but one arm it has to do the work of two.

I said nothing as the man sputtered and choked. When I released him, he stumbled to his knees, but he quickly gained his feet and ran for the gate. Strength often substitutes for authority.

Ignoring the gathering crowd, I followed the *servus* into the timber hall, through the door at the other end into Doged's private chambers. This time, we went through the further door and into a small antechamber with doors on either side and at the rear. I thought Doged's feasting hall seemed smaller than it appeared from outside.

The *servus* indicated the door on the right, which stood partially open. Taking a deep breath, I entered.

The very first thing I saw was Ysbail, dressed in a flowing yellow gown of fine linen. She looked just as imperious as she had at the feasting.

Doged was naked or nearly so. His death held no secrets. He lay on his back, an ordinary-looking dagger protruding from his bare chest. In the flickering light of the torch, I could see two or three other stab wounds. Whoever had done this intended for Doged to die.

"My husband is dead," Ysbail said, in a dull, dry voice, dead and lifeless as Doged.

"Bring torches!" I shouted. The sounds of *servi* scuffling to answer my call filled the room. I had absolutely no authority here, none.

"Why do you call for torches?" Ysbail asked, seeming to notice me for the first time.

"To better see what has happened here, to help determine who committed this murder."

She looked at me curiously, not hostile, but with real curiosity. "We know who killed him. He was caught running out the back door toward the kitchen. Some *servi* were finishing up their chores. They are holding him now."

"Might I see him, question him?"

Now the hostility began its ascent. "Why should I allow you to see him?"

"My lady, I have a certain reputation for helping to resolve matters such as this. Indeed, your own husband commissioned me to look into a similar affair just this evening."

Ysbail's eyebrows rose. "What similar affair? I know of no such incident."

"Harrumph." Bedevere cleared his throat. "Lady Ysbail, Malgwyn speaks the truth. We discovered a village on your eastern border that had been attacked, many people killed. Lord Doged asked Malgwyn to investigate. I swear it on my honor."

The new ruler of these lands looked first at me and then at Bedevere. "You indeed have honor. And I will accept your word. Your man may question the murderer."

I knew that I was about to shove a stubborn mule, but I had to take the risk. "And could I bother you not to disturb matters here until I have had time to study them? I guarantee you that if this man has truly killed Lord Doged, then I will prove it so and he may be punished. I am certain that the Rigotamos would make the same request of you if he were already here." Never before had I taken such liberties with the truth. But I knew this: With Doged dead, his lands would quickly fall into open rebellion unless we moved swiftly to maintain control. The prospect of gold and the safety of our trading port here were paramount. And who knew what havoc the Saxons would try to wreak.

"Do as you like," she said after a long moment. "I did not love him, though I bear his child. Besides, the killer has asked for you."

"Your prisoner asked for me?"

She finally turned and looked at me. "Well, not by name, but he screamed for the 'one-armed scribe' as he was tied up. You are the only one that I have ever seen."

Immediately, my mind flew like an arrow shot to Cilydd. If he was striving to avoid a prolonged war by assassinating Doged, I feared he had underestimated. Ysbail seemed as one who would and could hold on to her lands.

A scuffle sounded at the door, and I turned to see the antechamber filled with *servi* and others. Among them was Gurdur, the man who could speak all languages. I motioned him into the room.

"Gurdur, hurry to our camp and return with Bedevere and Ider. We must try to preserve some order to this or all will fall into chaos. As soon as Doged's death is widely known, the various factions will begin summoning their troops. War will be inevitable."

With a quick nod, Gurdur disappeared into the crowd.

I turned then to Ysbail. "A word, my lady?"

"Speak."

"I pledged to serve your husband as he saw fit. Lord Arthur often appoints me his *iudex pedaneous* to investigate such things as this. I—"

She stopped me with a hand. "I do not speak Latin nor understand it. Talk plainly."

"Call it an investigator, someone who studies these events and seeks the truth."

"Ha. The only truth you will seek is that which profits Arthur."

I stepped toward her, much closer than I should have. "You do not know me, my lady. Do not pretend you do. If I tell you

I will seek the truth, that is what I will do, no matter where it goes."

For her part, she gave not a step but stared into my eyes with those unrelenting blue ones of hers. "If you do that, you may not like where it takes you."

"I am willing to hazard that."

She turned away swiftly then. "Do as you like, but we already have my husband's murderer." But halfway across the antechamber, she pivoted. "I am sending for my brother, Ysbadden, to assist me. Cross me and you will answer to him."

Again, Ysbail made to leave, but something she said earlier, something that had nearly escaped my notice, came rushing back. "You are with child?"

For the first time in our short acquaintance, she smiled, and it brought a little warmth to her pale face. "I am."

My life was made of complications created by others. Well, and those I created for myself.

"You are certain?"

Ysbail looked at me with total disdain. "Yes, I am certain. Do not question me again or I will have you cast from the cliffs." At that, she disappeared across into another chamber. For a new queen, she had taken to the role quickly.

I gave a few more instructions to the *servi* and then went through the back passage. It opened onto the narrow lane between Doged's hall and his kitchen. Two soldiers stood guard outside the kitchen door.

Curious, I passed between the guards and looked into the kitchen, quiet now but for a single *servus* and a single torch. It would be yet another hour or so before they began to stir in preparation for the morning meal.

The man seated on the floor, his hands tied above him to a

post, looking completely miserable, could not have surprised me more.

Mordred.

And his words caused me to nearly burst out laughing.

"Malgwyn! You must save me."

"My lord Mordred. How surprising to see you here." In truth I was both surprised and confused, though I should have known that the story of his being held hostage by the Saxons could not have been true.

"Cut these knots and release me."

I will confess to great pleasure at seeing him so disposed. I had long wished to see Mordred trussed up like a suckling pig and roasted on a spit. But I knew that the story wouldn't be that simple.

"Mordred, you know I cannot do that." And I could not. But I was enjoying his discomfiture. Mordred's eyes flicked between the door guards. I understood and asked that they withdraw, which they did reluctantly.

"You are far away from home, Mordred. Aye, we have just received word that you are held hostage by the Saxons, and yet I find you here killing Doged."

His narrower face grew even narrower and anger marked every crevice. "Don't be a fool, Malgwyn. You are smarter than that. My killing Doged would throw these always fractious lands into even more turmoil."

I squatted in one corner. "I am neither a fool nor an idiot. But I have little authority here, as you must be aware."

"The woman? She is but recently the sister of a mere bully, and he all but a *latrunculus*. She will have to have a nobleman to rule with her."

"Ysbadden is hardly just a bandit. If denied nobility, he will simply cut someone's head off and take his lands. In this case, half of the work has been done." I paused for a moment while I considered how much to tell Mordred. "The laws of this land are unclear on these matters. True, that a woman has never ruled alone, but none of our laws say she cannot. Were I you, I would be more concerned by my own fate."

I cannot lie. I was taking more than just a little pleasure at Mordred's position, but the specter of Ysbadden taking over Doged's lands, with the possibility of gold within them, was a nightmare. For that matter, as pleasant as he seemed, Cilydd was an unknown. And with the Saxon embassy here at such an opportune time, I could see any number of people who wished Doged dead. Of course, I had to ask the question—was this confluence of events chance or planned?

I did not know. And I did not like it. With Arthur occupied at Tyntagel, the whole matter was in a state of chaos. One thing I did know: Without Bedevere's agreement, I was not about to let Mordred free of his captivity; indeed, I could not. This was not Castellum Arturius; this was not home.

"Malgwyn," Mordred began with a warning tone in his voice. "Now is not the time to settle our differences."

"It may not be," I agreed, "but proving you innocent may not be that simple either. For the gods' sake, Mordred, you were caught fleeing his chambers!"

"You think I do not know that?" He turned his head away, the most honest move I had ever seen him make. "I went there to talk to him, not to kill him."

"Talk about what?"

He turned back toward me then, squinting, and I could not tell if he was being honest or not. "I was attempting to negotiate a truce between him and Cilydd before a war began."

"A noble purpose. And he grew so frustrated that he stabbed himself in the chest?"

"He was already dead."

"I was in the feasting hall, Mordred. I did not see you pass."

Again that shadow passed his face which made the truth hard to discern. "I entered from the rear. Doged and I had an understanding."

At that, I laughed aloud. "Mordred, you cheer me. Bedevere and I spoke to Doged not four hours before he was found dead, and he spoke of you as an enemy, not a favored ally."

Arthur's cousin did not bother to argue; he simply shrugged. "I intended to press Doged to step down and allow Cilydd to take command. Your arrival was well known; I bribed a guard to let me in the rear entrance." I sometimes thought that Mordred preferred lying to telling the truth.

"But the rest is as I said it was," he continued. "When I entered his chamber, he was already dead. Knowing what it would look like, I turned and ran. But Lady Ysbail was in the passageway, and the guard I had bribed blocked my path."

This time, his tale sounded true. Wood smoke flavored the air, but I noticed that it had shifted, dampened, the scent of coals freshly wetted. Glancing at the great fire, I noticed one of the *servi*, still at his chores.

If I knew anyone in the world, I knew Mordred. He was no coward; I had seen him on the battlefield, fought alongside him. But assassination? No. Mordred would never do his own killing in that manner. He would hire others. He did not come to Doged's hall to kill him.

And he had made a good point earlier. While no one would mistake Mordred as one of Arthur's confidants, he was a lord of the *consilium*. If it was believed that Mordred had killed

Doged, we might lose this entire province, the port, the trade, aye, and these new rocks, the agaphite, and the gold, if there was any. I knew one other thing. Mordred was not stupid. He might threaten, intimidate Doged. He might try to bully him. But he would not kill him. He could not control the aftermath, and Mordred liked to be in control.

And then there was the matter of two or three or four Dogeds. I had not even had time to consider it. Bedevere and I saw one Doged go into his chambers. Then later, Doged reentered his chambers, but I had not seen him leave. Shortly thereafter, another Doged had fled past me at the gate. Finally, there was the true Doged, murdered in his bed. I could not pretend to know what it all meant, but something told me that unraveling the different Dogeds was the most important task before me.

Unfortunately, having settled Mordred's innocence in my own mind did little to prove it. And, I had to admit, the prospect of rescuing Mordred from this mess left a foul taste, like sulphur, in my mouth. So foul, in fact, that I wished only for some mead to wash the taste away.

Before I could send the *servus* for a cup, Bedevere joined us. His first words left no doubt of his reaction.

"Mordred, if you did this, I will see your privates ripped from you while you yet breathe."

"As much as I hate to admit it, Bedevere, he did not do it. There is something truly strange going on here." Quickly I sketched the evening's events. "What is being said in the town?"

Bedevere shook his shaggy head. "Chaos. People are gathering in the lanes in the *vicus*. Apparently, Ysbail has given orders to seal off the fort. I have sent a rider to advise Arthur and ask for instructions."

Somehow, I sensed that this chaos would last only until Ysbadden arrived. "Come. We need to study Doged's body and chamber to see what story they yield."

We turned toward the door as a yelp erupted from the floor.

"You cannot leave me like this," Mordred argued, a sweat breaking from his forehead.

I truly felt sorry for him at that moment. "I cannot do anything else, Mordred."

"He is right," Bedevere added. "To release you would only prove Ysbail true."

"You are safe for the moment, Mordred," I assured him. "Ysbail is unlikely to take any action until Ysbadden arrives."

My old enemy glared at me, shaking his head to move his braid from his face. "Which could be at any moment."

We left him at that, not at all unhappy that he was thoroughly miserable. Strangely, I feel bad about that now, but at the time I only regretted that his fate might be decided by someone other than me.

To my surprise, my requests had been honored. Ysbail was nowhere to be seen, but Doged and his chamber looked just as I had found them, if more brightly lit.

"Search the floor and furniture," I directed Bedevere. "I will see what else Doged can tell me."

"What do I seek?"

"Anything. Everything. Whatever strikes you as out of place."

With that I turned my attention to Doged. Under the flashing and flickering flames of new torches, the old lord looked only older and paler. No great pools of blood marred the furs, but I was certain he was murdered here. First, the dagger was such that it trapped the blood inside his body. Second, yet one more Doged wandering about was more than I could stand.

Nothing about the dagger was special, just the ordinary sort such that you might find at any man's waist.

With my one hand, I lifted Doged's body by his arm and saw what I expected: His back and side were dark as a Nubian. The blood had pooled within him.

I let him drop and stepped back. The dagger had struck him just below his breastbone, at an upward angle. "He did not expect his visitor to be his murderer."

"How do you know that?" Bedevere's question was a fair one.

"He was not struck from behind, as he might have been if his killer had lain in wait. He was struck from the front, but the blow was delivered underhand, as if the murderer had stepped in to him. Had it been a full frontal assault, Doged's arms might bear wounds themselves as he fought off his attacker."

As if to prove it to himself, Bedevere took up Doged's limbs. They bore old, white scars but no sign of a fresh wound. "You are right." He dropped the arm and turned to me with a question in his eye. "Could Mordred not have done this? What you are describing to me is an action suddenly determined and just as suddenly executed. Could he not have met with Doged, been infuriated, and killed the old man in a fit of passion?"

"He is certainly capable of it, but his voice rings true when he professes his innocence." I raised my hand before Bedevere could rebuke me. "I know. Mordred can sing a lie as sweetly as any songbird. But this time I think he sings the truth."

"You understand that if he is guilty, you now must prove his innocence to sustain the *consilium*'s authority here?"

I had not thought of that. In my disappointment at being away from Ygerne and the birth of our new child, I had thought nothing could make me feel lower. The idea of defending Mordred was bad enough. But my having to defend a guilty Mordred threatened to overwhelm me. I felt my feast seek a second appearance.

Still, I did not feel his guilt. "No, Mordred is guilty of only bad timing on this occasion." That, I could live with.

I returned to studying Doged's wounds, but nothing new drew my attention. Bedevere was leafing through some parchments and documents on a side table. Like Kay, he read, but not well. His youth had been spent more with playing at swords than at reading.

He held the papers out. "What do these say?"

I walked over and looked at them. "Some are reports of shipments at the port. Some are requests by ship captains to visit the port." Paging through the documents, I stopped at a small scrap, smaller than the others at any rate. The words were strange ones, strange for a king to have. "The key element," it said, "is to walk swiftly and with purpose, keeping the head low. When combined with the other preparations, one could easily be mistaken for another. Though I am confused about your request, I wish you great success, old friend." The writing ended there, but whoever had scraped the parchment to take a new document had done a poor job. Words from the older document could still be seen, still be read. "Come, Bedevere, bring me a torch."

Under the brighter light I could easily discern the earlier words, and it sent a chill through me.

"Look for the rest of this. It must have been at least two leaves." The parchment I held had no salutation, no ending or farewell.

And we spent the next few minutes sorting through the rest of the papers, but not one matched this queer bit of correspondence.

We finally gave up. "Bedevere, something very odd is happening here. I have told you of the seeming two or three or four Dogeds wandering the fort this night. This," I hefted the parchment, "would seem to be a primer in how to impersonate another person without detection."

"Yes," Bedevere said, now intrigued.

"These older words here, that were not well scraped?"

My friend narrowed his eyes.

"They are mine. Someone has taken a parchment I had written, scraped it, and composed this odd missive to Doged."

CHAPTER SIX

"Are you certain?"

"I know my own fist, Bedevere."

"How could someone have gotten a piece of parchment that you had written?"

I shrugged. "I write many things, for Arthur and some still for the abbot at Ynys-witrin." Pulling the parchment closer to the torch, I squinted, trying to read my own words. The faint, faint markings became clearer the longer I studied them.

"I think I recognize this. It was a message to Aircol from Arthur. But I made so many errors, I tossed this aside in frustration." Pursing my lips, I looked up at Bedevere. "This never left my house."

"Then how came it here?"

"I cannot fathom it. Perhaps Merlin? Surely he knew Doged. I have never seen Merlin write, though I know he reads well." Shoving the parchment leaf in my pouch, I tried to put it from my thoughts.

"Lord Bedevere?"

We turned to see Lady Ysbail entering. She had changed from her linen nightgown and put on a plain, black linen dress.

"Will you speed a rider to Lord Arthur? I wish him to participate in my husband's funeral, and I suspect that his presence will serve to calm things here."

Bedevere and I exchanged looks. We did not know the actual condition of Igraine at Tyntagel. But Ysbail was right in one thing—Arthur's presence might keep the most restless claimants to Doged's seat at bay, for a time. I did not know about Bedevere, but it seemed to me that Ysbail's request was somewhat out of character. She had shown her disdain for the *consilium*; why she would now request Arthur eluded me.

" 'Tis already done," Bedevere said.

"I have seen all that I need here, Lady Ysbail. I thank you for your patience."

Her eyes rolled upward, almost in jest, almost. "May I presume that you are now satisfied that the man in our kitchen killed my husband?"

Just as I opened my mouth, Bedevere placed a hand on my shoulder. "It is likely," he said. "But Malgwyn needs to make more inquiries tomorrow. There are several questions that have not as yet been resolved."

She started to speak, but Bedevere cut her off with a hand. "This is his way of divining these things. It is very effective, and your people will appreciate your loyalty to justice."

Ysbail had the most expressive eyes that I had ever seen, and at that moment I could almost see through them to the thoughts spinning in her head. From all accounts, she was just the sister of a bullying warlord who had never held a title that he had not murdered for or bothered with asking any questions of anyone. Justice was what Ysbadden said it was.

In this situation she was uncertain. I did not think that she had a hand in her husband's death, but I could not discount it either. When she accepted Doged's marriage proposal, she probably saw nothing but the luxuries that went with power, not the responsibilities or decisions. She hesitated, just a second longer than I expected, and I silently thanked Bedevere for intervening. The woman thought little of me, one-armed old man that I was, but Bedevere carried himself as a noble.

"Very well. My brother will soon be here. He may have until then to ask his questions."

"One last thing," Bedevere began. "Lord Doged had asked me to review his troops and determine what training they need. Forgive me for speaking bluntly, but rumors have spread far and wide that these lands are but an inch away from rebellion. With Doged dead, one or more of the claimants may attempt to replace your husband by force. If you will grant me your permission, I will assume command of the soldiers here and organize them into a defensive force."

Normally, Bedevere was so taciturn, he did not say more than five words in a row. But in this instance I was delighted to see him take a more active role. As he was a lord of the *consilium*, his request would go much further than mine. Still, it was a bold request.

For several long moments, Ysbail stared at Bedevere with those dancing blue eyes. Uncertainty lit them. She was not a stupid woman, but this was all new to her. Finally, a slight smile curved the corners of her mouth. "I have heard my husband speak of you as one of the best and most faithful of Arthur's nobles. Your word is said to be as strong as the gales that strike our coast. Will you pledge to serve me at least until my brother arrives?"

It was now Bedevere's turn to pause. We had been so often in the field together that I knew what he was thinking. Bedevere did not like having limits put on him. But he had no good reason to refuse her request. "I will, Lady Ysbail."

"Then you may go and make certain that no revolt breaks out until we have time to bury my husband."

One of Doged's nobles, one of the few that had been seated close to Doged in the feasting hall (and hence one of the more loyal), appeared in Doged's chamber.

"Go," Ysbail ordered. "Tell our garrison that Lord Bedevere will assume command for the time being."

The man nodded quickly and dashed from the room.

Bedevere turned again to Ysbail. "With your permission, I will bring our troop of horse within the fort. They are less likely to be confused by divided loyalties and can provide better security for you."

Again, she stared at my friend for a long moment. "Agreed. If you will now leave, I will begin the task of preparing my husband for burial." Though the demand was blunt, her tone was less so.

We departed quickly.

Once I was outside the hall, it occurred to me that I should go and let Mordred know what had been decided. But since I was not inclined to make his confinement more comfortable, I turned to Bedevere. "We should pull our camp inside the walls as well. I am sure that there are shelters here that we may use."

He nodded. "I had rather be behind the safety of the walls out on this headland than on the plain. Whoever sited this fort here was clever. Only laying siege and starving the garrison out would defeat it."

Bedevere was right. The only approach to the fort was across the one bridge. And the ravine was too wide to easily cross elsewhere. A handful of skilled archers and spearmen could hold off ten times their number.

And the wind whipping off the vast sea was broken within the ramparts of the fort. Out on the plain, it was an ever-present reminder of the world's furies.

I caught a whiff of baking bread and glanced at the stars. Morning was almost upon us. "Who has gone to Arthur?"

"I sent Aidan."

"A favor, Bedevere? Leave Ider here with me. I think I shall need him more." Only then, after speaking, did I look at Bedevere.

His mouth narrowed into a tight line. "You truly do not think Mordred did this?"

"Consider what we know."

My old friend just laughed. "I did not think we knew anything."

"True, but listen. We know that at least one other person was dressed as Doged and both entered and exited his chambers. We found a parchment in Doged's chamber that seems to be some sort of treatise on disguising yourself as another. As you yourself pointed out, the killing itself has all the marks of being done suddenly, but by someone that Doged knew or at least had let willingly into his presence.

"Mordred claims to have bribed a guard to gain entry into Doged's private chambers. We have not had time to search the truth in that. But undoubtedly, he was not dressed as Doged when he was captured, and no discarded clothes were found in his wake."

At that, Bedevere nodded reluctantly.

"Besides you and Merlin, Ider is the most experienced at helping me in my inquiries."

"Very well." He stopped and studied my face. "Malgwyn, a year ago you would not have asked. You would have demanded."

"A year ago, I was more petulant child than councilor to the Rigotamos."

He shook his head. "Petulant child when you and Arthur squabbled, but not in other matters. It was a mark of your self-confidence."

This time it was my turn to shake my head. "A year ago my petulance nearly cost the lives of several folk I dearly love, my cousin Guinevere and Ygerne among them, not to mention so many others. No, if by moving more cautiously fewer mistakes are made, then so be it."

"If you had moved more cautiously when Eleonore was killed, Arthur would not be Rigotamos and Ambrosius would be dead. Do not let caution rob you of that which makes you strong." At that, he strode off toward the gate, leaving me staring after him as the false dawn began to break.

"Malgwyn!"

The cry broke through the sudden buzz in the lanes.

I had taken advantage of the last remnants of night to seek some bread, cheese, and water. But when I emerged from Doged's hall, I saw true chaos.

Something was happening outside the walls, driving the people to seek refuge here. I strained to look over the crowd, but without climbing on a house I could not. Then I remembered the great burial mound. It rose over all the other structures in the fort.

Half-running, half-pushing my way through the crowd, I scrambled up its incline, my heart pounding at the effort. Though the thatched roofs of the houses obscured some of my view, I could see beyond the walls.

A mass of people, simple peasant folks it looked, were dashing for the bridge and gate. Far beyond them, back where the narrow spit of land broadened into a plain, I saw a mob of horsemen, running their mounts at an unbelievable speed, and yet another, more disciplined, formation of horse headed toward them.

"Malgwyn!"

Looking around among the bobbing of heads as people ran, stumbled, fell in the lanes in their haste to find the safety of the fort, I searched for its source.

There.

Ider's head appeared. "Malgwyn, Bedevere said you wanted me."

I motioned Ider up on the mound, giving him my hand for leverage. "Has he sent a rider to Arthur?"

Ider, his long hair already soaked with sweat, answered curtly. "He has organized our troops with Doged's and thrown up a defensive rampart further inland."

"Who are the riders?"

"The people are saying that it is Druce's men, intent on plundering Trevelgue now that Doged is dead."

"What is Bedevere's plan?"

"He is riding out with our entire force under a flag of truce to ask their intentions."

"He is that certain that they will honor the flag?"

"He is certain that if they do not, we have enough men to send Druce's rabble running."

I was not that certain, but Bedevere was a fine commander. "Malgwyn?"

Ider was calling me, and I was lost somewhere else. "Sorry, lad."

"What shall I do?"

"I need you to gather the soldiers who were on the gate at midnight last night, and the soldier who guarded the back entrance to Doged's hall."

"Very well. What will you be doing?"

I waited a long moment. "I will be on the parapet, watching Bedevere parlay."

"Should you ride with him? Perhaps he will need you."

"If Bedevere needed me, he would send for me. Now, go. Send a boy for me when you have gathered them. Oh, you should know that they captured Mordred dashing from Doged's chambers last night. He is being held in the kitchen."

But Ider did not move. He looked at me questioningly, as if he had not heard.

"Do you have a question?"

My young friend just shook his head and departed on his errands.

I did not like being here, so far from home. Ygerne was having my child. My daughter, Mariam, from whom I had been separated for so long, missed me on my long absences, and I missed her dearly. Recently, I had begun to worry about how my family would fend for themselves should I die. And I had come very close in the years since I rejoined Arthur's banner.

Pushing those thoughts from my mind, I trotted down from the burial mound and headed toward the front gate and the parapet atop the embankment.

I mounted the rickety ladder and found, to my surprise,

Lady Ysbail already there, studying the scene below intently. She glanced over her shoulder and saw me.

"Your fellow is courting disaster," she said.

"How so?"

"Druce is a barbarian and respects nothing. He has not a drop of the charm or nobility of his brother, Cilydd." I noticed an uncharacteristic warmth in her voice as she spoke of the young noble.

"So you predict that Druce will not honor the flag of truce?"

"I predict that unless your Lord Bedevere clearly signals that he is as strong and ruthless as Druce, we will see much blood spilled and a civil war begun this day."

"Truly?"

"Watch for yourself as the *consilium* loses my lands for me."

"If you will excuse me, Lady Ysbail. I think I may be needed below."

"What use could a one-armed man have in battle?" She turned away.

If what Ysbail said was true, Bedevere might need me; he certainly needed to know what sort of man he faced. I made the decision quickly.

Once down from the parapet, I snatched a soldier by his shoulder. "Bring me a horse and a sword."

The man looked at me as if I were mad, and to encourage the idea I drew my dagger quickly and pressed it to his throat. "Now."

Within a bare few moments, I was racing through the lanes of the *vicus* and out onto the plain.

Dust swirled about me as the winds pounded the land. Back in the distance, I saw a line of dark clouds roiling on the far horizon.

Pulling my horse up sharply as I entered our formation, sending half a dozen horses scrambling to clear a path, I glanced about for Bedevere.

"No, master," yelled one soldier. "He's gone to parlay."

I pressed on beyond them.

Once I cleared our lines, I could see Bedevere trotting toward the middle of the plain with a two-man escort. I stretched up as far as I could to see a single man riding out to greet Bedevere. He carried something in one hand, but I could not make out what it was.

Shoving my heels into the horse's flanks to speed him forward, I pushed him as fast as I could.

I had no idea what I would do or say when I reached them, but I suddenly felt that it was essential that I be there.

And I made it.

Just as Bedevere halted his party and waited for Druce's rider to arrive.

And he did, a young lad without the hint of a beard.

Not bothering to salute, he lifted the object in his hand and threw it at the hooves of Bedevere's horse. It rolled against them, frightening the horse, who reared up and stepped backwards.

The hairy sphere came to rest, and Bedevere's escort gasped.

" 'Tis Aidan."

I looked at Bedevere, confused.

" 'Tis the rider I sent to summon Arthur."

"Lord Druce," the boy said, "instructs you to withdraw from his path or you will all end up as this one."

"Is your master mad? Does he not know that killing a soldier of the Rigotamos is punishable by death?"

The fair-haired boy shrugged. "With Doged dead, the *consilium* has no power in these lands."

I was just barely listening to the talk. Instead, I studied what was left of poor Aidan. I knew him slightly. But he was like most of our young soldiers, a younger son, desperate to avoid life on the farm. His face was white where all of the blood had drained from it. The red/black stump that had been his neck had begun to dry and harden. A pair of flies found it and began feeding. Suddenly, I was back in Daron's village, and my village, looking at the dead. My heart began to pound, but not from the ride, from a deeper, darker place. A heat, stronger than any fire, rushed up my neck.

Someone screamed.

The next moments were lost in red haze.

It was only after, after my sword found its way through the lad's neck, that I realized that I had been the one screaming.

Bedevere and his escort stared at me in shock.

I did not wait for them to speak. Jumping down, I snatched up the newly severed head, the body sliding down from the horse and landing heavily on the ground. Swiftly wrapping the hair to a leather strap to secure it, I climbed back into the saddle, kicked the horse's flanks, and took off at a gallop for Druce's lines, all the while with Bedevere's voice in my ears. "No! Malgwyn!"

My horse laid his ears back, reveling, it seemed, in this mad race.

Time froze around me.

Only the horse and I seemed to move.

And then we were close enough to see the looks on their faces.

Druce was easy to recognize. He and his brother, Cilydd, favored each other greatly.

I jerked the reins, bringing my horse to a staggering stop.

Though he had two hundred men at his back and they could have killed me with little effort, they sat on their horses, stunned at the appearance of a one-armed man and the still-dripping, severed head, bouncing against the horse's shoulder.

Releasing the reins, I untangled the head and threw it at Druce's feet. "This is not the time for a rebellion. Lay down your arms and prepare to mourn your dead king. If you do not, I will gladly light the funeral pyre that will burn your bodies."

My words seemed to shake him from his stupor.

"That boy was my nephew."

"Then you should have kept him at home, playing at wooden swords."

He ignored my jibe. "Our king is indeed dead. These lands need a strong hand to lead."

"And you are here to provide that hand? I am certain you will not be the only claimant to Doged's seat. I have been charged by Lady Ysbail with finding Lord Doged's killer, to give him the justice that he deserves. I cannot do that with civil war raging about me."

Druce spat at my horse's hooves. "You should look to your own master. I do not doubt that he ordered Doged's death."

"Do not try my patience, boy."

"You are very foolish, riding here by yourself." Druce's voice was gravelly, holding nothing of the charm of his brother's. And his eyes held a dark mischief. But I saw a hint of fear there too. Killing a single soldier was one thing, the act of a petty bully. Launching a frontal assault against an equally strong opponent was another.

"And you are even more foolish for challenging the Rigotamos within the *consilium*'s domain. And it is the *consilium*'s domain. Lady Ysbail has not denounced the *consilium*, and Lord Doged was one of its oldest members. Indeed, Lady Ysbail has sworn Lord Bedevere to her service, and he has pledged to defend her against any enemy." I paused. "Your sloppy attempt to exploit Doged's death is both juvenile and laughable. As was your raid on those poor villagers." It was a weak thrust, but even at that, Druce did not flinch.

"What village?" His tone was flat enough that I could not decipher it. He could be guilty. He might not be.

Quickly surveying his host, I noted a conspicuous absence. "I do not see your brother among your men. Does he not support your claim?"

"My brother champions his own claim."

"And yet I do not see his army here, attempting to usurp Ysbail."

Druce smiled then, but it was a nervous smile, a tic jerking his lip. "More the fool he."

"More the man he."

"I have heard of you, Malgwyn, the one-armed scribe. They say you are a nuisance, an annoyance."

"I certainly was to your nephew."

My bluntness stole some of the sting from his words.

"We will encamp here and honor Doged," Druce announced.

In truth, it was the only logical decision. Now that I was close, I saw that Druce's men were little more than boys, boys puffed up by their braggart leader. Our men were seasoned veterans. No battle would honor this plain. It would be a massacre. And Druce was no idiot. Plainly, he had thought to strike in the confusion and our willingness to support Ysbail with force was unforeseen.

Druce directed his men with a wave of his hand to a meadow off the road. I turned my horse and started at a walk back toward Bedevere, watching behind me as I rode, just in case.

"Do not think that this is over between us," Druce's voice called at my back.

I did not turn. The civil war had merely been postponed, and I knew it.

Moments later I rode past the headless corpse of Druce's nephew and faced Bedevere.

"I do not understand you, Malgwyn. First, you preach caution and then you toss caution, like a thin parchment, into the wind, behead an envoy, and charge his army single-handedly."

I did not need Bedevere to tell me what I already pondered. Why had I done that? Why had I killed that boy? "Nor I you, Bedevere. You chide me for being cautious and then chastise me when I disregard caution. Besides, the boy did not carry a flag of truce."

At that, my old friend laughed. "I do not argue your right to kill him. All know that to kill a soldier of the Rigotamos is punishable by death, but you did it so quickly. Why?"

I was not prepared to answer the question, so I made an answer up. "I have had my troubles with puffed-up young nobles in the past. Remember Lord Celyn, the *monachus* Gildas's brother? I shamed him when Arthur was elected Rigotamos and now I must watch my back whenever he is present. It is easier to just kill them."

Bedevere cocked his eye at me, and I knew he did not believe me.

"In truth," I continued, "Lady Ysbail reminded me that I was more than just an old, one-armed man. And she reminded me that Druce was more bully than lord. Bullies only respect brutal strength. I rode to meet this threat with you, but when that child became so insolent something within me took over." I did not say it, but I was more than a little embarrassed by my actions.

"What will he do?" Bedevere asked, nodding toward Druce.

"Stop acting like a child. Pay due honor to Doged." I stopped. "You will need to send another rider to fetch Arthur."

Bedevere waved his wool-wrapped hand. "Already dispatched. What did he hope to accomplish by killing the first?"

I shrugged. "To impress us? If pressed he would probably claim that the man had done something to warrant his death. This is a strange land and these are strange people. Ysbail's brother, Ysbadden Penkawr, is likened to a god, and the people fear him. We will have our hands full with him; that is for certain."

"Come, let us return to Trevelgue." We turned our mounts back toward the village. "Have you learned anything new?"

"There was no time. I set Ider to gathering together the people I need to question. There is yet a separate question that must be resolved."

"I know. Can Ysbail reign in Doged's stead?"

The ancient laws of our peoples were complicated, and many had not been in use for long years past. And they varied from tribe to tribe.

"I have heard of a learned *monachus* not far from here. Petrocus is his name. He has established a community of believers between here and Tyntagel. Perhaps we should send for him," Bedevere suggested.

"No," I answered, suddenly remembering something very important. I was indeed getting old. "Ysbail told me that she was with child. If that is true, and I have little doubt that it is, Ysbail could rule in his stead, assuming that it will be a boy. The question is: Will Arthur and the *consilium* recognize such a situation?"

"I suspect that Arthur will recognize whatever arrangement entails the least blood and the least chaos. You believe her? This could just be a ploy to maintain control."

"She is clever, but not that clever, I think. In all honesty, Bedevere, we have more trouble than we need without counting Ysbail among our enemies. We must contend with her brother, Druce, Cilydd, and the Saxons. And I have little choice but to save Mordred's neck or there will certainly be war."

At that, my friend snapped his head around. "Could the many factions have joined with the Saxons in a plot to murder Doged and blame it on the *consilium*?"

I considered the idea for a moment. "They are not working in concert. We have only met Cilydd once, but while I do not doubt that he covets Doged's seat, I am not convinced that he would ever have declared open war with him."

We rode in silence for a bit longer.

Bedevere looked at me with his head cocked. "Malgwyn, you surely seem subdued. You are not acting like yourself."

I could have told him that killing a boy, as I had just done, was something that would change your behavior, but Bedevere already knew that. We had both seen more killing than we wanted, but that was our world. Life was as easily taken as air was to breathe. And yet that did not excuse my actions. "It is probably many things," I told him. "Ygerne is about to give birth while I am far away. Mariam needs me there, to be the father I was not for so long. Myndora is not well."

Myndora was an aged blind woman, sister to that old Pelagian *episcopus*, Agricola, whom I had encountered near Bannavem Taburnum nearly two years past. She had helped me in those last days before the late rebellion. When the fighting had stopped, Merlin and I went to her and moved her to Castellum Arturius.

"And what of Owain and the other children? And Rhodri and young Vala?" I continued. The last two I mentioned were from a family we had encountered the year before. They had been kind to us, and Vala had betrayed a curious ability. They too, like Myndora, had been resettled at Arthur's seat in the summer country. Kay had asked if I were trying to move all of Britannia to Castellum Arturius.

"Malgwyn, I have never heard you complain about your duty so," Bedevere pointed out.

I dismissed his comment with a frown. "Is it too early to drink some mead?"

"For you, it is always too early." He spoke lightly, but I did not miss the concern in his eyes.

He did not need to worry. For when we returned to Doged's hall Ysbail was meeting with the Saxon embassy.

CHAPTER SEVEN

Over the last five winters, word of Aelle, the Saxon lord, had rolled into our lands like a giant wave from the sea. Tall and ruthless, he was said to have massacred all of the Atrebati that opposed him, men, women, and children. Landing on our southeast coast, he had beaten a small force at one of the old Roman forts, and he was now the recognized *bretwalda*, overlord of all the Saxons in our island.

The year before, Ambrosius Aurelianus, the former Rigotamos, had warned Arthur that Aelle embodied the greatest threat that the *consilium* yet faced. "He is young and ambitious," Ambrosius had told Arthur. "And he is hungry for lands."

The Saxon embassy, at least those we saw, numbered five. The tallest of them, like his colleagues, wore the ubiquitous braided topknot, greased with animal fat until it shone. His *caligae* boasted leather straps that wound nearly to the knee on both legs. Around his torso was strapped a leather breastplate. His cloak was bear fur and pinned at the neck with a circular brooch.

They were seated near the back of Doged's hall, alone save

for Trevelyan, who seemed so forlorn that he probably welcomed any company, even that of Saxons. Ysbail, dressed soberly, was receiving the minor nobles at the front of the hall.

Then, one of the other four Saxons turned and glanced toward me and Bedevere. A cold, clammy fist grabbed my stomach as he smiled.

I reached for my dagger.

His smile grew wider.

The dagger was out.

He winked at me, with one milky eye.

I started across the room.

Until Bedevere blocked my path.

"Put that dagger away, Malgwyn. Are you insane? Those Saxons have been granted Ysbail's hospitality. We cannot touch them."

I moved to brush him aside, but he stood firm. "Look at him, Bedevere," I hissed.

My friend turned then and looked at the Saxon, who now approached us. Bedevere tensed, and his hand started toward his own dagger but pulled up short.

"Lord Bedevere," a voice said.

A soldier had appeared at the Saxon's elbow. Gurdur, the man who spoke many languages.

"This is Ceawlin," Gurdur continued. "He is one of the Saxon emissaries and wishes to speak with you. Unfortunately, he speaks neither our tongue nor Latin, so I will have to translate." Gurdur stopped and studied our faces. Mine was fully crimson, I knew, but I could not shake my glare free from the Saxon long enough to see Bedevere's. "Have you already met?"

Oh, we had met before. More than three years before, when

the plot to assassinate Ambrosius was revealed, Ceawlin had been one of the killers sent for the job, a task at which he failed. And in order to affect his escape, he took my baby, Mariam, hostage, held his dagger to her tender throat. By the favor of the gods, her life had been saved. And that of the Saxon as well.

But now, the gods had delivered him to me. And I could not touch him. This was no favor of the gods. This was a curse.

Yet I smiled also and willed the crimson from my face. "Ceawlin was once a visitor to Arthur's seat."

Gurdur launched into a flurry of words in the guttural Saxon tongue.

The milky-eyed Saxon smiled again, but this time with an edge. He looked to Gurdur and spoke.

"He commends Arthur's hospitality, but he says yours was somewhat lacking."

"Tell him that I disagree. We were very anxious for him to remain with us permanently."

When Gurdur translated this, the Saxon laid his head back and laughed deeply. With what sounded like a series of grunts and wheezes, Ceawlin spoke again to Gurdur.

The man of languages seemed also adept in understanding those words not spoken. He frowned and cleared his throat. "Ceawlin says that he would welcome the chance to discuss that with you in less formal surroundings."

This time it was Bedevere who answered. "Tell him that we look forward to it."

Ceawlin did not wait for Gurdur's translation and turned away quickly. I took that to mean that he understood more of our tongue than he would admit.

I drew Bedevere to the side. "This makes a difference. We know that Ceawlin is one of the Saxons' assassins. He is here and Doged is dead."

"How would he have gotten into the fort, or Doged's chambers?"

"I do not know. Perhaps he bribed a guard as Mordred claims to have done. Perhaps he was one of the many Dogeds running about last night. But I tell you this, Bedevere: I promise you that no matter what else transpires, that Saxon will not leave these lands alive."

I left Bedevere keeping an eye on the Saxons and went to find Ider. Almost immediately, a young boy that Ider had sent stopped me in the lane and led me to an old hut on the edge of the fort.

"Malgwyn." Ider stepped from the door. This was a rickety old hut. The walls had holes, and the thatch looked like it suffered from the plague. Inside were Sulien and Daron.

Before I could speak, Daron ran to me, her hand over her mouth. "You have been wounded, master!"

In that moment, in the dim light, she again looked so much like Gwyneth that I felt light-headed, dizzy.

"I am fine. Ider," I said, changing my focus and seeking some purchase in reality, "this will scarcely keep out the rain."

He smiled tightly. "Lady Ysbail said this would be good enough for us."

"She is such a caring hostess. Sulien, take Daron and find us wine and bread and cheese. Our guests may be hungry and I wish them to be honest with us."

Daron gave me an odd look, but Sulien, gently, pulled her out the door. I reached to pull the wooden door shut. One set of leather hinges popped free, and the door fell on my shoulder. More such hospitality and I would have need of Morgan ap Tud.

The men were sitting on the floor, playing at dice by the light of a single torch. At my entry, they scampered about, snatching up their coins. Something crackled on my skin, and I realized that I probably wore some of the boy's blood. It was just as well. Few men kept secrets before a bloodied madman.

"Who was stationed at the main gate?"

Two men raised their hands; from the sleep weighing down their lids I believed them. I recognized the *servus* left with me in the great hall, and the guard who had captured Mordred. I needed others to speak to, but these would do for a start. I watched one of the guards adjust his fibula, holding his cloak in. It was a fine stone, an agaphite. I remembered then that I needed to send a patrol to Doged's old seat and see what security there was at the mines.

"You." I pointed at Mordred's captor. "How came you to capture the man behind your lord's hall?"

"I had stepped into the kitchen, my lord, for just a second, and when I came out two or three men were running from the rear door. I grabbed one."

"Three?"

The man squinted. "Perhaps, master. It was late and dark. There was certainly more than one."

I drew him to the side, leaving Ider watching the others. "That," I began, "is a pretty stone, expensive."

The guard smiled through rotten teeth. "I found it in the lane last eve. Bit of fortune, that."

He extended it in his hand and I took it.

"Where were you when it was found?"

"Between the kitchen block and the main gate, master."

By the gods. It sounded as if half of Britannia had wandered through the fort. No wonder Doged was dead. He must have been trampled by the crowd.

We were interrupted then by Sulien and my "*servus,*" Daron. Apparently her minder had had a talk with her, and she behaved more like the slave she was supposed to be. They spread what food they'd found around the hut, and I gave them time to eat a little before I continued.

"Could one of the men you chased have lost this brooch?"

He shrugged nervously.

"It is unusual. Have you ever seen another like it?" I needed to put him at ease.

"Only two others. Lord Cilydd has one. I do not remember who had the other. . . ." He paused for a moment, then shook his head. "No, I cannot recollect, but it was recently. No matter."

Cilydd again. While this stone could have come from the quarry at Doged's seat, ships from Egypt traded with us, and such stones were found there as well.

I questioned the others, but none was willing to admit that they had let Mordred in, or anyone else either. I released them finally, when I had drained them of what information I could, which was far too little.

"How is the Lady Igraine?"

Arthur was not a happy man. The sun had set by the time he reached Trevelgue, and his escort had been challenged by Druce's men. Much like I had done, Arthur sorted it out himself, though he succeeded without killing anyone.

Ysbail had refused to greet Arthur personally, leaving the chore to one of Doged's more faithful nobles, a man whose name I no longer recall. But she had ordered a large house made ready for the Rigotamos, and it was there that we met.

"She is failing, but still difficult. She has already ordered Morgan's beheading three times. He says that it is only a question of time. It may be tomorrow or a fortnight. Judging by her complaints about Morgan, I would say she has a little time left, but not much." Arthur's hair hung in wet strands about his face. The weather had not been kind, storming and blowing all the afternoon. He looked more like a drowned dog than a high king. Morgan had not been in his party, and I knew that Arthur had left the *medicus* to see to his mother. "What has happened here?"

Bedevere and I quickly described all that had transpired. "In truth, Rigotamos, we have been much confused," I conceded. "The situation grows more and more uncertain with each passing hour. We still await Ysbadden Penkawr, though I thought he would arrive before you. Until then, Ysbail is satisfied to let me investigate her husband's death. But she is equally satisfied that Mordred is the killer. I fear only his death will satisfy her."

Arthur shook his head. "We cannot allow that."

"Even if he's guilty?" I had already accepted this reality, but I could not resist chiding Arthur.

Those quick eyes of his locked onto mine, but his voice was as gentle as I had ever heard it.

"I cannot fight another rebellion so soon, and David and some of the others would cry for my head if I did not come to Mordred's defense. And, quite honestly, I have nothing to purchase their loyalty with."

"Then Doged's death is a double tragedy." I explained how Doged had intended to transfer the mining rights to the *consilium*.

"And he died before signing the conveyance?"

"He did. And only Bedevere and I were present when he spoke of his wishes. I doubt that Ysbail would honor it even if it were signed."

"Malgwyn," Arthur began. "Bedevere has told me of the boy you killed. You have nothing to regret in that. His fortune was told when he took up arms with Druce. They killed one of my men. You avenged him. That is all that needs to be said."

I shook my head. "A man of my years and experience should control himself better."

"Well," Arthur answered, "I find no fault in you. Now, tell me of Ysbail."

"She is, as you said, beautiful, but very demanding," Bedevere began. "But she can be reasonable. When I offered our services to keep her safe, she accepted."

"After some thought," I reminded him. "She is not a stupid woman; she is actually very clever. But she was not prepared for this turn of events, and she moves slowly, cautiously."

"That speaks well of her."

"Aye, caution is always more to be wished for," I agreed. "But though she is cautious, she is unlearned in the ways of nobility. This is not Gwyneira, a girl groomed to be a queen from birth. She is the sister of a local bully, chosen by Doged for her beauty and youth and ability to provide heirs."

At that, Arthur nodded. "You are blunt, but correct. Have you any thought of who did kill Doged? Perhaps if we can do that service it will buy some goodwill."

"Do we care for her goodwill?" Bedevere asked. "She is but a woman and cannot rule by herself."

"That is not completely true. Just look at the Iceni queen, Boudicca," I said. "She not only ruled after her husband's death, but led troops into battle. I do not remember completely now, but I once read a manuscript at Ynys-witrin, a treatise on law, that gave a special name for women who ruled lands."

"He is right, Bedevere," Arthur agreed. "My mother ruled the lands around Tyntagel for a time after her first husband, Gorlois, was killed."

"That was why I was counseling that we send for this *monachus*, Petrocus, to advise us. He is said to be quite learned and has the people's trust as well."

"Send for him. It will raise the Church in the people's eyes that we trust him with this. I have understood Doged's reluctance to flaunt his belief in the Christ, but perhaps this is an opportunity. I have heard much of this Petrocus and would welcome the chance to meet him." Arthur paused before continuing. "Do you have any idea who killed Doged?"

I shook my head. Briefly, I explained about the many Dogeds tramping through the fort, about the manner of Doged's death, and finally about the strange parchment we had found in the old lord's chambers. "Who took it from my house, scraped it, and then sent it here I can only guess."

"This is unimportant," Arthur said abruptly, his face becoming grim. "You will have more fortune discovering who was with Mordred. Forget about these alleged impostors." He jumped to his feet and paced across the room. "You'll find no answers there."

I was used to people attempting to channel my inquiries, especially Arthur, but I had never seen him so suddenly agitated. "I disagree, Arthur. I think it was most likely one of these impostors." For once, I was not just being stubborn. It did seem most likely to me that an impostor had gained access and killed the old lord.

Arthur spun about, grabbed me by the tunic, and jerked me to my feet. "You will forget these impostors! You will forget the parchment! Look elsewhere!"

With that, he pushed me back and I fell against the wall. Arthur stormed from the room with a reddened face and the veins pumping angrily at his neck.

Bedevere stared after him for a moment, but then he crossed the room and helped me to my feet. "Malgwyn, I do not know what to say. I have never seen him in such a fury."

I brushed my tunic off. "Nor have I."

"What will you do now? What course will you pursue?"

Staring long and hard at the doorway through which Arthur had disappeared, I gritted my teeth. "I will do what I always do. I will seek out the truth, no matter where it leads. And Arthur should prepare himself for that."

With that, I too stormed out of the room, the sound of Bedevere yelling my name behind me, only this time I was headed for Doged's kitchen.

"Soon, you will no longer concern me."

Mordred looked even more miserable than he had the night before. Ysbail's men had moved him to a stake next to a pit for kitchen trash. The putrid smell of rotting meat filled the air, and it looked as if the *servi* had been careless about throwing the table scraps away; some of them hung off of Mordred.

"I fear that you have disappointed me, Malgwyn. You, the great finder of truth." Mordred was trying to be his usual self, but the strip of yellow-white chicken skin across his shoulder lessened the sting of his words.

"I will tell you this only once. Arthur is here and has agreed to let you be executed for Doged's death." Lying to Mordred caused me no pain. He had lied to me many times. "I still have until Ysbadden Penkawr arrives to find the killer, but he should be here any moment; indeed he may be entering the fort even as we speak. The guard who caught you claims that you had companions. Who were they?"

His hands were tied tightly together by the wrists; I saw how the leather bit into his flesh. The other end of the thongs was securely anchored to the stake. Mordred wanted to brush the chicken from his shoulder, but, try as he might, he could not reach it.

His shoulders sagged and his head drooped. "I do not believe you. Arthur has not the strength to allow my death. He knows that it would stir up an entire region against the *consilium*."

"He has no choice, Mordred. You were caught fleeing Doged's chamber. It is well known that you fomented rebellion against Doged here two years past. Ysbail has no love for the *consilium* and Ysbadden, her brother, has even less. In willingly giving you up to the sword's edge, Arthur may yet gain some goodwill. You are giving me nothing to aid your cause. Now, will you tell me who your companions were? Or shall I tell Arthur to sacrifice you for the sake of the *consilium*?"

"If I am to rely on their help, I am doomed either way."

I scarce recognized Mordred's voice then. It held a tone of defeat such as I had never heard before. "Who? Who were they?"

"Two of the Saxons," he mumbled, his voice so low that I had to bend over him to hear, catching a whiff of rotting fish as I did. "They forced me to bring them and to gain them entrance to Doged, to plead with him, to bribe him; I swear I do not know what their plan was."

"So you were held hostage?"

Mordred turned his head and did not speak.

"I must know everything."

"I was returning from David's lands to my own," he said finally, grudgingly it seemed. "It was just a small escort, five men and myself. We made camp for the night, drank a good bit of mead. When I awoke, the men were dead and I was held by a Saxon raiding party, from the sea."

"Why were you not killed as well?"

"Your friend was among them."

"What friend?" I asked, though I knew of whom he spoke.

"Ceawlin, the smoky-eyed Saxon that almost killed your child. He remembered me from Castellum Arturius, and he told his fellows that I could be of value to them."

Suddenly it all became clear. "So you bribed the guards at the gate as well?"

"They came much cheaper than the one at Doged's hall, and they were more faithful to the bargain," Mordred answered bitterly, spitting on the trash heap.

"How so?"

"Do not be so naïve, Malgwyn. The guard that gave us entry to Doged's private chambers was the same man who captured me as we fled."

"And Doged was already dead when you entered?"

Mordred nodded. "As we were entering the rear door, a man rushed past us."

"Did you know him?"

"We could not see him. He kept his cloak about his face, but I remember the guard saying something about the man not getting his way."

"Mordred, I do not know whether to believe you or not. How do I know that you were not a willing participant in all of this? I still believe that you allowed the Saxons into our territory to kill Ambrosius."

"Believe what you will, but I did not kill Doged. And neither did the Saxons with me."

I had known Mordred for more years than I could remember, and I had never trusted him. But this time, the rumbling in my stomach told me he was innocent. I had already determined this, but I needed to hear it again. "Did you see anyone about dressed as Doged?"

Mordred frowned and cocked his head. "No. Why would someone dress as Doged?"

The tone of his voice, the tilt of his head, the question in his eyes, all told me that he was truly confused. I noticed something else about Mordred at that moment. His hands tied tightly together, trash from Doged's kitchen hanging from his shoulders like some sort of rancid cloak, Mordred looked nearly bereft of hope.

"Take heart, Mordred. I will do my best to keep the sword from your neck. I prefer to save that pleasure for myself."

He glanced at me with dead eyes. "I am not sure that even you can get me out of this mess. What will you do now?"

"Find the guard you bribed. If anyone knows the name of

the earlier visitor, it will be him." I paused. "Mordred, I am going to send one of Bedevere's men to stay with you. He will have instructions to find me should Ysbail change her mind."

For the first time, in all the years that I had known him, Mordred blessed me with a sincere look of gratitude. I just shook my head and lumbered off in search of the guard.

And I found him, behind Doged's hall, but he would be doing no more talking. His throat had been slit.

CHAPTER EIGHT

I do not know why I was surprised. Nothing that had happened since our arrival at Trevelgue had made sense. But this did. Our pliable guard was a key player in all of this. And now I stood over him, sprawled in the moon shadows outside Doged's hall, his cut throat looking for all the world like a second mouth, grinning, the blood, black in the night, glistening with the flickering torches in the lane.

The lanes were busy with people, rushing about as if it were a festival. I grabbed a lad, a bit older than my little friend Owain, Merlin's son. "Do you know Lord Bedevere? Lord Arthur's man?"

The lad's eyes grew wide at my missing arm. He gulped and nodded. "Go and fetch him here; tell him to bring men with torches, that Malgwyn needs him." I pulled a single silver denarius from my pouch and pressed it in his hand.

He scampered off down the lane, and I retreated into the night shadows at Doged's rear entrance. Leaning against the wall, I avoided looking at the dead guard and tried to make some sense of it all.

Too many Dogeds. Agaphite brooches. Bribed guards.

Saxons. Mordred. Rebellious lords. Arthur in a seeming fury over nothing. And, perhaps, a hidden treasure. The one thing I knew for certain—the future of Doged's lands, aye, if Arthur spoke the truth, the future of the *consilium* as well, rested on untangling this puzzle.

I had never been more confused. And I knew why. I did not want to be here. I should be at home, at Castellum Arturius, playing with Mariam, seeing to Ygerne as her day grew near. I should be there to greet my new child. That was where Cuneglas, my dead brother, would be, were he living; he would not abandon his family to go chasing after some lord. Blasted Arthur! Blasted *consilium*!

And then I stopped, stopped condemning them. Were it not for Arthur and his blasted *consilium*, there would be no loving family for me. I would still be but Mariam's odd uncle, as she believed me to be before my brother's death. I would still be finding solace with servant girls. No new son's wail would greet me when I returned home. A son. Ygerne might have already given birth. Yet there I sat, condemning the very men who made it possible.

"Malgwyn."

At first, I thought it was Bedevere, but it was too hoarse, too throaty. I turned to see Sulien and Daron joining me. "Sulien, keep her away."

But it was too late. She had seen the smiling throat of the dead man. To her credit, the cry caught in her throat, and I quickly gathered her against my chest. "I wish I could shield you from such sights, Daron." In that instant, she was my Gwyneth, almost. And I released her quickly, too quickly, for I'm sure that it seemed to her that I had pushed her away. Aye, and it must have seemed so to Sulien as well, as he hurried to pull her back.

I did not wish to hurt her, but at times her resemblance to my Gwyneth was more than uncanny, and more than uncomfortable.

"Take her back to our hut, Sulien. Guard her closely. This affair becomes bloodier by the minute."

In my confusion and frustration, I failed to hear Bedevere approach.

"This way. Bring the torches up."

Just seconds later, the world brightened and I recognized my friend. "What has happened here?"

I pointed at the dead guard. "This is the man that Mordred bribed to let him in last eve. And before you ask, no, I did not kill him. I wanted to question him again and found him thus."

With the torches, at least I could see more of how Doged's man had been killed. One thing that this poor man's death accomplished was to lend credence to Mordred's protestations of innocence. For surely Mordred had no hand in it. Of course, the Saxons could have killed him to obscure their role, but as much as I wanted to feel my dagger slice through Ceawlin's gut, this did not smell of Saxon work. While that put me more at ease, it proved nothing.

Something bright glittered in the torchlight, and I rolled his head to one side. 'Twas the silver and agaphite brooch, still fastened to his cloak. I unfastened it, awkwardly with my one hand, and tucked it in my leather pouch.

"What was that?" Bedevere's eyes missed little, even in the night.

I rose. "A fancy brooch this man found last eve between here and the main gate. I do not know what significance it has, if any, but it is made with agaphite, which might mean that more than just Doged knew of its presence."

Bedevere shrugged. "Perhaps, but it could have been brought from far away, Egypt perhaps."

"Then I would see others being used. A trader does not bring just one of his wares. Though Lord Cilydd is said to have one just like it."

I motioned one of the torchbearers in closer. The stubble on his chin seemed marked by a smudge. Looking closely, I saw then that it was a bruise. Either the guard had taken a blow or, more likely, the killer had jerked his head back roughly from behind before slitting his throat.

Someone was eliminating witnesses.

As I thought that, raucous laughter boomed from the hall and Ider flew around the corner. "Bedevere, Malgwyn. Hurry!"

Bedevere motioned for two of his men to stay with the body, and we hurried after Ider.

Ysbadden Penkawr was the biggest man I had ever seen. He easily stood a head taller than Kay, whose height was renowned throughout our land. His tunic was made from rough-cut deer hide, as were his *braccae*. The belt wrapped about his amphorae-sized waist was studded with iron bits, filed to a point and shiny. Matching daggers were jammed into the belt, and in his left hand he carried a short club. He looked nothing like his pale sister.

You could hardly tell where his beard ended and his hair began. But oh, that hair. Though the rest of him was cut from the roughest, unscraped of hides, his hair was adorned with more combs than I had ever owned.

Among certain tribes, the practice of hair grooming and fancy combs was part of reaching maturity, and our nobles throughout the land loved nothing better than to decorate their hair with such trinkets as those Ysbadden sported. I counted three silver combs and two bone. His hair had been thoroughly brushed and decorated. Somehow, all the care did not soften his appearance; it only made him all the more menacing. But more frightening than his general appearance was the crooked smile that marked his red, pockmarked face. I had never called a smile evil until I saw Ysbadden.

As we pushed through the crowd, my throat caught.

They had pushed the tables back and the crowd was five deep all around. In one quick look I saw the Saxons, Druce, Cilydd, the sad Trevelyan, and many of the lords from the night before.

And on his knees in the center was Mordred.

My boast to him that Ysbadden could arrive anytime had come true.

I knew of no way to save him.

"Is this the one-armed scribe, Sister?"

Ysbadden's voice was deep and rumbling, like thunder. But the way in which he spoke to his sister, ponderous and belittling, irritated her; I could tell.

But Ysbail nodded.

Ysbadden turned to me and fixed that evil, crooked smile on me. "So you are the one that champions the killer of my brother-in-law? Perhaps I should just kill you too."

I glanced about quickly. Every eye was on me. I knew that I could not defeat him in regular combat. But I had no choice but to try. "Perhaps," I agreed. "But as your sister will tell you, I merely asked her for time to investigate, to make certain that this man actually killed Lord Doged. If you want to lop off his head, then do not let me hinder you. I have never liked him."

Ysbadden stopped and cocked his head at me even as Mordred spat at me, in frustration I am certain. "You have no desire to save him?" Ysbadden was confused. I am certain that he expected me to challenge him. "Then you have discovered that he did kill Doged?"

I shook my head. "No. I do not think he killed Lord Doged. As yet, I do not know who did."

The giant shrugged. "Then, he will do. He is of the *consilium* and I do not like them."

"Malgwyn." Mordred turned toward me, his hands tied behind his back and blood streaming down the side of his face. His eye was blackened, and he had clearly taken much abuse.

Ysbadden threw back his head and laughed. "Oh, this one is especially pitiful. He must beg a one-armed man to save his life." As he said this he turned his back on me, a mortal insult. And one that I could not ignore if I wanted to retain some semblance of respect, from our men, from Bedevere, from Arthur, from Ysbadden.

My left hand moved swiftly, but my aim was not true. Though Ysbadden howled like he was mortally wounded, I succeeded only in nicking his ear with my dagger, which continued on and stabbed deep in a timber post.

Ysbadden whirled around, club in hand, and advanced on me. "Perhaps I should kill both."

One-armed though I was, I crouched, ready to grapple with Ysbadden.

Then, my vision was blocked by movements from either side.

Arthur.

And Bedevere.

Ysbadden laughed. "So the cripple needs two men to protect him."

Arthur shook his head. "We do not protect Malgwyn. He has no need of our protection. We protect Lord Mordred, a senior member of the *consilium*."

"So you are the great Arthur? You are not much to look at, nor your fellow either. I believe that I will rid the *consilium* of its head. Sister," Ysbadden said to Ysbail. "That will make it easier to rule these lands." And he advanced toward Arthur and Bedevere, who both reached for their daggers.

I cast about for a weapon to use; I would not let my friends die in vain.

"STOP!"

The command rang in my ear.

Lady Ysbail strode forward and placed herself between her brother and Arthur. "Brother, you will put away your weapons. I rule these lands, and I say who dies and who lives. And I will not have my husband's funeral besmirched by your bullying."

To say that I was surprised cannot even touch my shock.

She turned then to Arthur and Bedevere. "In the morning, we will bury my husband. Even now, my *servi* are preparing his funeral pyre atop the burial mound here in the fort. I expect you, Lord Arthur, to light the fire to honor his service to your *consilium*. You, Lord Bedevere, have fulfilled your pledge to me, and I thank you." The common woman was becoming a queen.

Before anyone, including Ysbadden, could speak, she faced me, a faint smile marking her pale face. "Few two-armed men have the courage to challenge an insult from my brother. That you did raises you in my esteem. And I watched as you charged Lord Druce's army alone; that was not the action of a common man. You have bought yourself more time to investigate my husband's death. I grant you until the sun rises two days hence. If you cannot offer up another murderer, I will order Lord Mordred beheaded."

Turning her eyes once again to Arthur, she gave him a hard look. "If you wish to have any influence here in these lands, you will have to deal with me. Not my brother. We will talk more of this after my husband has been honored."

At that, she swept out of the hall and into her private chambers. Two of her soldiers appeared and hauled a struggling Mordred out, probably to tie him again in the trash. Two other soldiers posted themselves at her door.

The feasting hall fell strangely quiet in her wake. The Saxons, Ceawlin among them, wasted no time in leaving. Ysbadden came toward me, and I tensed again, but the now-gentle smile on his face eased my fear.

"You charged Druce's army alone?" he asked. "Yet, you live."

"Druce is more bully than lord. Bullies appreciate strength."

Ysbadden touched his still-bleeding ear and grinned ruefully. "I like you. You have courage. I will not kill you today."

"Then," I said, "I will not kill you either."

Ysbadden turned to Arthur. "So you are the great Arthur, Rigotamos of the *consilium*." He paused and looked Arthur up and down. "You do not seem much to me. Maybe someday I will kill you, but for now I will honor my sister's wishes."

Bedevere, quiet, taciturn Bedevere, was seething. "It sounded more like a command to me."

The giant turned and looked down at Bedevere. "I do what I please, when I please, and no woman will tell me what to do."

Arthur walked up to Ysbadden. "I have battled my whole life against men like you. And it is only out of respect for your sister that I do not challenge you to combat here and now. But when Doged is properly honored, I will come hunting you."

"A pretty speech," Ysbadden grumbled, but he turned and left, wiping the blood from his ear as he went.

The crowd thinned in the hall, leaving but the three of us and Cilydd and Druce, who were arguing, it seemed, in a far corner. Arthur drew Bedevere and me aside.

"What news have you, if any?"

"Rigotamos, I confess I am as confused as I have ever been. But here is what I know: Mordred admits now that he was a captive of the Saxons, and that they forced him to gain them an audience with Doged. Whether that is true I do not know."

Arthur nodded, pulling the ends of his mustache into his teeth as he did when thoughtful. "My agents to the north have told me as much."

"But someone else was there before them. And the same guard who Mordred bribed must have been bribed by this other man."

"And Mordred did not know who he was?"

"No. And now the guard has been killed. That is how I know that Mordred is being truthful with us. While the Saxons could have killed the guard, they are not stupid. And they realize that Mordred would blame them if only to save his own life. And Mordred could hardly have killed him, as he was tied at the trash pit." I did not mention the person disguised as Doged this time. Not because I was afraid of Arthur, but because I was even more confused as to how that fit into the events surrounding Doged's death. And I still believed it did.

"You have certainly made an impression on Ysbail," Arthur said.

"At the price of a boy's life." I hung my head at the admission.

"Malgwyn, you have no reason to be ashamed," Arthur assured me. "Indeed, Bedevere says that there might have been many more deaths had you not acted so swiftly and decisively. To allow the killing of my soldier without retribution would have emboldened Druce."

"Perhaps, Rigotamos, but I should have left it to Bedevere to respond. It was his decision to make, not mine."

At that, Bedevere laughed aloud. "Have you heard me complain, Malgwyn?"

"No," I conceded. "But tell me, had I not interfered, how would you have dealt with the situation?"

Bedevere turned and looked at me so intently that I became uncomfortable. "Malgwyn, as I stand before you and Arthur, I would have ordered the charge and more than just that one boy would have died. Your brash actions saved lives."

"And it won you the friendship of Ysbadden," Arthur chided.

"That," and I scowled at him, "is no honor."

"Perhaps," conceded Bedevere, "but it also raised you in Ysbail's esteem. I think, in fact, so much that were you so inclined you could easily capture that prize."

Rather than answer, I simply deepened my scowl. "Rigotamos," I changed the subject, "will you grant me a patrol to visit Castellum Dinas to check on the mining there?"

"I will do more. I have sent a rider to Gaheris, asking for two of his troop to join us here. I will give you a troop of horse and Ider to command. Leave them there when you have finished your inspection, but instruct Ider to avoid any loud demonstrations of our presence. In truth, Castellum Dinas is more hunting lodge than true town. And with Doged holding court here, it will be mostly deserted. While I do not want anyone else in control there, I also do not wish to show uncommon interest."

"What about those mining?"

Arthur shook his head. "Doged halted all mining after this new ore and the agaphite was found."

"Surely the workers were curious?"

"I do not know. But do not tarry there, Malgwyn. Despite your words to Ysbadden, we cannot afford for Mordred to be executed. It will virtually assure that Cilydd or Druce or whoever emerges as lord of these lands will not join the *consilium*, and it may indeed incline them toward a peace with the Saxons. And our failure to protect Mordred will further embolden our enemies, David, Mark, and others."

"I wish that Merlin were here," I admitted. "He knows so much more about these rocks."

"Oh, he will be at Castellum Dinas when you arrive," Arthur added. "I had word two hours ago that he and Kay were riding with all due speed. I dispatched a rider on my fastest horse to divert them there. When you arrive, send Kay on here. Use Merlin as you see fit, but bring him with you when you return. I may need his counsel on the morrow."

Bedevere and I turned away, off to do our duties, but I felt a hand on my shoulder and turned back. In the darkness, with only the flickering torches, Arthur looked much younger. The black of night hid those gray hairs conquering his beard. "Malgwyn, Bedevere, there is much happening here that I do not understand, and I suspect you are the same. But I know this: We have never faced so many potential enemies at one time. One misstep, one misspoken word, and we could lose our westernmost lands and the ports that go with them. We cannot afford that, not now. And we cannot afford a civil war with the Saxons here to watch." He paused. "There are those in the Empire who do not wish the *consilium* to survive. Before we were born, Malgwyn, this land provided much food for the Empire. We could do so again, but they would rather take it than pay for it. If we are to remain a free people, you must succeed."

And he was gone, leaving Bedevere and me standing alone. "Take heart, Malgwyn," Bedevere said finally, into the silence. "You will be so busy with this affair that you will cease to worry about Ygerne."

I parted ways with him then, even as I realized he was right. Since my encounter with Ysbadden, I had completely forgotten about Ygerne and our coming child. And that bothered me.

We returned then to the dead guard, but I could find nothing else of note. I sent a *servus* to fetch help so that he might be properly buried and left, straightaway, for Castellum Dinas.

"Merlin." I threw up my hand at the sight of my dear friend.

This was to be another long night. The journey to the mine at Castellum Dinas had taken only two hours, though the cursed wind that plagued our western lands made it seem twice as long. The cool blast wrapped around me like a Fury, ripping at my cloak, pushing me forward, it seemed, and then back. And, for what appeared to be good reason, Ider, myself, and our troop of horse were the only ones on the road. Reluctantly, I had left Daron with Sulien. She had seen so much devastation in the last days. I wanted to wrap her in warm furs and keep her safe from harm. But, for then, Sulien would have to do.

"I was very comfortable in our house, Malgwyn. I had no reason to come to these unfriendly lands." Merlin carried a sour look on his wrinkled face. He stood before Doged's hall. If it was possible, I believed Merlin had grown yet thinner since my departure. His tunic and *braccae* hung on him, and I worried about his health.

Arthur had been right. The lanes here were empty. A few dogs protested our approach, but apart from a single, surly guard at the gate there seemed to be no one at home.

"I did not call for you, Merlin. Blame Arthur for that," I answered, which was not exactly the truth.

"And why?"

Ider and I dismounted, giving instructions to the soldiers to await our return. We entered the hall to find Kay, alone at a table, drinking from a cup. The feasting room was filled with smoke. I looked up and saw that the hole to draw the smoke from the room was partially blocked. My brother, poor Cuneglas, would have repaired it quickly and expertly. He had been a thatcher, and a good one, until killed some years before. Though he was often sullen and sarcastic, like our father, I did miss Cuneglas, an emotion that caused me even more confusion, as his wife, Ygerne, was now my woman. But I pushed those thoughts from my mind and focused on the present.

"Kay, Arthur wishes you to join him at Trevelgue." I quickly explained all that had happened, and when I mentioned the numerous Dogeds from the night before I noticed an uncomfortable smile on Merlin's face. I said nothing but resolved to question him when we had more privacy.

"And you and Merlin?" Kay asked when I had finished.

"We will join you before Doged's funeral on the morrow. We have some chores to do here first." As I finished speaking,

I noticed a slight frown spread across Kay's face. "Is everything all right, Kay?"

"He is tiring of his role as Arthur's chief steward," Merlin explained.

"I wish to be in the field, commanding troops again. I fear that this is all that Arthur thinks I am good for." A bitterness tinged his voice that concerned me.

"There will be plenty of action for all in this affair, I fear."

"As you say. Ider is to stay here?"

"Aye. You should take two or three of his men as escort to Trevelgue. Saxons are about, as well as Cilydd's and Druce's men. They have already killed one of Arthur's soldiers and a village full of people." Quickly I told Kay of the massacre. True to his nature, he grew angry.

"They must be avenged, Malgwyn."

I laid my hand on his shoulder. "They will be. When Druce killed Arthur's soldier, I saw immediately that he would do anything to further his cause, even kill innocents. There was one survivor. I have her with a special guard. Apparently, Druce did not learn a lesson from Lauhiir." Lauhiir had transgressed against the Rigotamos as well, and suffered for it.

"Who did he kill?" Kay queried.

"Aidan. Bedevere sent him to bring Arthur back from Tyntagel. Druce stopped him and killed him."

"I knew Aidan. He was a good man. Very well, if a patrol is all I can command now, I will take it."

His bitterness surprised me, and I resolved to talk to him at the first opportunity. But just then, I only said, "Good. Arthur needs you. We will join you in a few hours."

At that, Kay spun about and tromped from the room, his *caligae* pounding the packed earthen floor loudly.

"How long has he been like that?" I asked Merlin.

My old friend shrugged. "Since you all left for this journey. He will leave these feelings behind," Merlin added dismissively.

I sat down, suddenly weary. A platter of cheese and bread lay on the table before Merlin, and I helped myself. As I ate, Merlin frowned. "Why was I dragged away from my work? What can I add to this affair?"

Reaching into my pouch, I pulled out the sample of the brown rock and the other stones. I tossed them onto the table and watched his reaction. To my surprise, his hand first went to the heavy brown ore.

"I have seen this before, but I know of no one who has successfully worked it. The temperature that is required to smelt it is higher than anyone has yet achieved. That does not mean it cannot be done, but it would be difficult and would require much time." He stopped and pawed the jumble of rocks usually found with gold. "These are more interesting. I am sure you know that gold is often found when these are present."

At that, I tossed the single bit of gold on the table.

"Ahh. Is there much?"

"Only this right now."

He picked up the piece of agaphite and turned it over and over in his hand. "This is perhaps the most useful of them all. These blue stones are popular for brooches and fibulae, but I have rarely seen them outside of Egypt."

"You have been to Egypt?" For some reason, I could not imagine my ancient friend outside our lands.

Merlin smiled that thin-lipped smile of his. "When I was a youngster, aye, before Arthur was even born, I worked on a ship that plied the trade route between here and the lands of the Christ, Egypt. It was a stunning introduction to life, Mal-gwyn, and some days I regret that I have left that part of life behind me."

"Is that where you learned about making someone look like another?" It was an arrow shot without aiming, but my belly told me it was true.

Merlin hung his head. "So Doged told you of our correspon-dence. I meant to ask you for some parchment, but I found a discarded leaf and used that."

"You should know, Merlin, that on the night that Doged was killed there were at least two other Dogeds wandering about the fort. And he said nothing of it to Bedevere and me. We found the scrap of parchment in his chamber, and I recognized that it was a cast-off of mine. But that makes no difference; you were wel-come to the parchment. What I need to know is why Doged wanted such information?"

"That is not a question that has a short answer, and truth-fully I would be guessing. I knew Doged many winters ago, when he was but a young lord following Vortigern's banner. We remained friends during his exile from the *consilium*, and, in-deed, I was one of those who petitioned Ambrosius to restore him to his former place. Doged was always a good man, without ambition to become Rigotamos, and he was ever a faithful ser-vant of the *consilium*."

I nodded. "Though I knew him but for a few short hours, I can say that he remained so until his death."

"Then he remained true to his nature." Merlin stopped and laced his pale, blue-veined hands together. "As to why he wanted my help on that particular subject, I cannot say. He merely asked about the best methods."

For one of the first times in my acquaintance with Merlin,

I readily saw that he was avoiding something, giving me part but not all of the truth. And because I felt these multiple Dogeds contributed in some way to these events, I decided to push him.

"Then why did he think you might have some knowledge of these things?"

My old friend turned away then. When he faced me once again, it was with a crinkled look of frustration, with me. "Malgwyn, are there not things of greater moment that you should be focusing on, rather than an old man's fancies?"

At that, I grew frustrated and slung the platter on the floor. "If someone would answer my questions about this, perhaps I would. But, like Arthur, you strew stones in my path."

Merlin's eyes grew wide. "You have spoken to Arthur of this?"

"I have."

"Malgwyn, do not travel down this path."

"How can I not? I, personally, witnessed at least two other Dogeds the night of his murder. How can that not be important?"

"I cannot tell you that it isn't. But there is only one person, yet living, who can help you in this. Lady Igraine."

"Arthur's mother?"

Merlin nodded solemnly.

"Merlin, this is a diversion. What could Igraine have to do with Doged's murder? She is herself on her deathbed."

"You need to know that Doged was a friend of Igraine's, as was I."

This was ridiculous. "Merlin, I demand the truth."

He began to speak and then stopped, began again, and stopped yet again. Finally, he said, "Malgwyn, though I love you like a son, I swore on pain of death to keep this secret. I cannot break that vow."

Merlin was much like Bedevere in that regard. Once an oath was taken, both would die before breaking it.

"But Merlin, Arthur was not even alive then. What could he know of it that would send him into such a fury?"

Merlin shook his old head. "It is not what he knows, Malgwyn. It is what he thinks he knows."

I cocked my head to the side in obvious confusion. "He does not know the truth?"

"No," and the old man smiled conspiratorially. "He does not." Merlin paused for a moment, shifting his thin frame and causing the leather in his belt to squeak. "Consider this, Malgwyn: If Doged was the one who asked me about these things, and it was Doged who was being impersonated, does that not tell you that he was thus aware of the impersonations?"

"Aye, or it tells me that something went horribly wrong."

"Have it as you will, but I cannot and will not tell you more."

I had known Merlin long enough to know how far I could push him. "Let us go to the mines."

You could hardly call them mines, more like great holes in the ground. Torches had been lit around the rim of each, but only Ider and his soldiers were about.

"No one was here, Malgwyn, when we arrived. I suspect that they all went to Trevelgue," Ider told us.

Before I could stop him, Merlin had descended into one of the holes on a rickety wooden ladder.

"One of you. Bring a torch down here. Now!"

A soldier snatched up a torch and, forgoing the ladder, hurried down the few feet to Merlin's side. I heard rocks clattering and dirt sliding as the soldier made his way down the slope.

For the next several minutes, all I heard was the sounds of Merlin breathing and that of rocks thudding in the dirt. I am not a metalworker, nor am I learned in the art of mining. Once, when I was fighting the Saxons with Arthur, we had ventured near the mines in the north. But they were mostly carved from caves already there. When I was much younger, my father took me to see the old flint mines of the people who came before. Though they were much neglected, they were much like Doged's mines, massive holes. If you looked carefully, you could see the remnants of scaffolding several feet down.

But Doged's mines were not yet that far advanced, and, through the flickering torches, I could still see the top of Merlin's balding head, bouncing up and down as he moved about. Finally, I heard his *caligae* slip on the dirt and gravel as he climbed out, and I gave him my one hand for aid.

He was huffing and puffing, and his pouch was bulging. "I am far too old to be climbing in and out of holes, Malgwyn," he complained. "Tell Arthur this." He led me away, out of earshot of the soldiers, and motioned for Ider to join us.

"There is gold here," Merlin affirmed softly. "How much and how difficult it will be to extract I do not know. The agaphite is good and profitable. This brown ore," and he hefted one of the odd, brown rocks, looking something like a piece of wood turned to rock, "is valuable only if a way can be found to smelt it. As I told you before, I know men who have tried but been unable to work it. What little I know of metalworking tells me that it would produce a strong metal."

I remained silent for a moment, assessing what I had just been told. "So, we are left with nothing, but maybe something."

"Oh," Merlin responded. "There is much here of value, if only the agaphite; it is of a very high quality. Properly mined and worked by craftsmen, it could provide a great profit."

"Then Arthur's urgency to keep Doged's lands in the *consilium* is not misplaced?"

"No, it is absolutely not misplaced. And if the gold is to be had without much difficulty, then whoever controls these mines controls the western lands, just as David is the most powerful lord of the north because he controls the old Roman gold mines."

I pondered all of this for a long moment, and Merlin took it for hesitancy.

"Malgwyn, we have trading ports to the south of Castellum Arturius, but they are constantly plagued by Saxon pirates. If we lose access to these western ports and the goods that pass through them, Arthur will be forced to tax the people more and to claim more of their goods and resources. You know Arthur. He will pay the people for what he takes (though David and the rest take what they wish without payment and consider Arthur a fool for doing otherwise), but the day will come when he too will have to simply take what he needs. He has become and remains high king because he does not impose burdensome levies on the other lords. But he will have to. And ultimately, that will cause the collapse of the *consilium*.

"Vortigern learned what happens when you abuse the people and the other lords. You can visit his grave and counsel with his bones if it makes you feel better." The last words were spoken with a sharpness uncommon to Merlin.

"I do not doubt your words. You have seen far more than I. But you know as I do that being right, being just, being fair, does not guarantee victory. Sometimes I wonder if the task that Arthur has set for himself, for all of us that follow his banner, is not an impossible one."

Merlin's expression softened, his lips curving into a slight smile. "If I heard those words from anyone else, I would thrash him. But I know what you have given in Arthur's cause, and I know something else as well."

"And what is that?"

"It is your cause too and always has been."

I grunted, since acknowledging the truth of his words was not something I was willing to do. "Ider, guard these mines well. At any hint of an intruder, send your fastest horse and best rider to alert us."

Merlin and I went to mount our horses for our journey to Trevelgue, but Ider caught my good arm. "Malgwyn, take two soldiers with you for protection."

Shaking my head, I answered, "No, Ider. I would rather not leave you with fewer men than you have. Merlin and I will be fine." I pulled a hood over my head; Ygerne had just sewn it to this tunic before our journey. "We are but one old man and a one-armed man. We threaten no one."

The wind had calmed a bit by the time we had left the mines behind. I said a prayer to Arthur's god and to all the gods to keep Ider safe. No man had a better friend than I did in young Ider. He had risked much for me, and I loved him as a son. But if even the small Saxon force took aim at the mines, Ider would have his hands full fending them off. And while he had taken to the soldier's life as if born to it, he still had much to learn.

"Do not worry for him, Malgwyn," Merlin said into the silence. "Ider will be fine." Uncanny! Merlin had a way of knowing what was in my heart before even I did.

"He is very young yet and has not been truly tried in battle."

"No man is tried in battle until he is."

A frown grew on my face. "What does that mean, Merlin?"

He grinned to match my frown. "We are, none of us, experienced at anything until we get that opportunity. Some will survive and grow wiser; some will die. Ider is a survivor. I feel it in my bones."

Merlin paused, and when he spoke again the timbre of his voice had altered, subtly. "Malgwyn, I do not know why Doged wished to know these things about disguise. And anything I say about that is but speculation."

"Sometimes speculation hits the target as surely as if it were aimed." I knew he was uncomfortable keeping things from me, but I knew also that he would keep his word to Lady Igraine, no matter how much guilt I laid at his feet.

"And how is young Owain's education proceeding?" I changed the subject.

At that question, Merlin returned to smiling. "He is a very bright child, Malgwyn. He understands numbers better than I, and he has learned to read uncommonly fast."

"He is your son, Merlin," I reminded him. Owain had been conceived in a stolen night of pleasure between Merlin and Nyfain, a lady of Arthur's court. She was a kind woman, but free with her pleasures during both of her marriages. The first had been to one of Arthur's early followers, but he was killed in battle. She then took Accolon to husband, an embittered soldier. But poor Accolon too soon tasted death.

"Sshh." The hiss came from Merlin.

I stopped and looked to him. He had brought his horse up short, and now Merlin was leaning over the horse's neck, peering into the darkness.

My breath caught.

"What?" I whispered after a long moment.

"Horses."

CHAPTER NINE

In tandem, we urged our mounts to the side of the road, into a grove of trees. After a few moments, punctuated by the whistle of wind through the branches, the source of Merlin's alarm rode into view.

They were ten in number and, like us, hooded and armed, some with spears, some with swords. Though they were too few in number to pose much of a threat to Ider, that they had swords bespoke resources that I would not have credited to a wandering group of bandits. Iron was expensive in those days. None was garbed with a lord's symbol, but they rode as soldiers will, straight backed and alert.

As they passed, I caught a few words of their speech, but either it was garbled by the wind or they were speaking a tongue that I knew not. I wished that we had brought Gurdur with us, a forlorn wish now.

In these days, it may seem odd that we were so quick to hide along the road at the first hint of passing riders. But that was a different time. Such stretches of roads through sparsely populated regions were the haunts of *latrunculii*, bandits, who killed and took what they wanted, what they needed. And if not bandits, in the later days it could as easily be Saxons or the Scotti.

Travel was dangerous. A cautious man learned to detect the little clues, the subtle hints that all might not be well. Wood smoke, but no sign of a house or village, could be from a bandit's fire. The sudden hush of night sounds might point to an unseen presence along the road. The pricking up of a horse's ears might also be a sign of danger; horses hear or sense much more than we do.

Merlin and I waited several minutes after the rattling chains and squeaking leather of the strange party passed before resuming our journey.

"Who do you think that was?" I asked Merlin.

"Probably some traders from Gaul," he said, shrugging. "Malgwyn, Arthur needs to send another troop to reinforce Ider. Too many people know of the agaphite and the possibility of gold. The steps you have taken are good, but the word will out, and you know it will."

"I chastised Arthur for releasing Illtud to the Church."

"And you should have." Merlin chuckled. "Illtud is a fine commander, one of the best. What think you of this religion?"

I jerked my head back in surprise. Never had Merlin even mentioned the Christ and Arthur's faith. "In truth, Merlin, I do not know enough of it to say. My father often said that we had not enough wealth to abandon the old gods."

"Aye." Merlin nodded. "It does seem to take much wealth to gain power in the Church. But it has always seemed to me that a religion should embody power, not be bought and sold like so many *servi*. When I journeyed in Egypt, I heard many stories of this man they call the Christ. Some there say He was but a magician; others hold that He was a philosopher. You know of the traditions that say He came here as a child, with the Arimathean."

"Do you credit those? Coroticus, at the abbey, has old parchments that speak of these tales. Aye, they even say that the Arimathean is buried near the abbey."

"You know of the thorn tree on Wirral?"

I nodded. On the summit of Wirral Hill stood a lone thorn tree, one that only bloomed in the winter. Legend had it that Joseph of Arimathea came here with some companions after the Christ had been crucified. They reached as far as the hill near Ynys-witrin, where Joseph planted the little tree that he had brought from the far east.

"I have only seen its like one other place," Merlin continued.

"Where?"

"Near Jerusalem on one of my voyages as a youth." Merlin paused and then chuckled. "As a child really. But still, if the Arimathean did not bring it, who did?"

"Who indeed?"

Silence ensued for several minutes. Even in the dark of night, I could see that Merlin was deep in thought.

"Malgwyn?" he said finally. "If something happens to me, will you promise to take care of Owain?"

"Merlin."

In the moon shadows, I saw his hand come up. "No, Malgwyn, I am not ill. But I am an old man, and I wish to know that my son will be well cared for if I die."

"You know that I will, but surely Arthur would be a better choice."

"Arthur has other things to occupy his time. You are already a part of Owain's life. Besides, your woman is not the only one carrying a child."

"Guinevere is with child?"

And then Merlin laughed aloud. "Did you think that they do not lie together?"

"But she has not said anything to me; I am her cousin."

"She does not tell you everything, Malgwyn. But, this time, she was not certain until just before you left on this journey. Even Arthur does not know yet. It is my charge to tell him."

"Poor Doged." I remembered then. "He did not live long enough to learn that Ysbail is carrying his child."

"In truth?"

"Aye." I nodded. "She told—"

Before I could finish, Merlin fell from his horse. I jerked my reins up quickly and scrambled from my seat.

"Merlin."

He was lying on the ground, facing away from me. As I knelt beside him, he rolled over toward me. "Malgwyn," he croaked. "I believe I have been struck."

And the arrow protruding from his shoulder proved him right. Something whistled in the air, and I saw another arrow embedded in the ground.

I felt a hand grasp my arm, tightly.

"Malgwyn, go quickly! Get to Arthur and tell him of this."

"Merlin, I cannot leave you like this." Another arrow struck the ground less than a foot from me. The rhythm of horses' hooves sounded down the lane.

My old friend smiled. "This is but a nick. You do not think that I would allow a band of *latrunculii* to kill me. Now go! Before you are struck as well. I will be fine."

Arrows sang through the night air. My mind moved as quickly as it could. They outnumbered us; I could tell that by the sheer volume of arrows. I saw that Merlin's horse sported three arrows in her flanks. By the gods, the horse was brave! But she couldn't carry Merlin any longer.

"Bring up the extra troop, Ider!"

It was an old trick I had used once before. Though they were probably certain that we were but two, my hoax might give us a few extra seconds. I dragged Merlin into the forest on the side of the road, quickly.

"Good," Merlin hissed. "Now go. I need to get into hiding and stop this bleeding. I will just slow you down and end up getting us both captured. Go."

And he was right.

And I did, though it nearly tore my heart from me.

I mounted my horse and urged him forward, screaming into the night air like a legion of Roman soldiers.

And praying that Merlin would be safe.

A *schoenus* down the road, I dismounted and led my horse into the moon shadows. My stomach roiled and I lost what little I had eaten in the weeds.

It did not matter that it was the smart thing to do.

It did not matter that it was Merlin's desire.

I had left Merlin behind.

My heart felt like it would split my chest open. I could not seem to breathe.

I was torn between two roads—return for Merlin or do as he commanded and seek help.

Falling back on my haunches, I pulled my knees up and willed my stomach to calm. In a few minutes, I succeeded in controlling my breathing. I was embarrassed. Too much was happening too quickly. But Merlin was right. I needed help to bring him to safety. And Merlin was a tough one, and he knew much about surviving in the forest.

No, Merlin was right.

I must ride for help.

And continue praying for Merlin's safekeeping.

"Malgwyn! Where is Merlin?" Arthur met me at the gate.

I slid from my mount and motioned for a boy to come and take him. "We were attacked, Arthur, not an hour from Trevelgue!"

"By who?"

I just shook my head. "I do not know. They wore no markings on their tunics. Merlin was hit with an arrow in the shoulder."

"And you left him?" Arthur was enraged.

"I had no choice. We were outnumbered, and he and his horse were hit. He demanded it and he was right. Had I not ridden on, both of us would be captured or killed. Besides, he was not wounded fatally, and I helped him secret himself in the forest before I left.

"Believe me, Arthur," I continued. "I did not leave him behind willingly."

"No, but you certainly saved your own precious hide," Arthur spat at me.

The next thing I knew, Bedevere had my wrist grasped firmly in his and I had a dagger between my fingers. "Step lightly, Rigotamos," I warned.

Arthur, his face red, seemed about to say something, but instead, he turned and stomped off.

"Are you mad?" Bedevere yelled. "Threatening the Rigotamos is punishable by death!"

"Then he should not have questioned my courage. Do you think I was happy about leaving Merlin behind?"

"No, of course not. Arthur is just upset over his mother and not hiding it well. And he had an argument with Kay."

"About what?"

"Kay demanded a field command. Arthur told him he would serve in whatever position it pleased him to offer."

I could sort out this problem quickly enough. "Call Kay here. Give him a troop and send him after Merlin."

"But Malgwyn . . ."

"Are you not Arthur's Master of Horse?"

Bedevere nodded.

"Then it is within your power. Arthur's too busy insulting his own men to remember Merlin's plight."

"Malgwyn . . . ," Bedevere began in a low, warning rumble.

"Would you trust anyone else?"

Bedevere shook his shaggy head. "Very well, but Arthur won't like it."

"Arthur will just be happy that Merlin's safe and sound, as will we all. Where is Kay? I will tell him myself. He will need information from me. I will go with him."

"There were how many in the party that passed you?"

"Ten riders, it seemed."

"Probably just a band of *latrunculii*. Merlin was right. Better that you came here. Kay and a troop will be enough to fetch him. We will need you."

"But Bedevere."

My granite-faced friend just shook his head. "I love Merlin as you do, but this fort is but tinder awaiting a spark. We do not even know who our enemies are. And unless you find who killed Doged, it will be laid at Mordred's feet." Bedevere paused and pulled me beneath the parapet. "A rider arrived this morning. Lord David has heard of Mordred's plight. He intends to march here with his forces and rescue Mordred by whatever means necessary."

I shook my head, disgusted at the very mention of David. We had crossed swords many times since Arthur's election as Rigotamos. My disputes with Arthur were but those of children compared to my feud with David.

"But you do not know that he is, indeed, coming?"

"No. But do you really believe that David will not exploit this for his own purposes?"

Bedevere was right. David would not allow a single opportunity for power to pass him by. Reluctantly, I agreed to stay.

Moments later, I had told Kay all I could about where I had left Merlin. Though Kay did not say, his eyes bespoke gratitude for this assignment. When Arthur made Kay his steward, I wondered how long Kay would be content with the job. He had done well, having lasted nearly three years. But Kay, who had once loved to tease others, had himself become the butt of jokes. I shrugged to myself. Kay was the perfect choice to find Merlin. He loved our old friend. He was a battle-hardened veteran. And, at present, he had little else to do.

The time had come to bury Doged. A great funeral pyre had been built atop the highest of the burial mounds within the fort. I knew that after the fire turned to cold ash, Doged's men would bury his bones in the center of the mound, and atop what could be dozens of nobles before him.

'Twas more a custom of the west than our lands. I had never attended a cremation. We buried our dead intact, wrapped in special cloth, interred in stone-lined graves or wooden boxes. But Merlin once told me that the Romans burned their dead. And our ancestors, back in the dark recesses of our history, had done the same. I would not know this, but once, when I was plowing a field with my father, we found a strange pot in the ground, with charred human bones, or at least the teeth seemed human. Father said he had seen the like before.

Arrayed before the mound were all of Doged's nobles—Druce, Cilydd, and the rest—as well as other nobles from far away, I suspected. To my surprise, I saw even a Scotti noble with his retinue. I bumped Bedevere and motioned toward the Scotti with my head.

"I do not know his name, but I have heard that he is the father of Mark's bride to be. Apparently, Doged played some role in negotiating the match."

"Perhaps Mark reneged on the arrangements and this Scotti killed Doged in revenge," I jested, and immediately regretted it. This was not the time to speak lightly of death.

As I stood with the crowd at the base of the mound, I heard someone clear his throat in a deep growl.

"Bedevere said that he had sent Kay after Merlin. Thank you." Arthur cleared his throat once again.

"Thank you."

"For what?"

"For not having me beheaded. Rigotamos, I truly do not seek to enrage you. I would have given my one good arm for Merlin. But he was injured; our enemies were closing in. I did not know how many we faced. Merlin was right to order me away."

"I know," Arthur said. "I know. And I should not have wasted time chastising you. I should have sent Kay immediately. No, I should have gone myself. I pray that he is not too late."

Glancing quickly at Arthur, I could see the fierce vein pumping at his neck and his whitened knuckles. I am not certain that Arthur was ever more frustrated than right then. His heart was with Merlin and his plight; his duty bade him stay.

"Kay will serve us well, Rigotamos."

He straightened his shoulders a bit. "The Christ will keep them both safe, if that is His will."

And then Ysbail motioned Arthur forward.

I did not stay to hear Arthur declaim. Slowly and silently, I slipped back through the crowd and went in search of Daron and Sulien.

Back down in the fort proper, a young boy came running toward me, bearing an arrow. "Lord Malgwyn!"

I stopped and he pulled up quickly. "Hold, boy. I am no lord."

"But you are Malgwyn?" The child leaned over, bracing himself with his knees.

"Aye. What do you want with me?" I was testy, from both my worry over Merlin and my verbal skirmish with Arthur. By all rights, I should have gone with Kay, but Bedevere insisted that I would be needed at Trevelgue.

"Lord Kay sent me to you with this."

And then I saw it. I snatched it from the child's hand, sending him stumbling back in fear. "Where did he find this?"

The boy's eyes grew wide.

"Where?"

"He said it was stuck in your horse's flank."

The arrow was exactly like those from Daron's village, a Saxon point on a Briton shaft, with Briton fletching. We had been attacked by the same band that massacred those poor villagers.

And I had left Merlin at their mercy.

"Where is Kay?"

The boy fell back once more. "He left some time ago, master."

"Bring me Lord Bedevere then, with all speed."

The boy raced back up the lane. Stupid child. He had probably spent too much time showing off the arrow to his friends. Perhaps even sealing Merlin's fate.

I whirled about in the lane. I found myself in a most unfamiliar situation. I did not know what to do, did not know what direction to go.

Then, I saw one of the strangest sights of my long life. Striding up the lane was a tall *monachus*, wearing a plain, brown robe with a mighty gold cross hanging about his neck. His nose looked more like a falcon's beak than a human appendage. He wore a strange tonsure. In those days, the *monachi* among us shaved all the hair above their foreheads. But the top of this man's head was completely shaved, leaving but a circle of hair around his skull. Coroticus, the abbot at Ynys-witrin, had told me of this. It was the custom in Rome.

He smiled as he came toward me. "You must be Malgwyn."

Whoever this man was, he was far more jovial than recent events dictated.

At that moment, however, I was more worried about Merlin than about meeting yet another *monachus*. I nodded at him and spun about, searching the crowd now descending from Doged's funeral even as the column of smoke from his pyre rose to the heavens.

I could not see Bedevere in the throng, but then I felt a hand on my shoulder and I turned, expecting to see my old friend there. But no, it was this odd *monachus*.

"Is there some way I might be of service?" I fair spat the words out, so impatient was I.

But the *monachus* showed no offense, just smiled in an oddly calming manner. "I was told to seek you out."

Why in the name of the gods would someone send a *monachus* to seek me out?

And then he answered that question without it being spoken. "I am Petrocus."

I was an idiot. Of course. This was the learned monk from the community of believers near Tyntagel. Too many things were happening too quickly. "Please forgive my temper. The situation here is changing with each and every moment."

"Is that arrow of some importance?" he asked, pointing. "You clutch as if it were."

"It was found embedded in my horse's flank. I've only seen its like once before."

"Yes." Petrocus nodded. "A Saxon point with our own fletching. An unlikely combination. I have seen this before as well, recently."

"Where?"

"A farmstead near our community was raided, the family killed, their livestock taken."

I nodded. "The other I found was in a village, near unto the border with the summer country. The entire village had been sacked and all the people massacred, save one." I stopped suddenly. Did I want this *monachus* to know of Daron? Long ago, I had learned that the robes of a *sacerdote* or presbyter were no guarantee of a good man. Caution bade me to keep silent.

"Near the summer country, you say," Petrocus repeated, not seeming to have really heard my last comment.

"Aye, just across the border in Doged's lands."

He nodded. "These are frustrating."

"I agree, but why do you think so?"

Petrocus pursed his lips. "Does it signify Saxons buying Briton shafts? Or does it signify Britons buying Saxon points? Both are freely available and freely traded up and down the coast."

"But we have no trade agreement with the Saxons."

"And we have no guarantee that the sun will rise tomorrow, save for the fact that it always has. Merchants and traders do that which is best designed to bring them a profit. Agreements between kings mean little to them."

I liked this Petrocus. Somewhat like Coroticus at Ynyswitrin, he was a man of the world. But Petrocus spoke plainly, not doling out his thoughts in bits and pieces. "Do you know why you were summoned?"

"To provide counsel on Doged's wife's legal rights. It is my understanding that the woman and Doged were only recently wed," Petrocus said, sounding much like Merlin.

Merlin.

What was wrong with me? I was allowing myself to be distracted at every turn. But before I could say aught, Bedevere came bounding down the lane with my little messenger at his side.

Without greeting, I thrust the arrow out to him, and he took it, studying its length closely. "The same?"

I nodded. "It came from my horse's flank."

Only then did Bedevere notice Petrocus. Though usually taciturn and reserved, Bedevere had great respect for the clergy. "Forgive me."

"Lord Bedevere, this is the *monachus* Petrocus, for whom Arthur sent. He has had experience with these arrows as well."

"Yet I'm not very helpful, I fear. Why the seeming panic?"

"Why do you think we are in a panic?"

The *monachus* laughed deeply. "A lord of the *consilium* running down the lane. The look of deep concern on your own face. It does not take a learned man to discern this."

I did indeed like this fellow. "I was attacked on my return from Castellum Dinas by a group of men using these." Merlin's plight was best left unspoken, especially to one that we had just met. "Having found these same arrows at the massacred village, I was greatly troubled that these murderers seemed to be ranging across a great sweep of these lands without challenge."

"Who is there left to pose such a challenge?" Petrocus observed. "Doged's nobles are here, all with as many of their men as they could muster. The lands are lawless enough when the nobles are at home. Take them and their men away and it is chaos."

"And you have heard nothing about who these people might be?" In my experience, the *monachi* hear much.

"No," he replied quickly. While the *monachi* hear much,

they say little. That too was one of the things that bothered me about the Church. They used information as currency, just as the lords did.

I suppose that they did these things for survival. Though the Romans had adopted this worship of the Christ, they had never fully succeeded in converting our people. Many had accepted Him; many had not. The Saxons were not believers, and they had brought their own gods with them.

This new religion had much to commend it; good men had embraced it. But I tended to rely more on things that I could see, and talk of wine turning to blood and bread to flesh sounded of alchemy to me. Yet I found myself drawn to it, a little more each day. This was something I had just noticed, and I wondered how much of it was that human need for understanding, for order, in a world that offered little.

Bedevere had remained silent during the exchange, but he spoke now. "I do not think this changes Kay's task, Malgwyn. If he encounters them on his patrol, he will almost certainly engage them and maybe then we will learn more of their origins."

"I thought that perhaps I should join Kay."

Bedevere shook his shaggy head. "But Petrocus is here now, and we will soon be in the midst of negotiations."

I marveled at how quickly Bedevere sensed the need for circumspection. I do not mean to imply that he was dense, but diplomacy had never been his strength. He was a warrior, and no man fought harder or more bravely. Yet now I was learning that he had unplumbed depths.

"I will send a rider," my friend continued. "Kay should be made aware of this absolutely. There must be a reckoning for those poor people at that village. And for those of your farmstead, Petrocus," he hurriedly added.

All this circumspection was becoming tiring. "Petrocus," I said, taking his arm in my one hand. "Let me take you to Arthur and Lady Ysbail."

Bedevere nodded and moved out of our way.

CHAPTER TEN

"So, this is the *monachus* who will proclaim me king of these lands?" Ysbadden was less than subdued by his brother-in-law's funeral.

Doged's hall had been rearranged, the center cleared and chairs and benches lining the walls. At the back of the room, before Doged's private chambers, Ysbail had taken her seat and, at that particular moment, was sending her brother a venomous stare. They were as different as two people could be. He was nearly twice her height and thrice her bulk. And she had all the grace and, yes, nobility, that evaded him.

Arthur sat next to Ysbail, a placement that I was certain was an effort to put Ysbadden in his place. But the giant seemed incapable of detecting such a slight.

"Brother, these are my lands now, and I shall rule them accordingly," she proclaimed.

"Bah. A woman cannot rule in her own right. All know that."

Shouts and screeches burst across the room between Ysbail and Ysbadden and their supporters.

And then the strangest thing happened.

While Arthur beat the floor with the hilt of his sword, pleading for silence, a guttural sound, the sound of a clearing throat, broke clear over the hall. In the din then sounding, it should have been drowned out like a mouse's squeak. But all heard it, and even more surprisingly, all quieted. Even Ysbadden found a seat, near the Saxon contingent, I noted.

"Lady Ysbail," Petrocus began, moving into the open area. "I understand that I have been summoned to offer counsel on the laws of these lands."

"Lord Arthur suggested you as a learned man in these matters," Ysbail acknowledged. It did not happen quite that way, but we gained nothing from embarrassing her.

"I thank the Rigotamos," Petrocus replied, nodding to Arthur. "These questions are not so easily resolved as your brother indicated."

I smiled. Petrocus was a skilled diplomat. By responding to Ysbadden through Ysbail, he established quickly who he saw as the most important. I was not certain that Ysbadden recognized the slight, but Ysbail did and she favored Petrocus with a smile.

"We have many ranks in our society, and the question of a female ruler has been at issue for many years." Petrocus strolled casually about the circle, as if this were nothing more than a lesson in a *ludus* and he a *magister*. "Among both the Scotti and our own people, women hold property, aye, even inherit property if there is no son. They have the same obligation to provide soldiers in time of war."

"But a woman ruler?" Druce bounded to his feet, interrupting Petrocus.

The *monachus* was not perturbed. "Yes, my boy. It is not unknown for women to lead troops into battle. The Roman

Tacitus wrote of a great queen, Cartimandua, of one of our eastern tribes. And do I have to mention Boudicca, of the Iceni? Sit, boy, and listen."

Most in the hall snickered, but I did not. Druce's face grew scarlet. Taunting the young can have violent consequences. Druce would have his vengeance for being belittled. But for now, he sat down, though I saw that his hand stayed on his sword hilt.

Turning suddenly to the Scotti king, who had stayed for this convocation after Doged's funeral, Petrocus smiled. "And I do not have to remind our Scotti guest of Macha Mong Ruadh, who ruled all the lands of the Scotti for nearly ten years."

Invoking Macha's name sent a low rumble circling the room. We had all heard her story, around the fires, late at night. Her father, the king, had died, and his council of advisors had elected Macha to replace him. But the old king had ruled in some complex way with two of his cousins, and the cousins did not want to share power with a woman. Macha was not a woman to be denied, and she raised an army, killed one cousin, and married the other.

Petrocus, ever the entertainer, let the power of Macha's name soak in. "And do I need to remind anyone that ancient tradition gives great authority to *arglwyddes*, female lords in the old tongue? No, both in our law and in our traditions there is ample evidence of women ruling."

"How come you to know so much?" Ysbadden challenged. The giant was confused. He had probably thought that taking these lands from his sister would be simple and less bloody than usual. But here he faced not only multiple claimants and the Rigotamos but also a surprisingly uncooperative sister. I almost felt sorry for Ysbadden, almost.

Petrocus smiled that endearing smile of his. "I studied in Rome, my lord. And I have been deeply interested in our laws and traditions for many years."

Ysbadden spat on the hard-packed floor. "So you studied in Rome? That does not impress me. What has Rome done for us but abandon us? Fancy words. But Ysbail is widowed; she will need a protector. As her closest relative that is my right."

This odd *monachus* turned his gentlest smile on Ysbadden. "That has no basis in either law or tradition." Which was not exactly true, but I would not dispute him.

"Rigotamos," Druce began, trying a more moderate approach, it seemed. "This woman is not even of our people. She hails from a tribe south of here. For her to dance into our midst and claim the crown on the strength of a marriage but two moons old is no different than her brother's practices."

I stood to get a better view of the room. I wanted to know how each faction would react to this, for, without question, this was the most important point.

Ysbail was unaffected. Ysbadden went for his sword but thought better of it. Arthur cupped his chin in his hand, looking thoughtful, but I knew he was concealing a smile. For Druce to appeal to him after killing one of Arthur's men and challenging him was, simply, laughable. And I noticed that Cilydd did just that, but quietly.

Ceawlin and the Saxons were still here, but they were lined up against the wall, far from the center of attention. Cilydd had chosen to stand next to them, though his brother was as close to Ysbail as he could get. The better to be heard, I suspected. The hapless Trevelyan and a handful of his men were next to Bedevere. At least a dozen other nobles, greater and lesser, were arrayed against the wall. I doubted that anyone of stature in a ten-*schoenus* radius was not here. Even a child or two could be seen, darting in and out of the audience.

Suddenly, the confident smile on Petrocus's face slipped, just a little. "Let me say that I am not here as an *iudex*. I am here only to offer advice."

I did not envy Petrocus his position. Only the presence of Arthur and a fraction of his troops stood between Ysbail and a rebellion. With Doged alive, the threat had been only that, a threat. But now it was more than a possibility, and all the major claimants were here in this hall. What Petrocus said next might spell the different between war and peace.

"The law lives in a world of absolutes," Petrocus began. "But we live in a world where right and wrong are hardly ever that easily defined. Is Ysbail's claim to these lands lessened by the short duration of her marriage to Doged? The law says no. Reality argues differently. Ruling lands is the same as ruling people. Law and tradition gives Ysbail the right to inherit these lands. But the law cannot force the people to obey her. In that respect, the length of her marriage to Doged is important."

"Ridiculous!" shouted the Scotti lord, as an audible gasp burst across the room. Even Arthur seemed confused as to why the Scotti would intervene.

Petrocus turned toward him. "King Anwas, you dispute my conclusions?"

Though we were constantly at war with the Scotti, they were but little wars. I still saw the Scotti as more nuisance than threat. The Saxons posed the greatest threat. So, I knew little of Anwas, and like everyone else, I wondered at why this mattered to him.

"If the match was properly made and all promises kept, then she is his lawful heir," the Scotti proclaimed. He was a tall man, though not as tall as Kay, with a round chest and a bushy beard.

"I believe that I have already said that." Petrocus allowed a bit of frustration to show through. "But we must also consider the realities."

"Bah." Anwas scoffed. "What does a *sacerdote* know of reality? Either the law is the law or it is not."

And then a thought struck me. "Is Lord Mark injured or in poor health, Lord Anwas? Or will he be?"

It was a chancy thing, to mock a king, but I was in safe company here, for the most part. Even the Saxons thought my jest funny. Arthur did not even try to hide his delight.

"You are brave for something that was once a man." Anwas spoke our tongue with a heavy accent.

"You are brave for a king in enemy country." I would pay later for that. It was impolitic and not completely true. But it served the purpose and shut Anwas's mouth, and I told myself to remember to warn Mark to add another food taster. I would not want Anwas as a father-in-law; he was altogether too familiar with our laws and traditions on inheritance.

Then something across the room drew my attention. Ceawlin, the Saxon pig, was whispering in Ysbadden's ear. After a moment, the giant nodded and struggled to his feet.

"This resolves nothing," Ysbadden shouted. "You, Arthur! You claim to champion justice and fairness. It seems that several men have a claim on Doged's lands. Submit this to an *iudex*. Let us have a trial to determine if my sister may rule."

Arthur was trapped. I was certain that Ceawlin had suggested this course of action. Once again, Arthur's insistence on virtue had turned into a root in his path, catching his *caligae* and throwing him to the ground.

Ysbail was alarmed. Her pale skin had turned a deep crimson. For the first time in my short acquaintance with her, that self-confidence that marked her had collapsed. Even the murder of her husband had not shaken her like this.

Perhaps it was Ysbail's reaction, perhaps it was the annoyance of children dashing about the hall, but at that moment I realized that Ysbail had failed to mention something important, something that could, indeed, make all the difference.

"Petrocus!"

The flurry of voices, swirling around the room, faded out. And all eyes turned to me.

The *monachus* looked at me expectantly.

"If Ysbail were with child, would that change the situation?"

I thought it but a simple question, but the reaction was anything but simple. Druce, Cilydd, even Trevelyan leaped to their feet. Aye, Ysbadden jumped up so quickly that I feared he would punch a hole in the roof, and truth to tell, more than a little dried thatch and dust hung in the air.

"Child! Child!" The word nearly became a chant, and through the wooden walls of Doged's hall I could hear it spreading throughout the gathering.

"She is not with child!" Ysbadden roared, finally quieting the room.

"But," Petrocus finally quelled the shouting mob, "if she were, it would change everything. The child would then become the heir and Ysbail its regent. That is law."

All eyes, truly, turned to the shaken Ysbail. Her crimson blush deepened. A moistness shone from the corner of an eye. Sucking in a deep breath, she began.

"I am not with child."

And the clamor began again.

Arthur looked at me curiously. He did not doubt my word, but he, we, all of us, had to wonder: Was Ysbail lying when she told me of her child? Or was she lying now? And if she was, why would she, as a child would secure her place?

While I pondered that, I noticed something truly ominous. Lord David had entered the hall and was whispering in Druce's ear. Arthur did not see; he was too busy whispering in Ysbail's ear, assuring her, I was certain, that he would support her cause. I also was certain that his mind was racing, trying to formulate a response to Ysbadden's demand.

But Bedevere had seen David as well, and he tripped over Cilydd's son, Culwhch, trying to reach Arthur's side. Just as he made it, a new voice broke over the din.

"I am Lord David, summoned here by my good friend Druce. I tell you all now that I support his claim on the throne."

"Bah!" exclaimed Ysbadden. "Sister, see how your friend Arthur works? He whispers his support in your ear while his dog, David, does his true bidding. You are far better off allowing me to rule."

Arthur seemed silenced by David's unexpected appearance. We had heard, of course, that he was on his way, but he must have ridden without stop.

"I speak for myself, not Arthur, not the *consilium*," David replied. "I support Ysbadden's call for an *iudex* to decide this matter."

No one responded immediately, and the low hum of whispering increased.

"Will Lord Druce commit to abiding by any decision reached by the *iudex*?" The words rang out, and it was a moment before I realized that it was I who had spoken. Arthur would not be pleased, and I avoided looking his way.

David turned toward me, seeing me, I knew, for the first time. He smiled in that way he had, that way that portended trouble for everyone. "Why, Master Malgwyn. So good to see you. Of course, Druce agrees to abide by any decision made." He answered too quickly, and Druce looked uncomfortable. I suspected that the young lord was not as accomplished a liar as David. He would be, if he lived long enough.

"You will?" Ysbadden asked, as puzzled as the rest.

"Truly. Lord Druce is no less a lover of fairness and equality than the Rigotamos, nor am I."

I choked back laughter. David loved mostly himself. After that, he loved gold. After that, power. But there was far more to this than just that. There was a reason that David wanted a hearing by an *iudex*.

"Then all that is left is the selection of an *iudex*," Arthur said, finally entering the fray.

Another lord of Doged's, a man in his middle years, stood up. "We have the perfect man already here. Petrocus knows the law and knows the traditions. He knows our ways. He is a man of the Christ. Let him be the *iudex*."

At that moment, Petrocus wished to be anywhere but here. He did not need to say it. The frown on his face sent the message much better than he could by speaking. For that I could not blame him. Petrocus viewed these matters as a scholar. His life was lived in theories. But this was about the real world.

"My lords, I am but a poor *monachus*, not a true *iudex*. Wouldn't you be better served by a man with more experience?"

"Do not belittle your own experience, Petrocus," I chastised him. "I would rather have a *sacerdote* or presbyter of your reputation oversee this matter than some *iudex* that measures his decisions by the heft of the claimants' purses."

Arthur frowned at me again, but he could not argue. We still had, in the larger towns, men who were called *iudices*, and they judged the occasional simple dispute. But the old Roman system of justice had long ago disappeared.

"I am satisfied with Petrocus as the *iudex*." Ysbail had recovered her composure. She turned her icy eyes to first Ysbadden and then Druce. "He has already acknowledged that the brief term of my marriage to Doged has a role to play in all of this. Certainly he is a fair-minded man."

"Then that is how it will be," Arthur said, rising. "We shall begin in three days' time. That should allow each claimant to choose an advocate and prepare."

Immediately, I saw smiles paint the faces of Ysbadden, David, Druce, and, oddest of all, Ceawlin. I wanted to scream, "NO!" But Arthur had left me no room. For some reason, they wanted this three-day delay. And what they wanted was almost certainly bad for us.

The crowd in the hall began to leave; Ysbail had had all the food withdrawn earlier. Looking toward the front of the hall, I saw Arthur wave a woolen-wrapped hand at me, beckoning me to join him.

"You are slowing down in your old age, Malgwyn."

In plowing through the lingering mob I had happened upon David. He was a handsome man with darker hair than Arthur's.

"How so?"

"The only question to be settled by this *iudex* is whether Ysbail can rule these lands on her own. It does nothing to determine who will rule if she cannot."

"And you are telling me this because . . . ?"

"I want you to tell Arthur that I intend to support Druce's claim to these lands. The *consilium* is not as one on this issue."

"That is as good as a declaration of war against Arthur, and the *consilium*."

"Only if Arthur is stupid enough to start a war. And you know as well as do I that Mark will join us." His arrogance was palpable; it almost oozed from his pores.

"Do not misunderstand me, David. I would love nothing better than to slit your throat on the battlefield, but know this: Arthur will not yield. Not on this matter." I stopped. If I said more, David would know (if he did not already) that there was more at stake here than a pair of ports and more lands.

But even that little bit brought the sly narrowing of David's eyes that never boded good.

"We will talk more of this later," he said, sweeping past me then.

I sighed and joined Arthur, Bedevere, and Ysbail near the door to the private chambers. Once the stout wooden door was shut behind us, I wasted no time.

"Ysbail. You told me that you were carrying Doged's child."

Though my outburst was intended to intimidate her, it seemed to strengthen her resolve. Now it was she who narrowed her eyes at me.

"I was mistaken. Would you like to see the proof?"

And that humbled me into silence. Arthur and Bedevere, standing behind Ysbail, grinned at my discomfiture. They would pay later. A *servus* who had brought a tray of cups of watered wine smiled a little as well. Fortunately for her, she was not my *servus*. But I still did not believe Ysbail's denials. Her earlier, unsought admission rang more true. And denying it now only weakened her position. I was greatly confused.

"Did you set a guard to watch over Petrocus?" I asked Bedevere, who nodded grimly.

"I do not think they would harm him now, but with this pack of rogues I do not wish to be caught off guard."

"The weight of the law is still on Ysbail's side," Arthur pointed out.

"But as Petrocus said, the weight of the law is not the only consideration. Rigotamos," I began. "David says that he will ally with Druce and support his claim. Even to the point of taking the field against you."

I expected Arthur to explode at that, but he began tugging at his mustache as he did when thoughtful. I think I was the only one that saw the vein pumping angrily in his neck, a sign of his anger.

"Malgwyn," Ysbail began in the lull, "perhaps it is now time to show my resolve. I shall order Mordred's execution for killing my husband."

"That is the one thing you cannot do," Arthur interrupted. "David and Mordred are old allies. David would use Mordred's death to further bolster his cause, to render a split in the *consilium*."

Ysbail's eyes narrowed in a hint of frustration. "But David is himself splitting the *consilium*, is he not?"

I nodded. "Aye, he is. But Lord David is a master at taking two opposed positions at the same time."

But then Ysbail's jaw became rigid. "That is of no matter to me. My husband's murder demands justice. You have found no other person who could have done this, have you?" She did not wait for my answer. "Then, it is settled. I can at least do that for him."

I looked to Arthur for help. He was still tugging on his mustache. "I cannot allow you to do that," he said finally, gently.

Only Ysbail's raised eyebrows showed her indignation. Her

voice was remarkably calm. "I do not see how you can stop me. Indeed, I think it might be a wise move after all. It will show the people that I will not blindly follow the *consilium*'s orders as my husband did."

I truly hated the world of lords. No one said what they meant. Each sought some advantage for themselves in everything they did. Moments like this were when I truly longed for my life as a farmer.

"No, Lady Ysbail. What that would do is force the Rigotamos into siding with Druce. For if he allows the beheading of Mordred, he may, very well, face civil war within the *consilium*." This was one of my tasks for Arthur, to state the blunt, sometimes brutal, realities without his having to do so. I was not fond of that part of my job either.

"And what of your vaunted reputation for fairness and justice? Which my husband so often mentioned?"

I began to answer, but Arthur held up his hand.

"I can scarcely champion fairness and justice while lying dead on the battlefield, Ysbail."

"Ysbail," I interrupted. "I do not like Mordred. Indeed, I despise him. Were it my decision to make, I would slash his throat this instant. But he did not kill your husband. I am more certain of that than anything else."

"Why?" 'Twas more challenge than question.

"Mordred swears that Doged was already dead when he sought entry." Telling her of the Saxons complicated my argument. "He says that a previous visitor ran past him as he entered the rear door. The guard that both parties bribed, apparently, was killed last night, to silence him. Mordred could not have had a hand in that. He was tied up by your own guards." The Saxons could have eliminated the guard, but Mordred could not have, so I was not telling a complete lie. And with Arthur there, I could scarcely bring up the many Dogeds prancing about that night.

A long moment passed. Ysbail hung her head finally. "I know of the guard's murder. He was one of my people, not Doged's."

Bedevere cocked his head to the side. "Doged allowed one of your men to guard such a vulnerable spot?"

She shrugged. "I demanded little. Very well, I will delay killing him, but he will remain my prisoner until such time as you can bring me something better than 'he did not kill the guard,' which does nothing to acquit him of my husband's death, or until this current crisis is resolved."

It occurred to me that she had no great desire to order anyone's death, and that raised her in my esteem. But there was a nervousness about her when she talked of Doged's death that I did not understand. A woman so disinclined to order a prisoner's execution is hardly going to commit murder herself unless forced to. But, as Bedevere pointed out, Doged had allowed his killer access and his death had come suddenly, as if he was unaware of his attacker's intentions. Ysbail would bear further observation.

"If I might ask a favor?"

Ysbail frowned at me once more. "What?"

"Do not allow Mordred to visit with David, Druce, or the Saxons. The longer we keep them apart, the more frantic Mordred will become and the sooner he will tell us everything he knows."

"You think he is still withholding information?" Arthur asked.

"I think Mordred always withholds knowledge."

I turned to Arthur. "Rigotamos, this three-day delay is but a ploy by David to stall for some reason."

Arthur smacked his head with his woolen-wrapped hand. "I am a fool. David arrived without an escort, riding at breakneck speeds. He needs the extra time for his army to arrive." Arthur spun about and grabbed Bedevere by the arm. "Speed a rider to Castellum Arturius. Have Gawain send an additional troop."

"A suggestion?"

Frustrated, he turned on me. "Yes, what?"

"Send a rider also to Castellum Marcus, but have the rider find Tristan. Tell him that I have asked him to bring two troop here."

"You?" Ysbail did not quite believe what I had said.

I just smiled at her. "He believes that he owes me a debt. He will come."

Arthur slapped a hand across my shoulder. "Good. They will have a shorter journey, and with good weather they should reach us before David's men arrive. How many men in arms do you have here?"

For once, Ysbail was truly at a loss. She looked to Bedevere. "Maybe two hundred or two hundred and fifty. How many are loyal I cannot say."

I counted in my head. "We have two troop here, one at Castellum Dinas with Ider and one with Kay seeking Merlin. If Tristan proves true, we will have a sufficient force to repel any assault."

"What if we must take the field against them? Defending a prepared, protected position is easier than defeating an army on an open field."

I looked to Bedevere, who screwed his face up in thought.

Finally, he looked to Ysbail. "Forgive me, but your husband's soldiers are ill trained, though I do not doubt their eagerness. But our men are veterans of many battles. Tristan's will be as well. Druce's men are in worse shape than Doged's; most are little more than children. David's will be like ours. It will all depend on how many David brings."

"It would not be like him to commit his entire force unless he was absolutely assured of success," I added.

"Then we should be safe in that event," Arthur concluded.

"Unless the Saxons join in, or Melwas." Melwas, the lord at Ynys-witrin, had plagued us the year before.

Arthur's shaggy head shook. "No, Melwas is licking his wounds, and David knows that he would court disaster by openly allying with the Saxons."

"Would he?" I should have remained silent, but I trusted David far less than Arthur did.

"You have doubts?"

"Mark has already counseled treating with the Saxons. Although Mordred has not said so openly, I suspect that he was more guest of the Saxons than prisoner."

"Yet you think Tristan will be eager to join us."

I chuckled. "Tristan is a young man who feels that he owes me a debt of honor. Such men are passionate about these matters."

"The *consilium* was fragmented under Ambrosius as much as it is now. Gawain, Gaheris, Bedevere, Kay, Aircol, Pascent, they are all loyal."

Arthur was right; they were loyal. The last, Pascent, was the brother of Vortimer and yet another son of Vortigern, who had brought the hated Saxons to our island. After Vortimer's death some four years before, Pascent had emerged as his successor. I had only met Pascent once, but he seemed a good man, as brave as his brothers and more trustworthy than his father.

But Arthur always wanted the *consilium* to act as one, and even the most loyal of members hesitated at that.

"What you must decide, Rigotamos, is whether these lands are important enough to risk splitting the *consilium* in half."

Only then did I realize that Ysbail was still there, listening carefully to all we were saying. She deserved to know what potential riches this land held, but I knew that Arthur would not sanction telling her, at least not yet, for fear she would use that knowledge against us.

And Arthur noticed her interest as well. "The ports here bring in much revenue to the *consilium*," he hurried into the pause. "What good is a united land if there is no money to govern it?"

He was telling me that yes, it was important enough. At the mention of ports and revenues, Ysbail's interest waned.

"Then," Arthur continued. "What is our plan?"

"I will see to the riders and begin organizing our troops," Bedevere said.

The Rigotamos nodded. "I will attempt to parley with David and the others."

"And I will join Kay in his search for Merlin," I added, but Arthur quickly shook his head with a rueful grin.

"You, my scribe, will prepare for this court, and you will seek Doged's true killer in earnest. Kay is capable of finding Merlin."

As I began to protest, Arthur rested his hand on my shoulder. "I am as worried about our friend as you are. But sending you to join Kay will not speed his quest. The Christ and His father will watch over Merlin, as they watch over each of us."

I did not like such answers. I preferred to make my own destiny. But Arthur should be more cautious about his desires.

"Then I will not brook interference, Rigotamos. And I believe that the false Dogeds hold a key to this affair. I will pursue that and all the evidence, no matter where it leads."

Crimson rose in Arthur's cheeks, but I was not moved. This was a familiar scene for us. "It is a waste of time," he replied, without half the fervor of before. More important events had taken his attention. He no longer had a will to fight me on this.

I did not respond, just stood firmly. After a moment, Arthur nodded jerkily, once. But as I turned away, I could not help but notice the shine of fear in Ysbail's eyes.

By all rights, my task should have been the easiest one that I ever approached. Poor Eleonore was killed in the lanes of Castellum Arturius, with hundreds of people as possible killers. Old Elafius was murdered in his cell at the abbey, true, but it was a community of brethren, each of whom could have killed the old *monachus*. But this was a lord of the *consilium*, killed in his own chambers with a guard at the door. I think that is why I found the whole matter so frustrating.

I left them then and wandered out into the fort, and even further, out into the village beyond the walls. Events had moved so swiftly that I had not had time to truly consider everything that had happened.

The delicate smell of sour wine drew me toward a stall on the road leading down to the port, but I ignored its pull. The lanes were full of visitors from the villages inland; though they came to mourn Doged, the flavor of a festival hung heavily in the air. I did not hunger for the company of others. I needed some solitude, a difficult commodity to purchase in that time and place.

"Malgwyn!"

Startled that someone shouted my name, I looked up to see Sulien urging me inside a small building, a public house of some sort where food and drink could be bought. Anger grew in my belly. If Sulien had abandoned Daron to drink, I would have his head.

But my fears were unnecessary. Inside, at a table, Sulien, Daron, and one other man were sitting. An old Roman pitcher held wine from the looks of it. Whoever owned the pitcher was lucky. It was of that bluish-green, wavy glass made by the Romans, and from the nicks and cracks had seen many a winter. Few of these survived now.

The stranger did not like my appearance. He cast his eyes at me with ill-concealed disdain, rose, and left, taking his beaker with him.

"Who was he?"

"A lustful man who wanted to purchase our friend here for the night."

I chuckled. "Was he unwilling to pay?"

"I told him that she was the *servus* of one of Arthur's councilors, a mighty man with one arm who would kill anyone that looked at her with evil intent."

Daron slapped Sulien on the arm. "I am not a *meretrice*, or a *servus*," she huffed.

In certain ways, Daron seemed to me as an adult Mariam, my daughter. She was a combination of Mariam and her mother.

"No, you are not, Daron. But until we discover who laid waste to your village, you must play a different role."

She looked away, brushing her hair from her face. "I thought you had forgotten my village."

"Now, girl," Sulien scolded her. "Malgwyn serves the Rigotamos. He has many duties to perform."

Daron flashed her blue eyes at me. "And it seems he gets none of them done."

Her shot was true, and I hung my head. "Daron, I want to bring your village justice more than anything. And I would have you safe when I do."

The light drained from her eyes. "My village is dead to me now. I have no village."

"And what village would that be?"

The sudden voice sent my hand groping for my dagger.

David. Leering over our table.

CHAPTER ELEVEN

Sulien leaped to his feet, placing his nose only inches from David's.

Lord David stumbled back two steps, grasping the hilt of his sword. "You dare attack a lord of the *consilium*?"

Sulien smiled. "No, my lord. My beaker is empty, and I am simply going for another. My apologies for frightening you." With that, he moved past, nodding and winking at me, and headed to the wine merchant.

David released his sword and straightened his tunic. "You should put that one on a leash, Malgwyn," he advised, sitting down.

"Why? Because he is thirsty?"

"Such thirst may get him killed someday."

"Are you here to threaten or talk?"

David chuckled. "We have no secrets between us, Malgwyn. Who is she?" He nodded toward Daron.

"My *servus*."

"I have never known you to hold *servi*."

"Time and people change."

He shrugged. "As you like. But she is a pretty one."

"Your business?"

"I no more desire to cross swords with Arthur than he does with me. It profits no one but the ravens."

"Good, Arthur will be pleased to hear that you plan to withdraw your challenge."

David shook his head. "Malgwyn, Malgwyn. You never cease to amaze me. You know that is not what I intend. These lands need a firm hand. Doged was a good man, but in his last years he ruled by virtue of his kind nature. People see that as a weakness. It was only a matter of time before Druce toppled him."

"Or Cilydd."

"Bah," David spat. "Cilydd lacks certainty. He is too cautious and would talk instead of act." He paused. "I will speak plainly."

"Please."

"If Arthur will agree to support Druce's claim, then no one will ever know of this dispute. The *consilium* will appear as one. Druce will become a lord of the *consilium*, and we will continue to profit from these lands."

No one would know until David sent his agents abroad to whisper it on the wind. He did not fool me. David would use any opportunity to undercut Arthur. But the neutral side of my nature, the one that looked at things from a distance, saw that his proposal had merits.

"You know that Druce killed one of Arthur's men?"

David flicked his wool-wrapped hand as if he were swatting away a fly. "Youthful enthusiasm. Besides, you repaid him by killing his nephew. Arthur should consider that debt closed."

"I will take your proposal to the Rigotamos, but I can nearly guarantee that he will reject it. He sees the law and justice on Ysbail's side."

"Or," David taunted me, "does he just fear Ysbadden that much?"

"Have it as you will. But I will explain your offer to Arthur."

David stood then. He stared down at me for a long, long second. "You and I have unfinished business, Malgwyn."

"We do," I agreed pleasantly.

"Do not try to resolve it in the days ahead."

"Nor should you."

With a quick nod, he was gone.

"Do you always talk so openly?" Daron asked, her blue eyes studying me.

"You are a *servus*. People always talk openly in front of *servi*. Though I agree with you that it is a bad habit." Recent history had taught me that lesson in a very painful way.

"I am not a *servus*." Daron stood and made to leave, but faithful Sulien caught her about the waist and guided her back to her seat.

"You are a talented man, Sulien. You caught my escaping charge and did not spill a drop of your wine."

The old soldier just grinned and sat.

I reached over and took Daron's hand in mine. "I will find the people who destroyed your village. I swear it."

Moving to release her hand, I felt her tighten her grip. Her eyes were a cold blue then.

And she narrowed them.

And I felt a sharp, piercing pain in my hand, and I jerked it back with a yelp.

The girl had stabbed my hand with a small dagger!

In the surprise of the moment, she bolted for the door and was gone into the night.

"Sulien!"

But before his name had left my lips, the old soldier was up and out the door after her.

I looked at my hand, but she had just barely pricked it, a small drop of blood marking the spot. Women! I never understood them and never would. Sulien would find her. Of that I was certain. I hoped before she had caused more mischief.

Bah. I was getting nothing done. I could not even find the solitude I needed to sort out these entangled threads.

With that in mind, I rose and headed down the lane toward the docks. At that time of night, only a handful of *meretrices* haunted the byway. In another day and time, I would have joyfully joined them. But I ignored their pleas and moved down until I could hear the waves lapping at the shore.

I saw a huge boulder on the cliff, overlooking the sea, and climbed upon it. On my right, the timber walls of Doged's fort rose high, and the glow of torchlights floated above it. The breeze was fresh and strong; I could taste the salt mist on my lips.

"My lord?"

I whipped about, my hand diving toward the dagger at my waist. The voice was soft, a woman's. But I saw no one.

"Be at ease, my lord. I wish you no harm."

"Make yourself known."

"It is better that you not know me. I have brought you a message."

It was so dark, and I could not see anyone near. "Then deliver your message and begone, ghost or spirit or wraith or whatever you are."

"The queen lied to you. She is with child."

"How do you know?"

"I am one of her attendants. I know."

"Why did she deny it before the others?"

"My lady has her reasons. She is confused and frightened. But she has said that she trusts you. She needs your counsel, though she will not admit it."

I searched the dark for my visitor but still saw nothing. "You are taking a risk by coming here, telling me this."

"Each day of life is about taking risks."

"An attendant and a philosopher," I noted.

This time, there was no reply. I climbed to my feet and quickly scanned the area.

Nothing, but the soft sound of lapping waves and the scent of salt in the air.

My invisible guest was gone.

So Ysbail had lied. But why? A child would further solidify her claim to the throne. This entire affair was confusing beyond all reason.

Ysbail's attitude about her condition had changed in a matter of days. What had changed in the broader picture? I felt, in the pit of my belly, that if I could explain Ysbail's reversal, I might be able to explain much more. I said a prayer for the gods to protect my unknown informant.

I looked out at the great sea, which seemed to stretch forever. I knew that Hibernia lay to the northwest but not what, if anything, lay yet further.

Somewhere, far away, a baby cried.

Ygerne! Our son! I had forgotten so completely, and I was immediately ashamed. Slamming my hand down on the rock, I let the pain fill my eyes with tears. Blasted Arthur! Blasted *consilium*!

Chuckling at myself, at my anger, I rose, intending to seek out Sulien and see if he had corralled our wayward girl. Clambering back up to the lane, I sighed. "Another day ended with nothing done," my old dad would have said.

As I reached the lane, I looked up toward Doged's fort. To my surprise, I saw Sulien and Daron coming toward me.

But then they stopped, and Sulien's eyes grew wide.

And he shouted, "Malgwyn!"

And all went black.

"By the gods. He should be dead!"

Only once before had I felt such a tremendous pain in my head, not counting the ones that I brought on myself with too much wine, *cervesas*, or mead.

I blinked my eyes open to the flickering glare of a torchlight. For a moment, but just a moment, I thought I had died, for reaching down from the light was my Gwyneth. She had come to take me to the afterlife.

But then she spoke.

"Quick, Sulien. He is opening his eyes." The vision had been a very earthly Daron.

"Thank the gods!" the soldier exclaimed.

I tried to sit up, but my stomach nearly revolted. Daron put her hand on my chest.

"Stay. Let yourself rest."

'Twas good advice, and I took it. After a moment, I ventured a question. "Who?"

I posed the question to Sulien, but it was Daron who answered it.

"Two of the ones who slaughtered my family."

"You recognized them?" And then I did sit up, the pain in my head and the nausea in my belly leaving me reeling.

Daron nodded.

"What of them?" I turned to Sulien.

"They turned and ran when I shouted. Good fortune for you, as they both had daggers out to finish you off."

"My own fault," I grumbled. "I was not on my guard. The gods know that in these lands such laziness will end in death."

"Did you raise the alarm?"

Sulien shook his head. "It seems that Doged had no *vigiles*."

"Bah." The pain in my head and the rumbling of my stomach were passing. "Daron, you are certain that they were of those who attacked your village?"

The voice that answered was colder than our most bitter winter. "Could you forget the faces of those who slaughtered your family?" she answered, as she dabbed at my head with a bit of rag.

It had been a silly question, so I simply grunted. "We will never find them now. They have had time to flee the village." I stopped as the ringing in my head returned. "Did you see just the two?"

"'Tis but a scalp wound. It looks far worse than it is," Daron said after a moment.

Sulien nodded. "We should get you back inside the safety of the fort's walls." He looked to Daron. "Both of you."

As I climbed to my feet, I realized that the attempt on my life told me one thing: Someone was afraid that I was getting close. But close to what?

"Thank you, Sulien." He was proving a good and loyal soldier, and Arthur taught me long ago that praise should always be given where due.

The old soldier turned and looked at me. In the faint light of the torch, I thought I saw moisture grow in the deep crevices of the corners of his eyes. "You do not remember, do you?"

The older I got, the more confused I seemed always to be. This time was no different. I shook my head.

Sulien sighed. "At the River Tribuit, when you received that," and he pointed at my half arm, "you had just saved one of Arthur's men, who was about to be killed by a Saxon sword. You ran the Saxon through, extending your arm fully. As you tried to withdraw your sword, it hung on the Saxon's ribs for just a second."

"Aye." I had done my best to fling those memories away, but Sulien spoke truly.

"And it was that second that allowed yet another Saxon to cleave your arm from your body."

"Aye."

"I am the soldier you saved, and I owe you a debt that these few days of service are but faint repayment for."

"Sulien . . ."

He held up a hand. "I have a son in Ynys-witrin, by my woman there. His name is Malgwyn ap Sulien, for without you, he would not exist."

I could not speak. Daron simply looked back and forth, from one to the other. Finally, I nodded quickly and began trudging up the lane toward the fort.

I did not know how to respond to Sulien's revelation. Aye, I was not even certain that I should. These were the thoughts that crowded my mind as I tried to settle into the simple hut that Ysbail had allotted us. Arthur had commandeered a two-story house closer to Doged's hall, but this hovel suited me. And with the certain knowledge that I had enemies within arm's reach, I preferred a more modest retreat.

As I unrolled my furs to make my bed, I noticed that Sulien was not doing likewise.

"You'll find furs are more comfortable than the earth."

He shook his head. "I will not sleep tonight. I will be outside, watching the door. Your attackers may try again."

"Here? Inside these walls?"

Sulien smiled. "I think that I do not wish to wager your life on the fierce edge of Doged's soldiers."

We both chuckled at that.

"Sleep well, Malgwyn. No one shall pass."

In the far corner of the room, Daron had already climbed among her furs and lay facing the wall. I could not imagine what she had gone through in the last few days, not truly. I had entered my village long after Gwyneth and the others had been killed. I did not have to watch helplessly as they died.

Sleep did not come easily that night. I do not remember ever feeling so hopeless, so overwhelmed. When I did finally drift off, it was to the visitations of a hundred Dogeds, all laughing at me.

Deep in the night, the dream changed, from wrinkled and creaking Dogeds to a lusty fantasy of Gwyneth and Ygerne. I awoke suddenly and found that I was greatly aroused.

And someone was caressing me. At first I thought it Gwyneth, but as I grew more alert I jerked back.

It was Daron.

She was naked. I did not have to see her; I could feel her.

"No! Daron!"

By the rustling of the furs I could tell that she was distancing herself.

"Am I not attractive enough?"

"Daron, you are a beautiful young woman, but I already have a mate."

"So? What of it? What man in this day doesn't take his pleasure anywhere he can?"

She was right. And in another time I would have eagerly taken her to my bed. But two things stopped me. Ygerne, at even that moment, was bearing my child. And I knew how deeply my brother's wanderings had hurt her. No, my heart would not let me do what my body would relish. I shook my head. "Not this man."

"You are a strange one," Daron said after a moment. I feared she would run away again, but, instead, she retreated to her corner, covered herself with furs, and spoke no more.

When morning came, I still felt the throb in my head from the night before. Unfortunately, it came without the memories of drinking and carousing that normally caused such pain. I threw back my furs and my heart leaped.

Daron was gone.

But as I scrambled to my feet, the creaky door swung open and she stepped back in, bearing a platter of bread and cheese and a pitcher of milk. She set them down on the one table and sat in her corner, braiding her hair.

"Daron, last night . . ."

"It is of no matter," she said without looking at me. "Eat.

You have work to do. And the sooner you do it, the sooner I can continue with my life."

Duly chastised, I broke my fast and went to find Arthur, leaving Sulien to watch over Daron.

"I was set upon last night, by some of the same rogues that sacked that village."

"Are you certain?" Arthur narrowed his eyes as I made my report.

I tilted my head forward and parted my hair so he could see where the blow had landed.

His stubby fingers fumbled at my hair. "'Tis hardly a scratch."

"Daron identified the men as among those who attacked her village." I did not argue with his judgment on my head.

"Did Sulien not account for any of them? Odd. He's a strong warrior."

"He was protecting Daron." I did not choose to share that Daron had run away and Sulien was retrieving her.

Arthur's eyebrows knit together. "Do you think David was serious in his proposal?"

"I think David was planting a seed to grow a delay in this matter." I paused. "But I cannot say without doubt that he is not serious. It would be unlike him to risk such an open break unless he was assured of the outcome.

"Let us be frank. No matter how Petrocus decides, Cilydd and Druce have some law and tradition backing them. We both know that Doged made this match simply to secure an heir. Ysbadden champions his sister's claims for no other reason than to ease his own path in annexing them to his. If it comes to open warfare, I foresee Ysbadden allying with Druce, and Cilydd striking a bargain with them both."

"And David?"

"As is his wont, he will avoid committing himself until he can be certain of victory. Do not doubt that he has his scouts out even now, watching the roads for signs of reinforcements." I stopped and glanced out the window. Roman glass was wavy, blurring detail, but the gray clouds gathering toward Tyntagel were easy enough to discern. "A fierce wind is blowing from the north. It may be the weather is causing his soldiers problems on their journey."

Bedevere nodded. "A rider came in from Tyntagel early this morning and reported a northern gale blowing down the coast. It is moving slow and will be here before nightfall."

"What have you learned about Doged's death?" Arthur asked.

I sighed. I knew that he would ask this question soon. "Very little. I still believe Mordred innocent. Unfortunately, to believe Mordred innocent also means believing the Saxons innocent, and they are innocent of nothing. But whoever killed Doged was most likely the man who hurried past Mordred."

"Why?"

"Because he was the only one with reason to kill the guard he had bribed. Bedevere observed that the manner of Doged's wounds indicated that it was a sudden act, that a friendly or at least neutral discussion had turned murderous. I agree. And that would imply, but not prove, that Doged knew his killer. That he did not raise any alarm supports that position as well. It was most likely Druce or Cilydd or one of Doged's lords."

"Why so?" Arthur asked.

"Doged would not have been completely on his guard with

someone as familiar as them. And who else has the resources to bribe the guard and would want or need to see Doged? Or," and I hesitated for a second, "the killer went in disguised as Doged."

I braced for an explosion, but Arthur just frowned and nodded. "It is possible," he grumbled.

Silence reigned for a moment.

"Arthur, you know that the Saxon who threatened to kill Mariam is here?"

Those big brown eyes of his narrowed. "Aye. I know as well that he is part of the embassy that has been granted Ysbail's hospitality. And if someone were to violate that grant, there is only one punishment. You know these things too."

I did not answer him; I simply brushed the hair from my face and met his stare with one of my own.

Though no words were spoken, we understood each other.

Arthur turned to Bedevere. "Send a patrol to the north to seek any sign of David's men." Tugging on the end of his mustache, he paused. "No word of Kay and Merlin?"

His Master of Horse shook his head. "And I am worried. The distance was not that great, and Malgwyn's directions were specific."

"No word from Ider?" I feared for my young friend.

"None."

"Calm yourself, Malgwyn," Arthur urged. I had not realized it, but I was actually bouncing slightly, so great was my concern. "Bedevere, take a patrol to Castellum Dinas and make contact with Ider there. As soon as you reach him, speed a rider back here with a report. If all is well, return with the rider. If not, send word with him, take command of the gathered soldiers, and resolve whatever problem exists there."

"Yes, Rigotamos." Bedevere gave him the salute and turned to leave.

"And Bedevere?"

"Whatever else has happened, find Merlin."

Arthur turned to me once more. "What else have you to tell me?"

"How did you know there was aught else to report?"

The grin that grew on Arthur's face stretched his mustache. "I am learning to read you as well as you read the signs left in the wake of these affairs. Now, speak."

"One of Ysbail's servants came to me last night before I was attacked. She says that our lady is indeed with child."

Arthur's eyes popped open. "Then why did she deny it?"

"I do not know. That fact in itself would render this entire matter moot.

"Unless," I began, the idea even then forming, "she fears that announcing such would make her a bigger target than she is."

"How?"

"All we have now is a thin crust of order, due to your presence alone. Beneath the surface, these lands are bubbling with intrigue. If any of the factions knew she was with child and that they could eliminate both her claim and the child's with one blow, I would not give a hide of land for her chances."

Arthur scraped past me, and I noticed that he was wearing a new kind of armor, designed by Merlin but supposed to have been used many, many years before.

"You should wear something that will protect you, not a suit of linen."

The Rigotamos laughed at me. "Do not let Merlin hear you say such." He paused. "Take your dagger and slash at my stomach."

"Oh, have you become a god now that you can survive the dagger?"

Arthur and Bedevere grinned. "Just do it."

Seeing Arthur's mood lightened was worth it. I pulled my dagger out and slashed across his midriff. My blade, as sharp as I could make it, did not even scar his breastplate.

"What? Is this some magic Merlin has wrought?"

"It is made with successive layers of cloth, melded together with the strongest glue. Shaped and allowed to harden, it is as strong as chain mail and lighter."

"As you say, but I will still place my faith in chain."

"What you say about Ysbail makes sense. But the question becomes, what do we do about it?"

Although I was becoming annoyed at the gesture, I shrugged. I seemed to forever be shrugging in this matter. "I do not know."

"What do you not know, Malgwyn?"

I turned at the voice.

Chapter Twelve

I will tell you what I know," Ysbail answered herself, gliding across the room. "I know that you have no idea who killed my husband. I know that you and your master here will do almost anything to keep me from executing Mordred, and that you only champion my cause in order to secure my allegiance to the *consilium*."

"And I know that you hide the fact that you are with child because you fear assassins."

Her eyes suddenly glistened with tears. "You do not know everything. And it is only in deference to Arthur that I tolerate you at all. You are cursed by the gods and should be turned out on the moors to die."

Though Arthur swayed at the ferocity of her words, they did little to me.

"Do you think you are the first to call me cursed? No, I hold that honor myself. And you maintain your position only because the Rigotamos is championing it. Would you prefer that he call his troops together and leave? Within hours, Ysbadden, Druce, Cilydd, the Saxons, all would be reducing these lands to burning rubble."

Now, Arthur recoiled at the ferocity of my words. But he did not dispute me.

Ysbail scowled at me and swept from the room, leaving a faint scent of lavender in her wake.

I turned to look at Arthur, expecting to see his now-familiar scowl only to be surprised at the grin stretching his lips.

"At last, my stubborn, disobedient scribe has returned. Now, perhaps, we can resolve all of this."

"Have you been dissatisfied with my service, Rigotamos?" The heat was spreading up my neck and into my face.

Arthur just laughed. "Since we began this journey, you have moped about, mad at me, mad at everyone. You would be mad at Doged, but he conveniently was murdered and hence spared himself from your ire. You showed a flicker of your old self back in that unfortunate village. But since then it is as if you are fighting with yourself."

My shoulders slumped.

"I know what worries you, Malgwyn. Last night, I sent a rider back to Castellum Arturius with but one task: to ride here on the wind at first word of your child's birth."

Those were the kinds of things that endeared Arthur's men to him. Yes, he was a lord, a king. And, yes, he sometimes had to take action that might seem cruel. But in a day when loyalty was both everything and nothing, Arthur was an exceptional man.

"Then our children will be cousins." I had meant to wait until Merlin was returned to us, but Arthur should know.

The Rigotamos drew his head back and blinked. "What?"

"It seems Ygerne is not the only one with child at Castellum Arturius."

"Guinevere?"

"Aye. Merlin was meant to tell you, but I could no longer keep it from you."

His eyes clouded over. "How long have you known?"

"Calm yourself, Arthur. Merlin told me just before we were set upon. I was hoping for his rescue so that he could deliver the good news himself."

Bedevere clapped him on the back, and I saw a true smile on Arthur's visage for the first time in many moons.

"Let us ensure that his father keeps his crown for a while longer," Bedevere said. He turned to me. "Your prediction about Tristan proved to be true. My scouts report that he is on the way with twice the number of soldiers that we requested."

"He was a boy, and boys make mistakes. He is proving himself to be a good man."

"Go," Arthur instructed our friend, and square-jawed, loyal Bedevere merely nodded once and left.

Arthur looked at me then. "Sit down, Malgwyn."

And I did, and he took a seat opposite me.

"I did not dispute you in front of Ysbail, but you understand what risk I would take should I repudiate her now and support Druce?"

"Aye, without doubt. You would lose your reputation for loyalty and honor. But for me to threaten such behind closed doors, out of the earshot of our enemies, costs you nothing."

Arthur nodded and smiled. "Good. And that is why I did not dispute you. But I wanted to be certain that you did not think that badly of me."

"Do not fear that, Arthur. Your consistency is at times boring, at other times frustrating, and on occasion dangerous, but I do not doubt its sincerity. Whether I like it or not, I have become your harbinger of ill winds. But, since I have never been all that well liked, I do not mind being the point of your sword."

"Malgwyn," Arthur began, leaning forward. "For a man with the sort of uncommon insight that you possess, you know little about how people view you. You ARE well liked, but more importantly you are well-respected."

"I doubt that David would agree."

"David respects you more than most. But he sees it as a weakness."

We sat silently for a moment longer. I wanted to say something to Arthur, something I had locked away long before. But a knock at the door stole the impulse from me.

Our visitor was one of Arthur's men. "Rigotamos, a man is here requesting to see you. He says that he has Lord Bedevere's and Master Malgwyn's permission."

"That would be Trevelyan," I realized.

Arthur looked confused.

"He is the lord of those poor folk from Ennor, pleading his case for lands on which to settle."

The Rigotamos nodded. "Poor folk indeed. I was told that many of them died when the sea swallowed their land." He shrugged. "I have little to give him but my ear. That shall have to be enough." He motioned to the guard to allow Trevelyan entry. I took the opportunity to leave. The last thing I wanted to see at that moment was another disappointed man.

As I wound my way through the narrow lanes, I realized just how alone I was. My three most faithful companions in these matters—Merlin, Bedevere, and Kay—were all away, or lost.

Even young Ider, who had proved himself so loyal and brave in the recent affair at Ynys-witrin, was at Castellum Dinas.

Remembering some cheese I carried in my ever-present leather pouch, I reached in and felt around, my hands coming to rest on a pair of square objects. I pulled them out. An ancient pair of dice, brown and worn, given to me by my old father. He claimed that they had passed from father to son from the old Roman soldier who started our clan. I suspected, though I never knew for certain, that my dad won our land with these. And then a thought struck me, and I picked up my pace.

"Sulien."

The old warrior appeared in the doorway of the hovel we shared, a questioning look wrinkling his leathered face.

"Go and ask among the soldiers; find the friends of the guard who was murdered. Tell them you have an amphora of Gallic wine and dice. Invite them back here to drink and play."

"The world is collapsing for these people, and you wish to play knucklebones?" His tone was beyond chastising.

"Trust me, Sulien."

He shook his head ruefully. "As you say." And with that he headed off to do as I asked.

The door of the hovel popped open and Daron slid out. She strode straight up to me and put her hand out. "Give me some coins and I will go fetch the amphora and some food."

I did not reach for my pouch, instead frowning down at her. She could not have reprimanded more powerfully with words as did the frown she threw my way.

"I will not run away again. If I am to have justice for my people, my family, I am wed to you until this affair is better."

The firm set to her jaw decided the issue for me, and I

pulled some coins from my pouch, giving them to her. Her fingers lingered on mine a second or two longer than was comfortable. But then she spun about and started off up the lane to Doged's kitchen.

Doged. It was no longer his kitchen. Indeed, I could still see a thin wisp of smoke ascending to the sky from his funeral pyre. But if not Doged's then whose? Poor Doged, old though he may have been, he gave his people stability, hope. Now, they faced nothing but division and chaos.

Three hours later, it would seem to a passerby that a new tavern had opened. Daron had been forced to slap all three of Doged's men for taking liberties as she served the wine. Sulien had tossed four men out who thought it a public party. And the friends of the dead guard considered themselves fortunate that the strange, one-armed man wished to enjoy their company. And they felt exceptionally fortunate that he was wealthy and horrible at knucklebones.

But suddenly, their luck turned bad. Worse than bad. Between the one-armed man and his soldier friend, they took every denarius the guards had; the poor fellows had even lost the old coins of the Durotrigii that weighed down their pouches.

But drunk from the good Gallic wine and convinced that their luck would change, they bet all they had on one roll of the dice: their freedom.

It wasn't uncommon in those days, but it was becoming more rare. In all honesty, I had maneuvered these poor fools into just this position.

And.

They lost.

I have seen the defeated in battle become *servi*. Once, when Ambrosius was yet the Rigotamos, I saw Lord David enslave an entire Saxon village. But these people were already defeated; they had had time to accept their fate. These soldiers had not, and the sudden turn from elation to defeat lined their faces in ways that even a lifetime did not. All in the span of a moment.

A flash of rebellion sparked in their eyes, but Sulien's sword, laid across the table, drowned that errant spark.

But I had no intention of taking their freedom. I simply needed them to answer my questions.

"A sad turn of events, men. But this is what happens when you risk everything for nothing."

"This is not fair."

"No, you cheated us; you must have."

"We can resolve this fairly, I think. I need information. And I will trade you your freedom in return."

"That is all?" said one, the leader, an old man with a ragged scar down his cheek.

I nodded with a smile. "That is all."

"Then ask and be damned." The glow of the wine had fled, and I knew that a headache was even then growing in the back of his neck. I had felt the same thing many times myself.

"One of your fellows was murdered two nights past."

"Aye," the older man said, "Rhys. What of it?"

"Rhys took bribes to give people access to Lord Doged. What do you know of this?"

All three put on their most shocked faces, but I was unimpressed. "I do not think that any of you or Rhys, for that matter, knowingly assisted in your master's death. And what you tell me now, here, will be carried on the wind no further."

They exchanged looks and then all nodded.

"Rhys was greedy. Each of us had chances to profit. But Lord Doged was a good man, and we took our tasks seriously. Rhys was new to Doged's service and felt no loyalty. He came with the Lady Ysbail."

"What chances? You were approached?"

All three nodded vigorously. "Of course," said the youngest. "Druce himself came to me. He offered me lands and coins if I would let him pass."

"To what end?"

"To kill Doged, I supposed."

"But you rejected him."

"Aye. The old master was a good man. He gave me leave when my mother was dying."

The others obviously agreed. The old one said, "I was with him the last time he took arms for the people. We tracked and killed a Scotti raiding party. When Lord Doged was a younger man, he was a ferocious warrior. We caught them plundering a village, and Doged himself waded into them and saved a child, killing three of the devils in the process. No, we all told them to pleasure themselves."

"Except Rhys," I prompted.

"Aye. He thought we were foolish for turning down their offers."

"So, who did he deal with: Druce? The Saxons? Who?"

"If we knew, master, we would tell you. Had Rhys not caught that lord running from the hall, we could have all stood accused."

He was right. Because of the ever-present threat of assassination, those who guarded their lords' persons were held equally liable should something happen.

Of course, all that they said could be simply lies, told to

placate me, but I was accustomed to sorting out the lies from the truths. That was one of my few talents. These men were not lying. I would stake my one hand on it.

"I would ask one last thing in exchange for your freedom," I continued after a long pause.

"Ask."

"Ysbail is your mistress now. I would ask you to be more vigilant in guarding her person. And I promise you this: a purse of gold greater than any that her enemies could offer you, if she stays alive until after this court renders its judgment."

The three exchanged serious glances. But it took little time for them to nod their agreement.

"Now, go sober up and get back to your duties. Wait." I had forgotten something. "Have any of you seen a brooch like this before?" I pulled the agaphite piece from my pouch.

"Certainly, master. All in these parts know that brooch. It belongs to Lord Cilydd."

"How can you be certain that this is his? Surely if there is one there are more about?"

"Aye," the older man said. "But this is the only one in these lands where the blue stone is set in silver, or at least the only one that I have seen that is set in silver. The others are set in pewter."

One of the other two twisted his face in uncertainty.

"You know of another?" I asked.

He shook his head. "In the back of my mind, I remember seeing another, but I can no longer remember who had it or where I saw it."

"Another silver fibula?"

"Just like Lord Cilydd's," he confirmed. "But it may have been a passing trader's cloak."

"Are you absolutely certain?"

"Not completely, master. But ask Old One-Eye. He's the only one that sells them. His shop is down by the docks."

"'Old One-Eye,' what sort of name is that?"

"He has another name, but no one knows it. He's a dusky one and comes from far away, from Judaea some say, from Egypt others allow. It is said that he was once a slave and his master took his eye for some crime. He wears a leather patch over it and some sort of hat of wound cloth."

The later in the day, the more threatening the northwestern sky became. I walked up on the parapet surrounding Doged's seat and sought the seaward side. A true gale was blowing to the north. On the distant horizon I could see the white peaks of wind-whipped waves.

"A rider from Castellum Dinas has arrived."

I turned to see that Sulien had joined me on the parapet. "A single rider?" My heart quickened. A single rider meant Bedevere had stayed there; a single rider meant there was something wrong.

"Aye." His tone was sober; he knew what that portended. "While searching for Merlin, they found sign of two, maybe three hundred horse, all seeming to converge on Castellum Dinas. They rode straight to the town and found that Kay and Ider had already suffered one assault, but had repelled it. And yet, they had been unable to identify their attackers. They had killed some, certainly, but they bore no lord's symbol on their tunics, nothing to mark their allegiance, and no one among our men or the people of the town recognized them."

"And no Merlin?"

Sulien shook his head slowly.

"Is Arthur seeking me?"

"Yes, but not for the reason you think."

"What then?"

"Druce and Ysbadden have gone to Ysbail and given her an ultimatum: Honor Lord Doged by executing his murderer, Lord Mordred, or face a true rebellion. Malgwyn . . ." Sulien paused. "With Druce and Ysbadden together, and this phantom band tying up Bedevere and Ider, our resources are halved; we might not win in a pitched battle."

The need to chastise him for such talk rose from my belly and near choked me, but he was right. Whoever these scoundrels were, they were effectively preventing us from being a factor in this affair. I respected Arthur's Christ and His Father. I truly did. But at that moment, I wished only that Illtud were still with us rather than studying for the Church in Gaul. He was one of our finest commanders, and I thought that we needed him far more than Arthur's God did.

"And the Rigotamos wants me to save Mordred's neck." It was not a question, but it should have been.

"No, Malgwyn. He wants you to help him sort out what manner of anger he will face from the *consilium* when he lets Mordred be executed."

I both hated and distrusted Mordred, and I had for many years. But I felt no satisfaction at the thought of his death. Not this way. Not when I knew he was innocent, at least of this crime.

Reaching into my pouch, I pulled out the silver and agaphite brooch and studied it in the fading light. I needed to confront Cilydd, but he had been conveniently absent from wherever I happened to be. If I had more time, I would go and question this "One-Eye" and see exactly how many particular brooches he had sold. But time was a commodity that I could no longer trade in.

"Malgwyn," Sulien said softly. "The Rigotamos awaits."

I did not answer. I would not go to Arthur until I had a solution to this problem. Mordred's life could brook no error. "How old is your son, Sulien, the one you have named for me?" The question was to stave off answering his.

"Eight winters, or thereabouts."

I chuckled. "Then you wasted no time when the wars ended."

Behind me, I heard him laugh a bit as well. "No, Malgwyn. I did not. Though it was difficult."

"Difficult?"

"Aye. I had to convince her that I was through with warring first. That was not easy."

Again, I laughed. "And not true."

"Well, it was at the time."

I will never know if it was in the way that he said it or in the words themselves. But something became clear then. My head cocked to the side and my eyes grew wide.

"Malgwyn?" Sulien called to me, but I barely heard him.

I understood what had happened. And many things of little note before now made sense. I believed that I knew who had killed Doged.

But I had one last chore to perform, one last fact to check. And that would take me to the north.

CHAPTER THIRTEEN

I have had enough of your delays!" Ysbail was furious. She walked right up to me and seemed about to raise her hand to slap me, but Petrocus intervened. She had been cautious enough to reserve this meeting to herself, Arthur, Petrocus, and me.

"My lady, Malgwyn is renowned for his ability in these affairs. Aye, for that and for his devotion to the truth."

"And I tell you now," Arthur said, entering the fray. "Malgwyn has no greater enemy than Mordred," which was not exactly true, but close.

"I have seen him do nothing but delay and protect his fellow while my husband lies unavenged." Her fury was such that her normal white pallor had exploded in red.

I had reached a critical juncture in this stew of affairs. Could Ysbail rule Doged's lands? Was she with child? Who were these strange mercenaries roaming the countryside, killing at will? And why were they attacking Castellum Dinas? Did they, or the Saxons, know of the riches to be found there? And how far was Arthur willing to go to protect the gold and agaphite? Finally, and truly most important, who killed Doged and why?

The last part of that query was still as ethereal as the mist, but I believed that I had sorted out the "who." The problem would be using that knowledge to delay Mordred's death until I had confirmed it. And Ysbail was volatile. If I rolled the knucklebones wrong, I might doom Mordred and thus the *consilium*'s future in these lands.

"I have what I believe to be a key bit of evidence, but I need to make one more inquiry to confirm my suspicions."

Everyone's eyes bulged open then.

Ysbail cleared her throat. "And what would that evidence be?"

This was the critical moment. "A brooch, a rather unusual one. It was found just outside the rear door of Doged's hall. I believe that the killer lost it as he fled."

The red fled from Ysbail's face and she turned so pale that I thought her dead for a fleeting moment. "And where is this brooch now?"

"Oh," I answered in an offhand way, "I have it in a secret place, to keep it safe until needed."

Petrocus pursed his lips and nodded sagely. "This is prudent."

"This is ridiculous!" Ysbail exploded. "I am to believe you?"

"I believe him," Arthur answered.

"Of course you do. He is your creature."

At that, Petrocus straightened. "I believe him as well, and I am no creature of the *consilium* or the Rigotamos."

This was one endorsement she could not ignore or dismiss out of hand, and she immediately knew it. She turned her back to us and her shoulders slumped.

A few awkward moments passed.

When she turned back, it was with a face without guile, a face marked with the tracks of tears. "Do you realize the position I am in? If I delay any further, I will lose Druce and my brother's offer to support my claim."

Arthur and I exchanged looks. His nod was nearly imperceptible.

"Lady Ysbail, you will lose their 'offer' regardless of what you do. Druce has the taste of power in his mouth, and it is impossible to wash away. Here is what will happen: Once Mordred is dead, Druce, Cilydd, Ysbadden, and all the rest will use it as an excuse to break ties with the *consilum*. The Rigotamos will be forced to withdraw his men from your lands. Then, as soon as we are gone, you will either be killed or forced into hiding and, eventually, the civil war you fear, that we all fear, will ravage these lands more effectively than the Saxons ever could.

"Doged's lands will remain in chaos for a generation or more. And if anyone should care to track this domain's decline, they will find that all the blood trails lead to this one moment. Your husband was a good and decent man. Honor him and let me do what must be done."

The tears streamed again. And she turned those blue eyes on me. "You have no idea what you are asking of me."

"Actually, I think I do. But it is the right thing. Once this is behind us, I can concentrate on finding who killed those poor folk near our border, Daron's people."

"Who?" Ysbail was confused and rightly so.

"A girl," Arthur said offhandedly. "She was the only survivor, and we brought her with us."

Had I two hands I would have locked both around Arthur's throat for revealing that. But he had other things on his mind and meant no harm, and, in truth, the error was of my making.

Ysbail too seemed to brush it aside. Her mind was elsewhere also.

In looking back, I think that it was at that moment that she truly became a queen. The slumping shoulders straightened and she took a deep breath.

"Do what you must. But know this, scribe: You must prove Mordred's innocence beyond any doubt. If you fail, he will lose his head by this time on the morrow. Do not doubt that." At that, she swept from the room.

"Who do you think did this?" Arthur asked quickly.

I shook my head. "I am not yet ready to say." Indeed everything pointed to only one conclusion, a conclusion that I was strangely reluctant to draw. I had decided that I was letting my own opinion of people color my efforts.

"Malgwyn," he began in that low, threatening voice I knew so well.

"No, my lord. If I am wrong, I will have accused an innocent man. It is much better that I keep my own counsel until I am certain."

I suspected that Arthur expected such an answer.

"How long will it take you to confirm this?"

I squinted at the sky, but the gathering clouds kept the sun hidden. "By just after the midnight, I should have returned with the proof I need."

"Well, waste no time then."

"And Merlin?"

Arthur sighed. "You know that I do love him like a father, but Kay has been unable to find him, and now they are fair besieged at Castellum Dinas. And Malgwyn?"

"Yes, Rigotamos?"

"Ysbail is right about something else, something none of us has been willing to voice."

"And what is that?" I asked, though I knew what troubled him.

"Just as Ysbail is frustrated with the state of affairs, so are Druce and Cilydd. I do not believe that you have yet more time. My scouts report that Ysbadden and Druce have met with some of these strange mercenaries. I suspect that it is their guiding hands that are directing the assault on Castellum Dinas." He stopped and paced across the room. Even at a distance I could see the veins at his temple bulge and pulse. "I cannot commit more troops to this fight. I did not come here prepared to wage war but to arrange peace. To withdraw more troops from Castellum Arturius will weaken it. Pray that Tristan does not fail us or the entire west country may be lost to us."

I just nodded sadly.

As I turned to leave, I thought of telling Arthur where I was headed, but I knew it would only cause him further distress. Because though the winds of the coming gale were already licking at Doged's fortress, I was headed north.

To Tyntagel.

"Malgwyn."

I mounted my horse to the sound of Sulien warning me.

"Malgwyn, you cannot go alone. I must go with you."

Looking down at him, I shook my head. "You must stay here with Daron. Ysbail knows of her presence here, and she might let it slip in front of the wrong people, though I think she is more concerned with her own situation."

At that, the old soldier screwed his face up in frustration. "I must tell you something."

"What?"

Sulien fidgeted a bit.

"What?"

"The night that Doged was killed, Daron disappeared for about an hour, right before the lord was discovered dead."

Stunned by his words, I jerked my head back. "What are you saying, Sulien?"

"It is possible that she could have killed Doged."

My world went spinning at that moment. I had never once considered Daron. But Sulien was right. She had seen her entire village sacked and plundered, and the lord responsible for their protection was bedding his new young wife. Daron certainly had reason. But if she did, why had she not fled?

"Why have you waited so long to tell me?"

"I did not want to believe that she could have done this thing."

"Then why tell me now?"

Sulien raised his head. "I do not like Mordred, but I know that his execution could split the *consilium*. I was there last night, Malgwyn, when David told you as much. And I thought perhaps you could use this information."

I did not answer him. It was certainly possible, and I believed that she had the spirit to carry it through. But I just did not see her hand in this. My present course was the right one; at least, that's what I told myself.

"Keep her close by, Sulien. If she did do this, I would have her at hand. If she did not, we will still need her to identify those who ravaged her village." At that, I steered the horse away, but a thought struck me and I turned back.

"Sulien, if—"

He waved me off. "You will return, Malgwyn. Now go."

And I did.

❖

I had not traveled to Tyntagel by this route before. The lands along the coast were bleak, but I could not tell if that was because of the mammoth black clouds, roiling and boiling out of the northern sky, or perhaps it was just a cold and discouraging place.

With the approaching gale stirring up the wind, few travelers were on the road. Most folk had scurried into their huts, added extra chinking to their walls, secured what few of their belongings were outside. In these lands, such storms were not unusual, and I found myself smiling grimly at the people's practiced movements, working swiftly but not in a panic.

On a good day, the journey from Doged's fort to Tyntagel would take but a few hours as we reckoned things. The road led along the coast, except as you approached Trebetherick, where Petrocus's community of brothers lay on the northern side of the River Camel estuary. The river's entry into the sea was a grand thing to see, the banks splitting away like a pair of arms opening wide, but it caused travelers to journey inland to its narrowest point to cross.

Above me, clouds scudded across the sky as if pushed by a giant's hands. They rolled black and purple and gray, and the smell of rain was heavy in them, heavier than even the salty scent of the sea. I could taste it on my tongue and in my chest.

The dark would be around me soon, so I kicked my horse in her flanks and prodded her forward. I knew this route, but I had never traveled it myself. I would not want to be caught out on it when the storm hit.

I pushed on.

Not far beyond Trebetherick, I dismounted and led my

horse into a small grove of trees near a pond. She needed the break and the water. Only a fool paid no attention to his horse's needs. And while I might be a fool in other ways, I would not fall afoul of such folly as to not attend to my horse's needs in that manner.

As I knelt beside her, cupping some water in my hand and quenching my own thirst, I heard the sound of leather and horses' hooves. Quickly I drew my horse deep into the surrounding copse. I held her muzzle in the fading light.

Twenty men appeared at the water's edge, not one hundred feet from me. The bile rose in my throat as I saw those self-same gray tunics, too many of them for me to engage. So, I remained quiet, listened, and watched.

In the coming night, blackened even further by the coming storm, I could not see individual faces, but I could hear voices. The accent was so familiar, very like that of the Gauls. Perhaps this was some new tribe of Saxons, just come from Gaul. But they did not wear the greasy topknot favored by the Saxons of my acquaintance. They certainly acted like Saxons, pillaging and sacking all in their path.

Their language was something like ours, some of the words seemed the same, but there was a difference. I frowned and waited silently until they had left. Soon, I would be able to focus on them, but right then, Tyntagel awaited me.

The raw beauty of Tyntagel's jagged cliffs was overshadowed by its dangers. One misstep and my horse and I were doomed to be crushed on the rocks below, and with the wind whipping about us like angry demons and the grayish-white blow of the sea spray, it seemed a likely prospect. I dismounted and led my horse along the narrow earthen bridge that tethered Igraine's home to the mainland.

On this night, the guard chambers were empty. Only a fool would tempt the gods in this weather.

Ahead of me was the wooden door to her outer ward. She truly had little fear of assault. The approach was simply too narrow to allow a force to mount an attack. A sudden gust of wind near blew me over the edge and I wrapped my one arm in my horse's mane. It would take more than a gale to move her; she was a stout horse.

And though my feet slipped on the wet rocks with every step, I finally arrived at the door, exhausted, sodden. I hammered it with my fist until the skin split and bled, while the storm seemed to pound away all sights and all sounds.

I had just determined to give up until the storm abated, turning away from the door, when something caught the back of my tunic. I swiveled around to see what it was and promptly lost my footing, and I went over the edge, feetfirst.

In that split second, that moment when you recognize that life is over, I surprised myself.

I said, "NO!"

With enormous effort, I twisted my body about and flung my one arm back up to the cliff's edge, clawing for some purchase, some hold to halt my fall.

My fingers found a crevice, a niche, but then the rock broke away under my weight.

This time it was truly over.

I cursed all the gods.

I died, inside.

But just as I had abandoned all hope, in that same second, a hand burst from the blast of the rain and the mist of the sea spray, as from some ethereal cavern, and fingers, real fingers, wrapped about my wrist and with some inhuman strength fair jerked me back on to the level and to my feet.

Morgan ap Tud, our little doctor.

He stood, blinking in the rain and wind, and shoved me through the wooden door and into the relative calm of the inner ward. My horse was already there, calmly grazing on a small patch of grass sheltered from the wind by the stockade wall.

"Malgwyn!" he shouted above the whining of the gale. "What sort of fool are you to travel on such a night?"

"I must see Lady Igraine. Now."

He led me away from the gate and into the feasting hall. "Malgwyn, she is but hours from death. I cannot allow you into her chamber. Any excitement might finish her."

"You do not understand, Morgan. I am not asking; I am commanding."

To his credit, our physician stiffened his back and stared me straight in the eye. "The Rigotamos gave me charge of Igraine's health, and I shall not allow anything that I fear will further harm her."

"Where is that sniveling little northerner?" The voice exploded from a private chamber at the back.

"Here." Morgan lowered his head, almost like a dog that has been beaten.

"I am not deaf, you insignificant spy. If someone wants to see me, I will decide if they may. Whence come you, stranger?"

"From your son, the Rigotamos, Lady Igraine."

"Then quit dawdling and come here."

I felt a hand on my shoulder.

"Be strong, Malgwyn," Morgan encouraged me.

Arthur's mother lay on a high pile of furs, covered over with a blanket. For such a commanding voice, she was a small woman. But I could see that she had given Arthur her penetrating eyes and high cheekbones. Her lips were thin, and she was very old. She had once had yellow hair, but it had turned gray and white, and not held up by bone pins, it framed her wrinkled face.

"You only have one arm," she said by way of introduction.

"That is true."

"Then you are Malgwyn. I cautioned Arthur not to enter you into his service. I told him that you would bring ill fortune on him."

I nodded. "Many say that is so."

She coughed, a wet, hacking cough, and I noted a pink tinge on the kerchief she used to wipe her lips. "I am glad to know that on this one issue, I was wrong. Arthur tells me you have been of great service to him. I thank you. He is not my only son, but he has risen higher than the other."

I knew nothing of a brother to Arthur, and though I wanted badly to ask, I held my tongue, simply bowing my head to acknowledge the compliment.

"You have questions, or else you would not be here. Ask."

Something in my belly told me that dancing a jig for her would be unwelcome, so I opted for the truth. "I assume you know that Doged has been murdered?"

Igraine nodded. "He was a kindly old fool, a good friend in days gone by but a fool nonetheless."

"Some odd things happened on the night of his death, and when I try to say that they were connected with Doged's death Arthur becomes completely unreasonable, almost irrational. When I spoke of these things to Merlin, he sent me to you."

Despite her illness, she smiled. "Merlin. You know, his name is really Myrddin, but it was Arthur who could not say it properly when he was a child, so 'Merlin' he became." A new coughing fit struck her and she dabbed at her mouth again. "Continue."

"There appears to have been more than one Doged traipsing about the hall that night."

At that, she burst into laughter. "Ahh, that old fool. Of course he would remember that." More coughing, and then she shot a penetrating look my way. "This made Arthur upset?"

"Aye."

She nodded. "He was always a sensitive child. And Merlin sent you to me?"

"He did."

"Sit." And she indicated a sturdy chair next to her bed. "Morgan Tud, you spineless worm! Bring mead for me and my guest."

"Morgan is a good man, a good *medicus*."

"Morgan is a creature of Lord David, and no more vile a man has drawn breath in this world."

Even I, who truly hated David, was taken aback by the venom in her words. "I do not dispute your assessment of David, but I am not convinced that Morgan is truly his creature, at least not any longer. He was of great service to your son in the recent affair with Melwas."

"When that pig kidnapped Guinevere?"

"Aye."

"Well, at the least he is a poor *medicus*."

"How so?"

"I am still dying, am I not?"

I could not argue with that.

"But you came to understand Doged's death, not to discuss Morgan ap Tud or that hyena David. Too many stories were told about those affairs, and all of them wrong. With Doged dead, only Merlin and I know the truth. I am told that you are a man who knows how to safeguard a secret. Both Merlin and Arthur speak of this virtue. In truth, I would have sent for you soon myself. At least one man living should know how it really was. Now, I must tell this in my own way; it may be the last time I utter these words and I wish no misunderstandings."

"As you wish."

And she began.

CHAPTER FOURTEEN

I was but a child when I was promised to Gorlois. At the time I was entranced by his strength, and his looks. He was a handsome man. And when you are but fourteen winters, you do not have the foresight to see that muscle turns to fat and wrinkles rut even the clearest skin, with time.

Then, one day, Ambrosius and Cadwy came to our hall at Celliwic. Gorlois had refused to pay his taxes to the consilium. Vortigern was then the high king, and he had thrown over his Briton wife for a Saxon one. Though not a good man in all things, Gorlois had strong principles, and he disagreed with Vortigern's actions.

Ambrosius and Cadwy were sent to treat with Gorlois and negotiate some settlement. With them was a young noble, more boy really than man, Uther. It was at a feasting, and I could not take my eyes from him. I think I loved him from the first.

I had seen my husband have notes slipped to other women at court, arranging rendezvous, and quite frankly, I pitied them. Gorlois, for all of his looks and fine figure, did little for me in the bed. He took my innocence, true, and I had had little experience with men before then. But after that first time, our couplings rarely lasted longer than a few minutes, and I found myself oddly uneasy afterwards.

Uther stared at me with an intensity I had never felt before. It was as if his eyes could lay me bare, and I could very nearly feel his hands on me. Calling one of my serving girls, one of the older ones who understood such things, I bid her take my message to Uther.

That night, I discovered what lovemaking was all about.

And it was lovemaking. We loved each other with a passion that seemed to consume us both, and afterwards, we lay, wet and spent among the furs, the scent of our mating wrapping us in its delicious warmth.

I grew uncomfortable with her telling of their coupling, and it must have shown on my face, because she paused.

You are no stranger to mating; stop acting shocked. It is as natural as sunrise.

I still believe that Gorlois was unmoved by our affair, but then he had other matters on his mind. Vortigern was adamant that he pay proper obeisance to the consilium. *Ambrosius and Cadwy were sympathetic to Gorlois, but they were good and dutiful lords and did as they were ordered, pressing the* consilium's *suit more with each passing day.*

Uther and I were, quite simply, besotted with one another and paid little attention to the growing crisis. Uther's dearest friends in those days were another young lord, Doged, and an unusual man from Carmarthen, Myrddin. I say unusual because he was not noble and, though he had been a soldier, he was prized more for his vast knowledge of things than any other attribute. They knew of our liaison and helped arrange our rendezvous.

But at the feasting that night, tempers flared. Words were spoken, hateful, spiteful words, and a blow was struck, sending the hall into a deep silence.

Frustrated and prideful, Ambrosius had told Gorlois one too many times what he "must" do. Gorlois rose and gave Ambrosius the back of his hand. And then he shouted the words that chilled my heart.

"You are no longer welcome in my hall. Take your men and go. These lands are no longer allied to that bastard Vortigern and the consilium."

And with that, Gorlois ordered Ambrosius, Uther, Merlin, and the rest to leave his lands. As they had come as guests, he could not have them killed, but I truly believe that he wanted to.

Uther and I had no chance for any sort of farewell.

Vortigern did not take Gorlois's actions well. He summoned his troops, supported by the Saxon mercenaries, and lay siege to Celliwic. I thought never to see Uther again. And then I learned that I was with child. It had to be Uther's, as Gorlois rarely touched me more than once or twice a year. And quite honestly, I had employed none of the devices with Uther that my serving girls told me noblewomen used to stave off conceiving. What's more, I wanted his child. I had never wanted to be mother to Gorlois's spawn.

Had my husband listened to his advisors, he would have fallen back on Tyntagel, which is very nearly impregnable. But he refused to accede to their requests. In all fairness to him, Gorlois believed that to fall back even an inch would do nothing but encourage his enemies. And he was right.

Assaulting Gorlois at Celliwic, while certainly something that could be done successfully, would mean a full-pitched battle, with many dead and wounded. No one wished for that. I was told later that there was much grumbling among the common soldiers about doing battle with other Britons in such a manner. Indeed, I have heard that some trace Vortigern's ultimate downfall to the affair at Celliwic.

It was a horrible time. I remained at Tyntagel, frightened to my very soul that something would happen to Uther. Each morning I woke with dread, worried that a new report would tell of his death.

In my despair, I came to a sudden realization that I loved Uther, really loved him.

You must understand that love was not a requirement, is not a requirement, in marriages between nobles. I respected Gorlois; he was essentially a good man, though not the one I would have chosen for myself. But he was supremely stubborn. And I knew that every man at Celliwic would die before Gorlois surrendered.

Fearing the worst, I sent one of my servi *to find Uther in the opposing camp. She was to tell him to come to me at Tyntagel.*

"You asked him to steal into your husband's fortress at a time of war?"

Do not interrupt me. I was but a child and did not think of the consequences. But as I sat in my chamber and fretted, the door opened, and I could have sworn that it was Gorlois striding into my chamber. When his cloak fell away, I saw that it was my own Uther, dressed as Gorlois.

Afterwards, after we made love, he told me of how Merlin had tutored him in looking like another, and of how Doged had helped him avoid patrols between Celliwic and Tyntagel, at great peril to himself.

And at that, I understood why Merlin had sent me here. If Doged had arranged for my many Dogeds, then I believed that I was beginning to see how everything fit together.

"You must have been distraught when the *consilium* launched its assault against Celliwic, for fear of Uther's death."

Igraine looked at me with narrowed eyes. "Are you as trustworthy as my son says?"

"I hope so."

"Then listen. There is more. You see, the *consilium* never assaulted Celliwic. Officially, Uther exploited a weakness in the defenses and entered the fortress with a small band of men. They discovered Gorlois in his hall and killed him in a fierce fight. With Gorlois dead, I sent an embassy to Ambrosius, asking for a truce and pledging fealty to the *consilium*."

"Though Gorlois was killed, you must have been pleased that the affair was settled without a larger battle. Poor Gorlois, victim of his own stubbornness." I shook my head. Such had led many good men to their deaths.

"You misunderstand me. Gorlois did not truly die at Celliwic. He died here, in this very room."

And I was confused once again.

And she continued her tale.

We lay together naked, on this very bed, pledging our love, planning the future. And then the door flew open and Gorlois entered.

I never dreamed that he would find us. He had not visited me in more than a fortnight.

Gorlois was not a stupid man; he knew that I was bedding Uther. But the situation had changed. He was now at war with the consilium, *Uther's master. And this was now treason.*

Uther fair leaped from the bed, his eyes frantically searching for a weapon. Gorlois drew his dagger and backed Uther against the wall.

And then a strange thing happened. Gorlois dropped his dagger; his eyes grew glassy; he fell. And I realized that I was then standing, naked, with a bloody dagger in my hand. I had murdered my husband to save my lover. But the reason mattered not at all. Should we be found there with Gorlois's body, his nobles would condemn us and summarily execute us.

The consilium *would never oppose it, for with Gorlois dead, by whatever means, they knew that the remaining nobles would sue for peace. Uther would be sacrificed for the sake of peace and I, well, I was a woman and did not really matter.*

We barred the door and immediately sent one of my girls to find

Merlin and Doged, who were hiding in an old Roman shrine not far away.

When they arrived, it was Merlin who took charge. Once, Uther, showing how young he really was, began apologizing for Gorlois's death. "Stop this," Merlin ordered. "None of us liked Gorlois. And if we do as I intend, you will receive credit for killing him, in battle, and you should never apologize for killing a man in combat."

I protested, "I killed him, Merlin."

And then he did something I never expected and have never forgotten. He slapped me. Not hard. Just enough to focus my attention. "Never say that to anyone else." And I never have until this minute.

The whole matter was over within hours. With Uther dressed as Gorlois and me at his side, we had no trouble taking the body into the fortress at Celliwic. Merlin and Doged wore tunics of Gorlois's service and no one dared question them.

We cleared the hall, arranged Gorlois's body in the doorway to his private chamber, ensured that his sword was in his hand, and then we inflicted more blows on the poor fellow, from the front this time so that we might say that he died in battle. At Merlin's insistence, Uther and Doged endured minor cuts and wounds to further the charade.

On the way to Celliwic, we had dispatched one of my girls to Ambrosius's camp with instructions for a small raiding party to arrive at the main gate at a time specific. And at the appointed time, Merlin and Doged, dressed as Gorlois's men, hurried to the main gate, told the men that Gorlois needed them in the feasting hall, and then opened the gate for the raiding party.

The rest was chaos for half of an hour, or a little more. When the shouting ended, it seemed that Uther, Doged, and their men had surprised the garrison, killing Gorlois and seizing the fortress. Vortigern was so pleased that he granted Uther all of these lands.

Later, when Gorlois's nobles began to whisper about the child I was carrying and how they had not seen their master near me, Merlin put about that he had cast a spell on Uther, making him the very image of Gorlois, and by such subterfuge Uther gained access to my chamber and my bed. It removed the stain of my adultery, and yet raised Uther's reputation among the men. Indeed, I understand that Merlin was continually pestered by men wishing the same spell cast upon them.

"That is an amazing story. So Arthur became so upset because he feared that your adultery would be revealed." That was my conclusion, not a question.

Igraine shook her head wearily. "No, I never told Arthur the truth. As he was growing up, he heard the story that Merlin put about. But Arthur was a sensitive child, and he was upset by the tale of his mother's infidelity, and his own illegitimacy. I knew he could never accept the actual truth." Her words trailed off into a wistful tone.

"Of your own willing adultery?"

Her eyes snapped back to me. "No, fool, that I murdered my husband, Gorlois. That his friend Merlin helped me cover it up."

Voices rose in anger in the outer chamber or feasting hall, but I ignored them.

"I will keep your secret, Igraine. If Arthur hears it, it will not be from me. But you bear no true blame. You killed Gorlois, yes, but to save the man you loved. If such killings are indeed sinful, then I am condemned to Hell a hundred times over."

The constant scowl on her face softened. "My son chooses well in his advisors."

"Your son will behead this advisor unless he gives me a

very good reason for disturbing you." Arthur burst through the door, and I almost did not recognize him. He was not dressed as the Rigotamos but in common garb.

"You will be silent, Arthur," Igraine rebuked her son. "I am still your mother, and Malgwyn has done nothing to disturb me. Rather, he has lifted a tremendous burden from me."

Her sharp tone brought Arthur up short, but not so much so that softened his tone. "And what burden would that be?"

"That is none of your business. I did not want you to bring this one-armed man into your councils, but he has proved his worth. And he will continue to, I am certain." She paused and seemed to see, for the first time, Arthur's manner of dress. "Now, tell me why you have braved this intolerable weather dressed as a common *latrunculus*?"

At that, Arthur turned rather sheepish. "I was told that Malgwyn was headed here. If we have any chance of saving Mordred and preserving Doged's lands for the *consilium*, I need Malgwyn focused on the problem at hand, not off chasing ghosts."

"We were finished, Arthur. Cease your whining. You were always a whiny child. Besides, I suspect that Malgwyn now knows who killed poor Doged."

And I did. Though the knowledge gave me no pleasure.

Arthur looked to me. "Do you?"

I nodded.

"Then let's return to Trevelgue."

"In this gale?"

"You braved it to come this far. We have yet more work to do."

"Listen to him, Arthur. It is a horrible night." His mother's voice had changed to a pleading tone I had not heard before.

The famous Igraine, known for her ill humors, was a caring mother after all.

"What escort did you bring?"

"Sulien and two others. Oh, and he insisted on bringing the girl Daron."

"Why did he insist on that?"

Arthur waved my question off. "He feared for her safety."

"And brought her out in this hell? Execute him," advised Igraine.

The Rigotamos moved to his mother's side and gently touched her face. "Morgan will care for you. I must sort out this mess." He went to remove his hand, but hers grasped his with a speed I did not know that she possessed.

"Yes, you must. Do not worry about me. I will survive that dratted Morgan's efforts to kill me."

"I will return as soon as I can."

And with that, we were out of the feasting hall and back in the storm.

The sky was beginning to lighten to the north and the wind, while still strong and treacherous, was steadier. Rain continued to pelt down but not as ferociously as before.

In the inner ward, Sulien, Daron, and the other two stood by their horses. As we walked over to join them, I asked Arthur what was uppermost on my mind: "Has there been any word from Castellum Dinas?"

He shook his head, the tangled, wet locks of his hair slapping his face. "No, and Tristan had not yet arrived from Castellum Marcus by the time I departed."

"He will come; of that much I am certain."

"You have never liked Tristan, Malgwyn. Why do you place such certainty in him now?"

"He was but a child then, Rigotamos. He grew during his confinement, into a good man, I think."

But Arthur, lit by the flickering of torchlight, still looked unconvinced.

Sulien rushed forward then and took my good arm, steering me a few steps away from the others.

"Something has gone much awry, Malgwyn. Since you left for Tyntagel, Ysbail has entertained a strange series of visitors."

I shrugged. "I am sure Arthur knows of this—"

"No, he was away from her hall, meeting with his soldiers, until he discovered where you had gone."

"Who were these visitors?"

"Her brother, Ysbadden; Druce and David; Cilydd; Trevelyan; and the one-eyed merchant from the wharves."

I thought for a moment. Her visitors, mostly, were far from strange. Ysbadden, Druce, and David were probably continuing to threaten her. Cilydd too, but for a different purpose. Trevelyan was probably pressing his plea for lands; I suspected he was thrown out on his ear. Ysbail had far greater matters with which to contend. But the one-eyed merchant? That made little sense.

"And Daron?"

"Malgwyn, we are running very low on soldiers at Trevelgue. Coming even this far with merely a three-man escort is lunacy. Our other men are assigned to other duties. We could not spare one more man to stay back and watch Daron. With those who ravaged her village about the town, I did not want to chance her safety."

"Agreed."

"Malgwyn, Sulien." Arthur was already on horseback. "Time to return to Trevelgue."

I looked to the sky and judged that the edge of the storm was even then pounding Trevelgue and all who called her home.

"So, who killed Doged?" Arthur had ridden up next to me.

"My lord, you know that I dislike revealing such things until necessary."

"Malgwyn, this is an affair of Doged's people. I can certainly influence events, but you have no reason to withhold this information from me."

"Rigotamos, I do not do this to be contrary. I do not like to withhold information. But oftentimes, my instinct may give me the answer, but it is only after reflection that I am able to explain it logically." I did not mention the real reason—that in times past I had been wrong and the truth only presented itself at the last moment. Better to be chastised for keeping one's own counsel than to speak prematurely and be revealed an idiot.

Even in the wind, I could hear Arthur grunt unkindly. "You would try a man's patience. But tell me this: Did what you learned from my mother aid in finding your answer?"

"I would say that it was the key."

And the change in his voice was apparent. "So, you know."

"I do, Arthur. And I promised your mother to keep the truth sacrosanct."

Silence. Then, "Good."

"I will drop back a bit and make certain no one is following us."

Again, Arthur grunted. And I slowed my horse and let the others trudge past me.

"So what have you discovered?" Daron had fallen in step with me.

"Unfortunately, nothing about your village. But I did encounter some of those same men not far from here. Very soon, the road will be clear to settling scores for your people."

No moonlight brightened her face, but it seemed to me that I saw her smile nonetheless. "So you have not forgotten your promise after all? May I ask you a question?"

"Certainly."

"You do not know me, not really. You did not know the people of the village. Yet, you take up our cause as if you are of our blood."

I looked at her and weighed my answer. "Once, I had a woman who looked much like you. Once, I lived in a village much like yours. One day I came home to find it ravaged, like yours. So, Daron, we are of one blood."

She simply nodded.

"But I must ask you, Daron: Where did you go on the night that Doged was killed?"

"I went nowhere."

"Sulien saw you."

"Then Sulien was mistaken. I did not stir."

"Well, it is of no matter. I have sorted out the question of Doged's killer."

"Indeed?"

"Indeed."

"Who killed him?"

"If I will not tell Arthur, I certainly will not tell you."

With that, she kicked her horse in the flank and flew forward. Her words rang false, and I felt a knot the size of my fist grow in my belly. I was grateful of only one thing: Whatever game she might be playing, it had little to do with our current crisis.

Before I could follow that thought further, Sulien, who had been riding ahead, trotted back down our little column.

"Horses ahead. Perhaps a dozen."

"Too many for us to take a chance with." Arthur's voice emerged from the darkness.

"Rigotamos?" An unexpected voice then sounded.

Daron.

"Speak."

"We are not that far distant from my village. I know these lands well."

I realized that she was right. We were at that part of the journey that took us southeast, passing not far from Celliwic. The idea of taking refuge there flew through my mind, but though it would provide walls, we had left no troops to guard those walls, and five men and a woman would provide precious little coverage.

"Can you guide us along a path that will avoid Celliwic? I have no soldiers there, and I would not endanger the people of the town by leading these assassins into their midst."

"I know a way."

So, our little band followed Daron through winding forest paths and across streams large and small. With the last breath of the gale still blowing around us, it was difficult to keep track of our direction, but I sensed that it was more or less a southerly one.

No more reports surfaced of mysterious horsemen, and we relaxed a bit. I began thinking about how I would convince Ysbail of the truth. She would reject it; that much I knew. Much would depend on the strength of my argument and how many people were present when I spoke. Why? I wished to place her in a situation where she could not simply reject me out of hand. Igraine had confirmed for me what I was already seeing in these events. It was a painful truth, but truths usually bring pain. Others would see the truth as well, and they would believe it, as it was not something that would profit me or Arthur or the *consilium*.

"Malgwyn."

Sulien. We were traveling without benefit of torches, just in case these marauders were about.

"Here."

"Daron has disappeared."

"What!"

"She rode ahead, claiming that she must check our route. When she did not return, I went forward. She was nowhere to be found."

Blast the girl!

But before I could continue berating the absent Daron, our horses began snorting and pawing the earth.

Others were near.

I turned swiftly to warn Arthur, but a break in the clouds above let a bit of moonlight slip through.

A ring of dark figures surrounded us. The first thought that ran through my mind was that Daron had betrayed us.

CHAPTER FIFTEEN

With but five of us, we stood no chance of defeating them in close combat. At least twenty-five of them encircled our small band. And they wore the now-familiar gray tunics.

None of them spoke a word.

Each of us gripped our swords and spears and readied our hearts for the end. I said a prayer to Arthur's God for the safety of my family. We would not escape this fate. My heart fair leaped from my chest and nervous sweat stung my eyes.

But they did not charge.

One said something to another in a tongue that was near incomprehensible. But I recognized enough of the words to be incensed. The speaker had said that we traveled as noisily as a bunch of women. "Or led by women," the other had answered.

Daron.

What else was I to believe? She had led us here and then disappeared. We were betrayed.

They were otherwise silent, for the most part. One barked orders to the others and about half the men moved toward us. We immediately raised our weapons, which prompted the leader to halt his men. One pointed at me and said something in their nearly comprehensible language, but which sounded a great deal like "we were told that the one-armed man was valuable and not to harm him."

So. They did not know that they held the Rigotamos of all Britannia. I saw Arthur's mouth open, but I put out my hand and touched his wrist. Better not to reveal his identity until we knew more. The band of thugs did not seem disposed to kill us out of hand. How they knew of me I could only guess. Perhaps Daron had been touched by my determination to avenge her village.

Ha. Her village? Now it seemed that she was more the attacker than innocent victim. They must have left her behind to plant a spy in our camp, a great deal of trust to put in a woman, but a shrewd ploy. We would never have believed a man. It told me much of our enemy's intelligence.

I spoke then, in our language, assuming that they could understand enough. "What law have we broken? We are but common soldiers out on a foul night."

The leader looked to me and smiled. "If what I am told about the one-armed man is true, you are anything but ordinary."

"Who tells you anything? Who are you?"

And he laughed at me. I noted his long, drooping mustache and shaved chin, a mark of many Gallic tribes. But he did not "feel" like a Gaul. Perhaps he was from Braga, where many Britons had settled in earlier days. Nimue, one of my favorites among the *servi*, had been from Braga. But she was dead now, on the very eve of her freedom.

The question remained, why was he here? And why were they killing Britons indiscriminately? They served no lord that I knew. They were not Picts nor Scotti nor Saxons for that matter. Mercenaries. Hired by Druce. I thought him fully capable of such. And David. This smelled like David. He was a duplicitous snake.

But I kept these thoughts to myself, though I longed to speak with Arthur about them. The less attention I gave him now, though, might mean the difference between life and death. I looked quickly to the others, but they were following my lead and staying silent.

Their leader motioned to a pair of his men, and they disarmed us and began the task of tying our hands together. Of course, my situation posed a special challenge, but they simply tied my good arm to my body.

They began marching us to the east, toward, I estimated, Castellum Dinas. Why they had not yet killed us I did not understand. But I knew that we were better off keeping Arthur's true identity a secret, or perhaps it was my own pride that made me pleased to be thought a more important man than he. I still do not know.

We reached our destination just as dawn began to grow in the east. Whoever these people were, they had established a marching camp just to the west of Castellum Dinas. But it was absolutely a military camp, no women. They were resourceful. I saw that they had scavenged some old Roman leather tents, now patched with a multitude of materials. We were thrown into one of those and our hands untied.

One thing puzzled me: They had no more than a hundred men, yet they were rampaging through the land at will. As I pondered this, I felt a hand touch my shoulder.

"They have the advantage of surprise, Malgwyn. And we

are far from our home, in what is truly a strange country, at least to us. It is also a country at war with itself."

"Do you still believe that Castellum Dinas and those rocks are so important to the *consilium*?"

"More than ever now. Because now, it appears that even more people know of them. And since we did not share what we knew with anyone, that indicates that our foes came to that conclusion with different information." His logic was complex, but it was there.

A breeze blew the scent of roasting chicken into our tent, and my nose crinkled at the smell. And my belly rumbled. It had been many hours since I had eaten.

"If we do not return to Trevelgue by sunset, Mordred will be dead and *consilium* influence in these lands will be but a faint memory," I reminded him.

Arthur looked at me then, coldly. "If we do not return by sunset, it will be because we are dead."

Sulien and the other two soldiers sucked in air at the bluntness of Arthur's words, and it did not escape his notice. I was curious to see how he would handle this. Arthur's title as Rigotamos caused men to follow him without question. But there, in that tent, we were all equal, all prisoners.

"Sulien," he began. "You have a woman and son near Ynyswitrin."

My friend jerked back in surprise. "I do, Rigotamos."

"And you men," Arthur said, indicating the other two men. "You each have families in the old Roman village below Castellum Arturius."

They nodded.

"Do they have ample food to eat? Can your children play without fear?"

All three men looked at each other questioningly, but they nodded nonetheless, though Sulien's face was shadowed with some doubt.

"Sulien? Your son, Malgwyn, is a playful boy, is he not? I believe that he bested the other boys in a footrace a fortnight past."

And now I was shocked. That Arthur knew my family was not surprising. That he knew Sulien's boy so well was amazing.

Arthur turned to another. "You have a young daughter named Nyfain, who is betrothed to a merchant near Lindinis." He turned yet again. "And your wife is a cousin of Kay's," he said to the last soldier.

Silence, not Arthur, reigned over the next few moments.

"Will you trust me to lead you now?"

No one spoke. But then no one had to.

He nodded.

"Rigotamos, you know that there is little chance that we will make it back to Trevelgue. We may die in the attempt, but it would be a forlorn attempt at best."

"What would you have me do, Malgwyn?"

"I do not know," I said after a moment. And I did not.

Arthur went to the leather door and looked out quickly. Dawn had not fully come yet. "We have time yet. Trevelgue is but two hours away by a swift horse. For now, we should watch and wait."

"Why not tell them who you are, Rigotamos?" Sulien asked. "And barter for our freedom?"

Arthur looked at me and nodded.

"These people, whatever their origins," I answered, "have already proved their brutality. Revealing his identity might just as easily seal our doom. It is a chance that we do not have to take."

Sulien was no idiot.

"Perhaps a rescue party will be sent," suggested one of the other men.

"By who? Bedevere, Kay, and Ider are besieged at Castellum Dinas. We have few enough troops left at Trevelgue. The Rigotamos is known to have gone to Tyntagel to see about his mother. No one will think anything of his delay in returning."

"But Lady Ysbail. She might—"

Arthur shook his head. "She would most likely welcome the opportunity to act without my pressure. Indeed it might solve many of her problems. I regret to say that we are on our own."

A thought struck me. "Perhaps, Rigotamos, it is time that we test our host's mead and *cervesas*."

He looked at me then, quizzically.

"We need an advantage, Rigotamos. I think I have an idea."

"You!" I shouted out the tent door. One of the gray-clad soldiers stopped and frowned. He said something in his hellish tongue. I did not know its exact meaning, but he seemed to reject my attempt at communication.

I took the chance to glance quickly around outside. Nine rectangular, leather tents formed in a kind of oblong. That number would account for almost a hundred soldiers as we believed. What we did not know was if this was the only encampment. One more might spell our doom. Who were these people?

My quarry appeared, spear in hand and frown on face.

"We need food, drink."

"Starve."

And that settled that attempt.

"Malgwyn, let us wait and watch."

And we did, as the sun climbed above the eastern horizon. The storm was completely gone, leaving that fresh smell of rain-washed earth, almost, almost, brightening my mood.

Roman tents were made of goatskin, or so my father had told me. The only ones to be found in those days were old ones, patchworked together like the one holding us. In the days of the legions, I knew that eight men would live in each tent, a *contubernium*. But that was all from a time long past. These ragtag tents had seen better days, and smelled better too. As the sun continued its ascent, the heat from our bodies, trapped by the leather, made the space nearly unbearable.

Two hours later they had apparently become used to seeing my face peering out from the flap. I counted some seventy-five different soldiers. One man seemed to be in command. He was tall, about my years, with a scar beginning under his left ear and running straight down his neck, disappearing beneath his gray tunic. He strode through the camp with quick, sure steps.

The tent next to ours was a center of activity. Soldiers came and went, always hurriedly. And it was into this tent that the scarred soldier turned.

But I still kept one eye peering out the tent flap, and thus was astounded when I heard voices nearly at my ear.

"Who are they?" The voice was familiar, but I could not put a name to it.

"The one-armed man you warned us about and four common soldiers."

"Keep the one-armed one alive. We will still have to kill him, but he may have value soon. Kill the others."

"Leave them where they will be found," the first voice said, and I knew then who spoke. Druce.

"Of course. You will honor your promise when this affair is ended?"

"You have my word," Druce said, smoothly, and I could fair smell the lie on his tongue.

Silence ensued for a moment, and a third voice spoke. This one needed no guessing.

"Honor nothing," Lord David said, apparently alone then with Druce. "These *latrunculii* are nothing more than common murderers. Use them to bolster your claim to the throne. Present their bloodied heads to the people and show that you are their defender, ready to take arms to protect them. These thugs will say nothing against you. They will be dead."

"You will honor your word, Lord Druce," and this voice shocked me to my very core.

Tristan. The young lord on whom I had staked our futures!

Behind me, I heard Sulien speaking to Arthur, but I turned and signaled for silence.

"What does it matter?" David asked.

"A noble's word should count for more than just another lie," Tristan snapped, and despite my horror that he was even in this camp, I felt a certain pride in the message he conveyed.

But David's last words chilled me even as Tristan's words warmed me. He said: "You will learn."

The voices faded then, as the speakers moved away from our tent.

Sulien spun and faced Arthur. "Rigotamos, if we do not return to Trevelgue by nightfall and Ysbail executes Mordred, you will discover Lord David's duplicity firsthand. I was with Malgwyn two nights past at that tavern. He has been right all along about David's loyalties."

I did not have to see the expression on Arthur's face to know that he was shocked.

"Malgwyn has told you of this?"

And Sulien laughed at his commander. "Rigotamos, do you imagine that your soldiers do not know everything going on? None of us doubted that Malgwyn was truthful in his judgment of David, at least not since the rebellion.

"Soldiers are much like *servi*," Sulien continued. "You use us; you depend on us. But you rarely see us."

I half-expected Arthur to mark him down for punishment, should we emerge from this. But I was not prepared for the smile on Arthur's face.

"I stand corrected, Sulien." He paused. This was an unusual situation for Arthur. He was not accustomed to having his wisdom questioned by common soldiers. "Once we emerge from this, I may find a place in my councils for a man such as you."

"Please, Rigotamos," I begged. "Do not ruin him by promoting him. Look what it has done to me." And I waved my half arm at him. At first, Arthur jerked his head back as if struck—I had never before jested so openly about my wound—but then he too joined in the laughter, a nervous laughter, but welcome nonetheless.

The tent flap flew open, effectively killing our laughter. A guard, one in a gray tunic, entered, glanced about quickly, and grabbed me by my half arm.

My companions, Arthur included, leaped forward, but a second guard, spear held at the ready, prodded them back, except for Arthur, who stared them down and whispered in my ear, "Do not hesitate to bargain us away if it will leave you free to protect the *consilium*."

I did not tell him what I was thinking: If I dealt him away, there would be no *consilium* to protect.

The first thing that I noticed was that no one was walking about the area of the camp in which we were held. I could only believe that this area had been cleared to keep us from finding out who was involved. But who would question us?

"Malgwyn. My dear friend."

Lord David. Who else?

"In the enemies' camp, of course I would find you here." I smiled.

David returned my smile and cut his eyes meaningfully toward the flap. Someone was listening. "I am here only as an observer to protect the *consilium*'s interests."

"Why would the *consilium*'s interests need protecting?"

"That's right. You would not know. You have been running about the countryside on one of your useless quests. Arthur is missing."

I searched David's face for any hint that he knew otherwise, but he seemed convinced of his own words. "I would not know. I traveled to Tyntagel and met with his mother and then began my return to Trevelgue in the night. I have not seen or spoken to him since yesterday eve. But I doubt that he has wandered far." The worst possible thing that I could do was admit that Arthur was with our little band.

David frowned, pursing his lips. "Although I would like nothing better than to slit your throat, I am compelled to seek your release. Who is with you?"

"My fellow, Sulien, the *servus* girl, and some common soldiers. 'Twas a terrible night to travel." I paused for a moment. "What is this you say about Arthur?"

My enemy shrugged. "He was in Doged's hall near the midnight last night, but this morning no one seemed to know where he had gone. When I heard you had been taken captive, I hurried here to see what you knew, and of course to secure your release." This last was for the ears around us.

"And how did you hear of my capture? At your own table?" I had no reason to pretend to like him, regardless of who might be listening. But his sharp eyes grew sharper still and pointed.

"I heard from my host, Druce. He does not like you."

"I am not compelled to like him either. I presume that these are his men besieging Castellum Dinas."

David's hand touched mine and squeezed slightly. "A general often has to take his armies where he can find them. The Saxons have declared their support for Druce's claim to Doged's seat. But their men are meant only as advisors."

The well of nausea rising in my gullet threatened to overflow. For a long, long moment, I weighed the cost of ending his life against that of my own. Though he would never know it, David owed his life to my daughter, Mariam.

"And the mercenaries?"

David waved them off. "Everybody uses mercenaries."

"Uniformed mercenaries?"

"Everyone has an agenda, Malgwyn. You do not need me to teach you that. Do not be distracted by side issues. Regardless of what I think of you personally, you have proved to have your uses in the past. We are in a precarious position here. Arthur is missing. Our primary body of troops has been trapped here at Castellum Dinas for some bizarre reason that only Arthur would know. The monk, Petrocus, is inclined to favor Ysbail's claim. Arthur favored it. But Druce has the force of troops. The Saxons threaten to take to the field en masse if Druce is denied his proper place."

"Mordred?"

"If Ysbail doesn't behead him first, he has agreed to support Druce's claim if Druce releases him. A wise position. Under these circumstances, as senior member of the *consilium*, I am inclined to side with Druce. We can ill afford a war this far to the west or to lose the goodwill of its leader."

David desperately needed me to follow his lead as he played the proper, mature leader. We jabbed at one another, but show me two men of strength who do not. He needed me, though, to acknowledge that in Arthur's absence he was his substitute, something that was not written in stone.

The one certainty in all of this was that were I to reveal that Arthur was in my little band, he would be dead as quickly as the dagger could be jabbed or the sword wielded. His body would be quickly disposed of and David would take over as Rigotamos simply by virtue of his presence.

It might be strange in this day to believe that people would not know Arthur when they saw him, but that was the way of it. The ordinary people recognized people by their clothes and their station. Images bearing the likenesses of people, a popular thing for the Romans, were still unknown by our people. Working and living and dying occupied our time well enough.

"Should we move so quickly? It could be that Arthur was called away on short notice and will return soon."

The evil gleam in David's eyes told me that that was exactly why we must needs move quickly. Arthur's sudden arrival could rip David's plans to shreds. David did not manipulate things to happen in this way, but he was a master at taking the strands of a situation and fashioning a rope best suited for his weight.

Someone, perhaps one or all of his co-conspirators, was not convinced of his ability to step in for the *consilium* in Arthur's absence. And in reality, I believed that under the circumstances, David had acted in a nearly proper way.

"My lord, I think you are yet on proper grounds, but Arthur's absence will need to be longer than just a night to convince Bedevere and Kay of your right. I'm assuming that that is your intent, to give me free passage to the fort. You know that Kay and Bedevere will listen to whatever I say."

David nodded. "Exactly. This is a stalemate that does not need to be. Arthur created this. Let Druce claim his title and lands. We can easily persuade Druce that treating with the Saxons will not profit him."

"And the mercenaries? Will they simply take their pay and leave our shores, as conveniently as the Saxons did?"

"These aren't ordinary mercenaries, and Druce will deal with them appropriately."

"So said Vortigern of the Saxons. What of my party?"

David flicked his tunic, ridding it of a bug. "They are of no consequence and you do not need the burden. We will handle them."

"As you will handle me."

And then something I never thought to see rose in David's eyes—sincerity. "No, Malgwyn. As Rigotamos I will need you. You have learned much with Arthur, and you certainly have proved your worth. I would have you as my counselor."

"And should Arthur appear?"

"That will be dealt with," he answered, his voice as cold as our winters.

I pretended to think for a moment. "It is possible that this could work. But allow me an hour to consider it more. The story presented to Kay and Bedevere will have to be as strong as we can muster."

"Good." David nodded curtly. "We have arranged a tent for you over here."

"No," I said almost too forcefully, too quickly. "Sulien and the others might attempt an escape and cause a distraction we can ill afford at this time. Return me to them, and I'll calm their fears."

To this day, as I sit here among the ruins of old Celliwic, I believe that it was David's sheer surprise that I would join him that bid him do as I asked. I never would have.

Within three minutes, I had been ushered back into the tent.

"Well?" urged Arthur.

"You are missing and with Bedevere and Kay besieged in the castle David has anointed himself Rigotamos."

"They do not know I am with you?"

"How could they? We left separately. You opted to dress as a commoner, without badge of office. We are in lands far from our own. More important, neither David nor Druce nor the others have seen you."

"And so?" Arthur pushed me.

"And so, we have very little time to try and leave this place. I have left David believing that I will support his claim as Rigotamos, and that I do not know where you are. I am to be given free passage to Castellum Dinas to apprise Bedevere and Kay of these happenings."

"And us?"

"You are to be killed, the more quickly so if they find out that you are Arthur. Rigotamos, I know that I have long condemned David as a traitor. But in this case, I believe he is simply taking advantage of a convenient situation. I did not get the impression that he was conspiring with the Saxons. But if he finds you here, he will have you killed. The crown is too deeply between his teeth now.

"There is only one way for this to be sorted out properly. If David's plan is to go forward, then Arthur's reign is over, forever."

"But can we succeed?" Arthur said quietly. "While I do not approve of David's methods or approaches, perhaps he is the better man to bring peace here." A wistful tone marked his voice.

For nearly half a minute, silence ruled our tent. Then, one of the other men, whose name has forever eluded me, leaped across the tent and snagged Arthur by his arm, yanking him to his feet. "I have warred with you longer than I ever dreamed possible. But you convinced me that you were worthy of my trust, of the sacrifice of my life if it be necessary. You'll not quit now if I have to kick your bleeding butt."

And the gleam that I knew was but hiding in Arthur's eyes sprang forth again. "That's what I was counting on. By nightfall many, perhaps all, of us will be dead, but it *is* worth the prize. The one thing that puzzles me is that I cannot believe that Tristan has broken his vow to me so quickly."

"What vow?" Arthur inquired.

I realized then that I had never told him of my encounter with Tristan on the eve of the young lord's release a year or so before. "Does it matter now? He is with our enemies."

"What vow?" Arthur persisted.

"He promised to be worthy of our trust, of your trust."

"And you believed him."

My face warmed. "He seemed earnest; now, not so much." I could not believe that I allowed the miscreant to convince me that he had changed. Seldom had I misjudged a man so completely. And the gnawing in the pit of my stomach made me hunger to thrust my dagger in his stomach and watch as his life drained away. That was how much I hated Tristan at that moment.

Arthur's face hardened. "I will deal with him later. For now, we know only one thing—everything depends on our ability to escape from this affair. We thought the civil war would be horrible were it just between Doged's lords, but now it seems that there is much more at stake."

I slipped a look out the flap once more, but they had placed us near the center of their encampment, making escape all that much more difficult. In the distance, I caught a glimpse of David and Tristan, making for their horses, probably sending riders to Trevelgue to bring word of his "negotiations."

Difficult, I mused. Escape suddenly seemed all but impossible.

"Come, Malgwyn."

I turned to see Arthur drawing in the dirt, Sulien and the other two watching closely.

"This is Trevelgue." Arthur indicated a rock. "This," he pointed to another, "is Castellum Dinas. I believe we are here," and he held a stick over a place between and north of the two rocks. "I will take these two men and head southwest to Trevelgue. Malgwyn, you and Sulien make for Castellum Dinas. Try with all your might to get through to Bedevere and alert him to the situation. If you can reach him, he will break out of this siege and take the field against this rabble."

"What will you be doing?"

"Keeping the sword from Mordred's neck, I hope. The affair is clearer now, at least in broad strokes. Druce hired these mercenaries to terrorize the people in order to boost his own claim to Doged's throne. At the appropriate time, he will produce the heads of these thugs and claim that he captured them. Druce will be seen as capable of safeguarding these lands, never mind that it was he who provided the threat. That will but add to his growing reputation with the 'new' Rigotamos."

I would not wager my purse on Arthur's assessment, but it was logical. More than that, it made sense. I learned a long time before that logic and making sense were two very different things. Take our little band at that moment, calmly planning our next move while ignoring one simple fact—we were prisoners with no immediate opportunity for escape. But should that opportunity present itself, we needed to know what came next. Logic required acknowledging the first fact. But it made sense to have a plan should that fact change.

"Keep your hood up. As a common man you may find entrance to Trevelgue easy. As Arthur you are as good as dead."

Over the next few minutes I kept my eyes focused out the tent flap, hoping for some sort of problem, distraction, that would aid our effort. Suddenly, I heard shouting and men began moving, not in a panic but at the quick step. And while there were still men milling around, it seemed they were fewer. I turned to Arthur.

"Rigotamos, if we are to turn this situation to victory, we cannot afford to wait longer. The right moment may not come. We must make this the right moment. Something has happened to draw some of their men away. Now is the time."

Sulien and the others hung their heads. They knew that the chances of their returning to their families had just all but disappeared.

Arthur saw their distress and turned to them, clapping each on his back. At last, Arthur came to me. "I will see you at Trevelgue when this is finished."

I could only nod my head; words were impossible to summon.

"You two, with me," Arthur ordered. "We will strike west. Malgwyn, you and Sulien go east. At the very least, we will confuse them by separating. Perhaps it will buy one of us time to lose ourselves in the forest."

I took a last chance to check the camp, turned swiftly and nodded to Arthur, and then plunged out of the tent.

And from the center of the camp an odd thing indeed happened.

An explosion shook the tents and filled the air with smoke.

CHAPTER SIXTEEN

We stopped. Arthur and I exchanged looks and simply shrugged. The gods or the one god or providence had thrown us a scrap from their table.

Arthur and his companions bent over and disappeared in the haze to the west. Sulien and I, true to our orders, struck out east, toward Castellum Dinas, as a second explosion shook the camp. Whatever caused the great blasts left a heavy fog in its wake. Men seemed to run haphazardly through the confusion, more frightened than not.

Within thirty seconds, we had left the camp behind us, a place of turmoil. Getting that far seemed almost like . . . magic.

Until I felt a hand grab my wrist.

A soft hand.

Daron.

Before I could shake my hand loose and wrap it about her slender neck, she pressed a dagger into it and whispered, "This way."

I looked to Sulien and, like Arthur, he shrugged.

Ten minutes later and we had covered nearly a half a *schoe-*

nus, half a Roman mile, from the camp, and I grabbed Daron by the shoulder.

"Why did you betray us? What price did they pay you?"

She laughed at me.

I could not believe it.

Was she mad?

"I did not betray you. I saw them before they saw me. There was not time to warn you. What purpose would it have served to have all of us taken prisoner? Free, I could at least try to help you."

"The explosion?"

"I had nothing to do with that, but your friend did."

"What friend?"

"The old man, Merlin. He found me."

My heart beat harder and faster than I ever dreamed possible. "Merlin? Where?"

"Here, Malgwyn."

I looked toward the voice and there was my dear friend Merlin climbing over the roots of a giant tree.

"But we sent Kay . . . and . . . others to find you."

He brushed my words aside as if they had not been spoken. "The wound was more minor than it looked. I hid until our attackers passed. I considered returning to Trevelgue, but I had not trapped rabbit in some time and decided to do just that. Come, I have prepared some for you."

"The explosion, Merlin."

Again, he waved my protests off. "You have seen me use sulphur in such a manner before. 'Tis but a simple trick."

"But what of Arthur and the others?"

"I made certain that they were safely on their journey."

"These mercenaries, Tristan, David, Druce."

That familiar schoolmaster face took shape. "Now, Malgwyn. You have seen a beehive disturbed. The bees fly about, striking everything in their vision, angry, confused, but ultimately they return to the hive." Merlin squinted at the sun. "About now they will be returning to their hive. It will be another half hour before they realize that their hostages are gone. But though you are away from them, danger is not past. You will be going to Castellum Dinas to treat with Kay and Bedevere and break the siege. I have given you but a brief respite. Though these thugs are unlearned, they are merciless."

"Is there nothing about this affair that you do not know?"

My old friend smiled. "It is not often that I can surprise people anymore. Now, we cannot waste more time here. All of this commotion will weaken the troops at Castellum Dinas, making it easier for Bedevere and Kay to raise the siege. We have yet more enemies to dispense with."

"Aye, David, Druce, and Tristan among them."

Again, Merlin's eyes twinkled. "Do not be so certain. Now, come. I have horses in a grove just over that rise."

"What about you?"

"I will join Arthur at Trevelgue. He will need me there."

I squeezed his thin shoulder. "Keep your head attached. You still have much to tell me. Now I can see you as Doged's co-conspirator all those winters ago."

"She told you?"

"Aye, but it is a story well hidden."

"Good."

"You must hurry yourself. Mordred's head may depend on your speed." I briefed him quickly.

"You know now who killed Doged."

I nodded.

"Is it as I guess? When Doged wrote to me, I suspected that he was unleashing troubles upon himself. Then, when you told me of the many Dogeds that night, well, I needed little else. The whelp let jealousy control his better sense."

"That is what I suspect."

"And which whelp did it?"

I had forgotten that Merlin never made it to Trevelgue before we were ambushed. So, I pulled him to the side and told him where my searches had taken me.

Like me, he was a bit sad. "I have heard of him, only good things really. Doged had spoken highly of him. But what you say makes sense, and you have evidence to prove it."

"As you know, love makes people do strange things. And I have the unique fibula he lost."

Merlin nodded. "I will convey this to Arthur, Petrocus, and Ysbail. You will have no friends at this court, Malgwyn, and Mordred will live to bedevil Arthur another day, but sometimes the truth is inconvenient."

"Are you certain that your wound is so minor?" I still worried about him.

He pulled his tunic back and showed me the ragged edges of the arrow wound, scabbed now and turning a healthy pink around it. "I have injured myself worse with some of my own inventions. Now, go. You and Sulien have little time to waste. But take this bit of information with you: Their leader is not among them right now. And they will not launch an assault against the fortress without him. I heard the others talking as I watched the pack of you brought in."

"Who are they, Merlin? What lord do they serve? There is a hint of Saxon in their tongue, but they are not Saxons."

Merlin shrugged. "I hear the same as you, and I have watched them for two days, and I do not know." He paused. "The girl speaks the truth; she did not betray you."

With that, he was gone.

I turned to Daron awkwardly. "I am sorry if I misjudged you."

She did not smile. "I gave you no reason to trust me. And that is unimportant now. The lands between here and Castellum Dinas are teeming with these mercenaries as well as Druce's soldiers. We cannot use roads and must stay to the countryside. It will slow us down, but it will keep us alive."

I admired her concentration. "While you were away from us did you have a chance to judge their numbers?" I was obsessed with that. In our world, strategy and tactics were important but not nearly as decisive as numbers. The more men you could field, the better the odds of victory. I looked about at our tiny band. We were not much of a relief force for our friends at Castellum Dinas.

"They are, perhaps, two hundred. Certainly not more."

"But between Ider, Bedevere, and Kay we have more than two hundred troops inside the fort. They would need twice or three times our number to successfully assault a fortified position."

Daron shrugged. "I am not a soldier. I am only telling you what I have seen."

"Very well. We have precious little time as it is. Let us see what manner of men are these."

Staying to the forest and off the lanes and roads, we took perhaps an hour to arrive at a ravine some one thousand yards from the fortress. Our refuge was too tree and bramble clogged to provide any benefit for a large force. But our group of three found it perfect.

We had no weapons save the dagger that Daron gave me and another we found on our escape from the camp. We were but two men and a female, more child than woman. And as we crept to the edge of the ravine and looked to the southeast, toward the rising prominence of Castellum Dinas, our eyes grew wide.

Truly, there were two hundred men here or more, arrayed in a massive camp directly in our front. And not all were clad in the ubiquitous gray tunics. Even from a distance I could see the greased topknots of Saxon raiders. In the furor that surrounded the death of Doged and the impending rebellion, I had completely forgotten about Ceawlin and his embassy. An embassy suddenly expanded greatly in number.

I should have known.

I slammed my one fist into the earth. This journey had been cursed from the start.

Ceawlin probably used the confusion at Trevelgue to sneak his men ashore. If they could take Castellum Dinas, leaving Trevelgue in their rear, the people would panic and flee and the Saxons could claim the port without much fighting at all.

I tried to calm myself, tried to put my anger to work. Tactics. I had always been able to see what angle of attack to pursue. And though we were but three and the enemy one hundred times that number, the task was still the same.

"Sulien, work your way around to the north side and see what is there. Come back here."

"And you?"

"I will look to the south side. Once we have a more complete idea of what is facing us, we can better plan. Regardless, we have little time. If we fail to free at least some of our soldiers besieged, I see no way for this to end well for us. Take no more than an hour to reconnoiter."

"And me?" Daron asked.

"Stay here and keep watch."

Her lower lip puffed out in a pout. "Have I not already proved my bravery and loyalty to you?"

I nodded. "You have. If I doubted either of those things, I would not leave you here alone. We need someone here to keep watch on them in case they begin to move while we're away. You will have to find us and alert us."

A smile lit her face then, one of the few that I had seen on it. It suited her well.

With a quick nod, we were on our separate ways.

The brambles grew thick in the ravine, but badgers and such had tunneled through them. Though we were not badgers and I carried more than just a pound more than I should, we used their purpose-built routes.

In truth we could have avoided such subterfuge. The nearest enemy were at least one hundred yards away. And they all wore these strange gray tunics or those of Druce's or the Saxons. But the Saxons were fewer than I had thought, in truth. Larger than any reasonable embassy, but not a decisive addition to the force.

I saw none bearing the markings of Lord Mark, the soldiers Tristan would have brought. He had not seemed a committed conspirator, but I was still stung by his treachery.

Finally, I saw something to smile about. What we saw was

what they had. There would be no reserves. And that made numbers even.

Which could only mean one thing.

I was wrong. They did not mean to actually take Castellum Dinas. They meant to trap our primary force there, leaving Trevelgue for the taking, to neutralize *consilium* troops as a force to be reckoned with in the coming struggle. Which meant that Druce was the ringleader of the conspiracy. And that fit very nicely with my conclusions about the killing of Doged. Indeed, it meant that Arthur's fears that others had learned of the rocks just quarried were not real. While that gave me some comfort, it did nothing to correct the situation as it now stood.

I appraised the ground. I knew that the main entrance was from the north, but there was an older trackway from the east. I suspected that Sulien would find the same thing that I had. The lines were thin, thinner than papyri, but that was not something that could be seen well from the ramparts. Druce had placed his troops at the exact position where the depth of his ranks was hidden by the slope of the hill.

Skirting well below the line of troops, I saw a cache of Druce's supplies stacked in the opening between the enemy and the lower tree line. He was certainly well provisioned, I thought, as I grunted and tucked my chin into my chest and contemplated the situation.

Bedevere would be in command inside the fort. Kay, chafing in his role as Arthur's cupbearer, would be anxious for action, to prove himself once more in battle. Young Ider, still a novice in battle, would be eager to match swords with an enemy. The three of them, with the troops I knew that they possessed, could rout the enemy.

Bedevere would have no immediate need to send parties out; the fort had its own spring. But what would Bedevere do? He was renowned for his caution—not that he was ever reckoned as a coward, yet he would move only after careful consideration.

I needed to craft a message that Bedevere would recognize, would understand, and his enemies would not. For if we failed in raising this strange siege, I would not give a silver denarius for Arthur's or Merlin's life at Trevelgue. Druce would be emboldened by Tristan's treachery, and he would not hesitate to move against even the Rigotamos; indeed, he might begin to harbor ambitions of his own for Arthur's seat.

An idea occurred to me finally, as I was returning to rendezvous with Sulien and Daron. It was a horribly risky quest, but we needed to accomplish two things—arrange a distraction so that one of us could slip into the fort and alert our fellows, but, barring that, a distraction that would reveal the true size of their force, or at least give Bedevere a hint of that reality.

A bit later, after dodging a three-man patrol and fighting the urge to slit their throats, I rejoined Daron and Sulien in our little badger sett. Quickly Sulien and I compared observations and found that we had come to the same conclusions.

"I tell you now, Malgwyn," he began, "I will take this Druce's heart from his chest as he watches and feed it to the dogs while it still beats. Anyone who brings the Saxons among us deserves no less."

With a cold smile, I explained my plan. And my companions' smiles grew just as chilled.

"Whoever starts the distraction will have little chance of surviving," Sulien noted.

"Has it not been that way on this entire journey?"

"We both know who it has to be," Sulien said. "You must be the one to reach Castellum Dinas. Your influence will mean the most with Bedevere. I will take care of the distraction. If God be willing, I will see my family again. If not, what better cause?"

"I will help him." Daron's voice sounded suddenly very tiny, very small. "I have no family but you."

She was brave. Of that I never doubted. "We will see each other again. If not in this life then the next."

And that was all the good-byes we said.

Minutes later I was in place at the most likely point. I would have more than an arrow's flight to cross in the open. And then there was a tree-choked gully in which I could hide, picking my way through to the northern entrance. Once there I would be in far more danger from our own men than I would be from Druce's troops. I did not think gaining entry into the fort was a problem. For once I gave thanks for my missing arm. It made me very recognizable.

As I crouched in the trees and waited, I shivered in my still-damp clothes, rubbed the cramping in my half arm, cursed Arthur once more for sparing my pitiful life. Every joint and every muscle pained me. I did not know if I had the strength to see this through.

Tribuit.

In recent years, I had not given much thought to that day on Tribuit. Before, I had gone to sleep every night dreaming of my outstretched hand, begging with me, pleading with me to join it in the next life. And an uncontrollable tingle of pleasure would go through my mind as I shuffled closer and closer to that disembodied hand.

Yet, just as the hand was about to grasp my shoulder, it would disappear, and I would howl in my anger . . . and then awake.

But that had been then, before Arthur rescued me from my self-pity. And here I sat, huddling from the damp, following Arthur's flag once more with even less chance of success than ever before. Once more, I wished that the Saxon's sword had been truer at Tribuit. Then, whatever future awaits us beyond this reality would have fed itself on us, engorged on us, and we would be happy in the next life.

I shivered.

And there would be, at least for me, no Mariam, no Ygerne, no coming child. I jerked back as if struck. I continued to be so caught up in this affair that I had nearly forgotten them. Whatever force created our lands and our people should have struck me dead at that moment. They were my very life, and to forget them even for a second was the only unpardonable sin in my holy book.

And that was enough to banish my self-pity and focus me on the task ahead.

The first hint of trouble came as a thin wisp of smoke, rising from near the enemy's main camp. At first they did not seem to notice, or rather no one said anything. But within seconds, the wisp turned into a column of smoke, heading for the heavens.

And the shouts began.

Just as I thought, starting a strong fire under their supplies distracted every man there. From my vantage point, I could see streams of men, like lines of ants, hurrying to extinguish the flames, now licking into the sky and growing further with each second.

Sulien and Daron had done their job well.

With a deep breath, I sent a prayer to the heavens and bolted from my nest.

My legs were no longer young and the path before me a gentle slope, but I pushed harder and harder and harder.

The heat within me seemed to boil my stomach and what little was there burned my throat and erupted into the air.

But I did not stop.

Behind me I could hear men shouting and cursing the fire.

Then the shouting changed, and I knew that they had seen me. I tucked my head, ignored the vomitus dangling from my lips, and willed my legs to move faster. I could not spare the energy to worry about Sulien's and Daron's fate.

But I had too much distance on the men, even over the broken ground. I heard the unmistakable whish of spears piercing the air close behind, but that was all. The rest was but fading curses and footfalls.

And the tip of the shallow ravine lay just ahead. My legs burned like Druce's supplies, but I pushed on, expecting guards to pop out at any moment. For that is what I would have done, hidden guards at the most exposed point of this ravine. But I entered the undergrowth unmolested.

And took three steps before a wrapped forearm crushed my throat and threw me backwards.

Blackness reigned and my head pounded. But in seconds the light returned to show a shocked Ider staring me in the face.

"Malgwyn! Forgive me! Lord Bedevere posted us here but bid us hide and wait until an intruder cleared the field before we struck."

"We must hurry. Take me to Bedevere and Kay now."

Within minutes we had navigated the ravine and emerged onto the trackway into the main gate. At Ider's signal it was cracked open enough for the two of us to pass. Rightly, he had left his men in the ravine.

"What has happened?" Bedevere hailed me from the rampart. "We have had no word from anyone, and it seems the force before us has grown. Where is Arthur?"

I braced my one hand on my knee and caught my breath. "Quick, what do your lookouts see around the fire?"

Kay called the order up the ladder. In just a few seconds, the answer came.

"The supplies are burned, my lord. And from the looks of it, they have far fewer men than we thought."

Still out of breath, I nodded. "But it is a good force nonetheless. Among them are Druce's men, Saxons, and these gray-tunicked mercenaries. More than two hundred, I judge."

"But they would need twice that many to take a defended position," Kay said.

"They don't intend to attack," Bedevere answered, a grin breaking across his stone face. He understood immediately. "They want to block this force from being an influence on affairs at Trevelgue."

"Aye," I agreed. "We were taken prisoner by the mercenaries last night as we returned to Trevelgue from Tyntagel."

"Who is 'we'?" Kay queried.

"Myself, Sulien, the girl, a pair of common soldiers, and . . . Arthur."

The explosion I expected did not come.

Both Kay and Bedevere hung their heads. "Then he is dead."

Kay spun away, slamming his fist into the parapet. "I warned him about going out unprotected."

"No!" I shouted. "He is not dead. He dressed as a common man. Those who took us did not recognize him. They were from among the mercenaries and did not know Arthur by sight. David was in their camp, but demanded only to treat with me. He never saw Arthur in our tent. When we escaped, with Merlin's help, he, Merlin, and two of the men made haste for Trevelgue."

"Merlin? So that's where the devil's been hiding. That was more than a bit of luck," Bedevere said with a sigh. "So tell us how it lays."

"Druce's men were spread thin to give the illusion that they had enough men to storm the Castellum. In truth they had fewer than half that many, and too few supplies for a long siege."

"Aye," laughed Bedevere, "and he bunched the supplies together like a novice. I see now what you did. You used the burning of the supplies to distract them while you slipped into the Castellum.

"But what is going on up here that concerns you so? So there are a handful of rebels, here. Perhaps some mercenaries as well, but they could never hope to take the Castellum."

And that was when young Ider proved that he learned his lessons well. "Of course, with Arthur's and everyone's attentions here, it would be easier to install Druce in Doged's seat. Mordred would find fewer defenders, and if he did conspire with the Saxons in the plot against Ambrosius, then it would make it easier to rid them of him."

"I fear the day when you turn your mighty mind to evil," I jibed Ider, whose eyes grew wide.

"Malgwyn, I would never—"

"I know." Turning then. "There are not enough Saxons for real trouble, but more than we would desire. Druce's troops are young and untested, but these mercenaries concern me. We do not know how seasoned they are. We must not so much abandon Castellum Dinas, but we must drive our enemies away, crush them, and make our face once more a factor in affairs at Trevelgue."

"Bah!" Kay exploded, swinging a long arm about Doged's hall at Dinas. "Forget Trevelgue. We need to run down these animals and crush them all. They have challenged the *consilium*, brought the Saxons among us, and must be slaughtered."

While I shared Kay's zeal, my immediate concern was breaking the siege and making certain that Arthur had made it safely to Trevelgue. But my old friend had too long been out of command and lusted for it like a young man would for a maiden, though why I never knew. "There are plenty of enemies to share, Kay. Have no fear. Do you have a plan, Bedevere?"

My square-jawed companion grinned. "If you will command a troop, aye."

Bedevere's plan of battle was complicated, but it could work. We knew that their numbers were just short of ours. It would be a magnificent fight by any measure. Castellum Dinas had three entrances—one to the west, one to the north, and one to the east. That in the east was the least guarded.

'Twas Ider who came up with the grand idea, and while it was genius, it was decidedly brutal. A rider was sent out to treat with their chieftain. A young boy, barely old enough to sit a horse; another might be killed out of hand.

The entreaty read: "With your explosive siege machines, our position is untenable. Allow us one hour to vacate the fort and it is yours."

I was guessing that they would wait no longer than a half hour. And all this while, we slipped our men a few at a time through the eastern gate, hidden in growth, and no one could observe completely. But our enemies were anxious, and anxiety counted for much. They accepted our terms.

And true to my word, at half the hour they stormed the western gate, pushing it back easily. Saxons, mercenaries, Druce's men, all milled about the interior, searching in the huts, reveling in our supplies, their own so recently lost.

As the last of the men streamed in, I saw that their leaders, mercenary and Saxon, were beginning to frown. Not a defender was in sight.

But their frowns turned to horror when a squad of our strongest lads slammed the main gate shut, bolting it from the outside.

Thus our enemies were devoid of any order or organization. Ider and Kay were given the honor to command the assault from the parapets. What men were outside the fort were easily killed, and Bedevere and I finished those up. Then we climbed the parapet and looked down on the carnage below. The mercenaries fought well: I will give them that. Ider himself accounted for the one that had treated us so roughly. The Saxons were pitiful creatures, seeking escape. I descended the parapet and sought out Ceawlin and found him trying to crawl into a barrel.

"Malgwyn, don't!"

Bedevere could have been speaking to the dead.

I strode across the battle, now broken into single combats, until I neared Ceawlin.

"Saxon!"

He ceased his sniveling and, to his credit, faced me like a man. "You should have died with your men," he growled in that guttural tongue. "For all that you are worth now is to clean scraps from the table."

"Then," I said, "I will clean them well, with one arm. Your mother had better brought you into the world dead, than subject us to your tortures. But where God has erred, I will set affairs straight. And I will begin with you."

Ceawlin snatched up a spear and a sword. I held but a sword, but it was one that I had wielded with skill before. "I should have killed your whore-child then, one less of your offspring to curse the world."

My sword hummed through the air before he finished, sending him dodging to his left.

"You are not fit to breathe the same air as she. She is an angel and you are but the shite of the Devil. Were she here, I would let her kill you, for you are more match for child than man."

We circled each other, knowing that this time there would be no escape. One or perhaps both of us would die on this ground. At that moment, I hated no man on earth more than him.

"We have a name for you among our people," he said, breathing a little heavily.

"That is nice," I said. "You are not thought of enough by our people to merit a name." His old milky eye blinked, and I just missed the point of his dagger, so swift was his thrust.

"I will feast upon your testicles tonight, though they be but dried prunes." He smiled.

"I would feed on yours but, alas, our *medicus* judges that you have none."

Our banter served only to mark our nervousness. We were not frightened but eager. "Smiling Malgwyn" had returned, and this time I was pleased.

"But I will feast upon your heart. Anyone who shields himself behind a child is a coward and no more." I would never forget this same pig's face hiding behind Mariam's, his dagger at her tender throat.

Around us, the clash of iron dimmed. Our thrusts and parries quickly became the only sounds echoing from the wooden and stone walls. Indeed, the chairs on the parapet rattled with each blow. What had once been a savage battle had now become a single combat with two hundred avid spectators.

He was strong. I give him that. We matched blow for blow. I had never danced so agile as I did that day, dodging his spear and his sword. But I made him dance as well. Early on, I noticed Ider, out of the corner of my eye, about to rush forward to aid me, but Bedevere held him back. And I was glad.

Confined to one arm, I had long ago built up its strength. But Ceawlin was no weakling, and he was equally skillful with either arm.

As I dodged the slash of his sword, the gods were with me and my own blade struck behind the handle of his dagger, ripping it from his hand and sending it flying.

But I paid for my success. The point of his sword ripped through my tunic and opened a gash down my back. My back was already wet from sweat, but I could easily feel the thick warmth of my blood soaking my tunic.

"You bleed easily," Ceawlin taunted me. "See that you don't lose all of your blood before I have the chance to drink it."

"The only blood you'll be drinking is your own." But even as I said it, I felt the weakness that comes with loss of blood. The storm of the night before had yielded to a bright sun, and though we craved such days, the heat sapped my strength as quickly as did my wound.

I have written elsewhere of my attitude toward superstition, ghosts, spirits, magic. Let me say here only that there are things in this world that I cannot explain. That hour, that minute, that second at Castellum Dinas was one. Just as I had resigned myself to Ceawlin's sword, a voice sounded.

It said: "You have a son."

Something sparked within me, and I looked up swiftly to see the Saxon pig rushing me, his sword well behind his head, at the beginning of his death blow.

And though my back was on fire, and though I wasn't certain that I had the strength to take another breath, I swung my sword up with my one arm and thrust it forward, taking Ceawlin in the chest.

As the blood gushed from his mouth, surprise forever marking his face, I thought for a fleeting second that he had never had a chance. Once he committed to that final charge, he was a dead man, his momentum alone impaling him on my blade. Only a handful of Druce's men and Saxons were still standing. They dropped their weapons and begged for mercy.

Bedevere looked to me.

I rejected their plea.

"Malgwyn," Ider scolded me, "the Christ preaches mercy."

"There is a time and place for mercy. This isn't it."

With that settled, I spun around looking for the voice that had moved me to action. "Where is she?"

Ider rushed out. "Where is who?"

"The woman who hailed me."

"What woman?"

Of two things I am absolutely certain. A voice did hail me, a woman's voice.

And there were no women there.

"Malgwyn, you have lost much blood," Kay laughed, "and your senses with it. Come, let Ider bandage you. We have yet more work to do."

I said nothing else about it. My companions already had enough reason to question my sanity. I walked up to Ceawlin to retrieve my swords, his eyes forever open and his mouth now a font of crimson. His death was assured four winters before when he took my Mariam as a hostage. With what little strength I had left, I wrenched the blade from his carcass and spat on him. He deserved no better.

I let Kay lead me away from the massacre. We did indeed have more to do, but that depended almost completely on Arthur having reached Trevelgue safely. I would not wager a Roman denarius on that. We had no time to waste. The sun was riding low in the western sky, and every moment we tarried was another moment stolen from Arthur's life, I feared.

Of the two hundred and more men under Druce's command, none were yet standing. Although Druce himself could not be found, I no longer considered him a factor. I suspected his own men had turned on him or he had taken to the forest to hide.

We had lost fifty to sixty men, men we could not spare. Arthur, if he was still alive, would not be pleased at the death of the Saxon embassy. I did not care. Our laws and customs controlling embassies and guests demanded great penalties for violating a safe-conduct or killing one of your own guests. But by fielding soldiers, no matter how few, they had violated the laws of diplomacy as we knew them. Arthur would see that finally, and the Saxons would whine and cry but do nothing to avenge Ceawlin.

I could not spare the time to search for Sulien and Daron, and they were nowhere to be found in the aftermath of the battle. Sulien was a good and loyal companion. Daron had already seen enough tragedy to last a long lifetime. I regretted it, but they knew the hazard.

As Kay, Bedevere, and I took two troop back toward Trevelgue, I considered the situation. We had left Ider in command at Castellum Dinas, as we could not afford for even a remnant of Druce's army or the gray-clothed mercenaries to coalesce.

Arthur had left portions of one troop at Trevelgue when he launched his ill-advised trip to Tyntagel. But what had happened to them in the wake of his "disappearance" and David's attempt to usurp his power I did not know.

David.

I had forgotten about that snake.

"Bedevere, did you see David during the battle?"

My friend screwed his face up. "No. I would have used the excuse to kill him if I had. Why?"

I explained to him and Kay about my interview with David, which I should have done before, but the excitement of our escape, the revelation that Merlin yet lived, and the battle had combined to drive it from my mind.

"This is good news," Kay interrupted. "We can now charge him with treason and get rid of him."

I shook my head. "As much as I'd love to, Arthur had disappeared and with Mordred still held for the murder of Doged David was the senior lord of the *consilium*. While I heartily disagree with his actions, I often feel the same about Arthur's. No, I suspect that he made certain to leave their camp when our message arrived. He could not be seen to be party to accepting the surrender of a *consilium* possession in league with *consilium* enemies. That would be treason.

"I doubt that he would do anything with the troops Arthur had left behind. Ysbail, however, is not going to be pleased with the real murderer of Doged. Indeed, I believe she is going to be highly displeased."

"Why?"

"Because she is in love with him, I fear."

"Then they conspired to kill Doged," Kay concluded.

"Oh, no. I don't believe that she will doubt the truth, but she will be very reluctant to act on it. Having submitted to Petrocus on her right to rule, I believe that when he embraces the logic and allies himself with us, she will be unable to do anything but have the killer put to death. Which is sad because I too like him."

Neither of my friends asked his name, and I did not offer it.

Despite the important questions still to be answered—Ysbail's right to rule among them—I felt satisfied, relieved. Such a feeling was not unusual in survivors of battles. But more than that, I could finally see an end to our mission. The destruction of Druce's army would effectively end the rebellion, no matter how Petrocus ruled. The Saxon embassy was eliminated, Doged's murder resolved. We had bought time for the exploitation of the minerals and ores at Castellum Dinas. And we had ensured that whoever ruled in these lands, they would be dependent on the *consilium* to stay in power. Happily, our losses had been minimal, if personally tragic. I knew that I would never forget Sulien's and Daron's sacrifice, and I mourned them as I would members of my family.

My satisfaction exploded in a heavy, satisfied sigh.

An hour later, we were well on the road to Trevelgue. I was a little surprised, because the lane we traveled was mostly de- serted. If events were bad at Trevelgue, I expected to see the people deserting the town, but word would have spread of the battle at Castellum Dinas and perhaps people were avoiding it. The stretch of road we were traveling was in open country, an occasional farmstead dotting the landscape. In the distance, where another lane emerged from a distant wood joined with ours, we saw a single rider atop one horse and leading another. We were too far away to see whether it was a man or woman and how it was garbed. Bedevere dispatched a ten-man patrol to our southern flank as a precaution and increased our pace.

As we drew closer, I noted with interest and not a little sur- prise that it was the strange, dark man with but one eye, the merchant. I had meant to question him, but events had moved beyond my control. And the need seemed hardly important at that moment.

We met him after a few more minutes, and I saw that two bundles were tied tightly to the back of the horse he led. His skin was dark, but not so dark as Africans, more like those of the Holy Land.

At the edge of the black patch covering his missing eye, I could see a hint of tanned, puckered skin. But his smile was genuine and he seemed pleased to see us, raising a hand in greeting and bringing his horse to a stop.

"My lords. You would be Lord Bedevere, Lord Kay, and Master Malgwyn, councilors to Arthur, the Rigotamos."

"You are well informed," Bedevere returned.

"I am Daoud, a poor merchant, living far from home. I had hoped to meet you earlier, but business called me away."

"You have not been at Trevelgue?" I asked, more to pass the time than anything else.

He shook his head and spoke in his deep bass voice. "No. I left the morning after you arrived. A customer offered me double the price if I could replace an item he had bought from me and lost. While my work sells well, I cannot refuse double the price. It was a task to find the materials, though. That is why I am just now returning."

"Some precious metal?" Kay asked.

"In a sense. I had the silver for the fibula he needed, but it had an agaphite stone and I had none handy."

My heart skipped a beat. "A fibula? Of silver and agaphite?" Suddenly nothing seemed settled.

Daoud nodded solemnly. "Strange. I only sold two and both customers lost them the same night."

And then I remembered that brief mention of a second fibula, a few words in another life it seemed. "Quick, man! Who wanted the replacement so earnestly?"

Kay, Bedevere, and Daoud looked at me as if I were crazy. But when Daoud answered, adding, "You must know him. His men are the ones wearing the gray tunics," a chill ran through me and my heels dug into my horse's flanks and the old girl leaped into the race.

"Malgwyn!" Bedevere yelled. "Where are you going?"

"To Trevelgue! Arthur is about to sanction the execution of the wrong man!"

CHAPTER SEVENTEEN

Though I heard the pounding of hoofbeats behind me, I did not look back; I could not look back. Once again, I had put the evidence together falsely. How could I have forgotten the guard telling me of a second brooch? It had been but a brief comment, yet on such things battles are lost. No one else had to condemn me. I was even then damning myself to an eternity in the Hell of Arthur's God. And even that seemed insufficient punishment for my deeds. For the wrongly accused's was not the only blood on my hands. My pride, my self-satisfaction, had already caused too many deaths in this affair.

Suddenly I understood why a hermetic life might be a good choice for me. I did not deserve to live among people.

And the pace of the horse's hooves matched the beating of my heart.

The fatigue of battle had vanished. I could not, would not, rest until I had cleaned up the mess I had made.

If I could.

I willed my horse to grow wings and fly us there.

Ysbadden Penkawr seemed twice as large sitting astride his horse as he did on the ground. I had heard it said that his sword was specially made to match his size. I did not doubt it. It seemed even larger held in his hand and pointed at me as he barred my approach to the causeway.

I slowed my horse, wrapped the leather reins around my half arm, and unsheathed my sword.

"You will not pass," he roared. "When her bastard child is born, I will become its guardian."

"And rule until he reaches manhood? No, I think he will meet a tragic end."

By then we had drawn abreast of each other.

"What do you care?" he began. "You are the one who pointed the axe at his throat. You and your Rigotamos quarter far from here."

I saw then his purpose. This was the only way he could control the situation.

"I will promise the *consilium* preference for trade over the Saxons."

I had no time for this. I cocked my feet, ready to speed my mount past him.

"You will be fortunate if the Saxons do not raid Trevelgue and massacre all there."

The giant frowned. "What have you done?"

"Slaughtered their embassy."

My answer shocked him, though he would have done the same if he saw profit in it, and he reeled a bit in his saddle. I kicked my horse's flanks, jumping at Ysbadden, who had to fight to keep his seat.

As I rode past, I swung the flat of my sword with all my

might, striking the giant bully in the back and sending him flying to the ground.

Seconds later, I had crossed the narrow causeway and entered the fort.

I leaped from my horse's back, almost before she had stopped, and hit the earth outside the hall, losing my balance and rolling in the dirt. A handful of guards were standing at the main door, and they laughed at my discomfiture.

Rising, I cursed their mothers, dusted the streaks of dirt from my already dirty tunic, and hustled into the hall, where Ysbail presided at the front with Arthur, Merlin, and Petrocus at her side.

Before her, on his knees, was Cilydd, head hung, hands tied.

Ysbail looked thoroughly miserable, and I heaved a sigh of relief.

It was not too late.

"My lord!" I shouted.

Arthur craned his neck around to see who had shouted. Merlin smiled at me, as did Petrocus. Ysbail's sadness turned to absolute hatred. And for good reason.

"Master Malgwyn," Petrocus greeted me. "Congratulations on a fine job of inquiry. I know something of the law as you are aware, and you would have secured a conviction by any court abiding by the Codex Theodosianus. And Master Merlin did a fine job in presenting it. And, let me tell you, Lady Ysbail was very difficult to persuade. But now Lord Mordred has been freed from his confinement and justice can be done and we can proceed with the issue of her right to rule in Doged's lands."

I was certain she had been very, very difficult to convince.

A hand landed heavily on my shoulder, and I turned to see Mordred cleaned of the food scraps and dung heaped upon him and smiling at me as if we were . . . friends, and he seemed . . . sincere.

"Honored Petrocus," I began, ignoring Mordred and pushing my way through the crowded aisled hall. It was stifling hot in there, miserably hot, I remember. Any more days like that one, I remember thinking, and they would be opening a grave for me.

I sucked in a deep breath and continued, "If this man is put to death for the killing of Doged, justice will not be done."

To say that voices buzzed around the hall did them a disservice. No hive of bees could match the hum of these voices.

"Malgwyn," Arthur's voice rose above the discord. "He was convicted on your evidence."

"I know, Rigotamos, and I apologize for my incompetence."

Merlin did not speak but looked at me quizzically.

Petrocus stepped forward and did speak. "I am sorry, Malgwyn, but Cilydd confessed after the evidence was presented. To ignore that would be to dishonor all that you, I am told, hold dear."

The fool. Of course he would have confessed. To contest the charges might have revealed what he and Ysbail were trying so desperately to hide—that her baby was Cilydd's, not Doged's. And Cilydd was in love with her. His last act would be to preserve her position and his child's right to succeed Doged.

I glanced around the hall, past Doged's nobles, past the whores hanging on their shoulders, past the embassies gathered. And there he was, lurking near the back, his head cocked to one side, a look of worry on his face.

"If you will permit me, Rigotamos."

I am not certain that I had ever seen Arthur so irritated with me. "I do not see what this delay profits us."

"Nor I, Rigotamos," echoed Petrocus.

"But this is my court, monk. And I will decide who has the right to speak, at least until that privilege is stripped from me." Ah, love! Ysbail saw a hope, a prayer of salvaging her man's life. And she would take up a sword herself against anyone that tried to silence me.

Even Arthur reeled in surprise at the sharpness of her tone. I pleaded to him with my eyes. No one but me saw an old wrinkled hand rise and gently touch Arthur's back.

Merlin had cast his vote with me.

"Proceed, Master Malgwyn," Ysbail ordered me in her iciest tone. "I am anxious to hear of your incompetence."

Two soldiers pushed the gathered throng back, making more room around poor Cilydd.

I took a deep breath and began. "First, I felt that under our customs of hospitality and because he was a member of the *consilium*, I had a duty to seek justice for Lord Doged. And I am cursed with a need to seek the truth in these situations, aye, more than a need, a compulsion that even I cannot control.

"Lord Mordred had been caught fleeing Doged's chamber immediately after his death. Anyone with knowledge of myself and Mordred knows that it would give me pleasure to see him summarily executed for his misdeeds, if such he committed." I knew that I had best temper my words, no matter how fatigued I was. Mordred helped by laughing almost embarrassedly.

"The Rigotamos, who has often called on me to be his *iudex pedaneous* in these situations, approved of my inquiry, and, eventually, so did you, Lady Ysbail."

"I do not need a history lesson," she snapped, but immediately thought better of it. At that moment, she needed me as man needs water to live.

"Of course not. I simply wanted to establish my credentials. What bothered me about Mordred's guilt is that I could not see a reason for killing Doged. Mordred is an intelligent man, and he would profit nothing from doing this thing." I paused. My next words had to be carefully chosen.

"What I also knew, what I had witnessed with my own eyes, was that someone, disguised as Doged, had gained access to his private chambers. It was not Mordred, as he was dressed normally when captured."

I paused for a bare second to steel myself for my next words. I am human, and therefore flawed. I had certainly lied before in my life, but rarely in one of these inquiries.

"When I questioned Mordred, he reported that just before they reached the rear entrance of the hall a man dressed as Doged rushed past him. I can verify this because I saw the same man rush out the main gate. I simply assumed that it was Doged, rushing to handle some problem. Upon my return to the hall, I learned that Doged had been slain and Mordred captured while fleeing the scene.

"Mordred says that Doged was already dead when he entered the chambers." I saw no need to mention that Saxons were with Mordred, as that would only make him look all the guiltier. "Later, the guard that Mordred had bribed was killed." That admission cost Mordred nothing, as such bribery was more a practice than a sin. "Mordred was imprisoned and could not have killed the guard."

Arthur grunted impatiently at me. Petrocus smiled gently and said, "Malgwyn, no one suspects Mordred of this any longer, but you have done well in proving that he did not do it. We have the man who did this thing, and he has confessed. I see no purpose in prolonging this. To do so is cruel to Cilydd."

"I will decide if there is no purpose in this," countered Ysbail. "Continue."

"With all due respect, Petrocus, this is my method. I was led to Cilydd as a suspect when I discovered an unusual silver and agaphite fibula that had been lost by the impostor Doged. I was told that only Cilydd had such a brooch."

"So, there is no question now," Arthur said, but I raised my one hand to stop him.

"But I have now learned that two were sold and two were lost. In truth, I was made aware of the existence of two such brooches at the outset of this affair, but I did not pay as close attention as I ought." I kept my eye on him at the back of the hall. I would almost certainly have bolted already, but he seemed strangely unable to move. But by that point, I had everyone's attention.

"Only one of the two owners was so anxious to replace it that he offered the one-eyed merchant Daoud double for another one. Only the man who had killed Doged would be so anxious."

Now, his eyes began darting back and forth, seeking an escape.

"Is that not right, Lord Trevelyan?"

He chose then to bolt. I plunged into the crowd after him, but the tightly packed bunch slowed my pursuit.

I hated revealing him this way, but I had really needed him to attempt to escape. I needed him to show his guilt openly, for that was the only way out of this dilemma. I should have brought Daoud, the dark-skinned merchant, but my only concern then had been trying to prevent yet another, needless, death. And our natural fear of strangers would have diluted anything that Daoud had to say. No, I saw quickly, even as I used my shoulder to split the crowd, this was the only path to success.

But Trevelyan had wisely stayed at the back of the hall and was already out the door. And in seconds so was I. I scanned the fort and glimpsed him headed to the main gate.

Though my lungs burned and my legs were cramping, I held tight to the pursuit.

"Stop him."

But Doged's soldiers were more interested in watching the spectacle than following my orders.

Behind me, I heard a horse snort and hooves slamming the hard-packed earth.

My body was about to give out when I felt a hand grasp my shoulder and pull up.

Arthur.

With all the strength I had left, I leaped and, with Arthur's help, swung onto his horse behind him.

"Malgwyn, do you do these things to me intentionally?"

Gritting my teeth as we approached the main gate and the narrow bridge beyond, I said, "Rigotamos, I am doing nothing to you or for you, but just trying to find out what really happened."

"So you say."

We threaded the needle that was the gate and crossed the bridge in two bounds. From horseback we could see Trevelyan commandeering a horse from some unfortunate citizen, and I feared for a moment that we would lose him.

But Arthur was a skilled and daring horseman; he urged the poor horse forward, bearing both our bodies.

In the distance, we saw Trevelyan about to reach the wooden and earthen defenses thrown up by Bedevere's men days before.

Trevelyan seemed intent on jumping the rampart, as we were drawing nearer. The horse he had appropriated was older than ours and not used to such rides. He thought better of it and headed for the gap in the works made for the road.

And past us, coming from our rear, the blur of a horse and rider slipped by.

Bedevere.

But his urgency was unnecessary.

Trevelyan stopped.

And dismounted.

We slowed as Bedevere, his momentum carrying him forward, was forced to turn his horse at the last minute.

Trevelyan ran forward and joined a gaggle of men entering the defenses. And as we reached them, I was not surprised at what I saw.

Lord David.

Others hovered behind, but it was David who strode toward us, leading the pack.

I kept my eye on Trevelyan, as I did not trust him not to mix with the crowd and attempt to disappear. But he seemed intent on throwing himself on David's mercy.

As Arthur and I climbed down from our horse, David wasted no time.

"This man is under my protection."

"Then," Kay, who had now joined us, said, "perhaps we should execute them both."

Arthur held his hand out to Kay, palm down, gesturing for him to hold.

"David, you do not understand the current situation."

"And what would justify the Rigotamos of all Britannia chasing down and killing this man, a poor noble who is simply trying to help his people?"

"Three things, Lord David," I began. "First, Trevelyan's men massacred and sacked a village in the far east of these lands. Second, Trevelyan murdered Lord Doged when Doged refused to settle lands upon them." I was certain that that was what had spurred Doged's death. "His men led a siege and assault on Castellum Dinas, as you would know since you were treating with them and the Saxon embassy."

"I did not," David replied.

"Yes, you did," Arthur answered. "Stop this pretense. I was one of the men captured by Trevelyan's forces and imprisoned in their camp. I heard your voice with my own ears."

For the first time in the years that I had known him, David was speechless. He was prepared to do verbal combat with me but not Arthur. Though David did not say it, I could see the thought behind his flickering eyes: *Idiots!*

"I acknowledge that I treated with an army of mercenaries in gray tunics, but I do not see a gray tunic on Trevelyan, and I did not see him or treat with him in the enemy camp," David said, handily dancing around the charges. "Who says that he has any connection with the mercenaries? They could have been hired by the Saxons."

"Who says that they were mercenaries to begin with?"

Mordred slipped over into David's group, easing up and whispering in David's ear. A quick nod of his head worried me no little bit.

"I have been told that they are all dead, Rigotamos. Massacred at the order of Malgwyn. If none of them yet survive, how will we ever know from whence they came?"

I understood then why they had worked so hard to keep Trevelyan from the camp, or at least to keep him out of sight. Without a witness that put Trevelyan and the gray tunics together, we had no way to prove the truth. He would argue that David's grant of hospitality protected him from punishment for killing Doged.

My shoulders slumped as the realization hit me. I had failed in my quest. Justice would not be served.

I began to turn away when a scuffle and shout arose from beyond the rampart.

Spinning about, I saw two horses muscle their way through David's mob. On one sat Ider, with a dirty, exhausted Daron behind him. On the other sat Sulien, looking equally as tired. Sitting in front of Sulien, with a dagger against his throat, was a soldier, in a gray tunic.

"Lord Arthur!" Ider shouted. "I beg your pardon for such an entrance, but we felt that we should arrive as quickly as possible, though we did not expect to find you at the rampart."

Arthur considered young Ider for a long second, a smile creeping across his face. "You have no need to apologize." He turned toward Sulien. "I see that the rumors of your death were premature."

"Fortunately, Rigotamos."

I was merely listening to this exchange. My eyes were now glued to Trevelyan, where horror grew the longer he looked at the man sharing Sulien's horse.

For his part, Sulien shoved the soldier in the gray tunic

from his perch, and he slammed into the ground with a thud and rolled over. "We found this one hiding in the forest."

The soldier scrambled to his feet, stumbling forward to grasp Trevelyan's knees. He said something in that almost but not quite comprehensible language of theirs. My eyes scanned the growing crowd, noting that Ysbail and her brother were arriving, until I found who I sought.

"Gurdur."

"Yes, my lord." The man of many languages stepped forward.

"Do you understand this tongue?" Arthur asked, seeing immediately my aim.

Gurdur nodded sharply. "Of course, my lord. It is an ancient form of our own language, used almost exclusively now by those from Scilly and Ennor. He," and Gurdur indicated the soldier, "is begging this man's forgiveness for his cowardice."

I had never, ever seen David so completely defeated.

Just as I was learning to enjoy the look, Mordred stepped forward. "Then this man," Mordred asked, "both killed Doged and ordered that poor village sacked?" He grabbed Trevelyan in a seeming fury.

"And do not forget, took arms against both these lands and the *consilium* at Castellum Dinas," I added, eager to pile on the humiliation for which David had asked.

"Then this pig does not deserve to live," and with a dagger that mysteriously appeared in his hand Mordred rammed the point in Trevelyan's gut, twisting it as he did.

A moment, a second, before the light left Trevelyan's eyes forever, I clearly saw the question: *Why?* I could have told him, but there was no time. The light was gone, a dull glaze settled in, and a fly landed on his eye, seeking a meal.

I did not hear the voices, the shouts, around me. The swiftness of Mordred's action had stunned me. That Trevelyan had earned such a death was unquestionable. That Mordred was the one to do it was surely questionable.

Ysbail shared my view, and also, apparently, her husband's dislike of Mordred. And it was her shrill voice that shook me from my reverie. "You have gone too far, Lord Mordred," Ysbail chastised him. "Tell me why I should not return you to my garbage pit until you decide to behave?"

Mordred recoiled as if struck. "Lady Ysbail," he said in almost a mocking tone. "All I have done is kill a murderer and an enemy of your rule. Surely there is no misbehavior in that."

"I have learned something of these matters from Master Malgwyn," she answered in a way that none of us expected. "Rushing to action is a risky path, and though I believe in Trevelyan's guilt, I would have insisted on a more formal process, one in which the facts were considered more judiciously. And you did not ask my leave." Now that was the Ysbail I was expecting.

I found it fascinating that Ysbadden stood silent behind her. Perhaps he was learning something too from this affair.

Moments later, Arthur gathered myself, Kay, Bedevere, Ider, and Sulien together, away from the others.

"Ider, what has happened?"

"Bedevere assigned me to command the force left behind at Castellum Dinas. After he, Malgwyn, and Kay left for Trevelgue, a patrol I had posted to round up stragglers returned with these three," and he indicated Sulien, Daron, and Trevelyan's man. "Sulien and the girl had him trussed up like a pig. They had apparently captured him."

We all laughed at that. Now that I could see they had survived, my heart lightened.

"I felt certain that you would need to question him here, since he seemed the only survivor of the mercenary band. I left someone in charge and brought them myself."

Arthur clapped him on the shoulder.

But despite my amusement at how events had transpired, I still felt remarkably unsettled. More so than even before. Trevelyan's people were nomads, poaching on lands as they saw fit. Which would not have been a problem had Trevelyan not so desperately desired a kingdom of his own. Ambition, one of those deadly things. David was more involved in the conspiracy than he would ever admit, but was he led into it by Druce or Trevelyan or the Saxons? What had brought these parties together? They were an odd collection for a conspiracy.

"Come, Malgwyn," Arthur said. "Petrocus has read all of the laws and heard all of the evidence. He has set tonight as the time that he will render a decision on Ysbail's right to rule."

"Have you any doubts that he will uphold her right?"

"No, I do not." Arthur paused. "But tonight is more important than that. It is a date that we should all celebrate in the future."

I did not see what he meant, and I did not hesitate to say it.

"Oh, Malgwyn. Of all the people that surround me, I was certain that you would understand. Tonight, our peoples will accept and abide by the rule of law, impartially determined. No bribes will change hands. No intimidation will be a factor. Do you realize how impossible this would have been just a few years ago?"

"I am not certain," I said with a dry chuckle, "that it is possible now. But perhaps."

"Forever the pessimist. I am proud of you, Malgwyn. You have played a true role in bringing this about. I will forever value your talents in war, but this, this is so much more important."

If I live another ninety winters, I will never forget the light in Arthur's eyes, a sparkle like that in the eyes of a young boy when he had won his first footrace. Had I the ability to capture that and store it in an amphora, I could cure the ills of the world.

"Forgive Malgwyn, Arthur," Merlin recommended. "He has been sorely used on this journey, and he loses himself too much in thought. I will bet even now that he is reviewing all that has happened and attempting to find some fault in what he himself has discovered."

"I am thinking that I should leave at first light to return to Castellum Arturius and my family." Which was not exactly what I was thinking, but I did not like Merlin's mind reading. He was too often right.

Arthur looked to Kay. "I have kept you too long from your lands and the needs of our army. Your service as my chief steward has been exemplary in every way. I wish you now to go to Ambrosius's old fort to our east, make it your seat, and begin construction of the defensive rampart that he has recommended."

I studied Kay's face to see how this would settle with him, and at first he seemed pleased. But then he asked, "And who is to assume my place?"

"I think young Ider has proved himself on this journey."

A dark, dark cloud covered Kay's face. He walked off without speaking. I saw that in the days to come I would need to speak with him as we used to; I would need to find out what tortured him so.

For Arthur's part, he chose to ignore Kay's ill mood. I did not like, though, the narrowing of Arthur's eyes as he watched his old friend walk away.

An hour later and with Merlin's help, I had secured an audience with Lady Ysbail. Only four of us were in the chamber where Doged had breathed his last: myself, Merlin, Ysbail, and Cilydd.

"I am impressed by the both of you, most especially with you, Cilydd," I began.

Cilydd shuffled uncomfortably from side to side. "Why is that, Master Malgwyn?" His tone was light, jovial, but the way he moved put the lie to his words.

"Oh, stop this!" The ferocity of Merlin's words stunned even me, and the force drove both Cilydd and Ysbail back a step. "He knows. Do him the honor of speaking the truth. He has earned it."

"When did you strike your bargain with Doged?"

Cilydd turned away, but Ysbail turned him back. "Tell him or I will."

"Shortly after the wedding," the young noble grudgingly admitted. "He sent for me one night. I had not yet challenged his rule openly, and he was appreciative." Cilydd paused.

"Go on," I urged. "Doged is beyond caring now."

Cilydd hesitated still.

Ysbail shoved him gently to the side, and I could not help but smile. She was a formidable woman. "Lord Doged was a good man. He made several attempts but could not . . . make it work. Doged was very apologetic." And then she paused. But the straight line that was her lips grew straighter still and she continued without prompting.

"Our marriage was arranged to provide Doged with an heir, to put a stop to all these rumblings of rebellion. I am a woman, chattel to be bargained for. But Doged was not a typical lord. He was both gentle and kind, and he never raised a hand to me. His failure brought a sadness to him, and I was touched by that.

"When he came to me with this . . . this . . . plan, I saw no reason not to agree. Sleeping with one man I did not love or another made little difference. But I was struck by how he solicited my approval. In truth, I thought the whole disguise business unnecessary."

I turned to Cilydd again. "What were the terms of your agreement with Doged?"

"That upon his death, given a decent interval, I would marry Ysbail and lead these lands as his, or rather my, son's regent. Doged was a very old man, and he was not in good health."

"So," Merlin interjected. "Doged wrote to me for help in how to use the disguise."

"But something happened that you did not anticipate," I ventured.

The new queen and the young lord grinned sheepishly and hung their heads. Ysbail spoke first. "Aye. We fell in love."

"Did Doged know?"

"He did, but he was not angry," Ysbail hurried. "In some way, I think he was pleased. He said once that we reminded him of another young lord and lady of his acquaintance." She turned to Merlin. "Do you know of whom he spoke?"

Neither Merlin nor I answered.

When the moment passed, I asked a question that had burned inside of me. "When you denied that you were with child, you were harboring a hope that the baby could be acknowledged as Cilydd's?"

She blushed, so unlike the imperious queen I had come to know. I decided that I liked the one who blushed more. "Yes," Ysbail said finally. "I was not thinking clearly."

What human in love did?

"It is more important than ever that this remain secret," I said. "As long as you carry Doged's child, you will be safe. I believe that you have gained much respect from the people by your actions in this muddled affair. Doged was well respected; in time I believe that Cilydd will be as well. But if the truth were known, it may very well foment the rebellion that Doged so badly wished to avoid."

"Let us swear an oath," Merlin began, and we did, with four hands clasped together.

"And how long must we maintain this charade?" Ysbail asked.

"I would wait several months, perhaps a year, before marrying," I began, but an idea sprang into my mind. "Let us do this," and I explained my plan.

What hours were left that day before Arthur's dawning of a new age I spent sleeping in the ramshackle hut that Ysbail had allotted to me earlier. Faithful Sulien kept watch over me, though I knew that he was as exhausted as I. Daron was strangely absent, but with Trevelyan as dead as the present rebellion in Doged's lands I did not judge that she was in any danger. She too had had a difficult few days.

Merlin came by and woke me in time to prepare for the feasting. I had no clean *braccae* or tunic with me, but I had the time and walked into the *vicus* where I sought out Daoud, now busy selling his wares to the great crowd that was gathering. Rumors of a new ruler assuming command were not dampened by the fighting at Castellum Dinas. A new ruler meant feasting and drinking. That was worth risking a little danger.

"Master Malgwyn," rumbled Daoud's deep voice. "Please, I have anything you need."

Of that I had no doubt. His stall was large and crammed with everything from fibulae to bone hairpins to combs to peplos gowns to tunics. I even spied a dozen amphorae of olive oil and a half dozen of wine, leaning against a wall. The wine, I was certain, was some exotic type from far away.

"I simply need some new *braccae* and a tunic for this evening's feast."

The dark-skinned man nodded. "Of course. Your recent duties have allowed little time for such niceties. Yet, a councilor to the Rigotamos is more than just a soldier."

"Unfortunately."

Daoud dug through his bins and emerged with *braccae* of the right size and a crimson tunic, just like those we, who served Arthur, wore. I had to ask the question.

"Do you stock items for every possible class of customer?"

He just grinned. "A merchant must. If I have what you need today, you will not bother with my competitors when you have a simpler request later. You will come straight to me."

"A wise practice." I paid him from my leather pouch. "How

long have you been among us? I would know something of
your history."

"Only about ten years or so, master. Before that, I was a
sailor with various merchant ships."

"From what people do you hail?"

"My people are desert nomads that ply the sands between
Jerusalem and Egypt."

"A desert nomad becomes a sailor. That is unusual."

He laughed again. "I tired of the sands. And then I tired of
the water."

"Well, I am pleased that you have settled among us. Should
you visit Castellum Arturius, you would be most welcome."

"That is very kind of you, master." He hesitated. "Master
Malgwyn? Is it true that the Saxon embassy were killed in the
fighting at Castellum Dinas?"

"Yes, unfortunately, they became involved in the fighting
between the *consilium*'s troops and Ysbail's supporters." I saw a
glint of frustration. "Before you chastise me, the Saxon envoys
involved themselves; we did not aim to involve them." Something made me pause. "I realize that you were not accusing me
of misdeeds, but I am curious as to why you, a foreigner, would
be curious about this?"

"I had two customers earlier who were, I think, soldiers of
Lord David. They were speaking of the Saxons, and one said
that David intended to use the law to 'bite off his other arm.'
Well, I immediately thought of you. Though I am certain that
you realize that you have many enemies, I thought perhaps
that you should know of this."

That David was contemplating bringing charges against
me was no surprise. Nor was I dismayed that he aimed to paint
it as a matter for the law to handle. And while I knew that Ar-

thur would protect me, I also believed that the law would protect me as well. After all, the Saxons had already dishonored the ancient laws of hospitality by taking up arms at Castellum Dinas.

I thanked Daoud again and returned to the fort.

CHAPTER EIGHTEEN

Three hours later, Petrocus faced what was assuredly his largest audience and his most important task, and the severity of his purpose had left wrinkles where once smooth skin held sway.

The aisled hall saw benches replace the regular seats. Kay told me that Petrocus had his *monachi* bring the benches down to Trevelgue. I chuckled a little. It seemed our *monachus* was learning a bit about theatrics.

The principals had not emerged from the private chambers at the back of the hall. I felt a strange tug at my *braccae* and saw that Cilydd's son, Culhwch, was working to get my attention. One hand was wrapped in my *braccae* and the other clutched a long, thin object wrapped in deer hide.

"Master Culhwch. How good to see you."

"Master Malgwyn," he began, trying his best to sound grown-up, like a man. "My father wishes you to have this in appreciation for the service you have rendered him." And then, in an instinctual move that showed how big the little boy's heart truly was, without saying a word, he stripped away the hide for me.

The gift was a beautiful, bone-handled dagger, the blade new, shiny, and sharp. Skillfully carved into the bone was the Cross, the symbol that graced the shields of Arthur's men and their tunics.

I pulled the old, well-used dagger from my belt and handed it to Culhwch. With a little flourish, to please the boy, I stowed the new dagger in my belt.

Culhwch stared at the dull, nicked blade of my old dagger as if it were made of gold. "Have you killed with this?"

"I have. But for now, I think you should worry about peeling apples with it."

He smiled up at me and grinned. "Yes, master."

"Where is your father?"

"With the Rigotamos and Lady Ysbail."

Young Culhwch ran off to play with his new dagger before I could ask him anything else. I thought about going back to the chambers myself, but, in truth, I had not the strength for the negotiations that were taking place there. But I was curious as to how my plan would work.

"Tristan has entered the fort," I heard Sulien's voice at my ear.

A wash of uncertainty covered me. I was not sure how to feel about Tristan now. Though he had not committed his troops to the battle at Castellum Dinas, neither had he fulfilled his promise and joined us.

Petrocus, Ysbail, Bedevere, Arthur, Cilydd, and David emerged from their seclusion. Leaning against one of the posts holding the roof, I settled in to see how all that had occurred would be molded to please the public.

The monk Petrocus looked decidedly uneasy, as did Arthur and Bedevere. Ysbail's expression was one of deep sorrow, as was Cilydd's. I straightened as I saw the joy in David's eyes. Something was amiss here. And it did not bode well for me.

"My lady Ysbail," Petrocus began. "I was charged by you and the Rigotamos with determining the right of a woman to rule over these or any lands in our domain. Your charge was agreed to by all those who opposed your rule. Hence, my decision will establish a sort of legal precedent for our peoples. With that in mind, I have considered all factors, consulted both the written records and scholarly books, as well as visited with elderly men who have lived long and know our ancient tribal customs well.

"First, let me say plainly that if Doged's marriage to Ysbail had been longer or if she had had issue with Doged, this controversy would not exist. Ample evidence exists in our annals of women ruling in their husband's stead. In other times I have mentioned Boudicca of the Iceni and examples from the Scotti, including Lady Igraine, here among the Cornovii.

"So, what we must come to is this question: Does Ysbail, herself, meet the requirements? No one argues that her marriage to Doged was not legally concluded. The question then becomes, is the short duration of her marriage a disabling fact? Does it change her right to inherit? I can only conclude that no, it does not. If a man sells a hide of land to his neighbor, and they agree on the price and such a price is paid, and then the man dies the next day, does that invalidate his arrangement with his neighbor? No, and no one would argue that it does. If the marriage was legally entered into, then no matter its length, all the attendant rights and responsibilities attached thereunto remain valid."

A collective sigh resounded through the hall. A couple of groans of disbelief marred the response to Petrocus's decision, but none with enough force to suggest that anyone would challenge it.

Arthur rose then. "Because of her short time here, Ysbail has decided to appoint Lord Cilydd to lead her soldiers and to consult with her on all matters relating to these lands. He has sworn to serve her."

Though a few grumbles could be heard, a wave of murmured approval easily drowned them out. This affair was coming to a most satisfying conclusion, and I was pleased.

At that, I expected that the feasting would begin in earnest, but Arthur, Ysbail, and the rest stayed in their seats. Including Petrocus. A rumble gradually rose across the room as an argument was in progress between Arthur, David, and Petrocus.

Only one thing could bring this group together. Daoud had warned me. For a fleeting second, I considered slipping out the door, but my pride would not let me. I was not ashamed of having killed Ceawlin, and since they had taken arms against us, I believed that they had lost any protection that their status afforded them.

Finally they separated. Petrocus stood. "Lord David has brought even more serious charges against Master Malgwyn, Lord Arthur's councilor. Since I am here, already serving as an *iudex*, and since it was Lord Doged's grant of hospitality that has apparently been violated, Lady Ysbail has asked me to continue and sit in judgment on this matter as well. Lord Arthur has no objection."

"Then have him taken into custody and trussed as poor Mordred was."

Petrocus dropped his head and looked down his long hawk's nose and shook his head at David. "Master Malgwyn seems to have no interest in fleeing. Will you join us here, Malgwyn?"

That Arthur did not object to my trial for killing the Saxon meant that I was completely on my own. Bedevere, blast his hide, could not bring himself to do more than tell the truth. For all the seeming politeness, I knew that David was out for my blood. In some ways, I felt a sudden relief. Perhaps "Smiling Malgwyn," the man who killed with pleasure, was to receive the justice he so richly deserved. To gain pleasure from killing was no virtue and should be punished. This was bound to happen sometime; I had flaunted convention and pridefully placed my judgment over others better suited.

But though my stomach was flopping around, threatening to revolt, I placed a smile on my face and strode, purposefully, to the front of the hall.

"Esteemed Petrocus," I began. "It is well known that Lord David has nothing but hatred in his heart for me. We have clashed since the day that the *consilium* chose Arthur over him to be Rigotamos."

Petrocus's face held a truly pained expression. "But, Malgwyn, did you indeed kill a Saxon envoy at Castellum Dinas?"

"Aye," I answered. "One by me, others by other of our men. And I feel no remorse. They had taken up arms against our forces. They had abandoned the protection of Lady Ysbail's hospitality by doing so."

That pained expression merely grew. "Malgwyn, the Saxon that you killed, in single combat if I am to understand correctly, was one that you knew, personally."

I shrugged. I could not see where he was taking this. "What of it?"

"Lord Bedevere tells us that you swore, several days ago, to kill Ceawlin before you left these lands."

And then I remembered. It was true. Bedevere had not betrayed me. He had done what he always had done, answered questions frankly and honestly. Arthur could not intervene for me because that would negate all that he had said to me earlier that same day. In truth, I had said virtually the same thing to Arthur. I was trapped by the truth that I had so long hailed.

"The Saxon envoy Ceawlin infiltrated Castellum Arturius, posing as a Druid priest, on the eve of Arthur's election as the Rigotamos. After a failed attempt to murder Ambrosius, he took my daughter, Mariam, hostage. It was only truly good fortune that kept him from slitting her throat."

The crowd sucked in a collective breath. Blood feuds they could understand.

"But you knew that he was protected by our laws of hospitality and yet swore to kill him anyway?" Petrocus persisted.

David's strategy was easy to see. He would counter explanations that included the Saxons taking arms against us by showing that Ceawlin was a dead man no matter what happened and despite Ysbail's hospitality. It was not a killing in defense of anything; it was an act of murder.

"This is nonsense!" David exclaimed. "I will ask the only question that needs asking. Lord Bedevere?"

"Lord Bedevere."

"Yes." Were Bedevere's tone more icy, I would have thought winter had come a season early.

"You were within the walls of Castellum Dinas during the fighting?"

"Yes."

"Did you see Ceawlin strike a blow against anyone before he was savagely attacked by Malgwyn?"

Bedevere's eyes flicked back and forth, from me to David and back again. He did not want to answer the question, but he could not stray from his nature. Still, he hesitated. "The fort was filled with men fighting. I was too busy to keep an eye on Ceawlin, or Malgwyn for that matter." But his tone said otherwise.

"You did not see him at all?"

My old friend's eyes again carried his heart's message. They said a silent apology. "I glimpsed him once, toward the end of the fighting."

"Doing what?" Somehow, in some manner, David knew what had happened inside the fort, though he had not been there. Or perhaps he was guessing, assuming.

"He appeared to be seeking escape. But," Bedevere hurried, "he was armed."

David smiled. "Who would not be when swords and spears are dancing about all around you? Did you see him strike anyone before he defended himself from Malgwyn's assault?"

The voice was very small now, belying the man who spoke. "No. I did not."

"This is not the time or place to sort out these charges," Arthur interrupted. "We should settle this at Castellum Arturius before a jury of the *consilium*."

"Why?" David sneered. "So you can assure the result that you desire? Malgwyn is no lord of the *consilium*. 'Twas Ysbail's hospitality that was offended, and it should be Ysbail's court at which it is resolved. If Malgwyn did murder the Saxon envoy, it must be Ysbail who carries out the punishment. It is her right."

With great obvious reluctance, Arthur sat down. David was

right. The offense had been to Ysbail, and, if she wished, she could summarily take my life, which was what David wished with all his heart.

I felt another tug at my tunic and found little Culhwch standing there. With my hand I brushed him away. I had no time for children at that moment.

But then the tug came even stronger, and a voice said, "Master Malgwyn."

I looked down at him, impatient and annoyed. In the back of my mind, I was aware of a scuffling at the front of the hall. Cilydd, seeing his son, was moving to collect him. But my aggravation had already overtaken me. "What, boy?"

Unblinking, with nerves of steel, he frowned at me. "You should not kill a Saxon envoy, no matter the cause. That is a mortal insult to his host."

I felt, rather than knew, that my face had turned red. This boy would not understand my reasons, no matter how I explained them. He knew only that hospitality was sacrosanct and had rules that must be obeyed.

The emotions ranging within me at that moment were almost more than I could face. I felt shame, shame at my arrogance, shame at my willfulness, shame at my murderous heart. Most shamefully of all, it took a child to show me. And as I looked from face to face of those closest to me, I saw, or at least thought I saw, something that pierced my heart as surely and as cruelly as a Saxon arrow—pity.

Mariam did not need such as me as her father.

Ygerne did not need such as me as her man.

If I were to deserve all the good things that had been said of me, all the praise heaped upon my bones, there was only one thing that I could do.

"My lady," I began, taking a knee before an uncomfortable Ysbail. "I submit myself to your judgment and apologize for violating our laws and customs in your domain. Do as you wish with me; I am guilty."

I just barely heard the clamor in the hall. Some cried for my head. Some cried for my forgiveness. Casting my eyes up for a mere second, I saw the self-satisfied look on David's face, and though it galled me to see, I realized that I had caused my own fall. I could not blame David with this.

The reluctance was strong in her face as she looked first from Arthur then to Cilydd and then Petrocus. "Take him," she ordered two of her soldiers. "Confine him, but make him comfortable. Tomorrow will be soon enough to dispose of this matter."

And they did.

"I did not believe that this would happen." David shook his head in mock surprise. "You always had such spectacular luck. But, in truth, you were always but a peasant raised high by a general's whims."

I was in the hut that Ysbail had originally assigned to me. Outside, two of her soldiers stood guard.

"I am to die tomorrow, David. They can kill me only once. Say another word and I'll reach down your throat and rip your black heart out."

David smiled, but I noticed that he edged closer to the door. "You thought you were so clever in sorting this affair out, and yet you missed the truth by a Roman *schoenus*."

"And what truth would that be?"

"You should have spent more time puzzling that out before

you murdered a Saxon envoy. Listen carefully. A man will shade the truth to protect himself. Always."

"My puzzling days are finished, David. As you can see." I was growing tired of this. "Why do you not go join your friend Mordred and drink to my death?"

Again he favored me with that cunning smile. "Mordred, yes, he and I certainly have plenty to celebrate. Until the morrow, Malgwyn. I shall look forward to seeing your head parted from your body."

And he was gone.

I did not need David to remind me of how shamefully I had behaved. But his comment about shading the truth locked itself inside my head and I could not shake it out. I had made many mistakes in my life, but I always seemed to find the truth before it was too late. Now, David said that I had missed a shading of the truth, from someone.

So, I sat and spent my last night in this world going through everything in my mind, sifting through it, looking for shades. It kept me from thinking about Ygerne and Mariam. I had written a message to them, trying to explain, and entrusted it to Merlin.

Between my musings, I had visitors.

Bedevere.

My old square-jawed friend, in many ways my best friend, simply put his hand behind my head and buried my face in his shoulder. He spun and left before I noticed the tears in his eyes, but I already had. He said nothing.

Kay.

As was his wont, he blamed everything on Arthur. "He could end this with a single word!" Kay raged. "You are the best of us, and you do not deserve this fate."

Petrocus.

"I have known you but a little while, Malgwyn, but I find much in you to be praised. On the morrow, I will consult with Lady Ysbail, and she will levy judgment on you. But after you confessed, there is little doubt as to what the punishment must be. You know this."

"I know that I am reaping the bad seed that I have sown throughout my life. But if you reckon my guilt is true, then why have you come?"

"To bring you to the Christ and assure you of a place in Heaven." His sincerity fairly dripped from his voice.

Coroticus, the abbot at Ynys-witrin, Arthur, Bedevere, Kay, young Ider, had all tried to convert me to this new faith. Even the great Patrick, *episcopus* to the Scotti, had tried. And all had failed. Though I found much to appreciate about it, I had not taken that final step.

And I would not in the face of Petrocus's efforts.

"You are a good man, Petrocus. But to embrace this faith on the eve of my death speaks of desperation, not conviction. I would not disgrace you or Arthur or any who truly believe by grasping it to simply save my neck. And, quite frankly, you should not want me to."

I expected another tongue-lashing, but Petrocus just chuckled sadly. "You will certainly be trouble for the Devil."

"Then I will serve a far greater purpose."

He was gone.

Merlin returned after the midnight. But he did not speak; he paced. Back and forth, back and forth, for several minutes.

"Merlin, have you nothing to say?"

He stopped, reached inside his tunic, and brought forth a small flask. "This draught will render your guards unconscious.

I will be waiting around the corner with a change of clothes. We can be halfway home before anyone realizes you are gone."

"No, Merlin. We cannot. My arrogance nearly cost Cilydd his life. My refusal to listen to anyone will now cost me mine. And perhaps that is how it should be."

"But Arthur—"

I shook my head. "Arthur can no more help me in this than he could when you were accused of killing Eleonore. We bested David nicely in this, and yet he will claim some small victory. Arthur has made justice and truth so much a part of his reign that to intervene for me, in such an obvious breach of ancient law, would cost him his seat. That which we have both strived for is being tested here and now."

"Bah. You are talking foolishly. This is not some lesson to be taught. When the sun rises tomorrow, they will take your head. The son that Ygerne carries will never know his father. Mariam will have lost a second father, and this time the real one."

He was telling me nothing new.

"That does not matter. Ygerne will find another, a better man than I. Mariam will yet have memories of me, and she will have the satisfaction of knowing that I took responsibility for my actions."

Merlin looked at me then, not with pity or sorrow but with disbelief. "You talk like a noble. We are not noble, Malgwyn. We are but poor men who have, for a season, the ear of a king. And kings are marked generally by their stupidity and their arrogance and their lust for power. It has been our good fortune to serve one that tempers his lust with a need to provide a better life for his people. That is truly noble. And for that we can be thankful. But, as you know all too well, we are each of us on our own when a king's seat is threatened."

His harsh words struck me as if by a fist.

"Merlin, you love Arthur."

"I do, as I would a son. As I do my own son, Owain. But while most kings are simply interested in saving their own hides, Arthur seeks to retain his seat because he thinks that is what is best for the *consilium*. But that makes him no more unlikely to glut the ravens with your flesh than David would be. Now, stop this nonsense and let us go."

I shook my head. "That simply confirms my decision. You see, Merlin, I believe that he is our best hope too."

Merlin's old wrinkled head shook so forcefully that I half-expected to hear him crackle. "Then, I have no more time to waste here. I must find some other way to save your scrawny neck." With that he stomped out with such vigor that he seemed a young, angry man.

Finally, Arthur.

Little of the night was left when Arthur appeared in the door. He did not look at me; rather he stared at the wall. I could not imagine what he would say.

"At daybreak, your guards will be relieved by two of our men—Sulien and another who rode with you at Ynys-witrin. They have been instructed to take you to Dinas Emrys, where you will stay in a kind of exile or confinement, much like Tristan did. You will be well on your way by the time that this arrangement is announced."

"No."

He spun around on me then. "No? I have been up the entire night negotiating this for you. Bedevere and Kay are threatening war against Ysbail if you are executed. David and Mordred are threatening civil war if you are not."

"And Ysbail and Cilydd?"

Arthur chuckled then. "They would throw you a feast and name you honorary lord of these lands. The only thing they feel more strongly about than each other is their hatred for all things Saxon. Ysbail has banished her brother from Trevelgue, and amazingly, he has left."

"He is afraid of her. She may be the strongest-willed woman he has ever encountered." I paused. "Mordred and David would use this against you. Aelle is young and anxious to return to warfare. This is an excellent excuse. Between a civil war and a new Saxon invasion, our lands would become a swamp of death. If you allow this deal to go forward, you will be signing the death warrants of hundreds of those same people you claim to champion." My one hand flew up to stop his protest. "My apologies, Rigotamos. Hundreds of those you do champion."

"I cannot allow your death, Malgwyn. Is there nothing that can stop this madness? What truly happened in that fort?"

I rubbed my forehead with my one hand. "I do not know, Arthur. There were indeed Saxons fighting alongside Druce's and Trevelyan's men. But I cannot claim to have seen Ceawlin strike a single blow against us. All that I knew, all that I could see, was that milky-eyed mongrel with his dagger to Mariam's throat."

"You are always hard on yourself, Malgwyn. Far more so than other men. Would Ceawlin be dead now if he had not been at Castellum Dinas? No. Would you have assaulted him here, in the lanes? No. I have negotiated a settlement that pleases everyone except the Saxons, David, and Mordred, and we have never cared all that much for what they thought."

A smile stretched my face then. "What did you tell me just yesterday? Something about this affair marking a new era, a new age for our people, one of justice and the rule of law? And yet, here you are, using your influence to arrange to save me. Arthur, either you believe in justice or you do not.

"Even if David and Mordred were to embrace this arrangement today, tomorrow they would be sowing the seeds of discontent from these lands to our northernmost regions. And the Saxons may well use it to invade, in force. Should they do that, you will need Mordred and David. But by your allowing me to receive the ancient punishment, they may think twice about challenging you.

"You were willing to execute Merlin when poor Eleonore was killed, to illustrate your devotion to the truth and to justice. And he was not guilty. I killed Ceawlin. No doubt exists about that. You must now be willing to sacrifice me."

"That was different. I was not yet the Rigotamos. Now, I am."

I walked up to him and put my hand on the back of his head and pulled it forward until our foreheads met. "And that is why it is even more important to follow the path of justice. Many men proclaim themselves just and honorable, until they grasp the power. And then that pretense falls away, and they are exposed as ordinary tyrants. You are more than that.

"I do not want to die, Arthur. But I have committed an offense that merits that punishment. Know this: I no longer curse you for stealing me from Death at the Tribuit. You gave me a life that has been good, and a purpose to serve that has kept my head high. You are the best among us, and though I have caused you much aggravation and annoyance, I do love you as only one old warrior can love another."

The Rigotamos's eyes overflowed then, and we hugged. Then he left without saying another word. Through the one, wavy Roman glass window, I could see a faint hint of red in the coming day. If a man had only one more sunrise to see, that one was not a bad choice.

The crowd was larger than that for Doged's funeral. The best of Ysbail's chairs had been arrayed at the foot of the big barrow on which her husband's body had burned. Apparently, it had seemed a propitious place for my beheading.

I blinked in the bright sunlight as Sulien and another drew me from my shack. As we walked through the crowd, there were no calls for my head, no cries for my blood. Just silence.

Sulien would not look at me, angry, I was certain, because I refused to allow my escape.

Soldiers had formed a semi-circular clearing in front of the chairs, some thirty feet at its deepest point. A place, it seemed, had been appointed to me as well. An old stump stood in the center of the semi-circle. Sulien and his mate led me next to it and then left me there alone, facing Ysbail in the center chair, with Petrocus to her left and Arthur to her right.

The woman I had once considered as icy cold as a winter's morn in the furthest reaches of our land looked less icy and more sorrowful on this morning.

Petrocus stood, and the buzz of the crowd settled. "Malgwyn, you have been accused by Lord David of having killed one Ceawlin, a Saxon envoy enjoying the hospitality of Lady Ysbail. You have admitted as much. Do you stand by that admission now?"

I knew that Arthur, Bedevere, Merlin, all of them, wanted me to denounce my admission, my confession. But I could not do that. I knew that I had killed Ceawlin, but I could not say that I had seen him raise a weapon against anyone other than me, and that in self-defense. And I could not deny that I had a bitter feud, a personal feud, with the Saxon. A simple nod answered the question.

Petrocus sighed. Though he was himself a slave to the law, this affair had unsettled him no little bit. "Lady Ysbail, as is your right, will you pronounce judgment on Malgwyn?"

Ysbail stood, a little uncertainly, and faced her people. "I have known this man but for a few days. Yet in that time he has proved himself a tireless warrior and clever man, and a true friend of my people.

"But he has violated one of our most ancient laws, that of hospitality. Any envoy granted that right is safe from danger or assault, and if such happens, the host is responsible for punishing the culprit."

She stopped. "Condemning a poor unfortunate to death is no little chore. And condemning a man who has served your flag is all the harder."

Ysbail straightened, and stared intently at her audience. "I have counseled with Petrocus, with Arthur, and with witnesses to these events. Malgwyn's guilt is clear. As is his punishment. Lord Arthur has agreed to wield the sword to ensure that one pass will suffice." She paused. "Does Malgwyn have aught to say?"

But as I opened my mouth, I could find nothing I had not said before.

Arthur came forward with his great sword. He knelt beside me and leaned close to my ear. "I will strike quickly and you will not feel it. Your songs will yet be sung in our halls."

The calm of my stomach was about to erupt, but I held it in check for just a moment. "Hurry, Arthur. I hear the calls of Tribuit; they are begging me join them."

He stepped away then. I heard the swish of air as he drew the sword back.

I sucked in a deep draught of breath and prayed for the safety and prosperity of my family, to whatever god might be listening.

CHAPTER NINETEEN

S top this nonsense NOW!"
     The voice was completely unexpected. It erupted from the rear of the crowd and roiled over the people like a great wave from the western sea. And strangest of all, I did not recognize it, but I should have.

Silence only was left in that wave's wake.

Arthur cleared his throat.

"Lord Tristan, I did not expect to see you here."

"I did not expect to need to be present; after lords Bedevere and Kay and your councilor Malgwyn put down the threat to Lady Ysbail's seat, I supposed that the affair was finished. But I see that if my friend Malgwyn is to keep his head, I must speak."

Tristan. Here? But I thought him a part of Druce's alliance.

I lifted my head and started to speak, but an almost imperceptible shake of Merlin's head kept me from it.

"I have not met you, Lord Tristan," Petrocus began, visibly uncertain at this newest event. "You have something to contribute here?"

"Many moons ago, I represented my father at the election of a new Rigotamos on the occasion of Ambrosius's retirement. I was much younger then, and I behaved that way. In so doing, I contributed to the death of a young girl, an innocent young girl. Though I was not alone in my guilt, the new Rigotamos found it meet to hold me in a kind of house arrest for more than a year."

"Have you come here to complain about Arthur?" David's red face showed that he was quickly becoming exasperated. I am sure that he had so relished the sight of my bloody head that he claimed a pleasure beyond the normal.

"Do not interrupt me," Tristan snapped, sending David, Bedevere, and Arthur swaying a little in surprise. Ysbail and Cilydd seemed more amused than shocked. I was simply lost in disbelief. This was not the Tristan that I recalled. This was a man.

"I learned much in that year. Though he was not aware of it, I gained much from watching Malgwyn sort out a pair of these affairs. Most of all, I came to respect Malgwyn for his single-ness of purpose and devotion to the truth. I believe, in this case, we can all profit from a little truth."

"Lady Ysbail," David cried. "I appeal to you. Must we endure the ramblings of this child?"

"David," Arthur interrupted. "You will cease your prattling now."

And then it was David that everyone leaned away from, as if even his breath was tainted and would color them as well.

A frown grew across David's face as he realized that he had pushed Arthur as far as he might. I knew him well enough to know that he desperately wanted to persist in his protests, but he acceded to Arthur's demands and sat down.

Tristan nodded to Arthur curtly in appreciation, and then he continued. "Malgwyn, on behalf of Lord Arthur, sent to me and asked for a mounted troop to reinforce the defenses here. I wasted no time, mustered two troop, and began my march to Trevelgue." He stopped and smiled at David, and I knew that his next words would not please the older man.

"When I had nearly reached this place, a rider interrupted our journey. He said he was from Lord David and that I was to divert my troops from Trevelgue and join David near Castellum Dinas. Assuming that Arthur and Malgwyn had need of me there rather than at Trevelgue, I complied.

"But when I reached the camp at Castellum Dinas, I saw David treating with a force of soldiers with which I was all too familiar. They were soldiers under the command of Trevelyan of Ennor. Because of my father's refusal to cede lands to them, Trevelyan has waged a Pict-like war against us, striking at smaller villages and farms, killing who they pleased and taking what they wanted."

"Why have I not heard of this?" Arthur interrupted.

"Because, Rigotamos, my father believes that to complain to you of such things makes him appear weak, as if he cannot safeguard his own lands. And because, until now, they were more like a bothersome fly than a true menace. But Trevelyan had ambition. His forebears were satisfied to steal the scraps from our tables. Not Trevelyan. In Trevelyan's eyes the old Doged presented opportunity."

Tristan turned to Petrocus. "Good monk, you are renowned for two things—your deep devotion to the Christ and your study of law."

Petrocus nodded humbly. "That is most gracious of you to say, Lord Tristan."

As Tristan began speaking, he moved toward the front of the gathering. "If I have an enemy, an enemy that I have sworn to kill, does that mean I am guilty of murder should his death come by misadventure?"

"Simply because you have sworn to kill him? No, not unless you were physically involved in his death, as in this case."

"Lord Bedevere, did you see any Saxons take arms? Were they fighting our men?"

"They were."

"Indeed, they were among the leaders of the assault," Tristan continued.

I looked up then. David was not protesting; aye, he was hiding his face. But Bedevere's face suddenly broke into a frown.

"And how would you know that, Lord Tristan? I did not see you at Castellum Dinas."

But instead of being insulted, Tristan just smiled. "I was in Druce's camp as plans were laid for the battle. When I saw that the Saxons were not just observing but actually concocting the battle plan, I wished nothing to do with it. I told them and led my troops away. But I held my men nearby; I had a debt of honor to pay Master Malgwyn, and I wanted to be close by if the Rigotamos's forces should need my help. Considering the duplicity of those arrayed against them, I felt it likely that I would be needed. When the assault came, I, with five of my best men, rode as close as we could dare to watch. And I arranged riders to call our troops in on a moment's notice.

"I did not think that Bedevere and Kay would surrender so quickly, so easily. I suspected that they would arrange a surprise for Druce's troops. When they did, we watched as our soldiers dealt with them." Tristan turned to Ysbail then.

"Lady Ysbail, the laws of hospitality are sacrosanct. It is only by abiding by these rules that we have any hope to resolve matters peacefully. But the obligation does not have only one face. It imposes responsibilities on both sides. Just as envoys and embassies should be safe from personal harm, so should the people of the lands they are visiting be safe from fearing that an embassy will take arms against them in a surprise.

"I saw with my own eyes Ceawlin at the vanguard of his men, even of the attack force itself. And he carried a Saxon battle-axe which he wielded against some of the outlying defenders that Bedevere had placed. No man serving the flag of Ysbail struck the Saxons before the Saxons themselves, most especially Ceawlin, had swung the first blow."

All was silent for a moment. Then, David, in a guttural voice that was as much anger as anguish. "This is all well and good, Lord Tristan, but it is simply your word against the rest."

"Do not count me among the fools that follow your flag, David. I have a dozen of my men ready to swear that they saw the Saxons strike the first blow. The grant of hospitality given by first Doged and then continued by Ysbail was broken before Malgwyn took up arms against the Saxon envoy. Once that had happened, the Saxons were but another enemy, and who among us would respect Malgwyn if he did not pursue them until his last breath."

So firm were his words, so solid his tone, he swayed the crowd. A palpable sense of relief swept across the plateau. Out of the corner of my eye, I saw Mordred turn away and walk toward the main gate. David opened his mouth as if to speak, but Arthur whispered something in his ear and he remained silent. Tristan, the boy whom I had reviled for his part in Eleonore's death, had become a man of great heart and eloquence.

Petrocus stood. "Thank you, Lord Tristan. You have borne witness to what you saw, and rightly so. If the Saxons had already begun fighting, if they led the assault, then Malgwyn bears no guilt."

Ysbail rose. She motioned her guards forward. "Release him. Malgwyn, you have our thanks for your services in our behalf and our apology for the accusations against you. It would please me greatly to call you friend."

I stood. The sudden reversal of my fortunes had sapped my strength. My stomach felt about to release all it held. I composed myself enough to thank her.

And then I was surrounded by my fellows, clapping their hands on my back and cheering me.

The guards drew back, and people began milling about. I stood, as if rooted to the spot. When you have concluded, when you have settled in your own mind, that your death is imminent, if by some miracle you are saved the rush of freedom seems to hold you tightly to its bosom.

But David was not yet finished. "This is so much sophistry. Ceawlin was yet an envoy of the Saxons."

It was the hawk-nosed Petrocus's turn to show his irritation. "Lord David, you are wrong. When Ceawlin took up arms in an assault on Ysbail's possessions any protection he had from her ceased. That is a law just as ancient as that of hospitality, and you well know it."

"Lord David," Tristan began, and I saw David cringe at the sound, ever so slightly. "Please do not force me to give a more complete description of matters."

With that, David departed in a huff, his face as red as the tunic on Bedevere's chest.

That exchange seemed to spark me from my trance, and I

approached Tristan with a grin. "I was ready to denounce you for a liar and a coward," I halfheartedly scolded him.

He smiled, and I noticed that his always youthful face now carried a wrinkle or two. "Had you truly needed me, I would have been there with my troops."

"Aye, I do not doubt it. I needed you today, and here you are."

"Thank Arthur and Bedevere for that," Tristan answered. "They had riders out all night, scouring the countryside for anyone who could shed light on the battle at Castellum Dinas. One of my men was at a tavern by the seafront. He had been one of those that I kept with me, and he told them what they needed to hear. 'Twas only an hour or so ago that they fetched me from my camp. We were preparing to leave for home. I am most glad that they found me in time."

"Your debt to me, if you ever truly had one, is more than repaid, Tristan."

"I am only happy to have been of some service to you, Malgwyn. But I must leave now; affairs are somewhat unsettled at Castellum Marcus. My father is bedeviled by his future Scotti bride, Iseult, and my responsibilities have increased."

"Old men," I said, "who take young brides often find life unsettled."

Tristan laughed, but in a way that suggested there was more to the story. He turned and saw Arthur heading toward us. "Good, I was hoping to speak with you both."

"Lord Tristan, I cannot begin to tell you how grateful I am that you came to bear witness for Malgwyn." Arthur's sincerity was obvious in every word.

"Well, my lord, someone has to save the stubborn old goat from himself."

We all laughed at that.

"Rigotamos," Tristan said. "My father wishes to extend an invitation to you, Kay, Bedevere, and, of course, Malgwyn to attend his marriage to the Scotti princess Iseult on the next full moon."

"Absolutely," Arthur answered.

"But Rigotamos—," I began my protest, but Tristan took my shoulder in his hand, squeezed it, and said in yet another odd tone, "I wish you especially, Malgwyn, to come."

How do you say to no to the man who just saved your life? I bit my lip and tried to smile graciously.

At that, I took my leave from them. I needed to see one other before this matter could truly be considered settled. My sudden reprieve from death had not really settled in. I knew that later my knees would shake and I would need a stout draught of mead to calm my nerves. But at that moment, there was only one person I wanted to see.

I found him hunched over a table in the same tavern where Sulien, Daron, and I had sat just a few nights earlier.

"You look much better without strips of pig fat dangling from your hair," I said, shoved into the room by three of Ysbail's drunken soldiers and a *meretrix* they had bought.

Mordred looked up at me and frowned. "So, you live to further torment me."

"I know you planned it differently, Mordred, but you did not count on Tristan coming to my aid. In all honesty, I would have thought you innocent in this entire affair had it not been for something David said last night."

"Hmmph," Mordred grunted. "David should talk less and think more."

"Agreed."

"When did you realize it?"

"Sadly, not until last night, after David came to me. He spoke of how naïve I am. How someone had told me a shadow of the truth, but not the entire truth. Despite my many visitors last night, I had much time to think, to consider all that had happened."

"And?"

"The only thing that I had been told that could, possibly, have shades of meaning was exactly what happened in Doged's chamber the night of his death. I knew this: Trevelyan killed him. He would never have panicked and run had that not been true. But who else might have been there? You told me yourself that someone, presumably Trevelyan, rushed out just before you and the Saxons entered to find Doged dead. I suspect that you entered with Trevelyan, you and the Saxons.

"What happened, Mordred? Did you and the Saxon envoys offer to support Trevelyan's bid for lands? I suspect that you soiled your pants when Trevelyan stabbed Doged in a sudden rage."

Mordred shrugged. "It is only the two of us sitting here. I do not mind telling you that we were there, and that Trevelyan did indeed stab the old man. The Saxons, however, were the ones who soiled their *braccae*. As soon as Trevelyan had stabbed Doged, I lunged for the door, though the others were right behind me. The guard who snagged me was the same that we had bribed for access."

"So, he had to be killed. Why wait?"

"Too many people were stirring by then. I heard a commotion from the front and saw immediately that it was Cilydd in his Doged outfit."

"Aye, I saw him as he fled through the hall. For a long time, I believed that that person was Doged's killer."

"It was fortuitous. We did not know that Doged had made arrangements with Cilydd until we collided with him in the corridor. He had no reason to doubt our story and much reason to keep his charade a secret."

"And what arrangement did you seek with Doged?"

"Trevelyan needed lands. I saw no reason that he should be denied. The Saxons supported the agreement."

"Of course they did. Trevelyan was already trading with them, buying Saxon points to put on his Briton shafts. A clear ally in this part of Britannia would be invaluable when the Saxons decide to invade our lands. That was why you had to so quickly and so permanently deal with Trevelyan. You could not allow him to bear witness to your misdeeds."

"I did us all a favor by killing that snake. He was becoming touched in the head and believed that he could do anything and kill indiscriminately in defense of his people. Good riddance."

"Is that how you found him so easily turned toward the Saxons?"

"Malgwyn!" Mordred feigned shock and surprise. "You think I would treat with the Saxons?"

"Enough, Mordred. You would treat with the Devil himself if it helped you gain Arthur's seat. Which, I am certain, is what the Saxons promised you."

My enemy shrugged. "What difference can it make now? Such did not happen."

"Oh, but you tried. And that is enough."

Mordred laughed, tiredly, hoarsely. "That is enough for what, Malgwyn? We are but two men spouting drunken nonsense in a tavern without a one of our fellows with us. No one has witnessed our conversation."

"Mordred, Mordred, Mordred. You should never take chances."

But the voice was not mine. Mordred stood and spun about the room but saw nothing but three soldiers, a whore, and the barkeep.

Until the soldier threw back his cloak. Arthur. The second proved to be Bedevere. The third was, to my surprise, Petrocus. And the *meretrix* a happy, satisfied Daron.

Like a trapped badger, Mordred searched for an escape but found none. He dove through the open door, with more grace than I thought he possessed, but Kay and Merlin herded him back inside. Behind them, Ysbail and Cilydd entered.

"Rigotamos," Ysbail said with a smile. "This seems very much an affair for the *consilium* to settle. If the wise Petrocus agrees?"

"As Lord Mordred is a member of the *consilium*, and it was that body that he conspired against, I think it meet that they should deal with him," Petrocus said with a wink.

Arthur nodded to Bedevere and Kay, and they hauled Mordred, cursing and spitting, from the tavern.

"I see Merlin has been making free with his expertise again," I said.

"He guessed that Mordred had more of a hand in this than it would seem, and he guessed that you would head straight for Mordred. So why not take a leaf from Doged's book?"

Why not indeed? I thought. But it was from Uther's book rather than Doged's, a secret that I would keep as promised to Igraine.

Though I relished the sight of Mordred tied up as a prisoner, I knew that such was not to be. "We cannot try him. Even if the *consilium* agreed, he has a mighty defense for everything and we have few witnesses against him."

Arthur nodded. "True, but we will keep him in custody a bit longer to teach him a lesson."

"Rigotamos," Ysbail began. "I believe that Malgwyn has a conveyance prepared at my late husband's request, granting the mines at Castellum Dinas to the *consilium*, assuming that the *consilium* will take responsibility for the mining."

My eyes widened in surprise, something that Ysbail did not miss. "My husband told me of his plan. The cleverness of it impressed me then and still does. Malgwyn, if you will alter the conveyance to reflect Doged's death, I will sign it and the bargain will be struck."

Arthur bowed his head to Ysbail. "My lady, you may not have been born a queen, but you have certainly grown into a fine one, a queen worthy of a great people."

At that, Cilydd ordered a round of good brandy for us all, and we drank to the health and fortune of the new queen and her commander, to the shade of Doged, even now protecting the next life, and to Tristan, who had assuredly saved my neck.

An hour later, we were all further into our cups than we should have been and there was a commotion at the door. A rider, wearing Arthur's tunic, stormed into the tavern. My heart sank. The Saxons were massing for attack. Or some other harm was visiting our lands. Celebrations were all too brief.

"Master Malgwyn," the rider croaked into the room. Petrocus hurried a cup of water to him, and forced a little past his cracked and dry lips. "Master . . . I have word for you . . . from Castellum Arturius."

A thousand disasters peopled my visions. "What, man? Speak plainly."

"Your woman . . . Ygerne . . ."

I was about to go mad.

"What?"

"She has delivered your daughter."

"A son! Ygerne has delivered our son!"

I drained my cup dry, but then I saw Arthur, and indeed everyone, looking at me oddly.

"What?"

"You have no son, Malgwyn."

"But," I stopped and pointed at the rider, "he just said . . ."

A daughter.

A sister for Mariam.

So much for soothsayers and prophets.

Well, there was nothing in the world prettier than a new baby girl, no matter how unsettled the world she entered.

And we were drinking to my new child when Ider, his head hung in embarrassment, presented himself to Arthur. "My lord, I wish permission."

We all turned. Ider's voice was serious. Arthur put his cup down. "Permission for what, boy?"

He drew a small figure from behind him, Daron. "I wish to pay court to Daron, Rigotamos, with your blessing."

"When did this happen?" I asked.

"You have been busy, Malgwyn," Ider answered. My little *monachus* had grown up. "She has no father or guardian from whom to seek permission. . . ."

"Malgwyn is my guardian, or at least I wish it so." She turned her gaze to me, and a hint of mischief crept into her eyes. "Now you know where I was the night that Doged was killed."

My face was a deep red, I knew.

"Both requests are granted," Arthur proclaimed.

During the celebration that followed, Arthur drew me into a corner. "Did you mean what you said last night?"

"That I had forgiven you for saving me at Tribuit? Yes, I did and I do. But remember this—I will still strive for the truth in all things, and if that becomes an annoyance to you, then so be it."

He laughed and clapped me on the back. "I would expect no less. When we return home, we must talk about Kay. He worries me."

I just smiled. Kay worried me too, but I truly believed that with me, Bedevere, and Merlin to help, Arthur would find a way to bring our old friend back into the fold.

And then yet another commotion erupted from the front. Emerging from the gaggle was the now-bedraggled Morgan ap Tud bursting into the room, looking thinner than he ever had.

My heart dropped. Igraine was dead. Arthur, for all of his blustering, would be devastated. I snatched Merlin by the arm and indicated Morgan. He took my meaning and we moved to flank little Morgan.

"Rigotamos," Morgan began. Arthur spun about, his face falling at the sight of the *medicus*.

"Lady Igraine has survived the current crisis and her situation has stabilized. She will live yet longer."

A smile lit Arthur's face and he raised a toast to Morgan, as the land's finest *medicus*.

But our little companion's face held no mirth.

"What, Morgan?"

"All that this means for me, Malgwyn, is that I will have to deal with that hellcat again. Twice she ordered me castrated and my testicles served to the dogs." He shook his head sorrowfully.

"You did your job well, Morgan; find cheer in that."

And the little *medicus* cast a jaundiced look at me. "So you say, Malgwyn. So you say."

CHAPTER TWENTY

And so, two weeks later, we crossed the River Cam and came within sight of Castellum Arturius. Those mighty ramparts were as welcome to me as a warm fire and a full belly. And that is exactly what they meant to me in reality as well.

I was heartily tired of our cook's food. 'Twas not really his fault; it was his first journey with us. Arthur's old cook, Cerdic, had withheld information from us nearly a year before, in the events surrounding Arthur's brief first marriage. Arthur had had Cerdic's eye taken as punishment for the lapse. Though Cerdic had been with Arthur for many years, we were no longer certain of his loyalty. So a youngster had been chosen, and he knew little more than how to boil beef and pig. Between his poor cooking and all the riding, running, and fighting I had done on this journey, I had lost much weight. Ygerne would be worried about me.

To my hearty disapproval, we had tarried in the west for another several days, helping Cilydd organize Ysbail's soldiers and negotiating those long-sought lands for the people of Ennor and Scilly. 'Twas nearly a comical sight as Ysbail and Arthur treated with the leader of those landless folk. All of their men were dead, and the oldest male left was but sixteen. Still, the young man comported himself well and won for his people the lands surrounding Daron's village, which required concessions from both Arthur and Ysbail.

Kay had taken most of our troops back to Castellum Arturius well before our main party departed. Merlin took the opportunity to go to Tyntagel and visit Igraine; he would join us later at home. So it was left to Arthur, Bedevere, and Ider to command on our return. But Ider left our party at Ynys-witrin to introduce his new lady to Coroticus, an event that I would love to have seen, but home called more strongly.

My old enemy Mordred had a most uncomfortable journey. Bedevere commissioned a great cage of wood to be built and mounted atop a wagon. That had served as Mordred's jail during a most rough journey. Mordred cursed me, Arthur, Bedevere, the Saxons, Trevelyan, and on and on.

"At least," I had told him, "you are spared the indignity of having our garbage dumped on you."

"I shall have the pleasure of watching your head bounce in the dirt yet, Malgwyn," he had promised me. But he bore his discomfort mostly in silence. I knew, though, that we both had scores to settle yet.

And such were my thoughts as we drew closer to the shadow of our home, thoughts of home and feuds and the future.

"We have come far," a voice said beside me.

"We have, Rigotamos," I agreed. "It has been a long and tiring journey. I am glad that it is nearly over."

"Oh, Malgwyn," he said. "I fear it has only begun."

I was tired, tired to the bone. "Please, Arthur, do not say that. I fear I have no strength left in me, not even a *schoenus* worth."

He laughed that deep laugh of his, and after the trials of recent days it was good to hear. "Do not take me so literally, Malgwyn. Look there," and he pointed to the ramparts. "It stands a little bit taller, shines a little bit more. Its reach is a bit wider."

"I nearly returned a head shorter," I reminded him.

Again that warm laughter.

"And that is why our world is a bit brighter. You helped me remember who I am, what I am."

The creaking of leather punctuated his words, and I gave deeper thought to them. "I am tired, Arthur. Perhaps if you spoke more clearly."

"It is what I said to you at Trevelgue, Malgwyn. The old world is changing. We are writing a new history, one in which the rule of law settles disputes, not the power of the sword. Your willingness to accept that rule, despite a host of attempts to circumvent it, including my own, has strengthened it beyond any of our individual abilities to do so. That future we both desire is finally within our grasp. And you have become a moving force behind it."

I heard his words, but the fatigue, deep in my bones, made them faint and confused. "I think, Rigotamos, that you make too much of my guilty nature." Having worked so hard to find truth, I had to accept my failure in so many ways. Was I right in killing Ceawlin? Tristan and the law said yes. But only my heart held that truth, and no matter how fiercely I searched it, it was not talking.

"You are guilty only of helping me find a way for our people."

Responding to him did not seem worth the effort. But I could not resist. "I am not sure of what we have accomplished, Arthur. Doged is dead. His killer gained the lands that he sought. We have further irritated Mordred and David, chancing a break in the *consilium*."

The Rigotamos laughed out loud at me. "Malgwyn, can you see no victories in this affair? True, Doged is dead. But the rebellion he feared has been averted. And his plan for the mining of the gold and agaphite at Castellum Dinas is in place. Yes, Trevelyan's people have found lands at last, but, in reality, either Mark or his father or Ambrosius or I should have settled lands on them long ago. And Trevelyan will not enjoy them. With so few men among them, they will soon intermarry with our people.

"Your head is still attached. My mother lives. Your daughter has been born. I will soon have a child as well. Malgwyn, we have much for which to thank the Christ and His Father. My father once told me not to borrow trouble. I would extend the same advice to you."

I was too exhausted to argue.

"Father!"

My beautiful Mariam met me at the great main gate, below Arthur's hall. The sunlight shone off of her blond hair, and my heart lightened with her smile.

Arthur and I dismounted inside the gate. Bedevere was busy conducting our companion Mordred to our cavalry encampment between the fort and the River Cam. Two *servi* rushed up and took our horses, leading them away to the stables in the barracks.

Mariam leaped up and I snagged her with my arm. She kissed my cheek and giggled as my unruly beard tickled her.

"Have you been a good girl?"

"Of course, Father," she assured me, but there was an extra twinkle in her eye that usually meant she had been naughty.

"Then, let us go and see your new sister."

She hopped down and took my bedroll and pouch and led me away from Arthur. "Come, Father! Mother is waiting."

Arthur waved. "I will come and see your new one soon. I have some homecoming chores myself. And he headed to his hall, a special bounce in his step.

"Did you behave yourself, Father? Mother worries about you."

I stopped and knelt beside her. "Do you remember the Saxon who tried to take you from me?" She had been much younger and I did not know how much she could recall.

But the merriment in her eyes died at my words. "Yes, Father. The one with the odd eye. I remember him."

"You never have to worry about him bothering you again."

She smiled then, a smile of relief. "I knew that you would avenge me someday, Father. But I did not think it would take this long." Again, she gave me that mischievous twinkle.

It took but a few minutes to reach Ygerne's house in the back lanes of the town. Feeling a welcome burst of energy, I banged my first on the door. "Ygerne, I am home!"

The door swung open, and I entered, half-expecting to hear the wailing cry of my new daughter.

Then the strangest thing happened.

A strap of cloth circled my head, gagging me. Someone covered my head with a leather hood, tying it tight.

Before I could react to that, hands quickly wrapped a rope around my body, holding my one arm useless against me. At the same time someone bound my feet with a second rope.

Nearly before I could speak, I was knocked off my feet and tipped over onto a deer hide.

I tried to cry out, but the gag held tight.

I heard voices, but none I could identify.

My captors carried me some distance, to the main gate if my senses were correct, where I was thrown onto the bed of a wagon. Seconds later, I heard and felt another person, trussed up as was I, land next to me with a loud grunt.

David. It had to be David's doing. Outraged by his failure at Trevelgue, he had somehow arranged my kidnapping.

But Mariam? Ygerne?

What had he done with them?

My bound companion was restless as well, rolling and struggling against his restraints.

We were in motion by then, headed who knew where.

I caught a whiff of the captive next to me. Mint. A chill struck my heart.

Arthur!

He constantly chewed mint leaves to freshen his breath. I would forever associate that smell with Arthur.

Kidnapping the Rigotamos? David would have to have a number of fellow conspirators. Perhaps Melwas. Perhaps Mordred's brother Gawain. Perhaps we had gone too far by imprisoning Mordred. If Gawain had turned against us, then mayhaps his brother Gaheris had as well.

The gag and the deer hide hood made breathing difficult but not impossible. But whoever had tanned the hide had done a poor job of it and it stank horribly. I would have given anything to speak with Arthur then. Who else might they have taken? Kay? Bedevere?

The bumps and lurches of the wagon told me that we were

on a road, not crossing open ground. I could not fathom where they might take us. Were this truly an insurrection, they would be better served by killing Arthur immediately. But that was apparently not their intention.

And the wagon rolled.

I thought I might go mad indeed. My death had faced me too often in recent days. No man is equipped to deal with such highs and lows so swiftly thrust upon him.

Arthur continued to struggle against his ropes. Aye, and I tried my own, but our captors had been expert in tying the knots.

And still the wagon rolled.

Finally, after what I judged to be some two hours, the wagon turned from the road and into a damper, cooler place. I had been there before; I knew it. The smell was familiar, though the scent of fresh-cut wood was in the air.

I could hear the murmuring of people but nothing distinct, nothing understandable. Our captives cut away the bindings around my ankles and pulled me from the wagon. I could have fought then, kicked, but I was curious. I was led, firmly but not roughly, a few feet and then I sensed that I was inside a building, a new building. The scent of construction was in the air. Seconds later, I felt and smelt the presence of Arthur.

Then hands were fumbling about me, removing the rope around my body and removing the hood and gag from my mouth. It was dark and I had to blink my eyes to clear them.

But when I did, I was astounded, and most thoroughly confused.

Arrayed before me were Kay, with a broad grin, the abbot Coroticus, Ider, Daron, Gawain, even Sulien and Morgan ap Tud. I turned to my left and saw Ygerne, holding a bundled baby; Mariam; and my dear cousin Guinevere. At that, I looked up and around and realized where I was.

Lantokay. "Kay's Chapel" in our native tongue. Nearly a year before, Arthur had granted these lands to Kay. Kay had torn down an old Roman shrine here and built a chapel, one that he intended as Arthur's wedding chapel.

And as I remembered, a smile spread on my face as I realized that I was about to witness Arthur's second marriage, to Guinevere. "But," I grumbled to myself, "Kay could certainly have let me in on the surprise."

Coroticus spoke first. "Lord Kay, while I applaud your intentions, I think you could have done this without so much subterfuge."

"But Coroticus, my good abbot, you know how contrary these two can be."

"That is absolutely true," I agreed, getting into the spirit.

But there was no accompanying chuckle. And I looked about and saw that everyone was looking at me, amused.

Feeling awkward, I moved toward Ygerne. "Let me hold my child."

But she handed the bundle off to Mariam, who moved to a corner.

Ygerne, her beautiful red hair glowing, narrowed her eyes at me. "You think we went to all of this trouble for just Arthur? If you wish to claim this baby, you must marry me before the Christ."

I was stunned. "Marry? You?"

And then, as was her nature, she advanced on me and slapped me across my stomach. "Yes. Marry me. Here and now."

All eyes in the chapel were fixed on me.

But I needed no time to think. "I cannot dream of anything finer, but is this not arranged for Arthur?"

And then the Rigotamos found himself the center of attention. He fumbled about uncomfortably. "This must be done properly, with invited guests. . . ."

But Guinevere stood before him and put her hand to his mouth. "It has been many months since Lord Aircol gave his approval." Aircol had been father of Arthur's ill-fated first wife. "Your child is even now growing in my belly. I have waited long enough. Marry me now, or you will never marry me at all."

At that, Arthur gathered Guinevere in against his chest. "I happily accept." But then he frowned. "Did Kay have to kidnap us?"

"If we continued to wait for the two of you," Guinevere said with a smile, "we would have grandchildren before you would consent to be our husbands. But do not chastise Kay. He was acting at our command."

"You are a fine leader, Rigotamos, a good man," Kay began. "But sometimes you need the flat of a sword against your bottom to get you moving." And he smiled, and I was most glad to see it.

Coroticus stepped forward and beckoned for Ygerne and me to approach. But just as he opened his mouth, the sound of horses galloping came from outside. And a mighty warrior rushed into the room, waving his sword left and right.

"Harm the Rigotamos and you will die today!" Bedevere had apparently not been privy to the plan.

"Lord Bedevere," Arthur said, "you are interrupting my wedding. Please put down your sword."

For the first time in all the years I had known him, Bedevere was completely without words. To his credit, he quickly surveyed the room and understood. As a great smile spread across his usually stern countenance, he tucked his sword into his belt and said, "With pleasure, my lord."

With that, Coroticus spoke the words that joined first Ygerne and me, and then Arthur ap Uther and Guinevere.

I remember wishing that Lady Igraine could see her son at that moment. She would have scolded him for his delay and then ordered Morgan beheaded.

At long last, as we were all being congratulated, I went to Mariam, still holding her new sister. With that same mischievous smile, Mariam handed the bundle up to me, and I cradled it in my one arm.

Someone gripped me about the waist. Ygerne.

"Do you approve of him?"

"Of course, he's— He? But the messenger said it was a girl."

I looked down into Ygerne's eyes and she pulled me close with a kiss. "I could not resist the jest."

At that, I swung about the chapel and shouted, "I have a son!"

I can remember no finer night when Arthur was king. Much death and devastation had marked our journey, but we emerged victorious. Slowly but surely, this was becoming a true country, a Britannia of which we could be proud.

Glossary and Gazetteer

Aquae Sulis—The Roman name for what is now Bath, England. Excavations have shown that many of its buildings were refurbished and continued in use throughout the fifth and sixth centuries.

braccae—Breeches worn by both Saxons and the Brythonic tribes. The only extant examples come from peat bogs in Europe. There was a certain disdain by Romans toward the Gallic tribes for wearing pants.

Breton—A native or inhabitant of Brittany, or the Celtic language of the Breton people.

Brittany—That area of Gaul known as Brittany. Settlements by some of the Brythonic tribes were located there during the fifth and sixth centuries.

Caer Goch—An Iron Age hill fort in South Wales.

Carmarthen—The legendary birthplace of Merlin.

castellum—Castle, but not in the High Middle Ages sense with thick stone walls, towers, and damsels in distress.

Usually a defensive position with stacked rock and timber defensive rings.

Castellum Arturius—For the purposes of this novel, Cadbury Castle at South Cadbury, Somerset, is the location for Arthur's castle. Excavations during the 1960s identified it as having been significantly rebuilt and reinforced during the late fifth century by a warlord of Arthurian-like stature, although no explicit evidence linking the site to Arthur himself was discovered.

Castellum Marcus—Castle Dore near Fowey in southeast Cornwall is believed to have been the site of King Mark's headquarters. Nearby was found the famous Tristan stone, a gravestone believed to commemorate the historical Tristan, making it the one contemporary piece of evidence for the historicity of a character in the Arthurian canon.

Celliwic—For purposes of this novel, is that place called Killibury Rounds north of the village of Wadebridge in Cornwall. Some scholars believe it to be a credible site for the real Celliwic.

cervesa—The Latin name for the beer made by the local tribes during the Roman occupation. According to tablets unearthed at Vindolanda near Hadrian's Wall, Roman soldiers were not shy about drinking *cervesas*.

consilium—A council. Gildas refers to a *consilium* ruling pre-Saxon Britannia that ended in Vortigern hiring Saxon mercenaries to help put down the raids of the Picts and Scots. It is safe to assume that any warlord who exerted influence over large areas in central and western England would have done so at the behest and the agreement of such a council of lesser kings.

Dumnonia (Dumnonii)—A tribe residing in the area of Cornwall and throughout the west lands. Mark is thought to have been a king of the Dumnonii during the general period of Arthur's life. Snyder suggests in *The Britons* that people in the post-Roman period referred to themselves by tribal designations.

Durotrigia (Durotrigii)—A tribe residing in the area surrounding Glastonbury down through the South Cadbury area to the southern coast.

fibula—A brooch used to pin cloaks and other clothing together. Sometimes fibulae were jeweled and quite ornate. Others were made in the shape of crossbows.

iudex pedaneous—A Roman official assigned to investigate crimes and offenses. It is known that such titles were still used in post-Roman Britannia.

latrunculii—A term applied to groups of bandits that ran rampant during the fifth century, not to be confused with a Roman board game of the same era.

Lindinis—A Roman town near what is now Ilchester, just west of South Cadbury.

Londinium—As would be expected, this is the Roman name for what is now London.

Meneds—The ancient name for the Mendip Hills of northwest Somerset.

peplos—A type of gown worn by women, having a Roman cut.

philologus—A teacher.

Pomparles Bridge—Located between present-day Street and the edge of Glastonbury. Legend has it that it was from this point that Bedevere set Arthur's funeral bier off for Avalon. Although the current bridge is not ancient by any means, fieldwork has shown that there may have been a Roman crossing in this vicinity.

presbyter—A term (originally Latin) applied to priests or other church officers. Remember that this was a time before parish priests.

sacerdote—A term used to describe priests, interchangeable with *presbyter*, above. There may certainly have been differences between these two terms at the time of this novel, but such distinctions, without documentary evidence, are impossible for modern readers to discern.

schoenus—A Roman mile.

tigernos—The Celtic word for "lord," sometimes used to designate local lords, but believed by some scholars to have been combined with the word "vor" to produce the name "Vortigern," or "overlord."

Via Arturius—"Arthur's Way." A roadway or lane actually ran from Cadbury Castle to Glastonbury. It has become known as Arthur's Way. Two major Roman roads near Cadbury Castle were the Via Fosse and the Via Harrow.

vigile—The Roman equivalent, in a sense, of both a policeman and a fireman. In Rome, *vigiles* watched for fires as much as any crime.

White Mount—Said to be the location of the White Tower at the Tower of London.

Ynys-witrin—According to some sources, this was the early name for what is now Glastonbury. It is believed that a Christian community may have resided there during the Arthurian age.

Author's Note

I like to say that I "ground" my plots in ancient stories of Arthur. I try to show how a certain myth or legend could have originated. In this instance, I consider the backstory to the Culwhch and Olwen story. The legends attribute Doged's death to Culwhch's father, Cilydd, but I opted to go another direction so that I might tie it into the legends of Arthur's conception. The stories do not give much about Doged but his name, so I have chosen to provide him with a life of some consequence. Putting his seat at Trevelgue simply fit into my plans and bears no connection to history, which seems only to indicate that his lands were in the West Country.

The ores at Castellum Dinas were and are there. The strange brown ore was wolframite, which was not profitably worked until the twentieth century. Agaphite is actually an early name for turquoise, and its value and use need no explanation here. Gold, also, was found near Castellum Dinas, but not in the quantities necessary to make mining profitable. Any leader of Arthurian standards would need every possible source of wealth. The refurbishing of the defensive works around Cadbury Castle would have cost a fortune. And dark, dusty rumors still link construction of the Wansdyke, the fifth/sixth-century great defensive ditch and bank that runs from Bristol (more or less) in a southeasterly direction, to Arthur.

The Welsh tales seem to indicate a gradual split between Arthur and Kay, and so that element is creeping in as well. I rely heavily on the pre-Galfridian texts, especially the tales contained in the Mabinogion. Gurdur, who plays a small but vital role in this book, is mentioned in the Mabinogion, though I have altered his name somewhat to make it more palatable.

Ysbadden, Ysbail's giant brother, is very prominent in young Culwhch's search for a bride. But that takes place some years after the current work. With the help of readers, maybe we will get there someday.

As always, I am indebted to the work of Geoffrey Ashe and Christopher Snyder, who have helped bring the Dark Ages to life for me. If I have erred, the blame belongs to me.